P9-DGO-130

THE GOLDEN ONE

Deborah Chester

ACE BOOKS, NEW YORK

LUCASFILM'S ALIEN CHRONICLES℠: THE GOLDEN ONE

An Ace Book / published by arrangement with
Lucasfilm Ltd.

PRINTING HISTORY
Ace edition / February 1998

The Putnam Berkley World Wide Web site address is
http://www.berkley.com

Make sure to check out *PB Plug*, the science fiction/fantasy newsletter,
at http://www.pbplug.com

Visit the Alien Chronicles Web site at http://www.lucasaliens.com

ISBN: 0-441-00561-6

ACE
Ace Books are published by The Berkley Publishing Group,
a member of Penguin Putnam Inc.,
200 Madison Avenue, New York, NY 10016.
ACE and its logo
are trademarks belonging to Berkley Publishing Corporation.

PRINTED IN THE UNITED STATES OF AMERICA

10 9 8 7 6 5 4 3 2 1

THE ALIENS OF

LUCASFILM'S ALIEN CHRONICLES™

THE VIIS...a race of seven-foot-tall, beautiful reptilian creatures. Their physical attractiveness has convinced the Viis that they are the most important, godlike creatures in the universe. This has led to an underground race of "uglies"— Viis that were cast off as unacceptable, worthless spawn...

THE AAROUN...the race of Ampris are powerful, golden-furred carnivores with sharp teeth. They have long been kept by the Viis as slaves, or as in the case of Ampris, pets.

THE KELTH...a submissive, doglike race with stiff, bristly coats and simian hands. Because they are so easily intimidated, Kelth are considered unreliable to handle important tasks. They are not to be trusted...

THE MYAL...renowned for their insight and memories, Myal stand barely three feet tall and are usually poets, musicians, and historians. They control the archives of the Viis empire.

THE ZHRELI…they are filthy, noisy, foul-smelling, and socially repulsive creatures. Yet they are unequaled at maintaining and repairing quantum hardware (the only reason to tolerate them).

THE SKEK…less than two feet high, furry, multi-limbed, and quick, the Skek live like rats in the ducts and garbage of the Viis. It's a common slave belief that if you dropped one Skek in a barrel, the barrel would explode with Skek offspring within a day.

THE TOTHS…Big, stupid, and Brutal, Toths roam the ghetto streets as thugs, but they are also used by their Viis masters as hired enforcers or brownshirts. Nearly as tall as the Viis, they have massive heads covered with thick mats of dirty, curly brown hair. Flies usually buzz around their long, floppy ears. Their faces are broad and flat, with wide nostrils, and their eyes are small and cruel.

THE GORLICANS…Merchants, shopkeepers, traders, the Gorlicans are a steady, hardworking, nonviolent race allied to the Viis. A heavy shell encases their torsos, rendering their balance sometimes percarious, and their arms and legs are covered with thick gray scales instead of skin. Their faces are ugly, with a prominent horned beak for an upper lip, and they have orange or yellow eyes. They must wear masks in public to avoid offending the Viis.

CHAPTER ONE

Three days of warmth and shadow . . . nuzzling against the solid reassurance beside her . . . squirming with her siblings in the moist milk scent . . . dozing while gentle fingers stroked her back . . . making the soft mew-cries in dawning awareness of a world large and new.

Vision cleared first, bringing her shapes to associate with the confusing tangle of fragrances filling her senses. Sibling shapes . . . four little wedge-shaped heads covered in tan and fawn fuzz, wobbling in exploration. Mother shape . . . large and infinitely gentle, crooning sounds of love, providing warmth and nourishment as she stroked her babies and sang softly to them.

Her single female child she held often, nestling her atop her stomach and letting the tiny one wobble and explore. A golden child with soft, downy baby fur and no markings at all save a light brown mask across her eyes that would probably darken with maturity. All the males were striped in brown and fawn, almost identical, fractious when together yet furious if separated. The golden female, however, was placid and calm, content to interact with her mother yet adventurous enough to explore on her own.

"My golden one," the mother crooned to her, smoothing

back the fur over sweet baby eyes. They all lay together in the bed. A small lamp glowed, pushing back the surrounding shadows. Many sounds came from far away, muffled and unimportant.

"Brave and strong, my daughter will grow up to be. Look at you, bigger already than your brothers. Straight-shouldered, you are. An Aaroun, you are, my darling, a daughter of a proud line of the Heva clan. All your history, I will teach you. Our songs, you will learn that you may teach them to your sons and daughters. Through you, we will go on."

Gentle, steady words. The golden one blinked up at her mother's loving face, drinking in the words she did not as yet understand. But she could understand the love in those words, and the pride. Her own heart opened in response, and she felt a sudden rush of feeling so intense it almost frightened her.

She mewed, and her mother kissed her, laughing softly.

"Yes, my golden one," her mother said. "Yes, you are wonderful and precious. I love you so much."

Love. The golden one blinked and rubbed her head against her mother's hand. It was her first lesson, to learn this feeling.

Without warning, there came a perfunctory pounding on the door. Before the mother could move, the door was slammed open, and a shaft of sunlight stabbed inside.

Startled, the golden one cried out. Her brothers awoke with screams. Their mother struggled up, hastily scooping her babies behind her.

"Get out!" she roared. "This is a birthing room! I have the right to privacy for these first days."

A pebble-skinned, blue Viis male in a dust-colored coat that hung long enough to cover his tail stepped inside. He wore a voluminous hood that masked his rill and face except for his vivid green eyes, and concealed his identity. Two Toth thugs carrying stun-sticks followed him.

Fear filled the Aaroun mother.

Standing well above two meters, nearly as tall as the Viis, with massive heads and shoulders covered in pelts of matted, curly hair, Toths were the worst kind of enforcers. Brutal, stupid, and dirty, they entered with a cloud of flies buzzing about their heads, chewing lazily, now and then flicking a big, pale tongue up inside their broad nostrils. They gazed at her with small, cruel eyes that danced with anticipation. Toths enjoyed inflicting hurt. Mercy was unknown to them. For the first time in her life, the mother felt the need to say the ancient Heva lamentations as a prayer rather than song-poetry. But her mind went blank, unable to summon the words. In the name of the ancient gods, what were these creatures doing here?

From outside her room, she could hear anguished screams down the row of cheap housing. Her fear intensified, and she began to pant. Whatever they intended, she would fight them to the death if necessary.

She watched the three intruders fan out at the foot of the birthing bed, facing her. Again she shifted her body to shield her crying babies.

"Get out. Get out!" she shouted, her voice thundering in the tiny room. "You have no business here."

"Watch her," the Viis said to his men. He was speaking in the common patois of the abiru, or slave races. "She's weak from birthing, but she's still dangerous."

The mother's alarm continued to grow. She panted with it, her rage mingling with her fear. She was poor, a grade-two worker in the docks. Her mate was on shift duty even now. With all her heart and soul she longed for him to come, but she knew it was impossible. He did not know she needed help. He thought her safe within the birthing room. Gods' mercy, why were these brutes here?

One of the enforcers pulled out a rope from his pocket and shook its coils free. The rope curled and straightened as though alive, suspending itself above the ground. A loop formed in one end. Dry-mouthed, the mother stared at it.

"No," she panted. "No!"

"Get back," the Viis said harshly to her. He pointed at the wall near the door. "Stand over there and be quiet."

She knew what they wanted then. It flashed over her like heat. Growling, she flung herself across the bed to protect her cubs, but the Toth moved faster.

He tossed the loop at her, and the rope settled itself over her head and throat. At once she felt a sharp pulse of energy enclose her throat, then a sizzle of pain.

Clutching the rope, she screamed.

"Hold her!" the Viis commanded as she struggled. "Take care, you fool! Don't hurt the cubs."

Despite the tightening of the noose, she fought harder. Through the roaring in her ears, she could hear her babies crying. Their helplessness and danger enraged her past all caution, and she roared with fury as she lunged for a floppy Toth ear, bit it hard, and tried to tear it off.

Oaths filled the room, mingling with her shouts and the screams of the cubs.

"Now!" the Viis said.

Another noose settled over her head, and the two enforcers dragged her bodily off the bed. She hit the floor hard enough to knock the wind from her weakened body. Lying there, she shook her head and tried to raise herself, but the Toths held her pinned, both of them sitting on her with cruel disregard for her condition or the pain they were inflicting. The Toth with the bitten ear shook his head, slinging splatters of blood, and huffed to himself. The Aaroun mother could still taste blood and hair in her mouth. She spat, wishing her teeth had caught his shaggy throat instead.

Helpless and seething, she was forced to watch as the Viis grabbed each of her babies in turn by its scruff and carried them over to the light by the open door. He dumped them on the floor and examined them one by one, checking fur quality, conformation, and tiny milk teeth. Instinctive infant growling filled the air, and the mother pressed her face against the dirty floor and wept in sheer frustration.

"Stripes," the Viis said in disgust. "Ordinary stripes, just like all the other cubs in this birthing row. Ah, but what are you?"

The mother heard the change in his tone, the keen interest, and her heart constricted. She saw him lift her golden child, her only daughter, high into the air to examine her thoroughly.

When he lowered the golden one to chest height and cradled her against him, the mother knew she had lost.

Grief consumed her. She howled until one of the Toths tightened the noose and choked off her cries.

"An extraordinary find," the Viis said. Although his voice was muffled by the hood, smug satisfaction registered in his tone. "This one will do very well. She'll bring a good price at market for Festival."

Stroking the golden one, who was trying to growl and cry at the same time, the Viis chuckled to himself. Stepping over the other infants, still squirming helplessly on the floor, he walked out into the street.

"Let her up," he called over his shoulder. "Stun her if she tries to follow."

The mother felt as though she had been shattered inside. She held herself still, defeated now, knowing that she had no choice in this theft, no recourse. But the Toths hurt her anyway as they stripped off the charged restraint ropes. She didn't rise, didn't try to regain her feet, but they beat her and kicked her until her pain was like fire, blazing around and through her body.

"Stupid Aaroun," one of the Toths mumbled. His wide, long tongue flicked up into one of his broad nostrils. "Always fight. Always lose."

The other one bellowed a laugh.

They stood over her a second more, as though expecting one last show of defiance from her, then at last lumbered toward the door. One of them clumsily kicked the infants aside, making them scream anew.

The mother tried to pick herself up, tried to crawl forward to the babies she had left. Although the bonding was new, it was so strong she felt as though they had torn part of her body away and stolen it.

"My golden one," she said, moaning as she dragged herself toward her tiny sons. They came to her, tottering and weak, seeking comfort.

But although they were soon pacified and settled, there was no one to comfort the mother, left bleeding and bereft on the floor, never to see her daughter again.

Carrying the golden one in the crook of his arm, his coat concealing her, the Viis strode through the squalid streets of the abiru ghetto, his hired enforcers lumbering behind him. A block away, his transport hovered on park a half meter above the unpaved street. Three more Toths guarded it with sidearms illegal for civilians. The Viis, however, had little fear of encountering a city patroller down here in this end of the ghetto.

Smiling to himself, he pulled off his hood and tucked it in his belt. The warm afternoon breeze blew across his skin and ruffled his rill, which itched after being confined in the hood.

"Hey, Poal," another trader called, walking up. "Any luck?"

Poal glanced around to see Tynmez, his chief competitor, hailing him. Stiffening, he checked surreptitiously to make sure the golden Aaroun was well-hidden beneath his jacket, then turned to face Tynmez with a false smile.

"Greetings of Festival," he said, using a tone that made the formal words a mockery. "May you fertilize many eggs."

Tynmez bowed, but his purple eyes kept straying to the lump hidden beneath Poal's jacket. "Luck?"

Poal flicked out his long, narrow tongue. "Not much."

Tynmez smiled and gestured behind him at the two Toths carrying laden crates of young Aarouns, Kelths, and Myals. All were crying with fear. Their cries, plus those of their anguished parents, made a din that echoed off the mud hovels. This was the very poorest end of the abiru ghetto, with the worst housing and most squalid conditions. Only the most desperate or greedy traders ventured into this area, but Poal now knew it was worth it. The Aaroun in his arms would fetch a handsome price. He had never seen her equal in all his years of trading.

"Your air sacs are full," Tynmez said. "You must be happy with your catch."

"I am."

"Show me."

Poal backed closer to his enforcers, glancing at them to see if they were alert. Two were gaping at something in the distance, chewing cud and flipping their ears at flies, but at least one seemed aware and on the job. Poal might need them all if Tynmez ordered his thugs to rob Poal's catch.

"You'll see my wares at the premarket selection," Poal said. "Until then, I don't show what I've got."

"Stupid," Tynmez said with irritation. "I might pay you well for your stock."

"I'll do better at premarket."

"You think those market vendors will deal fairly or generously with you?" Tynmez said with derision. "They are thinking of their markup. You and I are males of understanding. Let us come to terms."

"You would buy something you haven't seen?" Poal countered.

"If it has value. I see the smugness in your eyes," Tynmez said. "And I have looked at the stock on your transport. Oh, don't raise your rill at me," he said sharply as Poal glared at him. "The crates aren't opaque. I have eyes, do I not?"

Poal glanced at his guards, knowing now they were useless. Tynmez had bribed the fools. Poal would have to fire them and hire more, providing he escaped this situation with his hide intact.

More of Tynmez's enforcers appeared. They, like Poal's

thugs, were armed with illegal weapons, all aimed at Poal.

Gall poured through Poal, and he could feel his neck rill quivering with defeat.

"Will you force me to sell?" he asked.

"You have a good catch," Tynmez said, and now it was his turn to smile. "You are an excellent judge of conformation and pelt quality. You are much more selective than I."

"Yes," Poal said with a sneer as he watched his crates being loaded onto Tynmez's already-laden transport. "You would glean even Skeks from the sewer if you thought you could profit from them."

The insult bounced off Tynmez without effect. His smile broadened, and he jerked his head.

His enforcers moved fast, surrounding Poal in an instant. Poal's own hirelings made no move at all.

Seething with rage, Poal held the golden Aaroun tighter, hearing her faint sounds and knowing that he would never see the fortune this small creature was worth. More gall soured his mouth. With all his soul he damned Tynmez.

An enforcer stepped close and jammed the blunt snout of his weapon into Poal's ribs. "Don't move."

Poal obeyed, glaring at Tynmez with the blackest hatred.

Tynmez walked up to him and gently reached beneath the jacket. There was a bump, and a yip of rage drowned out by Tynmez's own hiss of breath.

He yanked back his hand and shook it.

Poal laughed. "Did she bite you?"

Tynmez backed up, glaring back. "You fool. You can't sell a fighter anywhere but the ring. And even the Bizsi Mo'ad won't take abiru this young."

As he considered the famous gladiator school and the high prices it sometimes paid for quality trainee stock, Poal's spirits lifted. "Ah, but when she's bigger, I'll have her to sell, won't I?"

Tynmez was still shaking his hand and examining his bitten finger. Poal did not think the skin was even broken.

His confidence came back. If he played this right, he could get rid of Tynmez and salvage this situation.

"Still want to rob me?" he asked. "I didn't know you had stooped to stealing gladiator bait."

"Bait?" Tynmez's eyes dilated in suspicion. "Or fighter?"

"What do you think?" Poal said, trying to keep his tone light. "In this wretched end of the ghetto, we are competing for the dregs. If you expect to find something better then may I sell you a cloud, or perhaps part of the sea?"

"Why cover this one, if it is of such poor quality?"

Poal flicked out his tongue, pretending indifference. "She bites and scratches like a cornered Skek. As you discovered."

Tynmez scowled at him. "You're a fool, wasting your eye and discernment on gladiator bait. Especially now, just before Festival. It doesn't make sense that you've sunk to such a low. I suspect you of trickery."

He was one to talk, after bribing Poal's guards and trying to steal everything in sight. Poal held down his anger, aware that he was still outnumbered and unprotected. Curling his tongue inside his mouth, he met Tynmez's eyes, hesitated, then placed one digit between his nostrils and sniffed.

Tynmez's eyes widened. "You?" he said in surprise. "You, caught by the dust?"

Poal flicked out his tongue, even as he despised Tynmez for being so eager to believe the worst about him. "When a male has debts, he must do everything possible to cover them."

"In debt for dust? A third time I say you are a fool." Tynmez backed away from him and gestured at his enforcers. "Finish unloading his stock. Quickly!" He swung back to Poal. "The two spotted Aarouns I saw in your crates will recoup what I've spent in bribes. The rest are no better or worse than what I found."

"Then leave them," Poal said. He tried to speak lightly, but there was an edge in his voice.

Tynmez must have heard it. "I will leave you your gladiator bait and a curse to go with it. May it bite you and turn on you. May your wounds go septic. May your brain grow riddled with abiru fever, that you wander the streets forever, witless and gibbering to shadows only you can see."

Poal drew in his breath to retaliate, and felt another warning jab of the weapon pressed to his side. He held his breath instead, fuming too much to feel relief at having tricked Tynmez. When his transport was stripped of its cargo, Tynmez and his guards departed in a whoosh of jetted air and flying dust.

Poal stood in the street, coated with dust, his neck rill at full extension. When he could finally command himself enough to speak, he turned on his enforcers with a glare, and flicked out his tongue.

"You're fired, the lot of you."

The Toth whose ear had been bitten by the mother of the golden Aaroun glared back at him. "I got no bribe. I—"

"Then make your brothers share with you," Poal said viciously. He brushed by the brutes, who stared at him with their mouths open, and climbed aboard his transport so fast he made it tip and scrape one edge on the ground.

Dropping the Aaroun on the seat beside him, Poal revved the engine and lifted it straight up just as the Toths finally figured out he was serious about firing them all. He roared away over their massive heads, leaving them bellowing insults in his wake.

Not until he flew under the curving arch of new dock construction bordering the side of the ghetto and tucked himself into the general stream of traffic did Poal relax his death grip on the controls. His temper calmed down, and he began to mentally add up losses. They were plenty. He had lost the wages squandered on his enforcers, plus their stun-sticks, restraint ropes, and sidearms. He had lost a day's worth of stock, good stock, all of it, despite what he'd said to Tynmez. He had nearly lost his life.

It was a heavy blow, especially coming this early in the year. If not for the prize still in his possession, he would be facing ruin right now.

Poal glanced over at the Aaroun crouched fearfully in the seat beside him. Her dark eyes were enormous in the light mask across her face. Her paws clung to the cloth with instinctive desperation. He could see her little sides heaving.

But, ah, that perfect fur. The broad shoulders, heavy with muscle and bone already, the sleek loins, and the balance of exquisite proportions. She was a beauty, as Aarouns went. Had he not lost everything else, she would have meant his fortune. Now she meant his salvation.

As a newborn, however, she presented him with a problem. She was too young, yet, to go long without proper care. Aaroun cubs could be slow to get started. Poal was not prepared to keep her for a few days, to hand-feed and pamper her.

Right now, freshly plucked from her mother, she looked in prime condition. Her pelt was shiny and soft, and her sides were plump. In a day or two, she might collapse from fright and grief. Often Aarouns this young failed to thrive away from their families.

He would lose money by selling her this early, but he wasn't going to be greedy now. He wasn't even going to risk the auction at premarket. He could no longer afford to take chances.

Poal knew of a dealer in the rare and costly, a Gorlican who specialized in supplying pets to affluent households. Like all his kind, the Gorlican possessed repellent manners and a visage so ugly he kept it hidden behind a mask, yet Gorlicans were a useful race, hardworking allies to the Viis empire. Most were merchants and shopkeepers, like his acquaintance, eager to partake of the buying and selling so repugnant to the middle and upper Viis classes. Poal decided to take a chance and go straight to the pet dealer. Tynmez would not hear about the golden Aaroun he had missed until it was too late to steal her.

Inflating his air sacs, Poal hissed to himself and gunned his transport even faster.

CHAPTER TWO

In the Chamber of Hatching, an ancient, rough-hewn place of stone and sand, antiquated torches blazed with unsteady radiance. Female Viis attendants, all blue-skinned and wearing identical saffron-colored robes, stood rowed around the perimeter of the sand, silently watching the imperial eggs.

Low drumbeats throbbed in a steady cadence that stirred primitive urges within Sahmrahd Kaa. Sighing with anticipation, he closed his brilliant blue eyes and let his senses submerge into the raw, ancient sound. Other musical instruments from antiquity joined in . . . the symstera wailing low and urgent; the flyta piping in swift staccato counterpoint. For a few bars, the music reprised the mating songs, then it descended into the simple, pounding drumbeats once again. All the collective anticipation, the waiting since dawn, filled the Kaa.

With his eyes still closed, the Kaa leaned forward on his throne. His will, his consciousness, surged toward the eggs. *Come forth, little ones,* he thought. *Come forth that we may rejoice over you.*

The drums stilled abruptly, leaving a silence heavy and profound. The Kaa gasped and opened his eyes. He peered

over the railing and heard a distinctive crack before he saw
the split appear in one of the eggs. The female attendants
raised their arms and sang in unison, the melody one of
rejoicing and encouragement.

Another egg rolled over. From the screened, secluded
gallery above the Kaa's throne, he heard a collective gasp
followed by a few muted giggles coming from his favorite
wives, those whose eggs he had fertilized this year. Their
excitement and anticipation fell like a hot breath on the
back of his neck.

The Chamber of Hatching vaulted high overhead, its in-
tricately carved ceiling lost among the shadows. The imperial eggs—large, faintly iridescent orbs of life—lay atop
warmed sand. Attendants in cerise-hued robes appeared.
With blankets folded over their arms, they hovered expec-
tantly near the eggs while the birthing song rose and echoed. Another egg opened, and another, spilling awkward
occupants into the world.

Now there were several damp, struggling youngsters
crawling amidst shell fragments, gawky in their first movements as they rubbed off their opaque membranes to reveal
their resplendent skin colors. The warm air grew fragrant
with the birthing scent, and the Kaa inhaled deeply, feeling
his own hatching memories stir in the vaguest recesses of
his mind.

Attendants swarmed about the hatchlings, blocking much
of the Kaa's view. He glimpsed wobbly heads, a tiny crimson rill as tender as a sigh, a flailing tail, miniature fingers
and toes gripping the hands of the adults. Grinning to himself, the Kaa rose to his feet in an effort to see better.

The Master of the Imperial Hatchery moved slowly
among the eggs, eyeing those not yet broken, now and then
laying his hand gently atop a shell. Fifty-two imperial eggs
this year. But how many hatchlings? The Kaa watched as
the master frowned and gestured for two unhatched eggs to
be lifted and taken away. The Kaa pretended not to see
those failures. Reseating himself on his throne, he switched

his tail from side to side and allowed himself no thought of the stillborn.

He was impatient to see the living.

"Sire."

The Kaa half turned on his crimson cushion, allowing the Master of the Imperial Hatchery to approach him. This was a private moment for the Kaa, one of the few permitted to the Father of the Empire, the Supreme Warrior, the Guardian of the Golden Seals, the Lord of All Things. He ruled countless worlds. His word alone was law. He could take life with a single glance at the green-robed guards standing alert behind his throne.

He could give life as well.

The Kaa's brilliant blue eyes widened and softened. He returned his gaze to his progeny crawling on the birthing sand.

His rill lifted above the jeweled collar supporting it, spreading in a magnificent deepening hue of crimson. His blood thrummed with excitement.

"Sire, your imperial hatchlings have been sorted."

This time the Kaa did not look away from where the saffron-robed attendants were filing out, each one carrying a hatchling swathed and concealed in a blanket.

The Kaa frowned, feeling the pain of loss beneath his breastbone. Those offspring he would never know. He would never see their faces. He would never hear their happy voices, or laugh at their chatter. They were as lost to him as the eggs which had not hatched. Ugly, deformed, weak, or merely plain—they had been deemed unworthy of his notice. They would live their lives outside the palace, joining other Rejects, unaware of the heritage which had been denied them by fate.

While the saffron-robed attendants did their grim work, the cerise-robed attendants moved slowly about, cuddling the acceptable hatchlings in their arms, cooing to them and singing.

The Kaa finally turned his gaze upon the master still

waiting at his side. "Master of the Birthing," the Kaa said formally. "What news do you bring us? How many born?"

The master bowed deeply and cleared his throat. His rill lay limp about his neck. "Good news, sire. The hatching was a splendid and most bountiful one."

From the corner of his eye, the Kaa saw another group of Rejects swathed in blankets and carried out. His pain grew, and from the gallery he heard a few hushed cries from his wives.

"How many?" the Kaa asked, although in his mind he was counting.

The master bowed again, careful to keep his gaze averted from the Kaa's face. "Twenty-nine blessed hatchlings are born to the Father and his gracious wives."

Twenty-nine acceptable hatchlings of the fifty born. Better than half. The Kaa blinked. Twenty-nine hatchlings and twenty-eight favorite wives. Tonight when the sunset marked the end of Festival, and the closing bells in the city's spires were rung, songs of joy would fill the wives' court in the palace. There were enough tiny, dewy-rilled hatchlings for every set of loving arms. And he would allow Myneith—First Wife, and still most favored—to have two. She would be pleased by the gesture, and perhaps she would forget that she was growing older, with less plumpness stored in her tail as her beauty became eclipsed by the newer wives.

"Congratulations to the Imperial Father," the master said.

"We are pleased," the Kaa replied.

The master released an audible sigh of relief and bowed with a smile.

The Kaa also smiled, and the drums began to roll with flourishes. Triumphant music soared in a rising series of fanfares. Now word would flash through the palace, and the waiting courtiers would be agog with the news.

Twenty-nine perfect, beautiful hatchlings . . . May the gods show mercy and let them all live, the Kaa prayed.

Satisfaction swelled within the Kaa. Rising from his throne, he bounced a little on his toes. At a time when fewer and fewer Viis offspring were born every year, at a time when beauty and perfection seemed harder to find, he at least need not fear that he was losing his powers or his virility. Yes, he was indeed the Father of the Empire.

But there remained one official question for him to ask.

He pinned the master with his gaze. "Do any of these newborns surpass the sri-Kaa in beauty?"

The master tucked his hands together and tilted his head. "One male is crimson, green, and gold. A most striking combination."

"Indeed, yes," the Kaa said, surprised. His thoughts flashed to Abiya, his newest wife from the southern continent. She was exotic and high-tempered. Perhaps she was the genetic mother of this son, not that it mattered.

"Still," the master continued, "unusual coloring does not in and of itself surpass the sublime qualities of the sri-Kaa. She remains supreme among the Imperial Father's progeny."

Relieved, the Kaa uncurled his tongue within his mouth and gave the master a nod. "Then it is done. We shall gaze upon them tomorrow when it is certain they will live. Inform our wives of the happy news."

The master bowed yet again, so deeply this time the folds of his rill shook free. "Yes, sire. It shall be done."

The Kaa walked away. By the time he reached the tall double doors of bronze carved with the legends of the First Hatching, the guards had snapped to attention, and two of them swung the heavy doors open for him.

Trumpets blared, and small Kelth lits of matched fur color, with upright ears and narrow muzzles, ran ahead through the passageway like small alarms in their red imperial livery. "Heads up! Heads up!" they cried in shrill unison. "The Kaa is coming!"

Surrounded by his guards, the Kaa strode along an ancient passageway of worn stone lit by old-fashioned torches that flickered and smoked with great inefficiency. House-keeping went to great lengths to keep the soot scrubbed away, grumbling at the extra work involved. But the touches of antiquity pleased the Kaa, for he was an admirer of history and its relics. Many times his courtiers had urged him to build a new Chamber of Hatching, one with modern seats, one with windows, one with a spectators' gallery so that the whole court might attend. They said the imperial Chamber of Hatching was crude and too old, little better than a cave, and far too small.

The Kaa had no intention of changing this most vener-able and sacred part of the palace. While he lived, there would never be room for spectators. To witness the emer-gence of the imperial hatchlings was the sole privilege of himself and his favored wives, and so it would remain.

Ahead the Kaa could see a handful of intrepid courtiers crowding into the passageway where it linked to the main section of the palace. Guards held these fawning sycophants back, however, allowing none of them near the Kaa's im-perial person.

One courtier ignored protocol and called out his con-gratulations, but the Kaa pretended not to hear. His servants opened the private door leading into his apartments, and the Kaa allowed himself a small sigh of relief.

Although the last day of Festival was always the best because of the hatchings, he still regretted seeing the week of pleasure and informality end.

Gaveid, chancellor of state and the Kaa's chief adviser, stood waiting inside the sunlit rooms. Heavy with much stored fat, his jaw rills sagging from dissipation that had not yet completely marred his good looks, Gaveid was lean-ing on his staff of office and yawning. He straightened hast-ily, however, at the Kaa's entrance and bowed deeply with an old-fashioned flourish both pleasing and graceful to the eye.

"Congratulations, sire," he said in his cool, unhurried voice.

"Thank you, chancellor," the Kaa replied.

The captain of the guard snapped a salute, and the Kaa flicked him a glance of dismissal. All the guards saluted and filed out, leaving the Kaa and his chancellor alone. Slaves moved unobtrusively about, one pouring cups of imported meccan wine while others laid out brushes, oil jars, and additional preparations for the Kaa's bath. The Kaa accepted wine and offered some to Gaveid, who respectfully gestured refusal.

Gaveid was the only Viis in the empire with the privilege to come and go as he pleased in the Kaa's quarters. He also possessed the privileges of being able to sit in the Kaa's presence and to speak his opinions as bluntly as he wished. Nearly as tall as the Kaa and very old, the chancellor was descended from one of the Twelve original lineages. Although in the past century Gaveid's family had been decimated by the Dancing Death, the noble bloodline had not yet been completely lost. Gaveid's golden, cynical eyes had seen everything. As the saying went, he had lived twice. Rarely did anything surprise him.

From the tall open windows of the rooms came the crashing sound of gun salutes being fired, one salvo for every accepted imperial hatchling. A distant crowd cheered in the city streets beyond the palace walls. The Kaa paid little attention, but the chancellor winced slightly and turned his back to the sunlight streaming in through the windows.

"Were you out gambling all night?" the Kaa asked him in amusement.

The chancellor puffed out the air sacs in his throat. Even as a lun-adult—well past his fertile years—he preferred to gamble and drink wine with the zest of a much younger male. No one at court had his stamina or his hardheaded ability to function and reason early in the day following a night of debauchery.

"Gambling?" he repeated. "Yes, sire. It is, after all, Festival, and I am not otal yet."

"You will lose your fortune someday," the Kaa said,

and drained his cup with a feeling of intense satisfaction. Father of twenty-nine new hatchlings. He restrained the urge to laugh aloud, and instead let the feeling bubble inside him like the effects of a superb dinner wine.

"Risk gives life its zest," Gaveid said.

The Kaa felt generous enough to tease the old one. "Gaveid, you will come to us one day a ruined male, lamenting and wearing the ashes of remorse on your head. Great Father, you will say, why did you not prevail on me to use more reason?"

The chancellor snorted. "I do not gamble my own money," he said. "I only risk the fortunes of others."

While the Kaa was laughing, a melodic chime sounded outside his dressing room. The Kaa's good mood vanished like a burst bubble. "Permit no entry," he said sharply to the slave who hurried to the door. "We will keep our privacy yet a while longer."

The slave bowed nervously. "It is Lord Telvrahd, sire."

The Kaa narrowed his gaze. "Most especially we do not wish to receive him. Deny him entry."

The slave obeyed, and Gaveid cocked his head to one side. "Is that wise? Telvrahd will be offended."

"We told our egg-brother we would not discuss his petitions until after Festival," the Kaa said shortly.

"The Progressionist Party is gaining popularity in the outlying areas, sire. Perhaps it is best to deal early with the matter, before it becomes a problem."

"The Progressionists are fools. Telvrahd is a fool," the Kaa said.

"Diplomacy, sire," Gaveid counseled. "Not confrontation."

"Yes, and next you would advise us to listen to the Reformists as well. Must we then give full rights of citizenship to the abiru?"

"It is not necessary to go to radical extremes to appease these factions."

"Factions." The Kaa flicked out his tongue in scorn.

"We are bored with factions and political parties. They should be abolished."

"Granted, they are a nuisance, but they allow citizens and nobles to vent their dissatisfaction without violence."

"Do they?" the Kaa retorted sharply. "Or do they encourage more grumbling against us?"

"Sire—"

"Enough," the Kaa said, and held up his hand. "This discussion bores us."

"Politics remain a necessary evil in the duties of the Imperial Father."

"But not today," the Kaa said with a grin of mischief. He was still swollen with pride, and he wished to savor the triumph of the Hatching as long as possible. "The Imperial Father has executed his most important duty. Twenty-nine new hatchlings," he boasted.

Gaveid bowed. "A splendid addition to your imperial progeny."

The Kaa cast him a sharp glance. Sometimes it was difficult to tell whether Gaveid was mocking him or not. "And how many hatchlings did you father when you were able, chancellor?"

Considering the low birthrate in Gaveid's family, this retaliation was not a kind one.

Gaveid's old eyes narrowed to slits. "A swift barb indeed, sire. You have reminded me of lost days, of vigor I shall never regain, of memories best left forgotten in the dust of time. I am honored by the Imperial Father's attention."

Annoyance flared through the Kaa. "And now in turn *you* remind us of the old days, when the royal hatching was double or triple this number."

Gaveid bowed. "Time sets its footprints upon us. Our civilization has changed. Our genetics have changed. We are in decay and decline as a race. The empire shrinks a little more each year."

"Don't say such things!" the Kaa said sharply, turning

away from him. Reaching for his refreshed wine cup, the Kaa drank deeply, too annoyed to savor its exquisite taste. "You speak as though we are finished."

"The end comes," Gaveid said.

His gloomy tone made the Kaa shiver. He loathed it when Gaveid was in one of his depressions. This should have been a time of rejoicing, but the old chancellor seemed to delight in drawing a curtain of pessimism over them all.

"Our empire will not end," the Kaa said decisively. "We shall restore it to its former glory. We shall spread our influence among the worlds until once again our supremacy dazzles the lesser races. We shall have our palaces restored, and our people will know prosperity."

"So your majesty's speeches have assured us before," Gaveid said in a dry, unimpressed tone.

The Kaa's rill reddened, and he glared at the old chancellor. Perhaps it was time for Gaveid to retire. He was becoming a nuisance. "We shall not hear another lecture against the expenses of restoration."

"No, sire." Gaveid bowed and placed his pebbly-skinned hand on the dispatch box atop a small table of polished blue jaepis stone. "There is not time today to discuss the depleted state of the imperial treasury."

The Kaa scowled. "Nor do we wish to receive the dispatches. They can wait until Festival is over."

"That time approaches."

"Not until sunset," the Kaa retorted, although he knew it was an infantile quibble.

"Some matters should not wait, sire."

The Kaa gestured, and the slaves came forward to divest him of his ceremonial robes. Even in private, without his courtiers to attend him, there was a ceremony and ritual to be followed in undressing the Father of the Empire.

Gaveid waited a moment, but the Kaa ignored him.

"Sire," the chancellor said at last, stepping forward. He walked slowly these days. For an instant, the Kaa almost thought he saw the old chancellor limp. But that was unthinkable. Were the chancellor to become otal—physically decrepit and infirm—he would have to be replaced at once, exiled from Vir, and sent to the country to finish his days far from the demands of public service.

Regret and grief touched the Kaa. No matter how angry he sometimes became with Gaveid, he did not truly wish to replace him. Gaveid had the wily shrewdness necessary to guide him through the tangles of galactic diplomacy, policy setting, and continued subjugation of the abiru races without inciting active rebellion. Most important of all, Gaveid was clever enough to concoct ways of keeping the treasury filled, which paid for the all-important work of restoring the oldest sections of the palace. *Let the gods preserve this old one for a few years more,* the Kaa thought.

"Sire," Gaveid said persistently, "the dispatches will not take long. The situation on galactic border nine—"

"Not that," the Kaa interrupted sharply, deflecting the matter entirely. "Not now. Send the dispatches away."

Without waiting for the chancellor's reply, he strode into his bathing chamber and walked down a series of shallow steps into a pool filled with warm, scented water. Pale moon blossoms floated on the surface, along with the oils of kaffyrd and eloa.

Slaves bathed and dried him, then his clothes for the procession were brought. Normally his courtiers would have entered for the ritual Dressing of the Day while Gaveid played the holograms of the dispatches. But during Festival many of the stultifying rituals of court were relaxed. There would be many parades to celebrate the return of the males who had left on their mating migration to other communities, and several courtiers had requested leave today to welcome home their sons.

On this final day, there would be no dispatches and no courtiers casting jealous glances at each other as they vied for imperial favor.

Instead, the Kaa allowed his slaves to dress him. When he had been assisted into a long-skirted coat of brilliant green cloth woven on the Isles of Vyria, and a heavy chain of gold studded with green Gaza stones—the most precious and costly of jewels—had been hung across his shoulders, he selected a tall jeweled collar, and gentle hands reverently arranged the folds of his rill above it.

He emerged from the bathing chamber to find the chancellor standing in the same spot. The dispatch box, however, was gone. The Kaa spread his rill in satisfaction and gestured for his mirror to be activated. The slaves pressed one of the jewel-encrusted knobs adorning a paneled wall, and a portion of the wall shimmered into a reflective surface. Standing before it, the Kaa watched as his attendants finished preparing him.

He was very tall, even for a Viis male in the splendor of full maturity, and towered over most of his subjects. Hued a magnificent deep bronze color, with dark green shadings beneath his jaw and across his hands, his skin showed patches of iridescence that shimmered multiple colors in the sunshine. Poets had lauded him for his splendid coloring, claiming in one epic poem that he "could blind his enemies simply with the radiant magnificence of his imperial person."

The Kaa did not consider himself a vain male as a rule, although he took great pride in his appearance. Today he studied his reflection as the slaves finished slipping gold tips onto the spines of his neck and jaw rills. He had chosen to wear an elaborate collar of gold, embossed with his name and titles in the ancient alphabet. It was quite heavy, especially in the back, where it supported his rill to nearly full extension. Narrowing his violet-blue eyes, as dark and vivid as the sky where it meets the curve of space, the Kaa twisted and turned his head to see the full effect.

Satisfied, he stepped back, and his reflection automatically vanished as the mirror became a wall again. The religious procession would not take long, and then he would have his outing with the sri-Kaa. How pleasant that would be.

Consulting his timepiece, Gaveid frowned.

The Kaa knew that look. "Are we late?"

"Very late, sire. It is coming on midday."

"Don't fuss," the Kaa said without concern. "We are the father of twenty-nine new hatchlings. Our wives are plump and happy. We are blessed."

"Blessed indeed," Gaveid said, inclining his head. "But still very late. There is the processional of thanksgiving to be made, the ritual at the old temple, the banquet, and the meetings with important visiting dignitaries. I think the Imperial Father should forgo his visit to the marketplace."

The Kaa had been picking through a tray of rings and bracelets. Now he tossed down the trinkets and swung around.

"No," he said sharply. "We made a promise to the sri-Kaa. We shall not break it."

"The sri-Kaa is barely two years out of the egg. She will quickly forget her disappointment. The emissaries from Ul-one-two-four have been waiting several days for audience. Their disappointment may be more difficult to repair."

Displeasure swept through the Kaa, and his tail stiffened beneath the long skirt of his coat. He faced his chancellor with a glare. "This will be the first public appearance of our daughter," he said. "It is important that all see she has become chune."

"Yes, it is well that the sri-Kaa has reached her second growth cycle, healthy and strong," Gaveid said. "But equally important are the sivo crystals mined on Ul-one-two-four, and the money they pour into the imperial coffers. Money which pays for the restoration projects planned by the Imperial Father."

"Can you not put them off?" the Kaa asked.

"Unwise, sire."

The Kaa's scowl deepened. He felt torn by these conflicting obligations. He did not wish to make a decision.

Gaveid watched him knowingly, as though he could read the Kaa's mind. "Perhaps—"

"Yes?" the Kaa said eagerly.

"Perhaps the sri-Kaa could accompany the Imperial Father in meeting with the emissaries," Gaveid said persuasively. "Combine both events. Please the chune, introduce her to the world, grant these dignitaries a double honor with both your presence and hers."

As always Gaveid's suggestions made excellent sense. The Kaa was tempted, but he remembered a pair of pleading eyes and the irresistible entwining of tender arms about his neck.

"We gave our promise to the chune," he said. "We shall take her to the marketplace as she has requested."

"Very well, sire," the chancellor said, frowning. "But should the sri-Kaa not learn that the duties of high office must take precedence over personal wishes?"

The Kaa returned his frown. For a moment he felt the crushing weight of his duties, his responsibilities, the fact that he had yet to find the time or opportunity to visit the far-flung corners of his empire, the slowness of building projects that he might not live to see completed, the constant pressure from his subjects and courtiers, each with dozens of requests, petitions, and intrigues. He lived enmeshed in duties and obligations. No matter how early he rose or how late he retired, the work was never done, the demands were never satisfied. Dispatches, reports, petitions, and audiences were pushed aside, only to multiply like the repulsive little Skeks teeming in the city's sewers.

This was Festival, a time of rejoicing and rebirth, a time of hope and renewal. The whole empire was at play for these few short days. Here, in his own capital, the Father of the Empire would also have a few moments of play with his daughter before Festival ended for another year of toil.

"Let the emissaries wait," the Kaa said. "We shall please our daughter today."

"The Imperial Father indulges her greatly," Gaveid replied. "Is it wise, I wonder, to spoil the character of one so lovely and graceful in physical form?"

"Israi is perfect," the Kaa said to him, thinking his worries foolish. "And perfection cannot be spoiled."

Gaveid's yellow eyes betrayed rare consternation. "Surely an unwise—"

"Let there be nothing more said on this matter."

At that sharp command, the chancellor closed his mouth tightly and bowed low. He stood in silence, his air sacs inflated, his old eyes disapproving, while the Kaa finished his preparations.

The Kaa ignored the disapproval and ordered the sri-Kaa brought to him. While his chancellor was wily and shrewd, never making mistakes, never steering him toward unwise decisions, the Kaa also disagreed with Gaveid in three key areas. One had to do with his restoration work. Another concerned certain policies regarding the outer worlds of the empire, especially the trouble spot of galactic border nine. The third revolved around the sri-Kaa, her training as a future ruler and Sahmrahd's successor, and the Kaa's own indulgence of the chune's whims and fancies.

Let the old one stand in sour judgment, the Kaa thought derisively. Gaveid did not quite know everything.

"Father! Father!"

The exuberant shouting came as music to the Kaa's ears. Seconds later, the door burst open faster than the attendants could move it and a small figure came hurtling through. She barreled into the Kaa's legs, nearly knocking him off-balance, and gripped him tightly in a hug.

"Father!" she squealed. "I have been waiting *forever*."

Although the Kaa's heart swelled with love, he put on an expression of mock disapproval and glared down at her. "Is this the way the sri-Kaa greets the Imperial Father?"

Israi's beaming smile faltered. Her eyes widened for a moment as she recollected etiquette. Swiftly she backed up, nearly bumping into her attendants, who had just now caught up with her.

One of them gripped her shoulders to steady her and bent down to murmur encouragement into her ear dimple. The sri-Kaa nodded and lifted her gaze to her father.

He stared down at her as though unmoved, although inside he was melting with adoration. Never had he seen a more perfect chune. Her soft, pebbly skin glowed a pure golden hue without flaw or blemish. Her eyes were as brilliant a green as the Kaa's own Gaza stones. That green spread from the outer corner of her eyes to curve up toward her ear dimples in markings that were very striking now but would, when she matured, make her beauty exotic indeed. Her tiny neck rill, supported by a miniature collar studded with glittering jewels, displayed variegated hues of gold, green, and blue. Although still very young, Israi already moved with incredible grace. Her physical proportions were perfect. She glowed with health and vitality. Even her tail, concealed today beneath the hem of her indigo-blue gown, was thick and already growing plump with stored fat. Lovely, intelligent, graceful, vital, precocious— Israi was his favorite daughter and chosen successor.

Just the sight of her filled him with joy and restored his spirits. He longed to laugh with her, to scoop her into his arms and breathe across her sweet face, to toss her into the air, to tickle her until she squealed, and to let her ride on his shoulders.

But today was to be her first public appearance. As sri-Kaa, she had to remember what was expected of her and act according to her rank and position. The first, most important lesson a sri-Kaa had to learn was to respect the Kaa. Completely, unhesitantly, and without fail.

He stood firm, meeting a gaze which could have melted the foundation stones of the palace, his stern expression never altering.

Israi's attendant whispered to her again, and Israi's green eyes lowered. Her rill blushed a dark blue, and with bowed head she walked slowly and respectfully up to him. She made her little obeisance flawlessly, and raised her gaze to his once more.

"Good morning, Imperial Father," she said, her young

voice grave and clear. "May—may the blessings of Festival befall you."

The Kaa bowed to her in return. "Thank you, our daughter."

Her eyes were getting bigger, and he decided the lesson had been reinforced sufficiently.

With a smile, he took her hand. Israi squeezed his long, slender fingers, grinning radiantly in return.

"Time for the procession, sire," Gaveid said from behind him.

Israi gestured urgently for the Kaa to bend down. When he did so, she whispered, "And the marketplace. You promised."

"We promised," the Kaa agreed. He gazed deep into his daughter's eyes, seeing his future in their fire and courage. He smiled. "We shall not forget, provided the sri-Kaa behaves herself through all the ceremonies that come before."

Israi lifted her head high and imitated an imperious gesture made by court ladies. "The sri-Kaa will behave herself," she promised.

From the corner of his eye, the Kaa saw Gaveid frown with doubt and misgiving. The Kaa smiled at him. "You worry too much, old one. The sri-Kaa has given her word."

"The sri-Kaa's word is her most excellent bond," Gaveid said, bowing to Israi, who puffed up visibly at the praise. "But will the Imperial Daughter remember it?"

"I will!" Israi said forcefully, stamping her foot.

The Kaa swallowed his laughter. "She will," he assured the chancellor. "Come, precious one. It is time to go among our people."

CHAPTER THREE

The spring sunshine blazed down, unseasonably warm. Surrounded by guards, courtiers, attendants, clowns, cupbearers, and musicians, the Kaa strolled along the dusty stalls of the abiru marketplace and felt the heat radiate off stone pavement and stone walls. He regretted bringing his daughter here. This was no place for either of them. Despite attempts to brighten the surroundings with gaudy festoons of ribbons and wilted flowers, the plaza remained drab, dreary, ordinary. The rounded daub architecture of the buildings offended the Kaa's eyes, especially since it dated from a neomodern style that he particularly despised.

Here and there, some shops or alleys leading away from the plaza had been closed off with walls of colorful silk gauze, such places deemed inappropriate for the Kaa to see. Yet the shops selected to remain accessible proved to be vile, scarcely large enough to turn around in, with wares of mediocre quality and execrable taste. Outside in the expanse of the plaza itself, portable stalls were set up in haphazard fashion. The hucksters running such places were mostly Kelths—cringing, fawning creatures in brindled fur. Their upright ears twitched nervously at every sound. Their keen eyes watched the Kaa's movements as though he would order them slain on the spot. Garbed plainly in colors of dust and muted greens, they seemed too awed by the Kaa's august presence to even call out their wares. One male Kelth, bolder than the rest, held out a cheap trinket as though expecting the Kaa to purchase it. One of the guards glared at him, and the Kelth hastily withdrew with an awkward bow.

The crowd behind the patroller barricades consisted mostly of the mingled abiru races, with a scattering of lower-class Viis among them. A few Rejects, cloaked and hooded, skulked on the fringes. Gripping Israi's small hand tightly, the Kaa averted his gaze from these, his basest subjects.

Sighing, the Kaa paused halfway across the plaza, ready to retreat from this ill-considered expedition. At once his clowns raced ahead of him to tumble and flip in a display of acrobatics that made the abiru folk stare in astonishment. Israi laughed aloud, defying etiquette, and the Kaa smiled at the simple innocence of chunenhal.

She tilted her head back to gaze up at him with sparkling green eyes. "Isn't this fun? I am fascinated."

He sighed again, and had not the heart to drag her away just yet. Turning from the acrobatics of his clowns, he strolled to the booth of a short Myal. Of all the slave races, Myals were the most civilized. The Kaa appreciated their intelligence and undertanding of art and history. This particular Myal was old and stunted, barely reaching to the Kaa's waist. His mane of reddish-gold hair was scraggly and sparse, but his dark liquid eyes held an expression of refinement. He dealt in handcrafted lamps.

Pausing at the booth, the Kaa allowed a guard to select one of the lamps and hold it up for his inspection. The workmanship was surprisingly good; clearly the maker possessed familiarity with historical artifacts. The Kaa found himself almost interested enough to forget how thirsty, hot, and uncomfortable he was. Almost. He longed for the cool, scented shade of his garden, and turned away from the

Myal without asking the question he had intended.

The guard put down the lamp, and the little Myal crafter curled his prehensile tail around one leg and sank down on his haunches in visible disappointment.

"What?" asked a cultured voice from behind the Kaa. "Is the Imperial Father uninterested in these humble wares?"

Recognizing that voice, the Kaa stiffened slightly, but masked his reaction by turning around. "Lord Telvrahd," he said without enthusiasm.

Telvrahd bowed low with dramatic flourishes of his green-skinned hands, displaying wide, fashionable cuffs sprinkled with pavé jewels that glittered in the relentless sunshine. His brow ridge and rill gleamed with oil. "A bountiful Festival to the Imperial Father," he said formally.

"A bountiful Festival to you," the Kaa replied. Inwardly he was fuming. Which fool in his entourage had allowed Telvrahd access to him like this? Egg-brother or not, Telvrahd was a pest with ambitions that outstripped his importance. Yet because he had made himself a leader of the Progressionist Party, it was unwise to dismiss him publicly. After all, there was the cheering crowd beyond the patroller barricades to consider.

When the Kaa acknowledged him, Telvrahd smirked. His ruby-colored eyes gleamed with mischief as he bowed somewhat less grandly to the sri-Kaa. "Greetings to the Imperial Daughter of Sahmrahd Kaa."

Although she had been tugging impatiently at the Kaa's hand, Israi now looked up at her uncle and gave him the correct half obeisance for someone of his rank and standing at court. She failed to make a verbal response as she was supposed to, but the Kaa did not bother to correct her omission.

Catching this most subtle of insults, Telvrahd's grin became more forced. His rill pinkened and extended itself slightly above the support of his collar. "There are matters between us, sire, that need discussion. My petition supporting the restoration of the jump gates between—''

Israi tugged at the Kaa's hand. Welcoming the interruption, no matter how rude, the Kaa lifted his long fingers to silence Telvrahd and bent down so that Israi might whisper in his ear canal.

"Father," she said impatiently, "I want to look at the hatchlings."

He hesitated, not understanding. "What?"

A courtier in attendance intervened with a languid gesture toward a shop across the plaza. "No, Imperial Father. No Viis have been hatched here. The sri-Kaa refers to young abiru, specially selected for presentation this day."

The Kaa's frown deepened, and from the corner of his eye he saw Telvrahd's impatient expression. For that reason alone, the Kaa extended the interruption. "Young abiru?" he repeated. "What sort?"

Fazhmind the courtier blinked at the question as though he had not expected it. Garbed in a heavy silk coat that clearly made him swelter, Fazhmind fanned himself with a delicate creation of lace-cut ivory, jingling the tiny silver bells that dangled from his rill spines, and consulted a lower attendant for an answer.

"All kinds," Fazhmind finally replied, still fanning. He was a fastidious, pompous toady, too well-connected to be dismissed from court, but pushy and never popular with the Kaa.

"Yes, sire," he continued, the tiny bells tinkling beneath his words. "I understand there is quite a pleasing selection of pet-quality animals. Kelth, Aaroun, Myal, even a Toth or two for those who find it fashionable to own the unfashionable—''

"Toths?" the Kaa said in alarm. "Certainly not. The Imperial Daughter may not go near such animals. They are too dirty. They carry disease."

"Father—," Israi whined.

"No," the Kaa replied brusquely.

He turned his back on both his daughter and the courtier,

facing Telvrahd once more. "Forgive the interruption. Young chunen do not always remember their court manners."

Telvrahd put on an indulgent expression. "It is Festival. Informality is expected. Now, about my proposal regarding the jump gates—"

"This is not the time or the place to discuss the matter."

"The Imperial Father has put me off for months."

The Kaa curled his tongue within his mouth, struggling to hold his temper. Flies buzzed around a segment of gristly bone that an Aaroun child was gnawing. A horrified courtier dispatched someone to shoo the cub from sight. The Kaa wished he might swat Telvrahd away as well.

"We have our reasons for the delay, Lord Telvrahd," the Kaa said. "We are not unaware of the problems involved, problems which your proposal addresses. We are not unsympathetic—"

"Sire!" Telvrahd dared interrupt. "Sympathy is not what is required. The jump gates are decaying, falling into disrepair—"

"Nonsense," the Kaa said sharply, conscious of too many spectators watching and listening. "Such reports are false, the work of alarmists. Our jump gates are functional across the empire, and they will remain so."

"Not without attention. When they stop working, nothing is done. Nothing!" Telvrahd said, leaning closer. He lowered his voice, his dark red eyes locked on the Kaa's. "This shrinks our empire's boundaries more. We cannot afford—"

"We are assured that maintenance is done according to the correct schedule. While we appreciate your interest, surely there are other matters more appropriate for your attention."

Telvrahd extended his rill fully, and it turned a dark crimson. The Kaa's personal guards stepped closer. "I have just returned from a visit to my estates in the colony worlds," Telvrahd said. "The ship was rerouted twice around failed jump gates, and I missed several important appointments—"

"Including your audience with us," the Kaa said coldly. "Now you have forced yourself upon our company, taken advantage of our time, and created a public spectacle around an insignificant matter."

"Sire—"

"Insignificant," the Kaa repeated with more force. He glared at Telvrahd with eyes cold and flat. As his rill extended and raised, Telvrahd's lowered.

Bowing low, Telvrahd stepped back. "I ask the pardon of the Imperial Father. My heart is much occupied with the safety and well-being of the empire. My zeal sometimes exceeds my prudence."

As an apology, it left much to be desired. The Kaa heard no sincerity in Telvrahd's tone. He saw no contrition in Telvrahd's red eyes. Telvrahd would persist, and make a great issue over something that was both costly and unimportant. As long as there were sufficient jump gates across the empire, why bother with a few gone inactive? Even more foolishly, why make a public issue of it and stir up the populace with irrational fears?

In the distance a squabble broke out among some Kelth lits. One of them nipped another, and their shrill yelping caught the Kaa's attention. He glanced around, and realized the sri-Kaa was no longer clinging to his hand.

Nor was she in sight. He stared at the small clusters of attendants, the wilting, bored courtiers, the tireless antics of the clowns. His musicians played light background melodies, but Israi was not with them either.

His heart froze inside him. How could she be gone? In an instant, he thought of a thousand possibilities, each one worse than the one before it. "Israi!" he said in alarm.

Telvrahd stepped very close to him. "I promise the Imperial Father that I shall not let this matter drop," he said in a low voice. "If I must, I will carry it to the public forum and—"

"Silence!" the Kaa roared, spinning around and turning his back to Telvrahd. Furiously, the Kaa gestured at his guards, and they pushed Telvrahd away.

"Where is our daughter?" the Kaa demanded. "What has become of her?"

The courtiers milled about in sudden consternation, making it impossible to determine what had become of the chune or her lady in waiting.

The captain of the guard hurried to the Kaa and saluted. "Sire, a search will be conducted immediately."

"Find her!" the Kaa commanded. He could not breathe. The air was stifling, laden with too many strange and unpleasant smells. He could feel his heart pounding. His rill stood at complete extension, and he realized he was lashing his tail back and forth beneath his coat with enough agitation to make it visible. But at that moment he hardly cared if anyone noticed. If anyone had hurt her, abducted her, *dared* touch the most precious treasure of his life, he would have them torn into pieces and burned in the forum of assembly. He would have every building, every shop, every residence searched until she was found. He would level this entire squalid section of Vir if necessary. Who had dared take his daughter, the light of the empire, the jewel of his soul?

"She is found!" came a shout over the hubbub.

A guard came running, and behind him trotted Fazhmind in his silk coat and filigreed rill collar, silver bells jingling.

"There is no alarm, sire," the guard said, halting and saluting the Kaa. "The sri-Kaa is found in that shop across the way. She is safe and unharmed. Lady Lenith attends her, as is proper."

"What is proper," the Kaa said around his flicking tongue, incapable of relief yet, "is that the sri-Kaa be in her place at our side."

Out of breath from having been rushed across the plaza in the heat, Fazhmind fanned himself and bowed low. "All is well, sire. The sri-Kaa slipped away while the Imperial

Father was talking to Lord Telvrahd. I followed her into the shop. As did her lady in waiting."

Only now did the Kaa allow himself to believe their assurances. He was flooded by a mixture of overwhelming relief and exasperation. "Where is she?" he demanded sharply, not certain whether to be angry at his daughter for slipping away from him or at this fool, for having let her do something so unwise. "Why did you not return her to us? Why have you left her insufficiently attended?"

Fazhmind bowed again, wilting beneath the Kaa's anger. "Forgive me, sire. I thought this area well-guarded and safe for—"

"Bring her forth now," the Kaa commanded.

Fazhmind hesitated, wringing his hands. "She will not come."

"What!"

"She will not come. The Imperial Daughter is captivated by the newborn abiru she has found in the shop. She cannot be enticed away."

"Do not entice her! Command her!"

Fazhmind's gaze lowered. He seemed unable to breathe, and a pulse jumped rapidly beneath his ear dimple. "Forgive me, sire," he said in a soft, frightened voice. "It is not my place to command the sri-Kaa."

Even before he'd spoken, the Kaa had realized the absurdity of his order. Israi knew she answered to no one but him. As sweet and delightful as she was, she could also be extremely stubborn when she chose. The Kaa hoped this was not going to be such an occasion.

Drawing a deep breath, he tried to restore his inner calm before striding to the shop in question. People parted before him, making way with deep bows. Someone stopped the clowns from their antics, and even the musicians ceased playing.

The Kaa realized his expression was thunderous. The way blood was pounding through his rill, he knew it was dark crimson and at full extension. The Kaa was not supposed to expose his emotions so openly, but at this moment he cared not. When they returned home to the palace, Israi would have to be punished. She would learn that correct public behavior did not involve coming and going where she pleased. Especially not when she was in the abiru quarter of the city. Gods, what if he had truly lost her? He needed wine for the shock, but he did not glance back for his cupbearer.

Instead, he quickened his pace. The two guards accompanying him had to run in order to reach the door of the shop before he did. The door stood ajar, and the guards thrust it open with a crash against the inside wall.

"Attention!" one of them thundered at the occupants. "The Kaa is coming!"

By then the Kaa was ducking his head and stepping over the threshold. The interior of the shop was low-ceilinged and dim, especially after the glaring sunshine outside. It took a moment for his vision to adjust, and his nostrils crinkled at the smell of damp litter, pungent cedar shavings, and tepid milk.

Repulsed, he twisted his head aside and closed his nostrils. Then he glimpsed his daughter sitting happily on the floor of this humble establishment, heedless of the dirt streaking her silk indigo court gown. She held something furry and small in her arms, and she was rocking back and forth, crooning to the creature. Her whole being seemed absorbed in what she was doing. She did not glance up even when the Kaa crossed the shop and loomed over her.

A flustered Lady Lenith—richly gowned and wearing perfumed skin oil—bowed and backed away, looking grateful that someone else might take charge.

The shop owner—a masked Gorlican with glowing orange eyes and bare arms covered with thick gray scales instead of skin—hastened forward, but one of the guards shoved him behind his counter. "Bow to the imperial presence," the guard ordered gruffly.

With an inarticulate sound, the shopkeeper lowered himself awkwardly. The shell encasing his torso made it difficult for him to bend in respect, but no Viis cared.

Ignoring them all, the Kaa stared down at his daughter, who paid him no notice as she sang, rocked, and stroked the back of the tiny creature in her arms.

Part of the Kaa had to appreciate the picture she made, his beautiful daughter with her exquisite coloring and adorable ways. She looked charming there on the floor, horrifying though the idea was, and when she crooned to the animal and rubbed her cheek against its soft golden fur, the Kaa almost wished the moment could be captured in an air portrait.

Yet at the same time, his horror and outrage were growing. Who had allowed her to touch this animal in the first place? Was it safe? Was it clean? Was it suitable to be gazed on by the sri-Kaa? Clearly her attendants were far too lenient. Their indulgence could lead to her harm.

"Israi," he said, and his voice was sharper than he intended.

She was whispering in the crumpled ear of the creature and apparently did not hear him.

"Israi!" he said.

His voice snapped in the shop's silence, and Lady Lenith jumped.

Israi glanced up and beamed at him. "Father," she said excitedly, "look at what I have found! Isn't she adorable? Perfect in every way. That creature said so."

Despite himself, the Kaa glanced at the shopkeeper, who bowed low again and said in an unctuous voice, "The very best animals, Great One. In honor of this day, this visit, only the very best, the very finest pets gathered, yes. See the quality of this one's fur. Look at the absence of markings—"

"Not a spot *or* a stripe, Father!" Israi said proudly. "That creature says she'll be extremely pretty. Prettier than any of the others. And I picked her out all by myself."

"Did you?" the Kaa said while he shot a look of displeasure at the shopkeeper.

Gorlican merchants the galaxy over were all the same—a greedy lot without conscience. The Kaa wondered why he had ever thought this visit among the common people would be a splendid idea. Instead, his senses and his aesthetics had been assaulted all afternoon. And now, Israi had clearly attached herself to what could only be an unsuitable pet.

"Splendid, our daughter," the Kaa said with dignity. "But now, the hour grows advanced. We must return to the palace. Put the animal down, and let us depart."

Israi jumped to her feet, but her face was a thundercloud. "No!" she said. "I want her."

In the doorway, courtiers and ladies exchanged glances. The Kaa's temper heated. "Daughter of the Empire, you do not say 'no' to your Imperial Father."

Israi's tiny face set itself stubbornly. She squeezed the golden-furred animal tighter, making it mew. "I want her. I want her for my own."

The Kaa drew back, feeling helpless and hating it. "What is this animal?"

Fazhmind minced forward and grimaced in distaste before he raised a scent cone to his nostrils. "An Aaroun, sire," he replied.

"An Aaroun?" Fresh alarm flashed through the Kaa. "No, Israi, you may not keep an Aaroun. They grow to be quite large and powerful. They do not make good pets."

"She is *my* hatchling," Israi insisted. She rubbed the tiny Aaroun's blunt muzzle with her fingertip and laughed when the animal tried to suck it. "See? Already she loves me."

"The Aarouns are very affectionate when young, sire," the shopkeeper said. "They bond into close-knit families. Very loyal. One that's only a few days old, like this, is rare, very rare. She'll bond to whoever cares for her. She'll never turn on the sri-Kaa. Not when hand-raised from this age."

"She's mine," Israi insisted. Her green eyes darkened

with impending temper, and her tiny nostrils began to flare. "It's Festival. Everyone has eggs. Everyone has hatchlings. I want a hatchling for *myself*."

The Kaa stared down at his tiny daughter, who was facing him like a little fury, ready to defend what she claimed was hers. Suddenly his own temper melted away, and he found himself laughing. Israi's logic was absurd . . . and adorable.

"Of course you want to be a part of Festival," he said, bending over to rub her head affectionately. "Of course you want a hatchling like the ladies at court. But do you really want an Aaroun cub? Why not a—"

"I want this one," Israi said stubbornly, cradling the animal against the bodice of her gown. Already the Aaroun had shed tiny golden hairs upon the indigo silk. "And I will take care of her. I know what to do. That creature told me."

The Kaa glanced at the shopkeeper, who dared to grin.

"Very fine specimen, Great One," he said. "Very fine pet for the sri-Kaa. Perfect conformation. Color superb."

"Superb!" Fazhmind said with a sniff of disdain. "Great Father, consider the unsuitability of an Aaroun in the palace. It will have to be fed meat. It is not even housetrained."

Israi turned on him, her eyes blazing, her tiny rill spread at full extension. "Silence!" she shouted, stamping her foot. "You can't tell my father what to do. I want her, and she's *mine*. I'm not leaving unless I can take her with me."

The Kaa frowned at this display of imperial temper. "Now, Daughter—"

"I'll scream and scream and scream," Israi threatened, glaring at them all. "I'll make myself cry, and then I'll throw up. I'll—"

"Silence!" the Kaa snapped.

Israi hushed, but her chest was heaving and her eyes glittered furiously. Her rill had flushed so dark an indigo it looked almost black.

"Is it wise to threaten your father, little one?" he asked her. "Is this the way a sri-Kaa behaves in public? Have you no shame?"

Israi didn't back down. She went on glaring up at him, stubborn to the end. Only her bottom lip trembled slightly.

That tiny sign of weakness undid the Kaa. His heart melted, and he knew he could refuse her nothing, not even this ridiculous pet she wanted.

She was too young, of course, for the charge of such an animal. But she would tire of it, perhaps by nightfall. Then the slaves could dispose of it quietly, and the matter would be ended.

"Put the animal down, Israi, that we may see it clearly."

Israi hesitated, her eyes full of appeal.

The Kaa kept his tone reasonable, even gentle. "Put it down. We cannot tell what it looks like or even if it is beautiful enough to be yours."

Israi bent down and put the small Aaroun on the floor. "She's very beautiful. She—"

"Allow me to take the animal away, sire," Fazhmind said, bustling forward unbidden. He gripped the Aaroun by the scruff of its tiny neck, and with a feeble growl the Aaroun snapped at his finger.

The courtier screamed and dropped the animal on the floor. Bouncing and rolling over with a yelp, the Aaroun crouched on shaky, newborn legs, lifted her wobbly head, and uttered a baby growl both ferocious and absurd.

"Have it killed!" Fazhmind cried, clutching his finger. His bells jingled furiously. "It's dangerous. It *bit* me."

Unexpectedly, the Kaa found himself admiring the little Aaroun's courage, for if anyone deserved to be bitten it was Fazhmind, with his airs and affectations.

The Aaroun advanced toward Fazhmind's foot, instinctively stiff-legged, a ridge of hair standing up along her spine. She growled again, louder this time, and snorted in disdain before turning and tottering back to Israi. Rearing up on her haunches, the Aaroun lifted her little hands in appeal, then fell over as she lost her balance.

Israi crouched on the floor and scooped up the Aaroun. "You poor thing. Are you hurt?"

"Hurt!" Fazhmind screeched. "It is I who am hurt."

Israi ignored him, cuddling the Aaroun closer.

"Careful," the Kaa said in alarm, concerned that the creature might attack her. "It could bite you, Israi."

"As it bit *me,* sire," Fazhmind said, still clutching his finger and grimacing dramatically in pain. "It is vicious and unpredictable. It will harm the sri-Kaa. Let the guards destroy it."

But Israi rose to her feet with the Aaroun clutched against her. The trembling animal thrust its head beneath her comforting hand. "Don't be silly, Lord Fazhmind," she said. "She couldn't really bite you. Her milk teeth are tiny things, nothing that could harm you."

"Right, yes," the shopkeeper said. "An Aaroun that little has no jaw strength yet."

A strange look crossed Fazhmind's face. He lowered his hand to his side and curled his fingers to conceal them in his fist.

The Kaa averted his gaze. He felt a tremor of humor all the way to his tail, and he struggled not to laugh aloud.

"Well." Fazhmind tried to regain his dignity, even as Lady Lenith spread her fan across her mouth and the captain of the guard coughed loudly.

Outside the doorway of the shop, several onlookers tittered in the crooks of their elbows.

"The dangerous instincts are there, sire," Fazhmind said. "The creature will grow real teeth soon enough, and then—"

"Defending the sri-Kaa a good sign of bonding already," the shopkeeper said. "Aarouns never turn on their own kind. She'll make a good pet. Loyal to the sri-Kaa always. Protect the sri-Kaa always."

"Within the safety of the palace, what need has the sri-

Kaa of protection other than that provided by the Palace Guards?'' Fazhmind asked.

Israi's eyes widened. ''Father, she has defended me. She will be loyal to me. I know it.''

''Nonsense,'' Fazhmind said with a sniff. ''Such animals can never be trusted. Never. It is most unwise. I strongly urge the Imperial Father to deny—''

The Kaa beckoned, and Fazhmind shuffled closer. Turning his back to Israi, the Kaa asked quietly, ''How are pets usually obtained for the imperial chunen? Suitable pets, quiet and well-trained?''

''Ah.'' Fazhmind rubbed his hands together and puffed out his air sacs, clearly pleased at being consulted. ''Something such as a coovie, perhaps?''

''Yes—''

''I don't *want* a coovie!'' Israi pushed herself between them and glared up at them both. ''They're stupid and boring. I want this one!''

Fazhmind's mouth curled in disapproval at the sri-Kaa's manners, but he replied to the Kaa, ''A request is sent forth via the office of the chamberlain, sire. I believe that individual then contacts a merchant who holds an official appointment of pet supplier to the imperial family.''

''Ah,'' the Kaa said, nodding. ''Of course.''

Israi stamped her foot. ''No! I want this one!''

The Kaa bent down and stroked her brow ridge. ''Dearest, this creature is pretty but—''

''She's beautiful. Like me!'' Israi said.

Again, laughter circled the shop. The Kaa sighed. Already his favorite daughter was growing vain. Yet how could she be otherwise, when what she said was true?

Fazhmind flicked his fan. ''Sire, I shall be most pleased to speak to the chamberlain about a different—''

''No!'' Israi shouted. ''I won't! I won't! I won't!''

Before the Kaa could silence her, she kicked Fazhmind in the leg and ran for the open doorway of the shop. Swiftly the guards moved to block her path. She screamed at them, and the Kaa knew from the expression of growing dread on Lady Lenith's face that a full-blown tantrum was imminent.

"Israi!" he said sharply. "Come here."

She fell silent, much to his relief, and obeyed him. But her face was twisted into a scowl. Her sides heaved, and her rill stayed an ominous dark color.

"This is not behavior for public display," the Kaa told her.

Israi glared at the floor and said nothing.

"You will apologize to Lord Fazhmind."

Israi's green eyes flashed defiance.

He held up his finger before she could speak. "Come here that we may speak privately."

She hesitated, kicking the toe of her sandal on the floor before she complied.

The Kaa gestured, and Lady Lenith and Fazhmind withdrew to the opposite end of the small shop. With growing exasperation, the Kaa leaned down and picked up his daughter, Aaroun and all, so that he could speak softly into her ear dimple without being overheard.

"Daughter," he said, "you belong to the imperial house. You are the sri-Kaa."

She nodded. "I am important."

"Yes, but that does not mean you can kick people, especially courtiers with titles and rank like Lord Fazhmind."

Israi scowled and glared at the male over her father's shoulder. "I don't like him."

The Kaa's tongue twitched inside his mouth. He barely kept his composure. "Neither do we," he whispered.

Her eyes widened, and she giggled.

"Shush," he warned her, fearful she would announce his rash confidence to the world. "That is a secret between us. Understood? You must never say it to anyone."

She nodded. "Yes, Father."

"Now—"

"But if we don't like him, I should have kicked him harder."

"No, Israi. It is beneath imperial dignity to kick our courtiers. We must show good manners to all those who are beneath us in rank. It is our responsibility."

"I don't understand."

He stroked her head, adoring the clarity of her soft, golden skin. She was so bright, so precious to him. How fragrant she smelled, cuddled here in his arms. Yet what a devil she could be.

"It is difficult," he said, "but one day you will understand. For now, remember your manners. Will you promise that?"

Her head tilted to one side, Israi thought a moment. "If I promise not to kick Fazhmind again, will you let me keep the Aaroun?"

The Kaa drew in a sharp breath, finding himself caught unexpectedly. Ah, she was bright and quick, this chune.

Israi went on gazing up at her father, her expressive eyes pleading. The Aaroun lifted her face and looked at him also. Something in the Aaroun's expression caught his attention. Her long-lashed eyes, set in their striking mask of light brown fur, held gentle, sensitive intelligence.

Startled, he gazed back at her, realizing this was no ordinary Aaroun.

"Father, *please*." Israi fidgeted in his arms, tilting her head from side to side.

He let her slide to the ground and stared down at her, this adorable daughter with whom he could never be angry long.

"How pretty," said a voice from the doorway behind them. It was Chancellor Gaveid's distinctive orator's voice, rich and measured. "A golden pet for a golden sri-Kaa."

Appreciative murmurs arose among the onlookers. Gaveid's poetic bon mot would be repeated endlessly around the court for the next few days.

The Kaa smiled to himself. Gaveid spoke true. The animal's coloring did complement Israi's. Besides, the creature had made him laugh and had bitten Fazhmind. Surely that in itself was worthy of special consideration.

"Very well," the Kaa said, relenting. "Our permission is granted, but—"

"Oh, thank you, Father! Thank you!" Radiant again, Israi hugged his legs tightly. Crushed between them, the little Aaroun mewed in fright.

At once, Israi sprang back and stroked her. "Hush, little one," she said to her. "I'll take good care of you. I promise."

The shopkeeper bustled forward, rubbing his palms together, before he was once again shoved back by the guards. "Excellent choice, Great One," he said. "This Aaroun is outstanding for her kind, yes. The best of—"

The Kaa glanced at Fazhmind, whose mouth had closed in a pinched, sour look. "Make the payment," he said, and walked out. "Come, Daughter."

Carrying the Aaroun herself and allowing no one else to take it from her, Israi hurried to catch up with her father's long strides.

"I am so happy, Father," she chattered. "Now I can be a mother too, just like the other females in the palace. I have my own hatchling to look after. I shall be very good to her. You'll see. I can take care of her. I won't forget her. She'll be house-trained right away. My slave Subi will take care of that. And she'll be good. I won't let her chew on anything. And when she's bigger, I'll—"

"You will have your slaves walk her regularly," the Kaa said, shutting away visions of a large, bulky Aaroun running about the palace, knocking over furniture and breaking priceless vases. But of course, it would never come to that. By the time Israi went to bed tonight, the Aaroun would be forgotten, just another discarded toy. Still, for the sake of parental authority, he felt he should give her a lecture on responsibility. "You will not forget to instruct your slaves to feed her. She is a small, helpless animal, very dependent on you and the care you give her. She is not like a Viis infant, able to take care of herself straight from the egg. The abiru folk are inferior to us in that way, as in many others. It must be your responsibility to think of her special needs.''

''I understand,'' Israi said with a serious nod. ''I won't forget.''

The Kaa sighed. Chunenhal promises: solemnly given, yet as enduring as puff-seeds blown by the wind.

Outside, standing in the dappled shade of a tree, the old chancellor leaned on his staff of office and bowed low to the Kaa, who paused.

''A wise decision, sire,'' Gaveid murmured without moving his lips. ''An abiru, however humbly placed within the palace and within the private circle of the imperial family, can only bring renewed love from the Imperial Father's humblest subjects.''

The Kaa frowned. In Gaveid's professional rhetoric, *humblest subjects* was a euphemism for abiru slaves. Although the Kaa had not indulged his daughter's whim in order to curry favor from the lowest ranks of the unwashed, he realized that his action would increase his popularity.

Their eyes met with perfect understanding.

''Father,'' Israi said, tugging on his sleeve for attention. ''Will the guns fire over the city to celebrate my hatchling, like they did today for yours?''

Behind them, Fazhmind gasped audibly in outrage, but the Kaa's heart swelled with pride. Truly his daughter was growing imperial. Already she reached for the privileges that could not yet be hers.

Holding back a smile, the Kaa said patiently, ''No, the guns will not salute your pet, precious one.''

Israi's green eyes flashed. ''Why not?''

''Because that right is reserved for the chunen of the Kaa only.''

''But I am sri-Kaa!''

''That is not the same,'' he said with more firmness.

Israi stamped her foot. "I want a salute. I want to be just like you."

He placed his hand gently on her head to urge her forward. "One day, our daughter. But we are the Kaa now, and you are not."

Scowling, she opened her mouth to protest further, but the Kaa's patience was over. He changed the subject as they walked toward their waiting transportation, saying, "And what will you name this pet of yours?"

Distracted from an imminent tantrum, Israi smiled up at him. "Ampria. For our Goddess of Gold."

The Kaa blinked and behind them someone gasped in affront. "Perhaps the name of our sun-goddess is a bit grand for such a small pet?" he suggested gently. It did not matter, of course. People named their pets after the lesser panoply of gods all the time, when it was fashionable. Presently, it was not. "Perhaps you should not offend the goddess in that way?"

Israi frowned, thinking it over.

They had reached the imperial litters at the outskirts of the marketplace. Beyond, the squalid streets of the abiru quarter twisted and turned in a maze of poverty and degradation. Guards ringed the litters, which floated above the pavement in readiness to go. The Kaa barely glanced around at his ugly surroundings. He was relieved to depart. He promised himself he would not return to this section of the city. Nor would Israi. She was too young for exposure to such grim conditions.

The Kaa climbed aboard and settled himself upon the crimson cushions. Israi was lifted in beside him. She snuggled close, with the Aaroun cradled in the crook of her arm. One of the golden animal's tiny feet dangled perilously, and the Kaa himself showed her how to hold the creature correctly.

"I shall call her Ampris," Israi said, holding up the Aaroun to blow gently into her small face. Brown fur formed a mask across Ampris's eyes, which were squinted against the slanting sunlight. The Aaroun squeaked and mewed, and Israi cradled her close once more. "That will honor the goddess and make everyone think of her, yet it cannot offend."

"Well thought, Daughter," the Kaa said in approval.

Israi grinned. "Yes, Ampris. A grand name, for her to grow into, for when she is bigger."

"Perhaps a bit too grand for a mere Aaroun?" he suggested again.

Israi looked at him. "Nothing is too grand for the possession of the sri-Kaa!" she declared.

He inflated his air sacs in pride. "Spoken like a true Daughter of the Empire."

She grinned at him, and for a second as their litter swung around and surged forward on a jet of air, they were in complete accord.

The Kaa hugged his daughter fondly and indulged her by blowing through her ear dimples. She squealed with laughter, and he laughed too.

"Faster!" he called to his driver, willing to give his daughter a treat. "Racing speed!"

The nose of the litter tilted up, and although it was built for stately processionals, not racing, the driver gunned it to maximum acceleration. Draperies billowed and swung free of their securings, flapping from the canopy. A cushion blew off, tumbling into the street to be fought over by the cheering crowd. The litter flashed by the people in a multicolored blur. The litters containing their attendants struggled to keep up, while Fazhmind and the ladies in waiting clutched clothing and squinted grimly against the wind.

The guards rode in a skimmer that was larger and faster. It caught up and paralleled the imperial litter, pretending to race them, yet never quite edging ahead.

Israi squealed in shrill delight and leaned forward. "Faster, faster!" she called to the driver. "Don't let them win!"

It was madness, surging through the streets of Vir at this reckless speed. The impetuous act of a ta-chune male, not a ruler over numerous worlds. Yet the Kaa's spirit soared, and he laughed in the sheer joy of speed, which he loved as much as his daughter.

Ahead of them, the magnificent spires of the palace reached to the sky, silhouetted against a sunset of blazing corals and delicate pinks. It was as though the sky itself celebrated the close of Festival with them. The Kaa saw the rising walls and scaffolding of the restoration project beyond the perimeter of the present palace compound, and his heart swelled more. Life was as it should be. No matter what detractors and political fools might murmur among themselves, his empire remained great. He was great. There was peace and prosperity for the Viis, and so it would remain while he held the throne. All was well.

In Israi's lap, Ampris squirmed briefly in an instinctive search for her mother. But there was only the reassuring touch of a tiny Viis hand pressed against her side, and momentarily, the stroke of a large hand down her back. Already Ampris had learned much in these short days. She had known excruciating loss and terror. She felt weak from hunger now, and her thirst brought pain. Yet the touch of these Viis creatures was gentle, not rough. The little Viis had saved her. That, Ampris understood. The little Viis loved her, and Ampris absorbed that love into herself, finding comfort in it. Already the memory of her mother was not as strong, not as painful, as it had been.

The fear and grieving in her tiny heart abated for the first time. Ampris sniffed, pressing her nose against the small hand upon her, and breathed in the strange scent of it. Viis scent. Not good . . . until now.

Not mother scent, yet here was love offered, along with comfort and security. Not mother scent, not mother love, but a good scent and a good love. Large Viis people could not be trusted. She knew that. When she looked at them she wanted to bite.

But this little Viis person was different. The little Viis person had promised to take care of her. There was no lie in her scent, no harm. Ampris relaxed her young muscles. She licked the hand that petted her, and found herself cuddled closer. Yes, this was good. She inhaled the skin scent of Israi's hand again and absorbed it into her memory, into her very being.

For the first time since being taken from her mother, Ampris felt safe. She did not know how long it would last. The last time she felt safe, terror had come. But for now, it was enough.

CHAPTER FOUR

Elrabin's stomach hurt so much he could barely concentrate on the display of meat globes just a few feet away. Crouched behind a stack of rotting, smelly fruit crates, Elrabin flicked his ears against the swarm of buzzing flies and peeked around the edge of the crates again.

Yes, the Gorlican shopkeeper was still haggling with his customer, a scrawny old green-skinned Viis with a heavily laden market basket. The Viis was clearly a cook in a small household. He gave himself far too many airs for his rank, and insisted on squeezing, sniffing, and haggling over every item.

Elrabin didn't mind the performance, for it distracted the shopkeeper, but the two adults were standing next to the meat globes. Elrabin could have stolen half the contents of the shop by now, but he wanted meat—juicy, synthetic, and flavored with spices to make it taste real. His mouth watered with anticipation, and he had to press both hands against the fierce ache in his stomach.

Gods, he was hungry. After a rough night crammed in bed with his younger lits, who yipped, kicked, and twitched in their dreams, Elrabin had awakened this morning to an empty larder and a note from his mother blinking on the data screen, saying to get two measures of Quixlix from the market on her payment card.

It was strange the way a sudden cool certainty had flowed through him. He stood there in the galley, staring at the open door to the bare larder, the grease-smeared cooker, the scuffed, cheap table, the grimy floor, and the fly-specked window that overlooked the next tenement building, and he felt suddenly calm and at peace with himself.

His lits, Vol and Mikar, were yipping in the other room in shrill argument, but even the noise seemed to dampen down and become insignificant in his hearing. He saw as clearly as though he gazed into a sivo crystal.

Their lodging stank of dry rot, rancid meat grease, and unclean fur. They had two rooms, both too small. The security locks didn't work. The bath sprayer didn't work. The water pipe leaked. The cooker was down to its last working burner, a bomb waiting to explode. The bottom panel of the door had been kicked in the last time Elrabin's da came by, drunk and howling for admittance. Maintenance had never repaired it. They had an old data screen that was illegally hooked up to the building's incoming vid signal feed. One of Elrabin's daily chores was to monitor any scans and keep the screen switched off at random intervals to avoid detection.

Yeah, like the building supervisor was going to be able to squeeze a fine out of Elrabin's mother if they did get caught. All he could do would be to evict them, and that was fine with Elrabin. The hopelessness of the place sometimes drove Elrabin to fury, and sometimes to despair.

"When things look up, we'll move," his mother often said. "When things look up, I'll change jobs, get a better shift. When things look up, we won't have to worry."

This morning Elrabin understood that things would never look up. Nothing changed in the ghetto, ever. His mother already worked double shifts, which meant she was never home. She slaved out there, breaking her back doing work too hard for her while she got the worst wages in the world. They came up short every pay cycle. Most of the time all they could afford to buy was Quixlix, and if Elrabin had to synthesize one more meal out of that stuff he would puke.

So he just stood there in the galley, with his heart thumping a little and his ears roaring and that strange calmness flowing through him. He picked up his mother's payment card, which had maybe one credit on it. He put on his coat. He switched the data screen to vid signal so the lits would have something to do when they came scrounging in for the breakfast they wouldn't get. And he walked out.

Just like that. He wasn't going back. Ever.

"Here, then, is all I will pay you!" declared the Viis cook to the shopkeeper. Flicking out his tongue, he fitted his purchases into his basket and left. Another customer came up.

Exasperation welled up inside Elrabin. He couldn't wait here much longer. Good thieving involved a quick dart, grab, and run. Lingering meant being seen. Being seen meant getting caught.

If luck rode on his shoulder, the patrollers would be kind, understanding individuals who would haul him home, strung up by the heels for all the neighbors to see. They would force his mother to leave work and make his bail. She'd lose pay. Elrabin would get an arrest mark on his record sheet. After that, if he got caught again, it was loss of a hand or sale to hard labor. That was the lucky scenario.

The unlucky one meant the patrollers would skip ahead past warnings and reform efforts and just cut off his hand on the spot for a first offense.

Not a good start to his first day as a thief.

But Elrabin had no intention of being a failure.

The shopkeeper turned his back to rearrange the scarlet pomas into a small pyramid, and Elrabin seized his chance.

He sprang forward, running right under the shopkeeper's coattails, and grabbed as many of the meat globes as he could. Stuffing them into his pockets, he wheeled toward the back of the stall.

But the customer saw him. "A thief! A thief!" she shouted, pointing.

The shopkeeper whirled around, banging the edge of his torso shell against the counter. "Thief! Stop! Robber!" He slapped a button, and a portable alarm blared.

Cursing them both, Elrabin flung himself through the slit he had cut in the back of the tent stall. Cloth ripped as he forced himself through the hole. The shopkeeper, hard on his heels, gripped his coat and dragged him back.

Fear burst in Elrabin's chest. He squirmed desperately and pulled free, only to trip flat. Several of the meat globes squished in his pockets, soaking him with juice and filling his nostrils with their aroma. The shopkeeper grabbed him by his left ankle now and held on, shrieking for assistance.

Elrabin twisted in the shopkeeper's hold and kicked free. He scrambled backward, scooting right under the Gorlican, then stood up. The move toppled the Gorlican off-balance. Staggering to one side, the Gorlican snapped with his beaked mouth, but Elrabin was already scrambling through the tent slit on all fours.

The alarm was still blaring. Gaining his feet in the filthy alley behind the food stall, Elrabin heard the sound of running footsteps. The shopkeeper's shouts for help grew louder. At any moment the patrollers would arrive.

Elrabin gulped in air, flattened his ears, and ran for his life. If he was lucky, he could reach the end of the alley and make the corner before anyone spotted him. All he needed was a head start and he could lose the patrollers.

"You!" an amplified Viis voice boomed behind him. "Small Kelth in the brown coat. You will stop and submit to arrest!"

Elrabin glanced over his shoulder and saw black-suited patrollers coming after him. He couldn't count how many. One or twenty, it didn't matter. In moments they would have a sniffer locked onto him, and then his chances would pretty much be over.

Panting for breath, fear running hot weakness through his pumping legs, he ran in a zigzag pattern, trying to elude the sniffer and knowing he had scant chance of success in the narrow alley.

It was stupid to head for the corner. They expected that. He could hear them talking into their comms behind him. Probably they were calling up more patrollers to block his path.

Abruptly, Elrabin turned left and ran through a narrow gap between two of the stalls. He jumped over tent ropes and ducked past a precarious stack of crates, spilling them behind him. A startled Skek burst forth, cutting directly in front of Elrabin on its stick thin, multiple limbs.

Elrabin tripped over it and went rolling into the soft side of a tent. He scrambled onto his knees, and for a moment he and the Skek stared directly into each other's eyes. Then the Skek lifted its skinny arms high over its furred head and ran, hands flopping almost bonelessly as it went.

Elrabin ducked and rolled in the opposite direction, scooting beneath the edge of the tent and finding himself wedged between another stack of crates. Baring his teeth, he squeezed through, waited until the shopkeeper stepped outside to watch the patrollers go by, then darted out past her and cut across the plaza.

People shouted and pointed, but Elrabin didn't care as long as he shook off his pursuers. He ran down another alley, sauntered casually through a crowded shop with his hands innocently in his pockets, lifted a comb adorned with fake jewels, and skipped out the back door without being noticed. Outside, he broke into a steady trot and headed into the dirty streets of the east side of the ghetto. Sounds of pursuit faded completely. He couldn't even hear the alarm now.

Elrabin's pounding heart slowed down. He drew in several deep breaths, glancing back often. A grin lifted his lips from his teeth. Now that the danger was over, his fear vanished, to be replaced by a rush of elation. Whirling around to face the direction he'd come from, he licked his palm and made the universal gesture of disrespect.

So much for the patrollers. They weren't so scary. Even with all their comms, sniffers, scanners, and surveillance nets they hadn't been able to catch one third-grown lit. Clearly he had been born to be a master thief. He had the moves; he had the talent. From now on he would be known on the streets as Elrabin the Quick. Everyone would soon admire how he could outthink and outrun the patrollers.

Still grinning to himself, he paused in a doorway and checked the contents of his pockets before fishing out a meat globe. It was sadly squashed, with most of its flavorful juice gone, but he ate it anyway, smacking his jaws and savoring every bite. He was tempted to eat all the globes; after the danger he'd eluded he deserved to treat himself like a kaa.

But he held back. He had to take care of himself, now that he was out on his own. He had to plan and think ahead.

Only for a moment did he remember his two younger lits at home, probably howling with hunger right now and wondering when he'd return.

Elrabin felt a tide of guilt surge through his throat, and his ears swiveled back. He could go home, take them the food, spend the rest of the day watching illegal vids. He could give his mother the comb he'd stolen from the shop. Pulling it out, Elrabin turned it over in his hands, watching how the fake jewels flashed in the morning sunlight. Even with jewels made of colored glass that were glued on, the comb looked bright and pretty to Elrabin, something that should belong to a fine lady. He felt sure that if he gave it to his mother, her tired eyes would light up. She might even smile and give him that fond lick between the ears the way she used to when he was really little.

A skilled thief could make forty times as much as a street

sweeper, not that Elrabin was even old enough to hold a legal job. As long as he brought home food and gifts, useful items they all could use, why should she mind?

She would, though.

Elrabin closed from his mind the memories of his parents snapping and fighting, the stolen loot from his da's latest escapade lying glittering on the battered table in the galley, the dust pouch dropped carelessly next to it in plain sight. They fought over everything, including Cuvein's inability to support his family, his dust habit, his gambling. He would stand there, leaning against the counter, charming and rakish with his head tilted to one side and his brown eyes gleaming. Now and then he would grin a little at her, then roll his eyes to the lits, crouched in the doorway in a watchful huddle. She would rail at him, her body worn and her fur dull, too many disillusionments in her eyes. He never listened. He never changed. Finally he stopped coming by altogether.

That's when she started working double shifts and talking about how things would change.

Yeah, Elrabin thought resentfully. Things had changed, all right. They had gotten worse.

Whining softly through his teeth, Elrabin tossed the comb in the air and caught it, then tucked it safely away in his belt pouch beneath his tattered brown coat. He was a gangly youngster, longer of leg and lighter-boned than most lits his age. Even at seven years, Elrabin was bright and observant, with a measure of cynicism worthy of one far older. His fur was short and dense, brindled a pale gray-brown color, and his eyes were a light, golden brown filled with mischief. His coat had belonged to his father, and was his only inheritance. Worn and grimy, the garment was made of strong, well-woven linen stolen and handed down many times until it turned up at a ragpicker's and was bartered for by Elrabin's mother. It was the only thing his da left behind, and Elrabin had claimed it immediately for his own. The sleeves were rolled up to hide their missing cuffs and tatters, and if it needed a good washing or if the lining had long since ripped out or if the pockets were stretched from having too many objects crammed into them, he didn't care.

"I'm not going back," he said defiantly to the empty street.

He had the spare meat globes in his pockets for lunch, and he would sell the comb to Berv, the junk dealer who worked near the docks. That would bring him enough to pay for his supper. A heady sense of freedom swept Elrabin as he turned his steps toward the far side of the ghetto. Life was getting better already.

"Come on, Ampris," the melodic voice crooned to her. "Come to me, my sweet. Ampris, *come*."

Crouched beneath the white, bell-shaped flowers that drooped becomingly on fragile stems, Ampris heard the voice calling to her but ignored it. She had discovered a fat worm with multiple tiny feet and a set of horns on its head, and the creature fascinated her. Rainbow-hued, it inched its way across the lower petals of a white flower, distracted neither by the twig Ampris held across its path nor by her gentle thumping of its posterior. She laughed at it and leaned closer, sniffing its length to gain a peculiar, leafy odor.

Lately Ampris had been collecting scents. Her nostrils were filled with a bounty of fragrances, some exhilarating and some pungent, some simply awful. She had to trace each smell to its source, so she could identify and learn.

Now she had learned what a flower worm smelled like. Pausing on the rim of the blossom, it reared up three-quarters of its plump length and reached for a leaf suspended above it. Ampris helped by moving the leaf within the worm's reach. It crawled onto the green surface, paused there, and began to eat steadily, again letting nothing she did distract it from its purpose.

Its leafy scent grew stronger, and she understood that it

was a creature devoted only to food—the gathering and the consumption of it.

Laughing to herself, Ampris sniffed the leaves of the flower and forever isolated the scent of flower worm in her memory.

"Ampris!"

Startled, Ampris looked up and saw a thin-armed silhouette looming over her with clear impatience.

"I have called you and called you," Israi said. "You are supposed to come when I call you. Don't you remember? I explained everything to you before we started."

Ampris rose to her feet, wobbling a little before she found her balance. It was still a new experience to walk upright, but it made her feel very grown up, a chune like Israi and no longer a helpless infant. When she'd ceased to crawl last week, Israi had praised her lavishly. They had celebrated with a party in the garden, just the two of them and Israi's favorite court of dolls. Servants had brought them savory dishes and served them banquet style. Ampris had been the guest of honor, and for a gift she had been given a new, very pretty ownership ring for her ear, one fashioned of real gold. From it dangled an elaborate cartouche of Israi's name, enameled in jewel-bright colors.

But now no approval showed on Israi's beautiful face. Her vibrant green eyes flashed with annoyance.

Dismay sank through Ampris. She hated it when Israi lost her temper. She could not bear to disappoint her beloved friend. "I am sorry," she said, bowing her head.

Already she understood that at court one did not make excuses for bad behavior. One apologized and took one's punishment. It was the brave way, the honorable way, the Viis way, according to Israi.

But Ampris's simple apology did not wipe the anger from Israi's face. Above her jeweled collar, her rill had turned a smudgy, dark hue. "Was I not clear?" Israi asked. "Must I explain the procedure *again?*"

"No, Israi," Ampris said hastily. "I remember the game."

"It is *not* a game," Israi said. "And you do not act like you remember anything. What are you doing?"

Ampris panted, eager to share her discoveries. "Sniffing."

"Again?" Israi asked, aghast. "Why?"

"It's important."

Israi glared at her. "Not as important as learning to come when you are called. Lord Fazhmind has told the whole court that you are a stupid Aaroun, impossible to train. I intend to show everyone how smart you are."

Ampris drew herself up, willing to please. "Yes, Israi."

"But I can't if you don't learn to do this! I have boasted about you. Will you now prove the sri-Kaa a liar?"

Ampris's ears flattened. She dared not meet Israi's eyes. This was real anger, not just a scolding because Israi liked to be bossy. Ampris realized she had made a serious error in disappointing her beloved friend. She wanted to weep. She would do anything to make amends.

"Please don't be angry," she said, throwing herself at Israi's feet. She pressed her face against the delicate enameled straps of Israi's sandals. They smelled of finely worked leather and the perfumed oil rubbed daily into Israi's golden skin. "I will learn all the games. I will make you proud of me. I promise."

"That's what you said when we started. Now the sun is getting hot, and I am tired," Israi said.

Ampris rubbed the side of her muzzle against Israi's foot. She knew that the feel of her soft fur usually pleased Israi. "Please don't pout," she said softly. "I promise I will be good."

"You promise, but then you *forget*." Israi pulled her foot back from Ampris's grasp. "And stop groveling."

Ampris sat up. "What's groveling?"

"It means licking my foot when you want me to like

you. Fazhmind flatters my father for the same reason, and he's nasty. I don't like him at all."

Ampris blinked up at Israi, her heart sinking inside her. "And you don't like me anymore either?" she asked.

"Silly." Israi swooped down and gave her a quick hug. "Of course I like you, except when you act stupid. Stand up."

Flooded with joy and relief, Ampris obeyed.

Israi clasped her hands behind her back, imitating her father, and circled Ampris for an inspection. "You have dirt on your clothes."

Ampris glanced down at herself and swiftly slapped at the streaks of dust on her fur. She wore no clothes, nor did Israi. During the hot summers, young Viis chunen of all ranks went unclothed within the privacy of their garden walls. It saved much unnecessary wear and tear on garments. Less laundry had to be done, and chunen could grow as they pleased without having to be refitted as often. But both Israi and Ampris loved to pretend they were wearing elaborate court attire.

If Israi was back to pretending, that meant Ampris really was forgiven. Tipping back her head, she squinted against the bright sunshine and lifted her palms to its warmth.

"Pay attention," Israi commanded.

Ampris lowered her arms and watched her beloved friend with concentration.

"I am going to leave you here in the flowers," Israi ordered. "Don't start sniffing them again."

"Yes, Israi," Ampris said.

"I will wait a few minutes and then I will call you. When I do, you are to come to me at once. Understand?"

"Yes, Israi."

"Good." Israi smiled at her and gave her a quick rub between the ears. "Now—"

"Israi!" called a female voice. "Israi! It is time for refreshments. Come indoors before you burn your skin."

Israi whirled around and waved to show that she'd heard.

Then she turned back to Ampris and bent close. "Lenith is watching. Now you have to do this correctly. *Will you?*"

"Yes, Israi," Ampris said.

"You won't forget? Even if I don't call you for a while?"

"I won't forget," Ampris promised. But even as she spoke, she couldn't help but look out of the corner of her eye to see if the worm was still eating his leaf. If Israi delayed calling her for a few minutes, she would have time to play with the flower worm a short while longer.

"Ampris?" Israi said doubtfully, letting her long slim tongue flicker past her lips.

Ampris looked right at her, eyes wide with sincerity. "I promise."

"Israi!" the lady in waiting called again. "Please. The sun is too hot for you."

"Yes, Lady Lenith," Israi said. She turned away to go, but not before she gave Ampris one last look over her shoulder.

Ampris smiled and crouched among the flowers again. They were slightly trampled now, but she didn't mind. The flower worm had vanished, and she could not find him, not even when she sniffed for him among the leaves. Perhaps he had gone into the dirt.

Dropping to her stomach, she burrowed among the flowers, sniffing the ground. In the process she discovered an entire new range of scents. The flowers were growing in loose, dark loam, and it smelled far different from the compacted soil of the—

"Ampris!" Israi called. "Come, Ampris."

Jolted from her thoughts, Ampris looked up. Israi was calling. She had to go.

But just as she started to climb to her feet, she smelled a scent so exquisite, so enticing, she reeled from it. Heady, intoxicating, it overwhelmed her senses and nearly suffocated her with its sweet perfume. Forgetting everything else, she crawled forward through the last of the white bell flowers and found a bush loaded with heavy bright blue racemes. Bees swarmed the bush, and its perfume filled the sunlit air.

"Ampris!" Israi called once more, then fell silent.

Torn, Ampris glanced over her shoulder, but she could not see her beloved friend anywhere in the garden. She knew Israi must have gone inside. Israi would think she had forgotten her promise, but Ampris couldn't bear to leave the bush without touching it. It might never smell this fragrant again. Israi said that many of the flowers bloomed for a short time, once a year.

Ampris did not completely understand how long a year could be yet, but Israi said it was a very long time, much longer than between breakfast and dinner.

But the garden was suddenly very quiet, except for the busy humming of the bees. Ampris looked around again and climbed to her feet. She felt lonely, isolated, strange.

Never had she been alone before. Not like this. For even the guards who always shadowed Israi had vanished from their place by the wall.

The sun blazed down, and Ampris felt suddenly pinned by its heat, pressing her toward the ground. She was small, and not very fast yet. If danger came, she could not outrun it.

And danger might come, for she did not have her beloved friend to protect her. Israi had called her, and Ampris had not obeyed.

She opened her mouth and began to whimper, then stopped herself. She would not fail her beloved friend.

Quickly Ampris jerked a handful of the blue flowers from the bush, then turned and ran on her short, awkward legs for the portico. At the steps she stopped, frowning. She could not do steps upright yet. She had tried yesterday and fallen, bumping all the way down and scaring herself. But to crawl meant leaving the flowers behind.

After a moment, she put the flowers in her mouth and swiftly scrambled up the steps to the column. Leaning against it, she found her balance, dropped some of her flowers and had to pick them up, then hurried inside.

The quiet coolness of the interior surrounded her. Her dirty feet padded silently on the polished stone floors. She skirted the atrium with its softly splashing fountain and bright, darting fish and headed down the broad corridor that led to Israi's apartments.

The tall doors of heavily carved bronze stood open. As Ampris approached, she could hear Fazhmind's arrogant voice:

"I have always felt the sri-Kaa should have a more elegant pet, something suitable for the Imperial Daughter's—"

"Here I am, Israi," Ampris said proudly as she pushed her way inside. She held the flowers aloft, and the room filled instantly with their fragrance. They were so beautiful, although they had already started to wilt, and she was pleased to offer Israi a gift worthy of her beauty.

She laid them on the table next to where Israi was sitting and smiled. "I am sorry to keep the sri-Kaa waiting," she said without stumbling over the formal words. She started to tell Israi that she'd found the bush and had wanted to experience it, but she glanced up at Fazhmind, who was glaring at her, and fell silent.

Israi sat up taller in her chair and extended her rill. When she looked at Fazhmind, her eyes held triumph. "You were saying my pet cannot be trained?"

His face looked as though he had eaten sour fruit, and his tongue flicked once into sight. "Well, perhaps some training can be achieved with this creature, your highness, if you call this straggling in *trained*."

Israi's face turned to stone.

Lady Lenith tried to intervene. "My lord," she said with a placating gesture. "Remember that the Aaroun is very young. Only this week has it been determined that she is reaching the age of accountability, when training can begin. Do not expect too much too quickly. I think she has done very well. She is far more intelligent than most of her kind. Otherwise, she could never have learned our language. That alone is quite an accomplishment.''

Ampris swelled with pride, but Fazhmind only looked at her as though she were something to be stepped on with his sandal.

He flicked out his tongue. ''Accomplishment? It is an abomination. Never should it have been permitted.''

Lady Lenith lifted her rill and glanced at Israi as though to warn him to mind what he said, but Fazhmind's tirade went on, unchecked.

''She comes to her mistress, covered with dirt, as befouled as a street urchin, and dragging in these hideous flowers which are an offense to the imperial eye.''

Ampris opened her mouth to defend her beautiful bouquet, but to her dismay the blossoms were wilted and curling up. Their bright blue color had already faded, and their delicious fragrance was gone.

''What happened to them?'' she cried.

''They cannot be picked, for their blooms will not keep more than a few minutes,'' Fazhmind said spitefully. ''You stupid creature, you have destroyed the symmetry of that shrub for no purpose, thus creating a double offense.'' He glanced across the room at a slave and flicked his fingers in summons. ''Take this mess from the Imperial Daughter's sight at once.''

The slave hastened to obey.

Fazhmind pointed at Ampris. ''Remove that as well. Wash it. Clean what it has touched.''

Ampris growled low in her throat. ''I am not an it. I am—''

''Ampris, hush,'' Lady Lenith said.

Backing her ears, Ampris obeyed.

Fazhmind gestured again at the slave. ''Take it away.''

Bowing deeply, the slave reached for Ampris's hand.

''Leave her here,'' Israi commanded.

The slave released Ampris's fingers as though burned and backed away, bowing.

Israi glared at Fazhmind. Her half-extended rill had darkened. "You may not dismiss my pet without my permission."

"Say *my lord*," Lady Lenith advised her softly. "Your imperial highness must be polite."

"My lord," Israi said coldly. She went on glaring at Fazhmind.

He sighed and bowed to the sri-Kaa. "The Imperial Daughter surely does not wish the company of a creature who is dirty. It will be a more pleasant companion if it is clean."

"I'm not an it!" Ampris shouted angrily.

Israi whirled on her and gestured for silence. Shame washed over Ampris, and she obeyed.

"Yes, Lord Fazhmind," Israi said. "*My* Ampris is dirty. *She* was wrong to enter my presence with dirt on her nose. But *I* will correct her, not you." She glanced at Lady Lenith and added reluctantly, "My lord."

Fazhmind flicked out his tongue. "The Imperial Daughter has made herself very clear. May I be excused from her presence?"

"Yes," Israi said coldly. "You may go."

She turned her back on Fazhmind, who bowed, extended his rill disrespectfully, and departed.

Silence fell over them, then Lady Lenith said, "Will you now drink your refreshment?"

Israi pouted, her rill rising and falling. She would not look at Lady Lenith. She would not look at Ampris.

This was not a good sign. Ampris watched her beloved friend worriedly. She understood that she had failed again to please Israi. Worse, she had somehow caused Israi to fail with Fazhmind. When he sneered at Ampris, that disrespect was somehow transferred to Israi. And for nothing in the world did Ampris want anyone to feel less than complete adoration for her beloved friend.

"I am sorry," Ampris whispered. Her eyes filled with tears, and she was suddenly afraid Israi would send her away as Fazhmind was always urging. "Please forgive me."

Israi said nothing. She would not look at Ampris.

"Please," Ampris whispered. She crept closer to Israi, only to be drawn back by Lady Lenith's gentle hand.

Lady Lenith shook her head and gestured for Ampris to be quiet.

Frightened by Israi's anger, Ampris flattened her ears and obeyed.

Lady Lenith kept her hand on Ampris's shoulder. "Have I the Imperial Daughter's permission to order a bath for Ampris?"

Israi flicked out her tongue but said nothing.

Ampris stared at the floor. She was whimpering silently now; huge tears rolled down her face, streaking and matting her fur.

"I think," Lady Lenith said in her calm way, "that little Ampris did very well. She is walking upright now, a great accomplishment. She probably tried to hurry when the Imperial Daughter called. Did you fall down when you hurried, Ampris?"

Ampris opened her mouth to say no, but Lady Lenith continued before she could answer.

"Falling down always gets Ampris dirty. Her fur is such a light color that she can't help it, can she? And she went to such an effort to bring your highness flowers. Wasn't that a splendid gesture?"

Israi kept her gaze averted. "They were ugly."

"Oh, yes, indeed, very ugly," Lady Lenith agreed, while Ampris quivered under her hand. "But when Ampris first picked them, they must have been exquisite. Too exquisite for a little one to resist."

Ampris nodded her head, grateful for Lady Lenith's understanding.

Lady Lenith smiled at her. "Now Ampris knows that she

must never pick the flowers again, don't you?''

Ampris nodded again. "Yes, Lady Lenith," she said softly. Her gaze never left Israi's averted face.

"Did your highness notice how splendidly she spoke when she first came in? Of course, she was not yet acknowledged. That was a small mistake of etiquette, which we can overlook because of her tender age. For even the Imperial Daughter can forget to wait for acknowledgment, sometimes when she approaches her father, for example. But Ampris said what was correct. She used the proper formality, and she spoke Viis without error. That is no small accomplishment for one of the abiru.''

Israi turned around to face them. Her green eyes were still flat and cold, but at least now she was looking at Ampris and her rill was fading to its normal color.

Fresh unhappiness filled Ampris. She was so sorry for all her mistakes. If Lady Lenith had not held her in place, she would have flung herself flat on the floor at Israi's feet.

"It is important to make allowances for the shortcomings of those beneath us in ability, Israi," Lady Lenith said. "Ampris is not perfect, but your highness loves her."

Israi nodded, and relief dawned in Ampris. She gulped in a breath and wiped her eyes.

"As one who is older and more accomplished, your highness must remember to have patience with someone so little and new to court life. Ampris will learn, and she will improve. Give her time, and she will eventually reward you by behaving perfectly."

"I will," Ampris promised fervently.

Israi's gaze softened before a fresh streak of dark blue appeared on her rill. "But Lord Fazhmind is horrid. I wanted her to impress him."

"She will, in time. You must not mind his criticism so much. After all, you are the sri-Kaa. He is forever beneath your highness, forever subject to you. Do not give him more power than he has by letting his remarks upset you."

Israi tilted her head, looking surprised. "Is that why he is so mean?"

"Yes," Lady Lenith said.

"Oh."

Ampris gazed up at Lady Lenith in gratitude. Perhaps Israi was going to forgive her after all, and if she did it was due to this gentle person's influence. At that moment Ampris loved Lady Lenith almost as completely as she loved Israi. She rubbed her muzzle against Lady Lenith's hand.

Lady Lenith patted her shoulder. "There now. All is right again. Will you two not make up? Or is Lord Fazhmind going to succeed in ruining your friendship?"

A strange look crossed Israi's face. She jumped off her chair and rushed to hug Ampris, dirt and all.

"Dear little Ampris," she said, squeezing Ampris tight. "I won't let him do that. I promise. You are going to be with me forever."

Happy once again, Ampris hugged her back. "I'll be good," she said. "I'll be very good."

Israi pulled free from their embrace and gently tugged one of Ampris's ears. "Now go and get your bath. I have a new game for us to play."

"The Imperial Daughter must take refreshment and a nap first," Lady Lenith said.

Israi grimaced. "I am too old for naps," she declared.

"All ladies take naps," Lady Lenith said. "It preserves their beauty and their skin."

Israi flicked out her tongue, but she made no further protest. "Go, Ampris, and bathe," she said. "I'll take a short nap while you do that. Then we'll play."

Relief was making Ampris feel sleepy herself. She beamed at Israi and bowed. "I can't wait," she said. "I like new games. But I want to play Squeak, too."

Spinning around, she rushed out.

Before she reached the bathing chamber, however, Lady Lenith caught up with her. Under the neutral stares of the slaves, Lady Lenith gripped Ampris by the arm and shoved her over against a wall. Her gentle expression of sympathy was gone, replaced by stern disapproval. Her rill stood dark, at full extension.

She slapped Ampris once across the muzzle, not hard enough to hurt, but hard enough to shock Ampris.

Surprised by the blow, Ampris stared at her in disbelief while fresh tears filled her eyes. Her mouth began to quiver, but she dared say nothing.

"Now you listen to me," Lady Lenith said in a clipped, no-nonsense voice. "You are getting too far above yourself of late. You are *not* the equal of the Imperial Daughter. Is that clear? You must *never* dictate which games her highness will play. Your opinion is not important, nor is it requested. Never again do I want to see you argue with her, or cause her distress. Is that clear?"

Shaken, Ampris nodded. "Yes, my lady," she whispered.

"You have been set far above your station because it pleases the Imperial Daughter to put you there, but never forget that you are just an Aaroun, nothing more. The fact that you are allowed to speak Viis does not mean you are one of us. You are abiru, just like those slaves standing there."

She gestured as she spoke, and Ampris stared at the expressionless servants in rising distress. She *wasn't* a slave. She belonged to Israi. She was beloved of Israi. She was special. Israi had told her so.

"Silence," Lady Lenith said as Ampris started to speak. "You are abiru, the lowest of the low. See that you remember it."

"Yes, my lady," Ampris whispered.

"And you can remember this also. The imperial promise is binding only as long as the Imperial Daughter wishes it to be. If you make her angry, she can send you away, just like that." Lady Lenith flicked her fingers. "Her cartouche will be taken from your ear, and you will be cast out."

Ampris clutched her earring in horror. "No!"

"Yes! I tell you this for your own benefit. You can be a good companion for her, if you will behave."

"She won't send me away," Ampris insisted. "She is my friend."

Lady Lenith slapped her again, hard enough to sting through Ampris's fur this time. "No, you stupid Aaroun. The Imperial Daughter is *not* your friend. She is your owner. Never forget it. Never, do you hear?"

Holding her aching muzzle and fighting not to whimper, Ampris said nothing.

Lady Lenith pushed her toward the pool. "Go take your bath. You've had your warning. It's up to you to remember it."

Without another word, she turned and walked away, her long skirts billowing over her tail.

Not until she was gone from sight did Ampris dare move. Running to one of the decorative columns, she crouched down behind it and glared at the slaves watching her.

"Leave me alone!" she said, growling.

They shrugged and filed out, while Ampris told herself she didn't care what they saw or what they heard. The opinion of a slave, after all, was nothing.

Alone in the vaulted bathing chamber, Ampris pressed her muzzle against the cool stone column and wept. She hated Lord Fazhmind, and she hated Lady Lenith. They said one thing and did another. Everything was a lie for Israi's benefit. Their kindness was false, and no one could be trusted.

No one, except Israi.

Ampris lifted her head at last, trying to stop the miserable ache inside her. She had learned a big lesson today. Never again must she risk Israi's displeasure. For only Israi mattered. She would make herself worthy of Israi's friendship in every way. She would make Israi proud of her. Never again would she shame her beloved friend.

"I am not a stupid Aaroun," Ampris whispered, resenting all the things Lady Lenith had said to her. "And Israi *is* my friend. As I am *her* friend. She will never send me away. She isn't mean. She isn't false.''

Slitting her eyes, Ampris glared into the distance and licked her palm before slapping it down on the floor and grinding it back and forth, the way she'd seen some of the slaves do when they thought no one was watching.

That for Lady Lenith of the two faces.

She licked her palm a second time and again slapped her hand on the floor, smearing her spittle across the stone. And *that* for Lord Fazhmind, her enemy. Both of them could do what they liked and say what they wanted. She would show them that an Aaroun was just as good as they were.

CHAPTER FIVE

The city of Vir lay wedge-shaped along the shores of the Cuna Da'r River. At its apex stood the vast palace complex, seat of the Kaa's power, and from the tall palace gates the broad Avenue of Triumph bisected the rest of the city. The fashionable west side, with its expensive shops and the villas of the nobility, filled the area between the river and the Avenue of Triumph. Bordering the banks of the river itself stood the Row of Palaces, grand edifices built long ago during the height of the Viis Empire. They were maintained now by the descendants of the Twelve, the original noble houses.

The east side of the city sprawled unchecked out into the dry, flat Plains of Filea. As the capital city of the Viis homeworld, Vir required a spaceport, but the terminal had been located eighty klicks away to spare the city from the noise of ground-space shuttles booming into departure velocity. Vir Station One stood at the farthest rim of the eastern side of the city, handling first-class passengers. Vir Stations Two and Three processed second- and third-class passengers, including military personnel. Vir Station Four handled only cargo, including domestic, intercontinental, and galactic trade. It constantly expanded to accommodate the heavy traffic between it and Port Filea, and many of the loading docks for cargo now extended into the abiru ghetto. Tenants never knew when they might return home from work to find their building marked for demolition. As a result, more and more tenements grew crowded, and more and more of the abiru folk were forced to live in alley shanties.

The ghetto was a place of decaying buildings, abandoned shops, and dirty streets. Sanitation Services came through sporadically. Public comm lines were usually broken, which also meant most of the vids didn't work. Public transit did not enter the ghetto. Cameras and security sniffers floated constantly along the perimeter dividing the ghetto from the rest of the city, with strong security networks clustered at the gates. The registration ID implanted in Elrabin's elbow lacked an authorization exit code, which meant he could stand at the barricades all day long and look at the sleek skimmers flying by, the well-to-do Viis citizens hurrying past on their business, the shops with fabulous wares displayed behind shimmering security bars, but he could never pass through the gates into the Viis part of the city. All those wonderful things out there might as well be located on the planet Mynchepop, for all the chance Elrabin had of ever getting closer to them.

Few Viis ventured into the ghetto besides slavers, patrollers, and members of the small religious order that ministered to the Viis Rejects, who were to be avoided at all costs.

Reforms were mentioned occasionally on vid news, but no one in the Viis government wanted to squander money on breaking the endless cycle of poverty, hard labor, and degradation of the inferior abiru races.

To Elrabin, standing at the barricade with his narrow muzzle almost pressed to its crackling energy barrier, there was an entirely unexplored world waiting for him out there. He pressed closer, yearning to experience a type of existence that seemed like a fantasy.

An alarm blared, startling him into jumping back. Heart pounding, he gazed up at the sniffer floating above him. Little frizzles of energy crackled over his skin, and he knew he was being scanned.

"You are too close to the barricade," a mechanical voice blared. It was scratchy, warbling at the ends of words in a way that would have been funny in other circumstances. "Step back six paces. Warning. You are . . . close to the barr . . . cade. Step back."

Elrabin scooted back, turned, and headed down the street with his ears cocked back, alert for trouble. The sniffer continued to float over the spot where he'd been, its message repeating itself as though stuck in a loop.

The stupid thing was probably five seconds from a breakdown. Elrabin flicked his ears forward. Half the machinery in the ghetto didn't work. No one maintained it, and anything that did function usually got stolen or cannibalized for parts.

Then the beeping alarm suddenly changed pitch to something shriller and more insistent. The sniffer came flying after him. "Warning," it blared. "ID chip five-five-seven-two-one-zero, you are in violation of city ordinance—"

Elrabin snarled a curse and ran, dodging pedestrians and stacks of uncollected garbage on the decaying street. At the corner ahead of him was a group of Toth thugs, seemingly idle and talking to each other in the guttural, broken phrases they considered their own language. In reality they were looking for their next victim to shake down. Elrabin veered instinctively away from them, because Toths were always big trouble, then reconsidered and ran straight toward them.

The sniffer followed, locked on him now and still blaring its message. If the stupid thing expected him to stand still as ordered and wait until a patrol skimmer showed up to arrest him, pass sentence, and utilize the wrist cutters on the spot, he wasn't going to behave like a good little slave-grade citizen.

Ahead of him, the group of Toths stopped talking and

stared at the approaching sniffer, their floppy ears extended. Uneasiness showed on their broad, ugly faces.

Grinning to himself, Elrabin stayed on direct approach. He figured they all had record sheets. Let the sniffer get in range of their registration codes, and it might short-circuit from trying to lock on everyone at once.

Muttering, the Toths could have scattered, but instead they spread out to face Elrabin. They were all adults, well above twice his height. Their massive, oversized heads were covered in mats of brown, curly hair. Their small, dim eyes glittered with brutal malice and little else. Originally brought to Viisymel for heavy labor, the Toths were rebellious and hard to control. Most ran in gangs or worked for slavers as enforcers. They respected no authority, followed no rules. Genetic bullies, they fed on fear and intimidation.

The sniffer was still blaring at Elrabin, ordering him to halt for arrest. He ran right up to the Toths, watching the sniffer from the corner of his eye to make sure it was close enough, then veered to dart around the thugs.

One of them grabbed him by the shoulder and brought him to a halt so sudden that Elrabin was nearly jerked off his feet. Snarling and snapping in fear, his plan suddenly cooked, Elrabin tried to break free of the Toth's grip and failed.

The sniffer halted and floated over their heads, still blaring its message. Elrabin glared at it, wondering why it didn't scan the Toths. The stupid sniffer's multiscan capability must be broken, he figured. Elrabin muttered under his breath and tried again to twist free. His captor only clamped Elrabin's shoulder harder, making him gasp with pain.

A small red light suddenly glowed on the sniffer's scuffed ovoid surface. Elrabin's heart lifted with hope, but one of the Toths pulled out an illegal sidearm and shot it, exploding bits of wire and circuitry over their heads. The bits came raining down, white-hot, singeing Toth fur where they landed.

Elrabin's captor bellowed in pain and slapped at his head. Elrabin took a chance, twisted around, and bit the hairy wrist of the hand clamped on his shoulder.

Toth blood, hot and foul-tasting, spurted across his tongue. The Toth bellowed again and slung Elrabin away. Elrabin went flying bodily through the air, arms and legs windmilling, and slammed into the graffiti-covered wall of a building.

The impact jolted his bones and knocked the breath from him. He lay on the ground, stunned and only half-conscious. By the time he managed to suck air back into his lungs, he found himself roughly flipped over on his back. Hands groped and patted through his pockets and belt pouch.

When he realized groggily what they were doing, he tried to sit up. "You—"

The Toth kneeling over him butted him in the chest with that massive head. Everything went black, and when the world came back again Elrabin found himself lying alone in the dusty gutter, with bits of garbage and food wrappers blowing over him.

Wheezing, he managed to sit up, and moaned from the effort. His chest felt caved in, although when he gingerly rubbed his ribs nothing seemed broken. The pockets of his coat were ripped out. His meat globes and the comb with fake jewels were gone. His belt had also been taken, leaving him minus his payment card and its one credit.

Elrabin rubbed his narrow muzzle, so angry he wanted to tip back his head and howl. But that wouldn't bring back his stolen property. He bared his teeth and muttered to himself. He'd taken those things because he needed them— well, the credit and the meat globes anyway. But the Toths were despicable thieves. They robbed for the pleasure of it. They had no morals at all.

"Loitering is not permitted. Keep moving. Loitering is not permitted. Keep moving."

The message blared overhead, making Elrabin jump at the arrival of another sniffer.

Gaining his feet, he trotted away and blended in with other pedestrians. Without scanning him, the new sniffer let him go, and by the time he'd dodged down several alleys and ducked in and out of a few businesses, his heart had stopped pounding and he was able to breathe normally again.

But his thoughts still raced around and around in his head, until he felt almost dizzy. This morning he had begun his new life in good shape. He had food and he had credit. Now, with late afternoon sunlight slanting across the city buildings, he had nothing to his name but his wits.

He sighed and rubbed his muzzle, telling himself not to worry, not to be scared. He was smart enough to take care of himself. He could figure something out.

But already his stomach was growling with hunger. He had nothing to eat. Nothing in mind to steal. Nowhere to go. Right now, freedom looked a lot bigger than it had before, and a lot less fun.

In the distance he could hear the throaty horns of barge traffic on the river. Most of the vehicles flying past on the streets in this section were industry transports. Warehouses shielded by security fields either buzzed with activity or stood abandoned. When the wind shifted fractionally, Elrabin caught a whiff of a stench that made his ears prick forward and the hair around his neck stand on end.

It was the smell of death, the stench of the meat houses, where condemned slaves were taken to be slaughtered.

He growled low in his throat and veered in the opposite direction. Picking up his pace, he hurried out of the district, knowing he had to look purposeful to avoid being picked up for vagrancy. He couldn't approach any public vid screens, because they would blare an alarm based on his registration code. If he went to one of the public food dispensaries and begged for charity, an alarm would sound.

One day on his own, and already he was wanted.

His ears drooped, and discouragement settled heavily on his young shoulders. Maybe he wasn't quite as streetwise as he thought.

Go home, ran a thought through his mind. *Go home.*

He thought of supper made from tasteless Quixlix, the cramped quarters, his quarreling lits, no privacy, no hope. A fresh sense of rebellion stiffened his shoulders.

No. He wasn't going home. He had no home. He was on his own, and he could make it. He would go to his old friend Berv, who would give him work and somehow get around the labor laws.

By the time he crossed the ghetto and reached the cramped streets and half-demolished buildings fringing the dock area for Vir Station Four, Elrabin's legs ached with weariness and he was famished. He dragged himself down a street lined with tenement buildings that made him think of home, ignored a handful of dirty Kelth lits and Aaroun cubs playing gollooball with chunks of decaying pavement gleaned from the unmended street, and cut across a vacant lot that had once been a city park with a statue of some dead Viis kaa surrounded by a grove of trees. Vines now grew over the statue, obscuring it. The grove of trees had died and been cut down for firewood by scavengers who couldn't afford cookers. Trash blew ahead of him. Now and then he stopped to kick through a pile of garbage that looked promising. So far all he'd found was a piece of circuit board, but he clutched it in his hand for hope. If he could sell it to Berv, he would be back in business.

But Berv's tiny basement shop was closed up tightly, the windows dark, a heavy iron bar locked across the door for security.

Elrabin sniffed at the door and windows, pounding on them, and yelled for Berv to come out.

No answer.

He whined softly in his throat, feeling frustration rising to mingle with sharp disappointment. Berv had to be here. The junk dealer never went anywhere.

Turning around, he glimpsed a pair of eyes watching him from the shadows across the street.

"Hey!" Elrabin said.

The eyes vanished.

He ran to the doorway and knocked on the door inside the shadowy alcove, but it remained closed against him. "Hey!" he shouted again. "I'm looking for Berv. Where is he?"

No one came to the door. No one answered his question.

Elrabin muttered to himself and turned around to glare at Berv's place. He had no right to be gone when he was needed.

A few blocks over, a departing cargo shuttle launched itself into the sky with a blast of fuel exhaust that lit up the twilight shadows. The thundering takeoff deafened Elrabin and made the windows rattle in the building next to him. There was an ordinance against flying the shuttles this close to inhabited buildings. But the abiru folk had no clout with the Viis government to make it enforce its laws, and the shuttle flights got closer and more frequent all the time. Word was that another dock and landing pad were to be built this year, extending the station yet farther into the residential district of the ghetto.

Elrabin listened to the powerful engines throbbing swiftly in the distance. He promised himself that someday he would leave the ghetto, would leave Vir, would go out to Port Filea and climb aboard one of those gleaming ground-space shuttles to get off Viisymel forever. Someday he would see the empire for himself, and not just watch vid broadcasts about it. He would see the wonder planets, like Mynchepop with its upside-down waterfalls and pleasure gardens. He would walk through exotic cities, breathing air that did not stink like Vir's. He would make his fortune, and he would live a life that meant something.

Someday.

In the meantime, it was getting dark. Upstairs windows showed lights now. The smells of cooking wafted on the cool night air. Elrabin's mouth watered and his stomach growled so hard he felt faint.

Go home, he thought again, but he shook it off, angry at himself for being weak.

Home was nowhere. Home was a dead end. He was Elrabin the Quick, and he was destined for better things than this.

There was only one thing left to do. He would go looking in the bars and dust holes for his da. Surely his own da would take him in, feed him, and teach him the ways of the good life.

That was, if his old da wasn't dead or arrested by now.

CHAPTER SIX

A chilly afternoon rain fell upon the eastern slopes of the Sivean Mountains and drizzled steadily over the Kaa's hunting lodge. A cold, wintry, disappointing rain. A plan-spoiling rain.

Standing at a window and gazing outside at the dreary, leaden skies, Ampris—fourteen now in Aaroun years and ta-chune in Viis growth cycles—heaved a disgusted sigh.

The imperial party had arrived earlier in the week for the Kaa's annual visit. Now that the hectic days of Hevrmasihd Festival had brought the year to an end, everyone felt lazy and bloated from too much feasting and activity. The Kaa came here to hunt across the breathtaking mountains, to take in fresh air, to eat simply, and to rest far from the cares of governing his empire. These were the slow days of Feval, the renewal. The courtiers had been released to visit their own homes or to go offworld if they wished extensive travel. Only a chosen, select few were invited to accompany the Kaa here to his beloved lodge. Some years he brought all his favorite wives and offspring; other years he did not. This year, only six of his most beloved wives were present, and of the many imperial progeny, only the sri-Kaa and her nine egg-siblings had been brought. Even the tutors had been left behind.

As a result, the galleries and corridors of the lodge seemed almost empty in comparison with the busy court at Vir. Here, the onerous burdens of court etiquette and protocol were relaxed a great deal; even clothing was simpler, less ornate and more comfortable.

Ampris loved Feval far more than the hectic Hevrmasihd. She relished the quiet days of renewal, the release from lessons that she had to share with Israi at the sri-Kaa's insistence, the freedom to wander and sometimes dream.

Israi's preferences, of course, were just the opposite. She loved festivals of all kinds, relishing the activities, the packed schedules of parties and preparations, the clothes, jewels, and finery, the music and games that seemed to spin on endlessly.

But there would not be another festival to celebrate until spring, when the best one of all was held. Sahvrazaa, the Festival of Fertility, brought the largest feasts, the greatest revels, and an atmosphere of kindness and goodwill, intense expectations and hopes. All the splendid old songs were sung in both palace and city. The bells rang, and many traditional rituals marked the occasion, including the grand mating migration of the males. Ampris loved the Sahvrazaa, for it marked the anniversary of Israi's finding her and giving her a home. Together, they had woven their own private traditions of gift-giving and feasting with each other. But beyond that, they both loved the opportunity of playing pranks and running free of supervision while the adults were occupied with hatchings and ceremonies.

Still, spring was a long time away, too far away to think about today. Outside, it was pouring rain even harder than before. Israi was gone, summoned to spend the afternoon with her father. In past years, when Ampris was younger, she had been allowed to enter the Kaa's study with Israi. She had found such times pleasing, for the Kaa would talk quietly of history or architecture, unrolling musty old

scrolls of dim drawings to show them. Often he would hold
Israi on his lap and allow Ampris to lean against his knee
while he rubbed her head between her ears. The Kaa's
voice was deep with authority, yet gentle. Ampris loved to
listen to him speak.

Sometimes he activated a screen, allowing them to watch
the twirling schematics of new architectural drawings prepared specifically for the restoration of the old palace. As
a treat, he would permit them to open a program and gen-
erate their own buildings. It was more fun than simple
drawing with a stylus. Ampris found she had a flair for
three-dimensional structures. She was quick to learn, and
inventive enough to earn the Kaa's praise. On the other
hand, Israi's walls never matched up. Her staircases went
nowhere. While she loved choosing colors and exquisite
details, she had none of Ampris's patience for the construction aspects of a building project.

If that was what Israi and the Kaa were doing this rainy
afternoon, then Ampris could not help but scowl at the far
end of the gallery, where the study door stood closed behind motionless guards.

Today, Ampris had not been invited to join Israi and her
father.

For the first time in her memory, Ampris had been shut
out.

Growling silently in her throat, she picked aimlessly at
a mortar joint in the windowsill. There had to be something
she could do. Something more interesting than just waiting
here until Israi came out.

Ampris's gaze wandered toward the opposite end of the
gallery, to a door standing ajar and unguarded. A door that
beckoned to her, leading to a part of the lodge she had
never explored before.

Israi would be furious if Ampris explored without her.

On the other hand, why should Ampris wait?

She glanced at the Kaa's study door, still firmly closed.

Israi had not ordered her to stay nearby. Israi had not given her any instructions at all.

"My father has summoned me to his study this afternoon," Israi had said.

"Will we draw houses?" Ampris asked excitedly.

"I do not know, but you may not come."

It took a moment for the remark to soak in. Then Ampris blinked at her in surprise. "Why not?"

Israi flicked out her tongue. She was wearing a bright green satin tunic lined with velvet that reached to her knees, worn open over a pair of golden trousers the exact color of her skin. Pretty pendants dangled from the spines of her rill in the latest fashion.

"The Kaa did not request your presence," Israi said.

Ampris waited for her to look annoyed, or to say that she had requested permission for Ampris to accompany her, but Israi said nothing more.

It was not polite to insist or beg. Swallowing her hurt and disappointment, Ampris bowed. "What shall I do?"

Again Israi flicked her tongue. "Anything you like."

And she walked away through the doors which the guards opened for her.

Anything I like, Ampris thought.

She looked around again, turning her back on the dreary rain streaking the windowpanes. She would explore, by herself, and she hoped with all her heart that she found something wonderful, something that would make Israi envious.

At once, she touched the cartouche hanging from her ear in automatic atonement for such an unworthy thought. It was wicked to make such a wish.

"But I don't care," Ampris whispered to herself, and hurried down the length of the immense gallery to the untended door.

She slipped past it without touching its ornate gold surface. For a second she held her breath, for there were alarms fitted throughout the lodge as part of the general security system, but she set nothing off.

Relieved, she looked around.

She saw nothing exciting, only another gallery as wide and long as the one she'd just left. This one, however, was fitted with dark paneling carved with scenes of ancient Viis battles waged long before the age of technology. She smelled archaic candles, cold stone, and wood well-polished with camphan oil.

She gazed at the panels, which were illuminated by the gloomy light that entered through the tall, narrow windows. Without someone to explain the significance of the scenes depicted, Ampris soon tired of them and walked on.

The lodge itself had been built more than two centuries before, at the height of Viis supremacy, and it was wedged onto the side of a dizzying slope. Balconies overlooked sheer precipices, and the crisp scent of narpine forests filled the air. On days of clear weather, fierce raptuls flew in spirals about the towers of the lodge, uttering harsh hunting cries that echoed forever into the canyons.

For Ampris, this was a marvelous place of nooks and crannies, stairways that wound and crooked unexpectedly, uneven ceilings, fabulous views from every window, the perpetual cooking scents of savory ragouts and leneek pies mingled with the fragrances of oiled leather, stone floors, musty tapestries, snow-frosted air, and the narpines.

Every year upon arrival, Ampris and Israi separated themselves from the other youngsters to explore the lodge as much as they were permitted. They had free run of the first two stories, which contained both public and private apartments, plus the common library, access to the gardens, and round towers with circular staircases that spiraled up to locked doors that no one would open.

This floor, the third, held the state apartments and the Kaa's quarters. Usually it was off-limits.

Ampris quickened her footsteps, nearly running to the end of the paneled gallery. Again, there was a door at its end, plainer than the previous one. No one guarded it either.

She curled her fingers around the cold metal latch and

hesitated a moment. Her heart was pumping fast. She pressed her ear against the door and listened for what might be on the other side.

Only silence came to her ears.

She sniffed, seeking Viis scent with the distinctive overlying fragrance of armor lubricant.

Nothing. No guards in the vicinity.

Suppose she actually walked into the Kaa's own chambers?

The idea made her shiver. Her heart pumped harder with growing excitement. No one entered the Kaa's private rooms without permission. Not even Israi dared do that.

Yet, it was surely the supreme adventure, the ultimate in daring. It would surpass even the day that Israi had dared her to walk the rooftop over the wives court, and Ampris had. Only the swift intervention of Lady Lenith had prevented Israi from making the attempt herself. Mortified by such interference, Israi had not spoken to her chief lady in waiting for three days. Then the matter was forgotten by all save Ampris, who still treasured her accomplishment.

Today, however, she would surpass herself. But she would have to prove she had actually entered the Kaa's chambers.

Ampris frowned in thought. She did not dare take anything from the Kaa's rooms. That was unthinkable. She could lose her head for that.

But she could leave something. Swiftly Ampris patted through her pockets and found three small, smooth pebbles that she had picked up on the hiking trail yesterday. They were intended for the pebble collection that she added to every year. Lady Lenith sneered at her collection, calling it ugly and foolish, and would not permit Ampris to display it the way Israi displayed her collection of exquisite sun crystals in a case built especially for them. But at the same time, Lady Lenith permitted Ampris to keep her humble collection of stones, for they had no worth and could not compete with Israi's possessions.

Hefting the three pebbles on her palm, Ampris turned them over with a fingertip, admiring their naturally smooth sides and the striations of color that veined them. Humble or not, they were not ugly to her eyes. She liked things that were natural, things that came from the ground.

Israi did not understand what Ampris liked in the stones, but Israi was too kind to sneer at them.

Ampris curled her fingers over the pebbles with satisfaction. Yes, she would leave these on the center of the Kaa's bed, for his valet to find. Word would circle around among the servants; questions would be asked. Israi would hear of it, and that would confirm what Ampris intended to tell her tonight.

Wouldn't Israi be wild with envy?

Grinning to herself, Ampris carefully turned the latch, pulled open the heavy door, and peered around it.

But the Kaa's quarters did not lie on the other side. Disappointed, Ampris found herself looking at yet another hallway. It was furnished with thick rugs imported from offworld, antique tables that displayed fine vases so old their glazes were cracked, chairs of antiquated, unfamiliar designs, and mysterious paintings with opaque surfaces that revealed nothing until Ampris stood close and peered at them for a long time.

Only then, slyly, would the painting surface shimmer to life, evolving into a portrait or a landscape of breathtaking quality that altered each time she changed her angle of looking at it.

She took her time here, peering into the paintings and catching her breath sharply at what was revealed to her. Oh, if only Israi could see these.

This far surpassed the pleasure of sniffing about the huge, hot kitchens, getting underfoot, and begging for treats from the harried staff.

Keeping her ears sharp for the sound of footsteps that would warn her someone was coming, Ampris finally moved beyond the paintings and stopped before a cabinet

that was tall and narrow, with solid wood panels that concealed its interior from top to bottom.

When she traced her fingertips across the lovely grain of
the wood, a stirring of sound reached her ears, barely dis-
cernible, like the soft lilting of a harp when air blows
through its strings.

She stroked the wood again, and again it sang softly to
her. Ampris had heard of songwood. She knew its rarity
was beyond price. Sometimes betrothed Viis couples would
exchange tiny slivers of the costly wood as tokens of their
impending nuptials.

But here stood an entire cabinet made of this lovely
wood, as beautiful in appearance as the sound it produced
beneath her fingertips. Ampris could barely tear herself
away from it, for its song fascinated her. Yet she dared not
linger in here forever.

There were surely many more fabulous treasures to find.
Even so, what thrilled her most was the thought of bringing
Israi here and showing her everything.

This passage ended with an open, vaulted doorway that
led into a spacious, round antechamber. Looking around,
Ampris saw a set of stairs carpeted in imperial crimson
rising to a magnificent door of hammered gold. Above the
door hung the grand seal of the Kaa.

Seeing it, Ampris gulped a little. Guards flanked the
door, staring straight ahead. Impassive and formidable, they
ignored Ampris, but she knew better than to venture near
the stairs. That, clearly, was forbidden territory.

Panting, she returned her humble pebbles to her pocket,
forgetting her plan of sneaking into the Kaa's quarters.
Such an attempt would not be daring; it would be stupid
and disrespectful.

Still, she had gotten this far without being challenged or
stopped, and that would surely be enough to make Israi
wish she had been here.

Overhead, the landing's ceiling was painted with scenes
from ancient Viis mythology, including Ampria the sun

goddess in her sky boat drawn by flying raptuls. The dark floor was inset with precious stones mimicking the patterns of constellations across the night skies.

Opposite the passageway Ampris had emerged from stood three doors, all closed, all unguarded. She stared at them, curious to see what they contained. But with the guards present, Ampris's curiosity flattened. She turned to retreat back the way she'd come, only to halt as she heard voices in the distance—fluty, well-educated Viis voices—that warned her several courtiers were approaching.

Ampris hesitated only a moment, then dashed across the landing to one of the doors. Although she did not think she was doing anything wrong, certainly she had not been given permission to be here, so near the Kaa's quarters. Still, it was better to hide until the approaching courtiers were gone. Then she would return to the area where Israi had left her.

Picking a door at random, she turned the latch and found it unlocked. She glanced up just as one of the guards turned his head to stare at her.

His eyes were yellow and cold. They stabbed right through her, and Ampris panted again.

The approaching voices were louder, closer.

Dry-mouthed, Ampris sprang inside without looking and shut the door firmly behind her.

She waited there with her face pressed against the door, listening for a shout, for the sound of hasty footsteps. But she heard neither.

After a moment she relaxed, relieved that the guards were not going to come after her.

When she was with Israi, she never feared the guards. But alone was a different matter. Ampris might live a happy, secure life now, but sometimes at night she still suffered nightmares of the Scary Time, those fearful few days before Israi had found and adopted her. While Ampris never remembered those dreams clearly, the heart-pounding terror they evoked haunted her, especially whenever she crossed paths with palace guards.

The courtiers walked past the door which concealed her, their chattering gossip loud. After a moment she heard them continue downstairs, and quiet came again in their wake.

She eased out her breath, not realizing until then that she'd been holding it. Sometimes the courtiers made cruel remarks to her when she was not safe in Israi's presence. Ampris was well-aware that few at court approved of her presence in the imperial household. No other Aaroun in all the empire was as well-placed as she. Lady Lenith reminded her of this fact at least once a day, if not more often, forever telling her to be grateful for the supreme kindness which had been shown her by the sri-Kaa.

Ampris sighed. The only problem with constantly being told to feel grateful was that it made her want to bite instead. Ampris adored Israi and knew she was blessed in the favor shown to her. But whenever Lady Lenith lectured her, Ampris hated being told how she should feel. She had to hide her resentment, of course, for Lady Lenith's punishments could be terrible. Nor could she go to Israi and complain, for then Lady Lenith would retaliate in even more horrible ways.

Ampris had learned the harsh realities of court life long ago. So many things were shielded from the sri-Kaa, so many things deemed inappropriate for Israi to know about or for Israi to see.

Ampris thought that the sri-Kaa should be told the truth about everything, but no one cared about the opinion of a young Aaroun. Truth, in the Viis imperial court, was a slippery concept at best.

In the meantime, however, Ampris decided she had been gone long enough. She knew she had better return before Israi found that she was missing.

She reached for the door latch, but before she opened it she glanced over her shoulder at the room she was in and found herself transfixed.

It was a hideous place, long and gloomy with narrow, antiquated windows. Preserved heads of all kinds of animals hung on the walls. Their dead, glassy eyes stared at Ampris in silent accusation. Bared teeth, yellowed with age, snarled perpetually.

Horrified, Ampris walked away from the door and slowly ventured deeper into the room. She felt as though she had entered a tomb. Her blood ran cold in her veins, yet she could not stop walking from one mounted head to another, staring at each and every one of the dead visages.

In one corner, she found a collection of five adult Aaroun heads mounted in a row. Severed pairs of hands, wizened into mummified claws, hung beneath each head.

Shocked, she stood like one frozen, unable to tear herself away from the sight.

On the wall with them hung an inscription relating to the incident. It described a battle between these five Aarouns, labeled assassins, and the former kaa, who had killed them single-handedly. The ceremonial sword he had used was also present, mounted in a special display case.

With a trembling hand, Ampris reached out and touched one of the Aarouns. Its fur felt silky soft, as soft as her own, yet the form beneath that thick pelt was stiff and alien. She jerked back her hand, hearing a faint, sobbing sound in the back of her throat.

The dead Aarouns loomed above her, dark and menacing, their teeth bared in eternal snarls. Their sightless eyes glittered in some trick of the pale light and seemed to follow her as she backed away.

Suddenly she could not breathe. The room seemed to be spinning around her. It was too hot. The Aarouns grew bigger and bigger, their open mouths ready to speak.

She stumbled back, suddenly convinced that if they said her name, she would be forever trapped here with them, and just as dead.

''No!''

The cry wrenched itself from her throat. Whirling

around, she fled, slamming her way out of the room and running back into the passageway with all the speed she possessed.

As she ran, arms and legs pumping, her breath rasping in her throat, she thought she heard the laughter of the Viis guards echoing behind her, mocking her and the dead.

CHAPTER SEVEN

A cold winter rain funneled down the back of Elrabin's collar, plastering his fur to the nape of his neck. Muttering to himself and hunching his shoulders tighter beneath his new coat, he dashed across the Street of Regard and ducked beneath a bright yellow awning that proclaimed the dwelling a brothel.

Three streets over he could hear the hourly chime of a temple bell in the historical district. Elrabin sighed to himself. Feval was the season for reflection of one's soul, for renewal of one's conscience, for rest following the vigorous celebrations of Hevrmasihd, the winter festival. Or so the high-and-mighty Viis claimed. In reality, the temple probably held about three contemplative Viis in the decrepit stages of otal, their final life cycle, looking at their future and finding it quite short. The city itself was all but shut down. The Kaa was out of town, with his court scattered to the far directions of the planet or beyond. Half the shopping district was closed for the season, the rest yawning through empty afternoons like this one.

Feval, the season of slim pickings and boredom, when even the slave labor went on half shift. Dozy and slow, many of the abiru races crawled into their cheap lodgings for winter hibernation, only venturing out for basic necessities and work mandates. Gullible marks were hard to find this time of year, making grifting almost impossible. Yet here Elrabin was, out in the cold, wet weather, scoping the brothels in search of Cuvein.

Standing under the yellow awning with its discreet black circle that also marked it as a gambling establishment, Elrabin shook water from his coat, hoping its bright blue dye wouldn't run and stain his fur. His last coat he'd worn until it was threadbare and the sleeves had grown absurdly short. Finally declaring him to be an embarrassment, Cuvein had given him some credit vouchers to buy a new one. Elrabin smoothed down the front, admiring the metallic thread embroidery that embellished it thickly enough to hide the cheapness of the cloth. It was not well-made, but he thought it made him look handsome.

He needed to look sharp if he was to continue charming the Viis widow he'd discovered in the Keskian district. Keskia was an old part of Vir, a crescent-shaped area of crumbling old houses, cramped shops, and a few struggling market plazas that bordered the fringes of the affluent Zehava district. Populated mostly by elderly Viis, including lun-adults and otals, Keskia housed retired merchants and minor aristocracy who had lost both fortune and favor at court.

The widow had caught Elrabin peering in her upper-story windows one day. Trying to avoid arrest charges, he'd fed her a glib tale of being a window inspector and told her that she had damage from worm rot (this last being pointed out to the lady to explain the gouges he'd made in trying to pry the window open). Her servants watched him with suspicion, but the lady herself was old, lonely, and eager for company, even if in the guise of a shabby Kelth grifter. She seemed to believe his story, informed him that he reminded her of a Kelth pet she'd had as a chune on her father's country estates, and grew worried enough about the bogus damage to listen to his proposal to sell her new windows (modern, flimsy ones that would be easier to pry open later).

Elrabin himself had never gone in for burglary. But he had a contact on the east side, a Kelth named Sant, who paid for information on good targets. The widow's house stood on a lonely street, jammed between two deserted dwellings with inheritance notices pasted to the front portals. If the heirs would pay the death taxes, they could have access to their property. From the look of things, no one was eager to redeem these crumbling edifices. So the widow had no close, snoopy neighbors to keep an eye on her. She was old and gullible and half-deaf. Best of all, her house was so crammed with goods and furniture that she probably wouldn't even notice if some of it got hauled off.

So Elrabin planned to sell the widow's address to Sant, plus he was hoping to sell her new windows. Either way, he stood to earn. He had an appointment to see the lady this evening, which was why he needed this fine new coat.

Except it wouldn't look so fine if the dye ran and the cloth shrank against its stitching. Damn Cuvein for making him come out in this weather.

Shivering, Elrabin rang the brothel's bell for admittance. The cold, moist air was clearing his head a bit from the slight buzz that made his thoughts sometimes crawl sideways. That meant the Dlexyline was wearing off. He had maybe an hour to be out on the streets with this dose, and then it would be time for trouble that he couldn't afford.

Impatiently he rang again.

Someone shuffled to the other side of the door and slowly slid it open. Behind it a security field shimmered opal white.

Elrabin squinted, trying to see through it. "Tiff?" he asked, hoping it was the owner who stood there. All he could see was a looming shadow. "Is that you? Let me in."

The speaker beside the door spat out a hissing crackle of static. "Get lost," the voice said. "You're underage."

"I'm legal," Elrabin said.

"You're under twenty."

"I'm close enough."

"Close don't count. What're you doing here? Trying to get us busted?"

Elrabin recognized the voice now through the hissing static. It belonged to Tiff's wife, never easy to charm. He tried, though, baring his teeth in his most appealing grin. "Hey, you can tell the patrollers you invited me in for lunch."

"Get lost." The door started to close.

"Wait!" He stepped closer, trying reflexively to block it even though the force field repelled his hand. "I don't want the wares, Oma, although Tiff did promise them for my nameday—"

"Get lost," Oma growled.

"Wait!" he said sharply, cutting out the patter. "I'm looking for Cuvein. It's important."

The door opened again, and the force field abruptly cut off, leaving the air smelling like ozone. Tiff's wife, a chunky Aaroun with brown and fawn stripes and a light brown mask across her eyes, stood there with her rounded ears folded back against her skull.

"Come inside before you drown," she said.

Grinning, he hopped over the threshold into the warmth. The place smelled good, with scent cones burning on stands in the corners. Soft music played unobtrusively from concealed speakers, sounding almost—but not quite—live. The interior lay swathed in shadow, dimly lit with tiny, radiant lamps, adrift in velvet cushions and plush hangings.

Elrabin glanced around quickly, hoping to catch a glimpse of one of the employees, but saw no one.

"Stop that," Oma said sharply, glaring at him. She pointed at a hallway behind her. "You go that way, straight through to the door at the back. He's in there."

Something in her tone made Elrabin glance at her sharply. "He pay up?"

"No."

Shame flashed through Elrabin. Always before, his da only came here if he could afford it, out of respect for Tiff's friendship. Now it seemed Cuvein was going to treat Tiff like everyone else.

Rubbing his muzzle, Elrabin dropped his gaze from hers. "I'll make it good," he mumbled.

"When?"

Irritated, he flashed her a glare in return. "When I can. Maybe a day or two. Things're slow."

She growled something he didn't understand, but the contempt in her tone was plain enough to make him cringe.

He was tempted to boast about the con he had going right now with the widow, but superstition held his tongue. Cuvein had taught him a long time ago never to brag about a deal until it was bagged. Tomorrow, when he had a fat credit voucher in his pocket, he could come back and make Oma's eyes bulge. Meanwhile, he kept quiet and took her scorn.

She pointed again at the hallway. "In there," she said gruffly. "Don't let him come back until he's paid up. Don't let him take advantage of Tiff that way."

Panting with embarrassment, Elrabin hurried past her hostile bulk and went to the door she'd indicated. His curiosity about what lounged upstairs had been quenched by his fresh annoyance with his da. Cuvein was already causing him enough trouble without putting them in debt with their only friends.

The door ahead of him was adorned by the painted gambling circle. Tendrils of smoke curled around the door's edges, and muted sounds of sour, keening music came from the other side.

It was Pixyl music and made Elrabin's ears hurt. Wincing, he flattened his ears and knocked on the door, then went inside without waiting for permission.

A thick haze of smoke and swirling mist engulfed him, and he stopped just inside the threshold, blinking until his eyes adjusted to the murky gloom. The music wailed and moaned, depressing stuff that could only appeal to stoned patrons. The decor was early cave—meaning low ceiling, walls made of faux stone, heavy beams, dark corners. A half dozen tables swathed in green baize cloth dotted the room. Fake candles flickered on each one. On the opposite side of the room, a trio of robots played the music.

Scowling at them, Elrabin wished he dared switch them off.

Three prostitutes were seated, maybe to welcome customers, maybe to conceal the fact that there were no customers. Two of them, both Kelths with their fur dyed vivid pink, sat together at a table, chatting in soft voices and playing Junta. Every throw of the carved pebbles made their bracelets jingle.

Elrabin caught himself staring, felt the fur around his neck stand up, and realized one of them was stealing glances at him in return over her shoulder. She and her companion giggled, and he wanted to writhe in embarrassment. Maybe it was the coat they were laughing at.

Fighting the urge to look down and see if the dye was running, Elrabin swung his gaze hastily to the third female, sitting alone, drinking alone. She was Viis, a Reject probably. Her skin was mottled in muted shadings of yellow-green. Her rill lay flat on her shoulders, smaller than usual and lacking spines. Her eyes met his, morose and dangerous.

Without a word, she pointed toward the back of the room, where two males sat hunched over a table.

Not daring to speak to her, Elrabin nodded and hurried on by while the pink Kelths tittered.

He had expected to see Cuvein sprawled in a stupor, dusted to the eyes and singing bawdy ditties.

Instead Cuvein sat perched on a wooden stool, bent intently over a drawn diagram spread out on the green baize tablecloth. Lean and long-necked, with dark gray fur marked distinctively with white on either side of his throat,

Cuvein was a handsome Kelth male of middle age, still rakish, still getting by on charm and insouciance. The dust was starting to take away some of his looks. His memory wasn't as good as it had been, either. He suffered from stiff-joint, a progressive bone disease that was a side effect of long-term dust addiction, but he wouldn't admit it. He was unpredictable, moody, capricious, and unfair, but he'd taken Elrabin in years ago, fed and housed him at least part of the time, trained him in a number of trickeries, and supplied him with Dlexyline, a nonaddictive chemical compound that masked Elrabin's registration implant and allowed him to venture out publicly without setting off any alarms.

Now he looked up when Elrabin came to the table, fixed his son with a long, unblinking stare of nonrecognition, and returned his gaze to the diagram on the table. ''Show me again,'' he said.

His voice gave him away. He was enunciating slowly, with too much care and a slight slur in his words. Elrabin looked at him and saw the telltale streaks of dust around his nostrils.

Dust wasn't as trendy as some of the fancier recreational drugs. It wasn't as expensive. As contraband, however, it was the most valuable commodity smuggled to every point of the empire. It had been sapping the life force from its users for the nearly four hundred years since its discovery, and no amount of laws, penalties, antidust campaigns, or slogans had eradicated its simple, inescapable lure.

Being cheap, dust lay within the reach of every laborer, every miner, every ship's crew member, every mechanic. One sampling of dust created an instant addict, and the habit was nearly impossible to kick. Because it proved futile to prosecute the users, patrollers worked instead to trap and catch the vast network of suppliers. Laws were simple and harsh: the sentence for dealing dust was death; the sentence for delivering dust was death.

The day he came to live with Cuvein, Elrabin was of-

fered a taste. Terrified, he refused. Cuvein had never offered it to him again. They got along by not discussing it.
When Cuvein was high, Elrabin tried to stay out of his way.
Now he looked at his father, feeling both disappointed and
resentful, and wanted to leave him here.

But first he had to get what he'd come for. "Cuvein,"
he said, trying to get his da's attention. "Let me talk with
you."

Cuvein flicked his ears and ignored Elrabin. Pointing at
the diagram, he stared at Tiff, who was sitting gravely next
to him, a big old spotted Aaroun run to fat, with sleepy
brown eyes that hid a brain like a steel trap.

"So the game is played like this," Cuvein said, tracing
a dotted line on the diagram. "Piece one goes this way.
Piece two here."

"You make the swap with piece three," Tiff said. His
voice was husky and very deep. He glanced at Elrabin and
jerked his head in invitation. "You come look. You should
learn this too."

Intrigued, Elrabin joined them at the table. Tiff explained
the game again, and Elrabin caught on quickly.

"I see," he said with excitement. "You palm the piece
as you move it—"

"No!" Cuvein said sharply, glaring at him. "Palm it
when it goes up to the next level."

"Like this," Tiff said patiently, showing him again.

"I've got it," Elrabin said.

"You sure?"

He met his da's vague eyes with confidence. "I said I've
got it. I'll try it tomorrow on—"

"No," Tiff said in warning. "This game is illegal. Betting on it will get you fined."

Elrabin scratched his ear. "Betting on a lot of things is
illegal. So?"

"So you take heed where you set this up."

Tiff had more to say, but Elrabin stopped listening. He

could feel his skull from the inside out. Impatient, he stood up. "Cuvein, we need to go."

"You go," Cuvein said without looking at him. "I'm busy."

"Then give me the combination—"

Without warning, Cuvein kicked the stool Elrabin had just vacated, sending it crashing hard into Elrabin's leg. "Get out!"

Cutting off a yip of pain, Elrabin dodged a second kick and gripped his aching thigh. He glared at his da, his temper flaring, and wrinkled his muzzle in a snarl.

Tiff coughed gruffly, catching his attention. Just for an unwilling instant, Elrabin shot his gaze to Tiff's. Silently, the Aaroun tapped his nostrils.

Understanding his meaning, Elrabin felt his temper fade as fast as it had come. He nodded to Tiff. If he didn't argue, Cuvein's temper would settle down. Maybe in a few minutes he would be happy and singing. In that mood, he might give Elrabin what he needed.

But right now, Cuvein stared at Elrabin defiantly, slyly, meanly, his ears twitching for sounds Elrabin didn't hear. "No combination," he said shrilly. "Get out."

"Maybe you better go," Tiff said. "Wait in the galley with—"

"Thanks, Tiff," Elrabin broke in politely, beginning to pant from the urgency he could no longer control. He was running out of time, and today time was important. "But I need a pill." Usually he didn't discuss it openly. No one, not even a friend, was supposed to know he was wanted by Viis authorities. Rewards for turning in petty criminals were collected every day. *Don't throw temptation in some-one's way,* Cuvein always said when he was sober.

"It's wearing off," Elrabin said. As he spoke, he refused to glance at Tiff, who probably now thought he was addicted to something that would shoot him straight to the gutter.

Stiff-spined and bristling, Elrabin tried to hold his da's gaze. "I need it."

"Go home," Cuvein said without interest. His eyes shifted in the lamplight, and he swayed slightly on his stool. "Wait it out like usual."

Elrabin glared at him, trying to break through the dust to the reason in his da's brain. "I need it," he said, his voice low and almost a growl. "I got work in an hour. I got to be out. If you ain't got any pills on you, then I want the combination—"

"No!" Cuvein jumped up, staggered, and nearly lost his balance. Catching himself against the table, he lowered his head and fumbled in his pocket. "No combination. Rule number one."

Elrabin mouthed the words, echoing him silently. Rule number one meant Cuvein was in charge. Cuvein guarded the combination to their tiny safe as his most prized possession. He kept everything important inside it: his payment cards and credit vouchers, his loaded tri-dice, his lockpicks, a vial of the tiny red Dlexyline pills, and his stash of dust. It was stupid of him not to trust Elrabin, who would never betray him. Stupid when he was starting to have memory lapses and blackouts. Stupid when sometimes he wandered off and couldn't be found for days. Rule number one had been established the day Elrabin persuaded his da to take him in. It said that Cuvein made the rules. Rule number two was Elrabin did whatever Cuvein ordered. Rule number three was Elrabin earned his own keep, but Cuvein kept control of the money.

"It's wearing off," Elrabin said, trying to keep his voice steady. "You didn't come home last night. I couldn't take—"

"I'll come home when I please!" Cuvein shouted. He pulled his dust pouch from his pocket and dropped it on the table. "Get out."

"But—"

Tiff came around the table and put his hand on Elrabin's

chest, gently pushing him back. "I'll handle him. He'll be more reasonable in a moment."

Anger was burning in Elrabin's eyes. "He just took some of that. He don't need more. Don't let him take more."

"Hush, now," Tiff said, still pushing him backward. "Don't watch it. This batch is bad dust. Cheap. Poorly cut. He'll be better in a moment. I'll ask him then. You go to the galley and get some food."

"But—"

Elsewhere in the house came the shrill frizzing sound of a security field on overload. Both Elrabin and Tiff froze. The Aaroun's hand tightened into a fist around the front of Elrabin's coat. He growled.

Elrabin heard a loud pop, and the lights went out. A second later they came back on, but less brightly than before. There was the sound of a door being slammed open and the rapid clump of booted feet.

Elrabin and Tiff looked at each other, realization dawning in their eyes.

"*Min deith el,*" Tiff swore in Aaroun. "It's a raid."

The prostitutes jumped up from their tables and ran past Elrabin in silence, leaving a waft of perfume in their wake.

Before Elrabin could respond, Tiff shoved him backward through the doorway and slammed it shut. Elrabin sprang to it, but he heard the locks activate, and a force field shimmered across the door's surface, repelling his hands.

In the distance, Oma roared something Elrabin could not make out. He whirled around and saw six patrollers in helmets and black uniforms crowding into the short hallway. Each held his stun-stick drawn and charged.

The prostitutes had already vanished upstairs.

Elrabin swallowed hard. He felt sick at his stomach, and his knees nearly buckled. A terrible rush of hot weakness passed through his body. He stood frozen for a split second longer, his mind racing in all directions.

He'd broken no laws today. He was carrying no contraband. He had no tri-dice in his pockets. But he was wanted for petty thievery, with a ten-year count of arrest evasion, and he had Dlexyline in his system. One scan over his body, and he would be hanging in a net faster than he could howl.

Just then he figured the wisest course of action would be to cooperate with the patrollers, not resist arrest, stand quietly, hope for leniency, and maybe talk his way into a reduced sentence. He had nothing but that one small offense on his record sheet. He looked reputable enough. He could, in a pinch, claim he had legal employment, and it might be believed.

Over two meters tall, their black uniforms padded with body armor, crimson stripes of rank on their collars and sleeves, the patrollers approached him grimly. Their Viis faces were concealed by the dark tinting in their helmet visors. The hum of their activated stun-sticks buzzed through Elrabin's hearing.

He stood there frozen, unable to think, unable to act. Yes, stay calm, he told himself. Act wise. Cooperate.

Yeah, right.

Panting hard, he whirled away from them and bolted upstairs as fast as his feet would carry him.

CHAPTEREIGHT

Darkness held her in its icy fingers, gripping tight, and would not let go. Trembling, too terrified to scream, Ampris tried to pull free of the sticky, invisible force which held her, and could not.

A terrible wailing rose in the distance, chilling her blood. Her heart lurched and seemed to stop. Still pinned so she could not run, she opened her mouth and panted hard.

"Go away! Go away!" she whispered, unable even to clamp her ears flat to her skull to close out the anguished wails and moans.

"Ampris?" a voice called. "Ampris!"

She gasped aloud, terrified to realize that they knew her name. She understood now that they were searching for her, getting steadily closer because she could not run.

"Get back!" she shouted. "Get away from me!"

As though her voice gave them direction, pale, wraithlike forms appeared suddenly before her. They surrounded her on all sides, pressing closer and closer.

They were the ghosts of dead Aarouns, some of them carrying their severed heads beneath their arms. Their dark eyes held centuries of suffering as they shuffled closer, moaning.

With a howl, she pushed through them, and ran. But this part of the palace was strange to her. No matter which passage she took, it always turned into a dead end. And the headless Aarouns kept hunting her, following her through the many rooms and passages.

Softly, their haunting voices continued to call her name.

"Ampris," came their unworldly cries. "Restore us. Give us back our lives. Avenge our mutilations. Restore us, Ampris. Only you can bring us life."

Again she cowered away from them, holding her hands over her muzzle, her ears clamped flat. "I can't," she said, sobbing. "I don't know what you want."

"Avenge us. . . ."

"No!"

"Ampris."

She could not bear their coming closer. They were suffocating her, so many of them, all horrible to see. She cringed back from them, screaming.

"Ampris! Ampris! *Ampris!*"

Blinking, Ampris opened her eyes to find herself being shaken hard. Illumination filled the room. Israi was gripping her by the arms, shaking her, and someone was knocking on the door.

Panting hard, still trembling, Ampris turned her head right and left. The dead Aarouns no longer filled the room.

She gulped in air and pulled free of Israi's grip. It was only a dream, she realized.

Relieved, she buried her muzzle in her shaking hands.

Israi climbed off Ampris's cot, making it creak. "Go away," she said to the person inquiring at the door. "Subi attends me. I do not require your attendance."

The knocking at the door stopped. From the adjoining bathchamber Subi emerged with a cup of water.

The slave would have handed it to Ampris, but Israi took the cup and held it to Ampris's mouth.

"Lap this," she said kindly. "Nightmares always make me thirsty. It will help."

Ampris drank rapidly, her heart still pounding. Israi was right—the cool water did help. She found herself able to breathe more normally. The horror of the dream faded. She looked around at the room, seeing the disarray of her blankets thrown on the floor, the nesting pillows on Israi's large round bed scattered and the silk coverlet thrown aside, the lamps burning bright, the disapproving impatience on Subi's face, the kind concern in Israi's eyes.

Israi sat next to her and gave her a hug. "My poor, poor Ampris," she said as Subi took the emptied cup away. "You mustn't let things upset you so much. Were you dreaming the same dream?"

Shame overtook Ampris. She found herself on the verge of sobbing, and fought for self-control. "Yes," she admitted, unable to lift her gaze. "The same."

"Silly," Israi chided her. "The ghosts can't get you. Put them from your mind."

"I'm trying," Ampris said. "I thought I had. But every night they come back."

Subi came stumping back through the room and began smoothing the covers on Israi's bed. Her muzzle was gray and her fur dull. She had a hip growing stiff with age, and her tall upright ears twitched constantly. Everyone considered her too old and too ugly to continue in service, yet Israi refused to dismiss her. Subi was grumpy for a Kelth, always grumbling beneath her breath, but she adored Israi and was fiercely loyal to her charge. Anything that made Israi happy, she approved of. Anything that brought even a frown to Israi's face, Subi was ready to destroy immediately.

She scowled now at Ampris as she plumped a pillow. "Night terrors, hmpf," she said. "Keep your nose where it belongs from now on, won't you?"

"Don't scold her," Israi said, rubbing Ampris between her ears. "She's had a bad enough shock as punishment."

"Needs more punishment if the sri-Kaa she awakens every night," Subi grumbled.

Israi straightened, dropping her hand from Ampris's head. "She sat up with me every night for a week when I had the sniffing fever. This is the least I can do in return."

Subi plumped another pillow, with even more vigor than before. "Prowling in the trophy room where she don't belong. Hah. She'll end up on exhibit there if her ways aren't mended soon."

"Subi!" Israi cried in distress. "Don't even *say* such a horrid thing. You may go."

Subi stopped her work and bowed low in obedience, but cast a swift, stern glare at Ampris and bared her teeth before she left.

Israi climbed back in her bed and rearranged the pillows to suit herself. Pausing, she listened a moment, then smiled at Ampris and patted the covers in invitation.

Ampris scrambled up to join her, grinning in spite of herself. This was a special treat. Together they dived beneath the covers, leaving the lights shining, and snuggled closer together in the bliss of breaking Lady Lenith's express rules.

"You won't have nightmares in my bed, will you, Ampris?"

"No."

Israi smiled and pulled her bead doll from beneath a pillow. As a ta-chune soon to be a vi-adult, Israi was too old for dolls, but this one remained her favorite. She handed it to Ampris. "You may hold her tonight while you sleep, and she'll protect you as she used to protect me."

Ampris took the doll reluctantly. It was a great honor to be permitted to hold the bead doll, but she was ta-chune also and, while she might be younger than Israi, considered herself too old to be comforted like a hatchling. Ever since she'd entered the trophy room, she'd felt peculiar, as though stretched too far. She couldn't seem to snap back to the same Ampris she had been before.

"Thank you, Israi," she said politely.

"The sadness is returning to your eyes," Israi said.

"You promised me you wouldn't think about it."

"I'm trying, but sometimes I can't help it."

"Then try harder."

Ampris snuggled against a pillow, hunching up into a knot around the bead doll. "I bet if you saw a room full of Viis heads that had been preserved, you'd find it hard to forget."

Israi's rill rose to full extension and she slapped her tail hard against the bed. "That's a terrible thing to say! You'll get into trouble if anyone hears you talk like that."

"I don't care," Ampris said sullenly. "Why were the Aarouns in there with the others? Like animals?"

"They *are* animals," Israi said.

Astonishment flashed through Ampris. She sat bolt upright with a growl. "They are not! I am not! How can you say Aarouns are not people?"

Israi gripped her arm and pulled her back under the covers. "Hush. Not so loud."

"I want to be loud," Ampris said. She felt her anger rising, bringing rebellion with it. "I want to yell. Who dared do this to them?"

"It was my grandfather's trophy room," Israi said sternly. "You may not criticize it."

Some of Ampris's defiance faded. "Forgive me," she said more quietly. "I do not mean to criticize. I want to understand. Aarouns are people, aren't they?"

"Yes. Well, almost," Israi amended. "All the abiru races are intelligent. Otherwise, they wouldn't *be* abiru. You know this."

"Yes. That's why I don't understand why Aarouns are in the trophy room." Ampris shuddered. "Their heads and hands hanging there, mounted as though they never thought or spoke or had feelings."

"They're there because they were traitors," Israi said. "Insurrectionists who broke into the palace and tried to assassinate my grandfather."

Ampris stared at her. "I saw that word on the inscription. What does *assassinate* mean?"

"It means to kill someone for political reasons."

Ampris stared at Israi in amazement and horror. "That is a terrible thing."

"Oh, yes," Israi said, flicking out her tongue casually even as pride swelled in her voice. "No one talks about it because the rebellion was a tiny one, very unimportant. The Aaroun traitors were crushed right away, and all the abiru races were punished in retaliation."

Ampris said nothing, but she felt uncomfortable when Israi talked about the slave races this way. So offhandedly, as though they barely mattered. "But how did the Aarouns get past the palace guards?"

"They were garden workers," Israi said in a flat voice. "When my grandfather went into his private garden for a nap, they attacked him. He defeated them all single-handedly. He had nothing except his ceremonial sword, while they had tools and bludgeons, yet he came to no harm. He was a very great warrior."

"He must have been," Ampris said.

"Yes, and afterward he ordered them all executed. He had their heads and hands cut off and brought here as a reminder that—"

Dilating her pupils, Israi stared at Ampris a moment, then looked away. She didn't finish her sentence.

"A reminder of what?" Ampris asked.

Israi turned her back to Ampris and slid a pillow beneath her plump tail. "Let's go to sleep."

Ampris poked her spine. "A reminder of what?"

"It isn't important. It happened a long time ago. You mustn't dwell on it."

Ampris could hear the discomfort in Israi's voice. She knew Israi was evading her, but she didn't understand why. Ampris sighed. She hated it when everyone seemed to comprehend something she did not.

"Please tell me," she begged. "I want to know."

"You'll have bad dreams again."

"No I won't."

Israi tilted her head to one side, clearly not believing that promise. "You won't like what I have to say. I would rather not discuss it."

"Thank you for sparing my feelings," Ampris said politely, "but I do want to know."

Israi's rill rose behind her head in annoyance. "Very well. Since you *insist*. The Aarouns hang there as a reminder that no one of the abiru can ever be trusted."

Ampris waited a moment, but that was all Israi said. As the silence between them lengthened, Israi's words soaked deeper into Ampris's understanding. She flattened her ears in hurt. "Ever?"

"That is the warning," Israi said. She met Ampris's gaze. "I told you that you would not like it."

"Do you distrust me?" Ampris asked in a very small voice.

Israi sat up and drew her close in a hug. "Silly fur-face," she said with affection, tugging on one of Ampris's ears. "If I did, would I share my room with you? My bed? My lessons? My toys? You're different."

"But I am Aaroun."

"I know, but not really. You've been mine since your first week of life. You aren't like the others. You're special. Never consider yourself one of them."

Some of Ampris's distress faded. She hugged Israi back, closing her eyes. "I would *never* hurt you, Israi. I would never turn against you."

"Of course you wouldn't," Israi said. She wriggled free of Ampris's strong embrace. "Now don't crush me. And don't think about this again. It happened a long time ago, and it has nothing to do with you or me."

"I'm glad," Ampris said in relief. Then another thought occurred to her. "Is this why the courtiers do not like me? Lord Fazhmind and the others? Because of what those other Aarouns did?"

Israi yawned. "Fazhmind does not like you because you bit him when you were little. Everyone laughed at him because he is such a fool."

"Yes, but the others—"

"They are stupid grown-ups, with stupid prejudices. We do not regard their opinions," Israi said, sounding very imperial. "Now will you promise to go to sleep and have no more bad dreams?"

"I promise," Ampris said.

"And you will not think about it, or brood, or let your feelings be hurt?"

Ampris nodded.

Israi clapped her hands in satisfaction. "Good. Then let us go to sleep."

She curled herself on her side around her nest of pillows and closed her eyes.

Ampris sat there, however. Her thoughts were spinning. There was too much to think about for her to feel sleepy.

Israi poked her. "Go to sleep. That's an imperial order."

Ampris stuck her head out from under the covers. "Lights, out," she commanded, and the lamps dimmed at once.

In the gloom that engulfed her, however, she shivered, feeling once again the ghostly touch of her kinsmen who had died in the Kaa's garden, a garden where only a few days before she had played games in ignorance. Understanding where hatred came from did not make it easier to endure. She was blamed by Lady Lenith and others for something she had not done. She was amazed that Israi had ever been permitted to keep her.

Israi poked her again, harder this time. "Get settled and go to sleep," she said sharply. "Or I'll make you go back to your own bed."

In obedience, Ampris lay down and snuggled against her share of the pillows. Soon she could hear Israi's measured breathing, deep and slow. But Ampris could not sleep.

Every time she closed her eyes, memories came leaping back, too sharp, too horrible.

What had driven the Aaroun gardeners to attack their kaa? What had filled their hearts with so much hatred? What had turned them so far from obedience and respect? Ampris had never heard anyone call Israi's grandfather unjust or cruel. Had the Aarouns themselves been evil? Had they been insane? What political reasons could they have had for trying to kill the Imperial Father? It was a shocking, unthinkable, blasphemous act.

She thought of the present Kaa, who was regal and terrifying, yet kind and gentle. He was a scholar, a historian, with countless interests and infinite patience. He had given Israi permission to keep Ampris. When they were younger, he used to come by once a day and watch them playing together. He had permitted Israi to teach Ampris the Viis language. While all the household slaves understood Viis, none of them save Ampris was allowed to speak it. He had consented to Ampris's attending Israi's lessons.

As a result, Ampris could read and write. She knew most of the coordinates of the empire, most of the names of the principal inhabited worlds which composed it. She even knew which constellation contained the Aaroun homeworld, not that she had any desire to visit it. And she was beginning to understand the connection of mathematics to other things more interesting, such as music and the drawing of houses. Her life was good, and now and then the Kaa would rub her between the ears or smile at her casually. Such moments were blessings that she treasured. At times she almost imagined him to be her father too. It was good to have a pretend father, good to be praised by someone so glorious.

Ampris could not conceive of why anyone would want to hurt the Kaa. Troubled by the possibility, she pushed the matter from her mind, unwilling to think about it anymore.

But instead, the ghosts came crowding back inside her thoughts, many more than the five mutilated assassins in the trophy room. Hundreds of ghosts, thousands of ghosts, all Aaroun, all crying out to her with words she did not understand. Was the ghost of her mother among them? The mother she could not clearly remember? What did they want from her? Why did they haunt her sleep night after night? Why did they cry out for vengeance? And vengeance for what?

Her thoughts chased themselves endlessly, but Ampris found no answers through the long, empty night.

CHAPTER NINE

Elrabin raced up the stairs, his coattails flying out behind him. He wanted to howl at his own stupidity, but he knew it would be a waste of breath. Right now he had to focus on getting out of this brothel with his hide intact. He wasn't too worried about Cuvein downstairs. His da had the gift of getting out of any situation, no matter how tight. Long ago the two of them had agreed that if trouble came, it was every Kelth for himself.

Shouting, the patrollers came thudding upstairs after him. With every bootstep he heard, Elrabin's confidence seeped farther away. Fear squeezed his heart, and his ears kept flicking back, swiveling to the sounds of pursuit.

Never lead the patrollers on a chase unless you know the territory, he reminded himself. Well, it was too late to second-guess himself now.

He gained the landing by leaping over the last two steps, gripping the railing, and using his momentum to sling himself up and around the corner. A rapid, whipping sound passed by him, missing him by scant centimeters.

Elrabin's mouth went dry. He slammed his back against the wall and panted there for a second, realizing just how close he'd come to being stunned.

He'd never been hit, but he knew the sound well enough. Cuvein had described it.

"Like needing to throw up, only you can't. Like being jabbed all over with red-hot needles, itching bad while all your nerves go crazy. Like knowing you got to run, got to move, but you just lie there, helpless in the dust like the garbage they think you are. And then they drag you off, tank you, sell you to a slaver, or give you to the lab creeps for experimentation. Think ahead. Don't get yourself into anything where they're going to come after you with stunsticks."

So much for fatherly advice. If it weren't for Cuvein, he wouldn't be here now.

Muttering to himself, Elrabin glanced around swiftly to gain his bearings. He was in a narrow, gloomy hallway, dimly lit by lamps placed between a double row of closed doors. A window at the end of the hallway looked like his only hope for getting away. If he could gain that, he had a chance.

But the patrollers were nearly to the top of the stairs, nearly upon him. He'd never get to the window before they rounded the corner and saw him. They'd have a clear, easy shot. Already the hide between his shoulder blades was itching.

Feeling a surge of near-panic, he ran to the nearest door and touched the pad.

Locked.

He ran to the next.

Locked.

Fighting the desperate urge to pound on the cheap panel, he flung himself diagonally across the hallway to another door and touched the pad.

The door slid open silently, and he stumbled inside, off-balance and nearly falling.

The inside of the room was pitch-black, with a cloying scent choking the air. Someone giggled, then twin pairs of hands gripped him and pulled him forward.

He recognized the giggling, recognized the scent, and his heart skipped a beat in a rush of exhilaration mingled with dismay. By luck or fate, he'd found the quarters of the pink Kelth twins who'd laughed at him earlier. This was the opportunity of his life, and he didn't have time to take advantage of it.

They were laughing now as they tugged him from side to side, reaching for his coat, fingers ruffling through his fur, a slim, scented muzzle sliding along his.

He drew back, his heart pounding too fast, trying to keep his head, trying to keep his coat on.

"Wait," he said desperately, his voice two notches shriller than normal.

One of them was licking him between the eyes, finding a place that made him shiver. His senses were swimming. He couldn't think, couldn't get away from them.

"Stop!" he said, his ears straining for sounds of the Viis patrollers outside. He panted for air, then jerked himself free with a violent twist of his shoulders.

As he did so, he heard a rip of cloth, and his new coat became a casualty.

"I need a way out of here," he said, his voice low and urgent.

Although he half expected them to rush him in the darkness, they stayed back.

"The only way out is the way you came in," one of them replied. Her voice was throaty for a Kelth. She had a way of speaking that made every word suggestive.

But he was too worried to think about that now. He had to get out before the room became a trap.

"They're in the hallway, searching the rooms," the other twin said. Her voice was thin and high, but she spoke softly. "I can hear them. I think they're questioning Tenia."

Panting, Elrabin listened through the door to the harsh, authoritative Viis voices and soft female replies.

Dismay leaked through him. He wanted to race around

the room, to fight, claw, bite. He wanted to howl. He wanted to sink to the floor and curl himself into a tight ball.

But he could do none of those things. He was a male, nearly grown, and supposed to be able to handle himself.

"I'm wanted," he said, spilling his secret. "If they scan me, I'm—"

"Too young," one of the twins said.

He bristled at once. "I've been on the streets since I was a lit. I know about—"

"Illegal, but plausible," the other twin replied as though he hadn't spoken. "He's old enough. And what's another minor charge on our record sheets?"

Elrabin glared, wishing he could see them in the darkness. "What are you talking about?"

"A stupid one, but cute," the low-voiced one said with a sigh. Her partner giggled, and a flush of embarrassment spread beneath Elrabin's hide. "For seventy credits, we'll save you."

"Done," he said without hesitation. "But how—"

They swarmed him, giggling in a way that gave him his answer. Pulling off his coat and belt, they pushed him into a soft pile of cushions and snuggled up against him, just a split second before the door circuits fried and the panel was shoved open.

Light spilled into the room, momentarily dazzling Elrabin and revealing to him how narrow and cramped the space actually was. The bed cushions filled most of the area, along with a couple of wooden chests and a small curtained alcove off to one side.

Squinting, he stared at the patroller looming in the doorway. The Viis seemed to go all the way to the ceiling. The black visor of his helmet permitted no glimpse of his face. His crimson stripes of sergeant rank stood out boldly against his black uniform. Slung about his hips was a heavy belt holding his comm, sniffer link, stun-stick, and a standard-issue sidearm. Body armor protected his tail, and he held a circuit-cutter in his hand.

Smoke from the ruined door control pad curled its tendrils about the patroller, who stared down at Elrabin in silence.

Sprawled on the floor with the twins, Elrabin found himself frozen with terror.

"Name!" the sergeant demanded.

Elrabin opened his mouth. He couldn't speak, couldn't think. At any moment, he knew, he would be scanned. Then the patroller would have his identity, his record, and full knowledge of the illegal drug in his system.

The bolder of the twins giggled, and her pink-furred hand gripped him unexpectedly in a way that made him yelp. He sat bolt upright, gasping, while both of them giggled harder.

The other one stroked his muzzle, opening a tiny vial under his nostrils with a quick, practiced motion. The world suddenly went blue and white. He opened his mouth, feeling his eyes cross, and his terror floated to one side as though it now belonged to someone else.

He watched the sergeant approach them as if he were covering a great distance.

"Get away from him," the sergeant commanded. "Now!"

Someone giggled as the twins complied, and finally Elrabin realized that he was the one laughing. He dropped back bonelessly into the cushions and smiled up at the Viis.

The scan buzzed through his body, and he enjoyed that too.

"Get up," the sergeant said, kicking him with his boot toe.

Elrabin waved at him with his foot and let his gaze wander appreciatively over the pink twins. The light was very strange, making them seem more purple than pink, and they shimmered at the edges.

"What did you give him?" the sergeant asked.

The twins circled each other before one stood behind the other and rested her chin on her shoulder. "The usual," she replied. "He was nervous, the stupid lit. Like they all are their first time here."

"He's not legal age."

The twins shared dumbfounded looks. "He's not?"

The sergeant's tail switched once before he brought it under control. He reached for his comm. "Get in here. I've got an underage customer who can't be scanned."

The other patrollers appeared at the doorway a few seconds later. To Elrabin they all seemed extremely tall. He wondered hazily how they could fit into the room, but when he tried to ask the question his tongue seemed to wrap around itself, and nothing came out of his mouth but a giggle.

"Take him downstairs," the sergeant ordered. He opened a small data screen and entered some codes. "I got two Kelth females, prostitute grade," he reported verbally to it. "Working in the Street of Regard. Owner is an Aaroun named Tiff. License number one-zero-four-four-eight. Violation of city ordinances ten, four, seven, and nineteen. Sixty-credit fine for the prostitutes. Eighty-credit fine for the owner. Other charges pending against owner. Stand by."

He closed the data screen and returned his attention to the twins. "You will pay those sixty credits within a one-day cycle, or your fine will be doubled."

The twins sighed. "You make it rough for working females—"

"Silence! Give your compliance, or the fine will be doubled right now."

Resentment filled their eyes. "We'll comply."

The sergeant swung away from them to face his squad and gestured at Elrabin. "Take him downstairs."

By the time they carried Elrabin down to the opulent receiving room, the scent cones were burning out, the lamps had been switched to bright, and Oma and Tiff were standing silently in one corner while a patroller scanned their transaction records.

Elrabin's potion was wearing off. He no longer felt any desire to laugh, and nausea boiled in his stomach. Shivering, he lay on the floor where the patrollers dumped him and wondered what the twins had given him. While the substance had protected him initially, he wasn't sure how long its effects would last. The downside felt so bad he almost wished he'd been stunned instead.

The patrollers herded all the employees downstairs and grouped them in the receiving room as well. It was getting crowded, but Elrabin realized he didn't see Cuvein anywhere.

Despite his physical misery, he had to admire his da. Obviously Cuvein had slipped out during the initial confusion. He had a gift for avoiding trouble. He could vanish like smoke, without a trace. He knew every side street, every back alley, every sewer main access point. He had taught Elrabin how to take to the rooftops if necessary. How to blend into a crowd, never running to attract attention, always staying calm, always keeping his head.

Right then, lying on the floor with his stomach cramping and his limbs under no control at all, Elrabin felt disgusted with himself. He hadn't kept his head. He hadn't stayed calm. Instead, he had run for it, and landed himself deeper into trouble.

The sergeant saluted an officer with a crimson collar of rank and pointed at Elrabin. "He was coming out of the gambling end of the establishment when we first saw him. When he ran from us, we figured he must be up to something. We pursued and made target acquisition upstairs."

Elrabin groaned to himself. If he'd only stood his ground. If he'd only stayed calm. He could have bluffed his way out. Damn.

"What's his identity registration tell us?"

"Nothing, sir."

The lieutenant raised his black visor to reveal dark blue skin and Viis eyes of vivid crimson. His eye color extended on either side of his head in striking contrast, blending purple streaks into the shades of blue and dark green that marked his rill.

"Nothing?" the lieutenant repeated. He flicked out his tongue and turned his cold crimson eyes on Elrabin. "Is his implant in place?"

"Yes, sir."

"Run a drug scan on him."

Two other patrollers gripped Elrabin by his arms and pulled him to his feet. Small spasms of returning life ran through his muscles, but he hardly cared. He was finished now. It was all a matter of what kind of sentence they would deal him on-site. Wrist cutters would be the mildest fate he could hope for. Being sold to hard labor would be worse. The labs, he wasn't even going to think about.

Panting, he tried to face those black visors without showing fear, tried to look brave, tried to look defiant. But he was whining softly in the back of his throat, barely able to keep himself from howling in despair. His bowels were water. His legs wouldn't support him. Thumping inside him like his own heartbeat were the self-recriminations: you shouldn't have run; you shouldn't have come here; even high on dust, Cuvein is smarter than you; he's free and you're doomed.

"Lieutenant," Elrabin said, gasping out the word.

The Viis didn't even glance at him in response.

The sergeant struck Elrabin across the muzzle with the grip of his stun-stick. "Silence!"

Reeling back from the blow, Elrabin bit off a yelp of pain. The patrollers lifted him higher on his sagging legs, forcing him to stand. Gasping, he struggled to master the pain and ran his tongue gingerly along his mouth where blood was trickling, hot and salty.

He couldn't give up, he told himself. He had to think of something. And he would.

The scanner buzzed across him, making him dizzy. The sergeant looked at the readout. "Traces of Venoyl and Dlexyline."

"Illegal," the lieutenant snapped with harsh satisfaction. "Venoyl rates a fine. Dlexyline usage is a major offense, meriting sale to hard labor." His gaze bored into Elrabin, who had forgotten to breathe. "I could change that sentence if you tell me the name of your supplier."

Elrabin nearly blurted out Cuvein's name, then bit it back, horrified at his own weakness. He wasn't going to betray his da, who'd given him a home of sorts, raised him, taught him how to make his own way. It was what the Viis always wanted, he thought bitterly, trying to turn abiru against abiru, trying to keep them divided and suspicious of each other.

"You have one chance," the lieutenant said to him sternly, flicking out his tongue. "Who is your supplier?"

Elrabin's gaze shifted around wildly before he mastered himself. He shivered in the patrollers' hold and forced himself to meet the lieutenant's gaze. "Go fertilize a Toth," he said.

Someone in the crowded room gasped. The lieutenant's gaze grew still and cold. Because of the confines of his helmet, he could not extend his rill, but its folds turned a bright crimson that matched his eyes.

The sergeant drew his sidearm, but the lieutenant stopped him with a gesture.

"Do not waste your ammunition," he said, and his voice was very calm and brittle.

Elrabin swallowed, flicking his ears back, aware that at any moment the patrollers would beat him to a pulp.

"Run the scanner again. Burn through the Dlexyline on maximum setting if you must. I want this creature's identity."

Elrabin cursed silently to himself. The lieutenant could not be rattled or deflected, it seemed, not even with insults.

"I will have your name," the lieutenant said coldly to him. "I will have your lodging address. I will locate every friend, every acquaintance, every contact you—"

"Save the speech," Elrabin said rudely. "My registration code will tell you my name and not much else. Most of your central data banks are old, out-of-date, corrupted, or not working. So why not charge me, give me my fine, and let me go?''

He was struck again, hard enough to make his ears ring. Sagging back, he let his head loll on his shoulders while little black dots bounced across his vision.

By the time he could blink, remember his name, and determine which way was up, the scanning was over. His skin itched under his fur. His mouth felt dry, with a queer, metallic taste. His eyes burned, and he had a headache.

"His name is Elrabin, sir," the sergeant reported. "Born to Kelth registrants, Cuvein and Magathin. No known street address. Magathin is listed in the dead registry—"

"No!" Elrabin burst out, too shocked to keep quiet. "She—"

"Silence!"

His protest stopped, and Elrabin lowered his head with his ears flattened. Inside he had to fight an unexpected surge of grief. He hadn't seen his mother in years, not since the day he'd walked out and abandoned her and the younger lits. He hadn't called her in all this time. Hadn't spoken to her. Hadn't sent her a single message. Now he felt ashamed of himself, realizing he had been cruel to leave her that way. Had she worried about him? Had she searched for him, walking the streets until hope left her? Or had she been relieved that there was one less mouth to feed?

A burning sensation filled his throat. He wanted to tip back his head and unleash the grief howl, but he choked it back.

The lieutenant was watching him like a predator, merciless and intent. "What else?" he asked.

"Wanted for petty theft. Arrest evasion at least ten years."

The lieutenant's thin tongue flickered out, and his cold, crimson eyes dilated slightly. "Ah. That alone warrants the wrist cutters. Take him outside to the street, where he can be an example.''

Elrabin's ears roared, and all the strength melted from his body, along with his defiance.

Someone else in the room spoke out, and the lieutenant turned sharply to sweep the room with his gaze. ''Viis justice is swift,'' he said to everyone. ''Viis justice will not be mocked.'' His gaze flicked back to Elrabin and lingered there just long enough for Elrabin to see the cruel satisfaction in his eyes. ''The arrest evasion plus usage of Dlexyline indicates a hardened criminal mentality. He cannot be reformed, but he can be stopped. Sergeant.''

''Yes, sir?''

The lieutenant's gaze remained on Elrabin's face as though waiting to see his reaction. ''Take off both hands.''

The sergeant saluted and made his response, but Elrabin could barely hear the words for the increased roaring in his ears. His heart pounded like thunder in his chest. He could not feel his hands, could not feel his feet. Panting in fear, he tried desperately to think of something he could do, something he could say, but his throat choked up and he could utter nothing.

They dragged him around, and he had one glimpse of the gathered prostitutes, huddled as far from him as they could get. None of the females would meet his eyes, not even the twin Kelths with their dyed pink fur. He would never be able to pay them their seventy credits, and they all knew it. The Reject had hooded her face in the presence of the Viis males. She stood apart from the others, in the corner, with her back to everyone.

Elrabin understood, even in the throttling grip of his fear. He was sentenced and doomed. No one could help him.

How would he live? How could he work with no hands? How could he feed himself? He would be forced to beg, a disgusting cripple holding an alms bowl in his mouth, drooling for mercy. He would never be able to afford synthetic replacements for his severed appendages, not that marked thieves were allowed to own prosthetics anyway.

Or maybe he wouldn't live at all. Maybe he would bleed to death out there in the gutter outside Tiff's establishment.

The whining started in the back of his throat. It shamed him, but he couldn't control it, couldn't stop it.

The patrollers heard him and laughed.

Tiff stepped forward. "Wait."

"Stand back, you," the sergeant said harshly. "Interference will cost you additional fines."

"Have mercy," Tiff said, ignoring the warning. Oma glared at him as though he had lost his mind. Even Elrabin—although grateful—was astonished that Tiff would risk himself like this. "This Kelth is underage, not even fully adult yet. Do not maim him for such a small crime, committed so long ago. What did he steal? A trinket or two? Some food perhaps? Is that all you can find on his record sheet? Is it worth this terrible penalty?"

The sergeant hissed behind his visor, but the lieutenant stepped forward to gaze at Tiff.

"What is your interest here?"

"Elrabin is the son of a friend," Tiff said without flinching.

"Do you supply him with Dlexyline?"

Aghast that Tiff had brought himself under suspicion, Elrabin opened his mouth, but the chunky old Aaroun lifted his sleepy eyes to meet the lieutenant's. "I know nothing of such a drug," he said, honesty firm in his voice. "I keep a clean establishment. There has never been trouble with drugs here. This is known."

The lieutenant gestured impatiently. "Then keep quiet. This is no affair of yours."

"Have mercy," Tiff said again, while Oma growled in her throat at him. He ignored her, his gaze steadfast on the lieutenant. "I will pay his fine, and Elrabin will not steal again. I give you my word."

Several of the patrollers laughed inside their helmets. The lieutenant inflated his air sacs, saying, "The word of an Aaroun? Do you dare equate yourself with the Viis, that you think your word is valid?''

His scorn was brutal. Shame flashed across Tiff's spotted face, and he glanced down submissively before stepping back.

Oma grabbed his arm and growled something in his ear. He didn't look up.

"Enough of this place," the lieutenant said, glancing around impatiently. "It stinks of cheap scent and meat. Our tip was a false one. We have netted nothing but this one pathetic thief. Take him out, and let us be done here."

Panic filled Elrabin. He struggled with all his might, but the patrollers held him easily. They forced him outside into the twilight. Cold rain still fell in a steady downpour, washing across the street and gurgling in the drains. No traffic passed by. The other brothels had lit their yellow lamps over their doors, but otherwise looked closed. No one took chances with two patroller skimmers hovering on park in the street, lights flashing in broken refractions through the rain.

"Put a restraint bar on him," the sergeant ordered. Little droplets of rain beaded and ran down his visor. Behind them, the lieutenant lingered under the awning, as though reluctant to get his uniform wet.

Or maybe, Elrabin thought with scorn, he was afraid Kelth blood might spurt all over him.

While a patroller brought a restraint bar and the wrist cutters from one of the skimmers, the others surrounded Elrabin, each taking firm hold. He panted hard, unable to believe it was happening. He had feared this so long, yet he'd never actually believed he would finally get caught. Not like this, not today.

They weren't going to be kind enough to give him a sedative first. Laughing among themselves, they spoke in Viis as though believing he couldn't understand their words.

He didn't care what they said. The wrist cutters filled his

attention. Even in the gloom of approaching night and the steady patter of rain he could see that the steel blades were stained with blood dried black, except at the edges, which had been freshly ground and sharpened. The metal there gleamed bright.

"Pull his hands forward," the sergeant ordered. "Then lock his elbows with the bar. I don't want it getting splashed. If blood corrodes its finish, Supplies will insist on docking our wages."

Elrabin fought and struggled with all his might, but they were too strong for him. One of the patrollers held his stunstick to Elrabin's throat, and Elrabin froze in mid-struggle, breathing hard and keening in his throat.

He no longer cared if they saw his fear. He no longer cared if they laughed at him.

When the wrist cutters did their work, his life would be over.

The restraint bar was fitted across the inside of his elbows, but before it could be locked on, a shout came from down the street.

The sergeant turned, and even the lieutenant stepped out into the rain as an additional squad of patrollers came marching up. Their uniforms were mud-splattered, and they came dragging a prisoner in an arrest net, floating on its antigrav field.

By the time they arrived, Elrabin recognized the prisoner's gray fur with the distinctive white markings along throat and muzzle.

His heart sank with fresh dismay. So Cuvein's luck had also run out. Truly, this was an evil night.

The lieutenant bent down to peer at the prisoner, ignoring the salutes. "Is this the one?"

"Yes, sir."

"Good work."

"We found him hiding in a ventilation tunnel. We also found this." The patroller making the report produced two dust pouches, one the slim one Elrabin had seen his da using earlier, the other larger and fatter. "And this." The patroller held out a data crystal, which the lieutenant took eagerly.

"A list of his network?"

"We think so."

"Excellent."

Astonished, Elrabin stared at Cuvein, unable to believe it. Since when had his da become a supplier? And who had laid the tip, bringing the patrollers here tonight for this raid? What was going on?

"Cuvein?" he called.

"Shut up," his da said, growling. "It's planted evidence, every bit of it. Run if you can."

The lieutenant was laughing. He tossed the data crystal in the air and caught it before tucking it safely away. "That promotion is now mine," he said in triumph. "See that the Aaroun female gets her reward."

Rage burned in Elrabin. Oma had betrayed them. Why? Just because Cuvein hadn't paid for a few bad throws of tri-dice? Just because his bar bill was bigger than his purse? Elrabin wanted to throttle her. He'd promised he would settle his da's debt. He'd given his word.

But promises meant nothing. He knew he wouldn't have paid it, not all of it, not unless forced to. It seemed Oma understood the rules of the street too.

The sergeant snapped to attention. "Do you want an execution on the spot, sir? Or an arraignment at head-quarters?"

"Don't be a fool," the lieutenant said sharply. "Mark the death penalty on the official report, but don't ask me to waste good money when he can be sold to a labor camp. Fear not. You will all get a share," he added, glancing around at the patrollers.

Elrabin snorted to himself. Viis corruption. You could count on it like the rain of winter.

Then he realized no one was paying him any attention. Even the patrollers holding him were watching the officer and the new prisoner. Elrabin had made plenty of mistakes tonight, but he didn't intend to make any more.

Swinging around, he twisted sharply to break himself free of their grip. One of them reached for him, but Elrabin rammed the Viis in the midriff with the end of the restraint bar clamped on his arms. The patroller went staggering back, and Elrabin swung around just in time to duck the grab of the other one.

Crouching low, he scuttled away a few steps, dropping to his knees and skidding around. As he did so, he pressed the end of the restraint bar against the rain-slick pavement and used the leverage to pop it off his arms. He thanked the gods that it hadn't been locked yet.

Viis fingers grabbed at him from behind, scratching through his wet fur without much purchase. Elrabin picked up the restraint bar and swung it around like a club.

It cracked across a patroller's legs and brought him down with a bellow of pain.

Staggering to his feet, Elrabin nearly lost his balance, but managed to get upright. He started toward the patrollers with the club upraised, intending to rescue Cuvein, but the sergeant aimed his stun-stick at Elrabin and fired.

It clipped him on his right side, making him feel as though he had been cut in half. Dropping the restraint bar with a clatter, he fell heavily, landing on his stunned side and never feeling the impact.

His right side was dead. Nothing worked, no matter how much he struggled. Floundering desperately with his left arm, Elrabin got to his hands and knees, tried to crawl forward, and fell again.

He could hear bootsteps, and fear drove him up once more. This time he half crawled, half dragged himself into the gutter. Water swept along its channel, icy cold and making him gasp. With his good fingers, he felt along desperately, seeking a grating that he could pull up.

"Get him!" the sergeant ordered.

He fell again, facedown in the water, and the mild current swept him along the gutter, faster than he could drag himself. Bumping and sputtering, he lifted his muzzle from the water and glanced back at his pursuers. He didn't have a chance.

"Let the creature go," the lieutenant said. "I have what I need. Our night is proving profitable enough without hunting down one worthless thief in the dark."

Relief sagged through Elrabin. Lowering his head almost into the filthy water, he used his left arm to guide and pull himself along, buoyed by the gutter current. Behind him, he could hear muted sounds in the distance as the skimmers were loaded up. They flew off in the opposite direction, searchlights stabbing the darkness briefly before they were gone.

Elrabin bumped against a heavy grating. The water rushed over and beneath him, sucking itself down into the sewer main below. He clung there, braced half out of the water, and tipped up his face to the still-falling rain.

Only then did he cry out, his grief and anger throbbing harshly from his throat.

A fit of coughing interrupted his howl of mourning and brought him back from the dangerous edge of his emotions. He knew he couldn't afford to give way, not here, not now.

He was free, and he was alive. But he felt far from lucky. For now, he had to hide himself, avoiding anyplace those who knew him would think of looking. That meant he couldn't go home, couldn't go to any of the usual haunts. Oma's betrayal meant his da's cronies might also sell Elrabin out, now that they knew he had a record.

It was a cold thought of no comfort.

Shivering, Elrabin swallowed his grief and pulled open the heavy grating. He hesitated there, a hunched figure in the rainy darkness, fearing to lower himself into a still-greater darkness. Skeks lived in the tunnels beneath the streets, along with other creatures. But Skeks were merely scavengers, no matter how loathsome, and he knew he could fight them off if necessary. Tonight, the only predators he knew about were aboveground. And they all wore the name *friend*.

CHAPTER TEN

In the morning, Ampris awakened to find herself back in her own cot, snugly tucked beneath her blankets. Subi had put her there, she supposed. Subi always did, so that Lady Lenith would not catch them.

Israi sat up in her nest of cushions, yawned hugely, and stretched her rill to its maximum extension. "The sun is shining," she said. Bright-eyed and cheerful, she was already brimming with plans. "Let's have a picnic."

Ampris panted with excitement. She loved it when Israi planned a special occasion. "When?"

"Today. We'll make it a grand, outdoor luncheon. By midday the sun will be warm. And I know the perfect spot."

"The clearing by the stream," Ampris guessed.

Israi laughed with approval. "Of course! I shall wear fur robes, and you wool. There are those old costumes in the storage rooms that we can dress up in. We'll pretend that we are grand court ladies in the old dynasty of Ruverl."

"Who?"

"My great-grandfather. He who built this lodge," Israi said impatiently. "Because we are having a historical picnic, we must not ride up to the clearing on skimmers. Instead we will walk.''

Ampris blinked. ''It's a long climb.''

''Don't be lazy. We will walk,'' Israi said. ''We will take thick blankets to spread over the ground, and only one slave to serve us.''

''Let's take Moscar,'' Ampris said. ''He's strong enough to carry everything.''

Israi's green eyes gleamed. When she emerged from her morning ablutions, her skin oiled and glowing, her fur-lined tunic cut loose in the back to conceal her tail as modesty required, she grabbed Ampris by the hand and went dashing down the corridor to the central section of the lodge.

There, they halted by the main staircase, breathless and giggling. Israi beckoned for a page to approach her.

He came at once, bowing low. ''Yes, highness?''

''Take a message to the cook. I wish a picnic feast prepared for today. I shall want carnela cream, plenty of fruit tarts, candied granapes, and spiced antas.''

The page bowed again. ''Forgive me, highness, but it is supposed to rain.''

Israi eyed him coldly. ''Did I request your opinion?''

''No, highness.''

''Then be quiet.'' Israi turned to Ampris. ''You may pick two of your favorite foods as well.''

Ampris beamed eagerly. ''Thank you. I want—''

''But no meat,'' Israi said sternly. ''I refuse to watch you gnaw on bones.''

''Spicemeats?'' Ampris asked hopefully.

Israi flicked out her tongue. ''That's slave food.''

Ampris lowered her gaze to mask her disappointment. Spicemeats were delicious, but she knew when Israi would not relent. ''May I have civa cakes?''

Israi laughed. ''You *always* want civa cakes. What else?''

Ampris thought hard but she couldn't think of anything permissible she wanted besides those tiny, mouthwatering confections. They melted on the tongue with the most exquisite flavors. She swallowed, already longing for them.

"Lots of civa cakes," she said.

Israi sighed indulgently and returned her gaze to the page. "You heard that."

"Yes, highness."

Israi flicked her fingers in dismissal. "See that it is done."

"Yes, highness." The page hurried away, and Israi turned to Ampris with an air of satisfaction.

"There," she said. "I like my idea very well."

"I like it too," Ampris said.

"Then let us go and select our costumes."

Together they started upstairs, but a voice called them back.

It belonged to a ta-chune Viis male, scrawny and with skin variegated in tones of bright blue and green. He was one of Israi's egg-brothers, named Oviel. Both Israi and Ampris despised him.

"Where are you going?" he demanded.

Israi lifted her head very haughtily. "I do not answer to you."

He frowned. "It was a civil question. You could at least be polite to me, Israi. After all, one day I shall be your chancellor."

"Not while I live."

The two Viis siblings glared at each other. Ampris, feeling uncomfortable with the argument, tried to edge past Israi and keep going up the stairs, but Israi stopped her.

"Go and bite him, Ampris," she commanded. "Bite him and shake him hard enough to snap his skinny neck."

Ampris stared at Israi in surprise, even as her fur stood on end in mingled embarrassment and annoyance. She did not like it when Israi used this tone with her. It was rare, and done only in public, but it made Ampris feel as insignificant as dust. It was the tone all Viis nobles used with their slaves, creatures who were ignored and used like furniture was used. The command itself was in poor taste, not even funny, and that embarrassed Ampris even more.

Ampris said nothing.

After a moment, when Ampris made no move toward him, Oviel managed to stop looking alarmed. Ignoring Ampris, although his gaze flickered to her more than once, he gave Israi a thin smile. "I am glad your pet does not always obey you."

"The taste of your flesh would poison her teeth."

He frowned. "You are unkind, my sister."

"You are ambitious, my brother," she retorted. "I have been warned about you."

"By whom?"

"I know that you are hoping to get the throne for yourself. You think I am weak because I am female, but you forget the examples of history. We have been ruled by three other female kaas, all of whom were ruthless, bold, and courageous. None of them were deposed by their male relatives. Nor shall I be."

Courtiers were approaching. Pages went by on errands, glancing at them in curiosity. The lodge was stirring in the new day, and this argument could not continue.

Oviel seemed to sense this, for he backed up a step and bowed. "I only asked where you were going today, Israi. Nothing more. You need not be so defensive, you and your pet."

"I am not defensive," Israi replied coldly, "but I am on my guard against you."

His eyes glittered in response, but although a tremor passed through his rill he did not extend it. "I will discover who has dripped this poison into your mind. I do not like to find I have enemies."

"You should concentrate on growing your battle teeth, brother. You'll need them."

Flicking her tongue, Israi turned her back on him and continued upstairs. Ampris followed her, glancing over her shoulder in time to see Oviel's rill turn bright crimson as he walked away.

"Why did you speak to him like that?" Ampris asked once they were safely out of earshot. "Why did you make him angry on purpose?"

Israi glanced at her as they entered the storage room, with its musty shadows and draped cobwebs. The sri-Kaa did not immediately answer. Instead, she opened a chest and started pulling out quaint old garments that smelled of dust and camphan preservative.

Ampris sneezed. "Israi, please explain," she said.

"Very well, but it is a secret I tell you."

"I understand."

Israi cast her a sharp glance. "You will chatter about this to no one. Is that clear?"

Hurt, Ampris widened her eyes. "But I never share your secrets. Never. Do you distrust me now?"

"No, but you must be careful."

"I promise."

"Then I will tell you that my father has been giving me special lessons of late."

Ampris nodded. She knew about those sessions, from which she was excluded.

"These are lessons which a ruler may share only with one who will one day rule."

A shiver passed through Ampris. She said, "Sometimes, when we're playing, I forget how important you are."

"How important I shall one day be," Israi corrected her. "Yes. I am old enough now, my father says, to begin to study politics and intrigue. It is my father who has warned me to beware of Oviel. His tutor is ambitious, my father says, and the tutor has taught Oviel of the old custom of an egg-sibling serving as primary chancellor of state. This is dangerous for me, and my father says I must not allow it."

"Oh," Ampris said, impressed by such adult talk. "Couldn't the Imperial Father just dismiss the tutor?"

Israi laughed and tilted her head from side to side. "How simple that would be! Ampris, you are priceless."

Ampris swelled with pride, until she realized that Israi was laughing *at* her. Backing her ears, Ampris asked, "What is wrong with my suggestion?"

"It's too simple. Too obvious. My father says it is better to keep a known enemy nearby where you can watch him than to send him away, where he can work his mischief unobserved."

"Oh," Ampris said again. She thought about this, understanding that complexity was always desirable to a Viis, even Israi. Ampris herself preferred things kept simple and direct. If the tutor was imprisoned or even put on a labor gang for his wickedness, he would have no opportunity to cause mischief. But she did not utter this thought aloud. She had no desire to be laughed at again.

By the time they selected their costumes and came downstairs, the morning was well-advanced. A page came to tell Israi that Lady Lenith wished to see her.

"My compliments to the lady," Israi replied, "but inform her I am otherwise engaged and not at liberty this day."

The page backed away to deliver her message.

Israi caught Ampris's eye and giggled. "Come," she said, gripping Ampris's hand in hers. "Let's go before she finds a way to stop us."

They ran headlong through the lodge, sending servants, advisers, and courtiers backing out of their way. According to court protocol, Israi's personal guards were supposed to accompany her outdoors, but the sri-Kaa was in a mischievous mood today. She and Ampris slipped down the servant stairs into the vast kitchen complex. A place always boiling with frenetic activity, the kitchen provided perfect cover for two youngsters to escape outdoors without being noticed. In the stables, they dug out old Moscar—a massive Aaroun whose spots had faded on his dull fur. A gentle creature, slow of wit and harmless, Moscar could not speak, but he bent willingly to the task of carrying their blankets and food baskets. Silent and steady, he trudged behind them up the long, steep trail that led higher into the mountains.

Ampris loved being outdoors. The wintry sunshine warmed her shoulders, offsetting the chilly air. She lifted her nostrils to the breeze and inhaled a myriad of scents, all intriguing and fresh. Overhead a pair of raptuls sailed and circled on the wind currents. Their wingspans were enormous, casting swift shadows across the steep ground. Now and then they uttered a cry that echoed down the mountains, a cry so savage and primitive it sent shivers through Ampris.

Tossing back her head, she threw up her hands to the sky and tried to roar.

The cry came out thin and guttural, embarrassing her.

Israi glanced back. "Stop that. Why are you making such an ugly sound?"

"I don't know. It felt natural."

"It is hideous. I don't wish to hear it again."

Ampris frowned beneath Israi's rebuke. "Forgive me," she said politely. "I'm not doing it right. Perhaps if I practiced—"

"No."

Ampris's gaze met Israi's. She saw only unyielding sternness in Israi's green eyes. Sighing, Ampris bowed her head.

"Yes, Israi," she said in obedience. "I won't do it again."

"You are a lady of court," Israi said, struggling not to trip on the hem of her long robe as the trail grew more rocky and steep. She paused, panting in the thin air, and gripped the trunk of a narpine sapling. Her rill lay limp and wilted over the edge of her collar. "Help me here."

"Maybe if we took off these costumes until we get to the picnic spot," Ampris suggested. She was finding her robe cumbersome and hard to manage. It also reeked of camphan, clogging her nostrils so much she couldn't stop rubbing her nose.

"No," Israi said. "I don't want to take off the robe. It's part of the game, remember? We are fine ladies of the court, and we are climbing to a proper vantage point to watch the lodge being built."

"We may break our necks," Ampris grumbled, boosting Israi forward, then clambering awkwardly over the rocks herself. She pulled up the hem of her robe and tied it in a knot out of her way.

"Hurry," Israi said. "And stop complaining. You are spoiling the game."

"Yes, Israi."

"Help me over this rock."

"Yes, Israi."

Again Ampris gave her friend a boost from behind. Both of them were panting loudly. Hunger rumbled inside Ampris's belly, and she thought about the feast that was soon to come.

"It's not far now," she said with satisfaction, looking ahead up the trail.

"Thank the gods," Israi said, puffing hard. She yanked at her dragging hem once again, and nearly lost her balance. "This is the shortest way up, but I didn't realize it was so steep."

Above them, the huge old narpine with its wind-twisted trunk and spreading branches stood in welcome, waiting for them to take their favorite spot among its gnarled roots. There was one last climb over a jumbled pile of rocks between them and their objective.

"We shouldn't be court ladies coming this way," Ampris said as they paused to rest. "We should be invaders, trying to breach the palace walls."

Israi flicked out her tongue, too winded to speak.

From below them came a shout.

Startled, both Ampris and Israi looked.

"Oh, no," Israi said.

Ampris saw a small contingent of guards and courtiers about halfway up the mountain trail. The person in front was waving at them. Another shout echoed up the mountain and sent the wheeling raptuls flying away.

Ampris flattened her ears and growled. "Fazhmind," she said in disgust.

Israi leaned against her, peering into the distance. "Are you sure?"

"Yes."

Israi blew a most nonroyal snort through her nostrils. "That *toad.* What does he want?"

Ampris sighed. "He wants us to go up the ordinary trail. To ride in a skimmer. To take your ladies in waiting along. To wear our cloaks against the cold. To have your guards in attendance."

"To be utterly and completely *bored,*" Israi finished. "Why must he always ruin our games? Who asked him to interfere?"

"Come down!" came the call, rising to them while echoes tumbled off the rocks and gullies.

Shoulders drooping, Ampris turned to obey, but Israi gripped her arm. Israi's green eyes were flashing. "I shan't," she said defiantly. "Who is he, to give me orders?"

"But, Israi—"

"Quickly," Israi commanded, turning Ampris around and pushing her toward the rocks. "We'll keep going. We can hide from them, and it will be a better game than before. If he has to spend the whole day searching for us in the mountains, won't he be tired and filthy and put out when he gets back?"

She laughed unpleasantly, a calculating expression in her eyes. "Let's make him run off all the stored fat in his tail. That will teach him to interfere."

Ampris liked the idea, but she was busy thinking ahead. "What if your father has summoned you?"

"No, he hasn't," Israi said. "Besides, I hardly care. I

shan't have my fun spoiled like this. Come, Ampris. You stand there and boost me up.''

Ampris looked at the rocks they had to climb and pulled off her costume. ''It would be better if I went first and gave you a hand.''

''Then do it quickly,'' Israi commanded.

Already Ampris had evaluated the climb. She started up, finding hand- and toe-holds quickly. Ahead of her was a ledge where she could lie flat and extend her hand to Israi. But even as she reached it, she heard scrambling sounds and Israi's quick panting. Glancing back, Ampris saw Israi climbing right behind her.

She started to tell Israi to wait, then held her tongue. When Israi lost her temper, she listened to no one.

Ampris hauled herself onto the ledge and knelt there in time to grip Israi's reaching hand. She heaved, and Israi came scrambling up in a flurry of long legs, tail, and the cumbersome fur robe that she refused to take off.

Streaked with dirt, Israi closed her eyes and gasped for breath. Below them, old Moscar stood at the base of the rocks and shook his shaggy head slowly from side to side.

''He can't make it,'' Ampris said.

Israi opened her eyes and flicked out her tongue. ''Then send him back. He'll only slow us down.''

''Will the Imperial Daughter please return!'' came another shout from the group farther down the trail.

Israi muttered something beneath her breath and started climbing again.

Ampris leaned down toward Moscar. ''Go back,'' she said in the abiru patois he understood best. ''Go back. Follow us no more.''

Puzzlement filled his dull eyes. He stood there, swaying back and forth, then finally turned and started back down the steep trail.

''Ampris, come on!'' Israi called.

Ampris rose to her feet and turned around just as Israi screamed. Suddenly Israi came tumbling down the rocks, skidding and flailing. She rolled past Ampris and went tumbling toward the ledge.

Horrified, Ampris threw herself bodily after the screaming Israi and just managed to clutch her leg. Israi hung there, half on the ledge and half off. For a dazed moment there was only silence.

Ampris lay there, feeling bruised and stunned, astonished that she had managed to catch Israi at all.

"Israi?" she whispered. "Are you hurt?"

Israi did not answer at first, then moved slightly in Ampris's grasp. "Help me," she said, her voice muffled and afraid.

Gripping Israi's leg with both hands, Ampris pulled with all her might and finally managed to drag Israi back to safety. The sri-Kaa lay there, streaked with mud. Her clothing was torn. Blood smeared her head and hands. She lay unmoving, her breathing shallow, her eyes half-shut, little pulses jumping beneath her ear dimples.

Terrified, Ampris stroked her rill. "Israi," she said in rising alarm. "Are you badly hurt? Israi!"

The sri-Kaa's eyes fluttered open and her gaze fastened on Ampris. "You saved me," she whispered. "You didn't let me fall."

Ampris gripped her hand tightly and licked it. "Of course not," she said, hardly paying attention to what Israi was saying. "You could have gone down the whole mountain. You could have died."

"Saved me," Israi whispered, and fainted.

Fear formed a lump in Ampris's throat and would not let her swallow. Certain that Israi was badly injured, Ampris tried to rouse her friend, but could not. Dropping Israi's slack hand, Ampris scrambled to the ledge and looked down at Moscar, who had stopped and was staring at them transfixed.

The guards and Fazhmind were waving and coming as fast as they could, but they were still too far away to help.

Ampris beckoned to Moscar. "Come," she said urgently. "Hurry."

The old Aaroun shuffled forward, and at Ampris's bidding he put down the food basket and climbed up to the ledge where Israi lay unconscious.

"Hand me one of the blankets," Ampris commanded. "We must wrap her in it so that she doesn't grow cold. Careful. She may have broken bones."

Moscar nodded his shaggy head. His hands were gentle as he lifted Israi and pulled the blanket around her.

"Can you carry her down the mountain?" Ampris asked.

Moscar gathered Israi into his powerful arms. He moved slowly, with infinite care, while Ampris scrambled down off the rocks so fast she nearly lost her balance.

In agony she watched him climb down, never putting a foot wrong, never slipping. He was steady and sure as he carried his precious burden.

Once he was safely off the rocks, Ampris could contain her impatience no longer. "Come," she urged him. "Hurry as fast as you can. I'll get the others."

Leaving him, she headed down the steep trail, skidding and dropping to her haunches more than once. Going down was much harder than going up. She paid no attention to her recklessness, however. Her heart was slamming hard in her chest, and in her mind ran a continual prayer.

Please don't let her die. Please don't let her die.

When she reached Fazhmind, she stumbled and nearly fell into his arms. He fended her off roughly with a hiss.

"Get out of the way," he said, and gestured for the guards to precede him.

"She's hurt. She's fainted," Ampris said breathlessly, gulping for air. "There is blood—"

"Great gods," Fazhmind said in horror, and rushed past her, leaving her behind.

The guards took Israi's limp form away from Moscar, one carrying her down the trail with rapid strides while the other grimly shepherded Moscar along as though the accident had been his fault.

Ampris went with them, feeling very small and young now, more frightened than ever at the grim adult faces around her. Seeking reassurance, she looked up at Lord Fazhmind. "Will the sri-Kaa be all right?" she asked.

"Silence!" he snapped without even glancing at her. "This is all your fault."

"But—"

He turned on her and struck her across the muzzle. "Silence!"

Ampris pressed the back of her hand against her quivering mouth and stared at him, her ears flat to her skull. Holding back a hot rush of tears, she followed him down the mountain and through the towering gates of the walls.

Inside, impatient hands shoved her aside when she would have followed them into Israi's quarters. The doors were shut firmly against her, and Ampris was left to hunker on the floor, heedless that her muddy fur was streaking the priceless carpet. She waited for word, and prayed that all would be well.

It was nearly dark, and long purple shadows filled the corners of the corridor when at last Subi came to find her. Growling to herself, Subi pulled Ampris to her feet without a word and marched her off for a bath, then a hot supper that Ampris would be too miserable to eat.

"Is the Imperial Daughter all right?" Ampris asked.

Subi's gruff expression never softened. Her eyes were hostile and worried, and she looked ready to bite. "Better you keep quiet and ask no questions," she said as she took a clean Ampris down into the oppressive warmth of the kitchens. There, the air was redolent with the scents of the feast being prepared for the Kaa's evening meal. Baking ovens stood open, and fresh breads and pastries were being pulled out by perspiring cooks.

Subi seated Ampris on a stool in a quiet corner out of everyone's way and ordered a plain dinner for her. In minutes it was brought, and a tray was set up on legs to form a small table.

Ampris barely looked at it. Her eyes beseeched Subi. "But she's hurt. She—"

"Big trouble for you. Keep quiet," Subi said, her upright ears twitching nervously. "You eat now."

Wretchedly, Ampris picked up her spoon and toyed with her food. Every bite she swallowed felt as though it might come up again. After a moment she put down her spoon and shoved her bowl away. The cold lump of worry inside her kept growing, sharp-edged and painful. Why wouldn't anyone tell her what was happening? The evasions and grim looks frightened her.

The constant babble of noise in the kitchen hushed momentarily. Looking up, Ampris saw Lady Lenith standing on the stairs, looking over the room.

Ampris's heart stopped. She couldn't breathe.

Lady Lenith was attired in a glittering court gown, too formal for the lodge, and all the more imposing because of it. Jewels winked in her rill collar, as well as in her necklace and many rings. A long scarf of sheer silk gauze trailed from her shoulders. Her rill stood at full extension and was stained a dark indigo. Her eyes were cold with disapproval.

Her gaze traveled across the room and its many workers. Subi pinched Ampris, who rose to her feet.

Lady Lenith gave Ampris a long hard stare. There was something so implacable in her gaze that Ampris was certain Israi had died. The room started to spin around Ampris, and her head grew so cold it no longer seemed to be hers. She blinked, feeling strange and hollow. Her ears roared as Lady Lenith beckoned to her. Somehow she pushed herself forward, walking in jerky motions as though detached from her feet.

The workers stepped out of her path, but Ampris did not notice them. Nor did she hear the silence. There was only the fateful *ka-boom* of her own heartbeat and the tense rasp of her breathing in her ears.

She reached Lady Lenith and stared up at her, so tall, so angry. The world seemed to be ending.

Dry-mouthed, Ampris had to swallow twice before she could manage the words. "Is Israi dead?"

Her voice came out a tiny squeak, sounding nothing like her own.

Lady Lenith's fierce expression did not change. She flicked out her tongue once, twice, then said, "The Kaa has summoned you to his august presence. Come."

Ampris followed her out of the kitchen, up to the main floor, up the grand central staircase. When they turned onto the second floor, Ampris expected to be taken to the state receiving room, but instead Lady Lenith walked to the door of Israi's quarters.

A Viis page running ahead of her knocked softly at the door, which was opened before Lady Lenith reached it. She walked inside, the hem of her long gown brushing the carpets. Ampris followed, gripping her jaws together tightly to keep herself from growling nervously. She could feel the hair standing up along her spine. The door shut behind her with a firm snap that made her jump.

Inside Israi's sitting room, the lamps were dimmed to a low level that filled the chamber with shadows. Myneith, the First Wife, and two others sat there with their ladies in waiting. They talked in hushed voices that fell silent as Ampris entered. They stared at her with cold Viis eyes, accusing her with silence.

Chilled, Ampris felt more wretched than ever. She tried to imagine a world without Israi in it and couldn't. She tried to think about what she would do and couldn't. Her heart was breaking. She wanted to howl and weep, but she did neither. Instead, she panted for air, her eyes hot and her tongue dry, and walked past them in Lady Lenith's wake.

Imperial guards stood before the double doors leading to Israi's bedchamber. Lady Lenith paused and gestured to her page, who told them, "Lady Lenith's compliments to the

Imperial Father. She has brought the creature, as requested.''

Ampris flinched at that single word, *creature,* as though a whip had been laid across her shoulders. Behind her, she could feel the hatred in the room from the other females, a hatred that pounded into her back from every pair of eyes.

Her bottom lip trembled, and she sank her incisors into it to make it stop. Inside, she had begun to grieve for her friend with a misery that had no boundary. *Israi,* she thought. *Oh, Israi.*

The guards permitted Lady Lenith's page to step between them and tap very softly on the door. It opened a crack, and no more. The page murmured to someone on the other side, then the door was closed.

Returning to Lady Lenith, the page bowed and said quietly, ''Your ladyship is asked to wait until the physician is finished with his examination.''

Lady Lenith nodded and stood in place, motionless, her back ramrod straight, her rill half-extended. Behind her, Ampris closed her eyes and found that she could breathe again.

Not dead, she thought as joy spiraled into her heart, thawing it. *Not dead. Not dead. Not dead!*

But her joy and relief proved short-lived as the silence wore on. Worry returned to Ampris once more. Everyone was acting too serious for Israi to be all right. She must be badly injured, perhaps near to dying.

Clearly, the blame for this had been assigned to Ampris. She wanted to deny it, to explain what had happened, but she dared not open her mouth. She knew no one would listen, no one would permit her to speak, no one would believe her. Their minds were already made up. Without Israi to speak up for her, what would happen?

The door opened, and a tall green-skinned Viis in a physician's cloak emerged. He passed Lady Lenith without a word, and Chancellor Gaveid himself beckoned to Lady Lenith from the doorway.

Ampris blinked. She knew that the chancellor was not staying here at the lodge. He must have flown in by shuttle this afternoon from Vir or his own estates. Her fear came back, stronger than ever.

Lady Lenith glanced down at Ampris. Normally she would have fussed over Ampris's appearance, given her several last-minute instructions and reminders about how to behave. Tonight, however, she said nothing.

Her gaze raked across Ampris with contempt, and her tongue flicked out once; then she walked forward.

Ampris followed, wishing she could run, wishing the floor would simply swallow her up.

The door swung open, and Ampris walked between the guards into Israi's bedchamber. The lamps here were very dim, casting out a feeble glow that made everything shadowy and unreal. Israi lay nestled on her side among the pillows beneath a silk coverlet, a small, still figure swathed in bandages.

Drawing in a quick breath, Ampris wanted to run to her side, but she dared not.

A crimson ribbon of carpet stretched across the floor, leading past the foot of Israi's round bed to a tall-backed chair flanked by four imperial guards in green cloaks.

The Kaa himself sat there, bronze-skinned with green shadings along his jaw and throat, glittering in a magnificent coat made of cloth of gold and jewel dust. His slightest motion, even his breathing, set the coat reflecting the light in a thousand winking refractions. His rill collar rose very tall at the back, very formal. Fashioned of gold, the collar was studded with a solid array of yellow tafirs that flashed as though containing fire.

Stern-faced, the Kaa narrowed his cold, space-blue eyes to slits when Ampris entered, and his extended rill turned an ominous crimson.

Lady Lenith made deep obeisance. The Kaa's gaze flickered to her in brief acknowledgment, but he did not speak.

"I have brought Ampris, as the Imperial Father requested.'' Lady Lenith's voice quavered slightly as she spoke.

Chancellor Gaveid walked forward with stiff, slow movements. Handsome still despite his very advanced age, he gestured to her as protocol demanded.

''Thank you, Lady Lenith. That will be all.''

Lady Lenith hesitated, glancing down at Ampris, then to the chancellor, then to the Kaa. ''I wish to say . . . if I may be permitted to speak . . . I had nothing but misgivings from the first as to—''

''Thank you, my lady,'' Gaveid said smoothly. His yellow eyes held no mercy. ''That is all understood. Nothing else is required of you.''

She bowed, looking stricken. Again she started to speak, then pressed her hand to her ear dimple and rushed out.

The door was closed behind her by a guard, who then walked over to one side of Israi's round bed and stood there at attention.

Ampris, left on her own, remained on the crimson carpet, which made her think of a stream of blood across the floor. The silence grew more ominous than ever. The chancellor's yellow gaze was like stone. The guards stared beyond her, as though she did not exist. The Kaa's eyes held nothing at all—no affection, no gentleness, no memory of past days when he had smiled at Ampris.

She watched him, her heart hammering wildly inside her, and felt the awful weight of his majesty and power as she never had before.

For an eternity he said nothing, did nothing except stare at her. She thought she would faint beneath his gaze. He seemed to probe to the depths of her, this Viis whose empire spanned an entire galaxy. Surely he was all-wise and all-knowing. Surely the gods had granted him special wisdom, so that he would know she had done nothing wrong. She hadn't caused Israi to fall. She had tried to save the sri-Kaa's life. Certainly the Kaa had enough mercy and pity in his heart to listen to the truth.

Ampris's ears flattened, and she felt a slight tug on her ear as Israi's cartouche swung on its ornate chain. She tried to find the courage to speak, to make an appeal.

But he was the Kaa, and she dust beneath his feet. She stood there trembling, and dared do nothing unbidden.

Finally, his gaze shifted, releasing her from that terrible stare. He sighed and looked infinitely weary, as though facing a task he dreaded.

Lifting a single digit from the arm of his chair, he crooked it, beckoning to her.

Afraid, Ampris felt her feet root in place. She could not move.

Chancellor Gaveid prodded her in the shoulder with the tip of his staff of office. "Approach his Imperial Majesty, cub. Do as you are told."

Gulping, Ampris walked along the crimson carpet, one slow, frightened footstep at a time, until she stood before this personification of supreme power. She knew better than to meet the Kaa's gaze this close. Instead she stared humbly at his feet, and even that seemed a sacrilege.

"Kneel!" Chancellor Gaveid barked the single word, making it a harsh command.

Ampris lost her breath. She sank to her knees, trembling, and bowed low, certain she was doomed.

CHAPTER ELEVEN

Elrabin moved slowly to one edge of the thronged plaza outside the gladiator arena. He took care to bring no attention to himself, to stay on the fringes of the crowd. He always kept a group of people between him and any patrollers stationed there for crowd control.

It was opening day of the games, the first of the winter fighting season that would last until Sahvrazaa Festival. The marquee above the ticket booth was flashing the names of popular champions. Famous schools of gladiators such as the Bizsi Mo'ad and Utar Dan flew their pennants above the arena. Hucksters called out prices for souvenirs. Opening day brought big crowds of spectators, many of whom had fat credit lines. Elrabin ignored the aristocrats, with their retinues of family, friends, attendants, and bodyguards. Anyone clad in expensive clothing would be wearing body alarms. Instead, Elrabin searched for much smaller game, the gawking country visitor fresh off a small estate, one who had never been to court, one without city ways or city wariness.

Trying to look casual, Elrabin leaned against a stone pillar away from the bookmakers and illicit dust dealers. His elbow brushed against the stone, and he winced. Swiftly he cradled his swollen elbow in his hand, flexing his arm in an effort to null the flare of pain. Three days ago he'd had his registration implant cut out in a back alley shop. The illegal operation had been an expensive butcher job, performed fast and without any anesthesia. Now the incision was infected, bringing fever with it. Elrabin fought off a wave of dizziness and forced himself to concentrate.

Since escaping arrest a few days past, he'd been living like a Skek, scavenging through garbage, stealing food when he could, starving when he couldn't. Afraid, trusting no one, he'd kept low, rarely venturing out during the day, sleeping in the sewer tunnels. He'd sold scrap, fighting Skeks for the best of it. He'd stolen anything he could find, taking more risks than he should have. Finally he'd managed to scrape together the fee for the implant removal, but it had taken everything he had.

Now he was truly illegal, a ghost in the registration system, able to walk into public areas freely. Of course, if a patroller saw him and grew suspicious, a quick scan would betray him as a ghost. But he couldn't be tracked with a sniffer for his past record, and hiding became easier.

A ghost . . . yeah, he would be a real one soon enough if this fever didn't clear up. Fighting off the shivers, Elrabin straightened again and moved to another pillar. More people were arriving, but the crowd was starting to line up outside the entry. They were going in. From inside the arena, a fanfare of trumpets sounded and cheers went up.

Desperation curled through Elrabin. He hadn't seen the kind of target he was looking for. The more organized the crowd grew, the smaller his chances. He needed a hit today. He was so sick and hungry he couldn't think. He couldn't hang on without something to eat or somewhere warm to go. Merciful gods, he pleaded, let him find an easy mark.

As though his prayer was heard, there came a sudden commotion a short distance away. A battered, dusty litter pulled up at the steps leading from the street to the plaza, and a Viis family climbed out. Arguing and complaining among themselves, they issued contradictory instructions to their driver, collected wraps and a food basket as though unaware that concessions were sold inside the arena, and came hurrying across the plaza to join the line.

Elrabin forgot his misery and grinned to himself. Exactly what he wanted. The family patriarch was very tall and thin, dressed in outdated fashions, and oblivious to the stares and snickers of city-dwellers. His gawking, half-grown sons pointed at the gaudy marquee and colorful flags. The wife fussed with her rill collar and skirts, talking nonstop. The young daughter didn't even bother to look around. She was too busy sneaking food from the basket and popping it into her mouth while no one was looking.

Elrabin let them walk past him, then followed in their wake, taking his time, although it was tempting to grab the food basket from the Viis female's hand and run with it.

They moved with the line, the father busy counting up the admission price, the sons nudging each other and whispering sly remarks. Elrabin caught up with them and moved closer, bowing several times, until the father's eye noticed him.

At once the Viis scowled and made a shooing motion with his hand. "Begone, beggar!" he said sharply. "You'll not find me softhearted."

Elrabin bowed again but didn't step back.

The father glanced at his sons. "You see? You must take an authoritative tone with these inferiors."

"Shoo," the mother said to Elrabin, shuddering as she averted her gaze from him. "Such a dirty, tattered creature. Aethea, don't look at him."

The daughter stared right at Elrabin, chewing fruit with her mouth open. "You stink," she said.

The mother grabbed her by the shoulders and pulled her close as though she expected Elrabin to steal the chune.

"I told you to go," the father said. "We have no money for you."

"Please, sir," Elrabin said in his most obsequious man-

ner. "I am no beggar. The arena employs me to assist its
spectators, those who come attended by no servants. I will
carry your basket, your wraps, your cushions. If you wish,
even your bets I can lay for you."

The father's eyes flashed. "Hah, I'm sure you'd like to.
But would my money ever reach the booth? Eh? No, I'm
sure it would not."

The Viis sons nudged each other and snickered.

"This basket *is* heavy," the mother said, then slapped at
her daughter's hand. "Aethea, stop nibbling. You've eaten
too much already."

The repellent brat went on chewing, staring at Elrabin
the whole time. He swallowed and tried not to think about
food, although the smells coming from the basket nearly
made him swoon. But he had to concentrate, had to keep
his wits on what he was doing.

"We'll manage our own belongings, thank you," the
father said sharply. "I carry a payment card only, which is
secure for travel. I have no coins for tips."

"Kind sir," Elrabin said with another bow, "no tip is
necessary. The arena employs me. I require nothing except
to serve you."

"Hmm." But the father was caught by the bait. Stingy
to a fault, he couldn't resist the chance to get service without paying for it. "Very well, take the basket and our cushions. Wife, watch him closely. I shan't have anything
stolen."

The family piled him up with belongings, so many he
staggered to hang on to everything. It was all he could do
not to run with it, but he was too smart for that.

Instead, he stood patiently in line behind the family, ignoring their stupid chatter and rude remarks. He waited
until the father had paid admission at the ticket booth and
was turning around. No patroller was paying attention. Another group of late arrivals were walking up, making the
opportunity perfect.

Without warning, Elrabin heaved his armful at the father,

forcing the male to take the things or have them dropped.

"What the—"

Elrabin stepped closer, juggling the handle of the food basket over the Viis's wrist and bumping into him as he did so. "Service ends here," he said over the Viis's startled protests. "Go in quickly. The games are starting."

"But—"

"I must attend to other people."

"But you were to carry our things inside," the father called after him.

Successfully having lifted the Viis's card from his pocket, Elrabin barely glanced back. "Not part of my job," he said, and threaded his way quickly into the crowd.

He milled around the spectators for a few minutes, resisting the urge to run. He knew to stay calm and casual. But he was panting with excitement. His unsuspecting marks had gone inside the arena. With any luck, they wouldn't miss the stolen card for hours. By then it would be fenced, and his stomach would be full.

A hand came out of the crowd and gripped his injured arm like a vise. The pain was instant—hot and debilitating.

Close to panic, Elrabin bit off a cry and kicked out blindly. But the fingers holding him tightened so hard he nearly blacked out from the agony. All he could think of was patrollers . . . arrest . . . disaster.

"No," he said, gasping. "No!"

"Shut up," growled a voice in his ear. "Make no sound and come this way. Fast, now."

Elrabin realized it was no patroller's voice. Reeling and half-blinded with tears of pain, he staggered along as he was pulled through the crowd. A Kelth gripped his arm, a grim-faced youth about his age who was missing one ear. White fur grew along the scar, which ran down his head beneath his eye and under his jaw. Scar tissue had twisted his lip on that side, revealing strong yellow teeth.

The pain in Elrabin's arm throbbed hard, but he was over his initial fright now. He gauged his moment, and when the scarred Kelth paused at the top of some steps leading away from the plaza, Elrabin set his feet and jerked hard.

He nearly freed himself. Even as the Kelth turned on him, Elrabin reversed tactics and pushed with all his might. The Kelth went sprawling down the steps with a muffled grunt.

Elrabin spun around and ran, angling down the steps and heading for the street. But seconds later he was tackled from behind with a force that knocked the wind from him. Stunned, Elrabin found himself wrestled around and dragged to his feet.

The scar-faced Kelth glared at him. "Stupid, that. You come now, fast, before the patrollers get wind of us."

Before Elrabin could try another trick, or even retort, his captor twisted his bad arm behind him in a ruthless hold that made resistance impossible.

Gasping in agony, burning with fury, Elrabin found himself marched along toward an underground service access leading beneath the arena. It was a delivery area, busy with activity, but lacking any patrollers.

On the other side, they entered an alley, then cut across several streets until they reached a dead end littered with garbage. Tall, windowless buildings surrounded them on three sides.

There, the scar-faced Kelth stopped, spun Elrabin around to face him, and hit him hard.

Reeling from the blow, Elrabin staggered to one side and barely kept his balance. Before he could recover, he was hit again, then shoved hard against the wall. Expert hands patted him down, fingering both pockets and lining of the coat he'd bartered for yesterday from a ragpicker, plucking out the card he had just stolen from the Viis.

Released, Elrabin dragged in a deep, unsteady breath and managed to straighten. He was shaking with humiliation and rage. Who did this *nolo* think he was?

The scar-faced Kelth stood a short distance away, holding the card up to the sky while he read the numbers embossed on it, mouthing them to himself.

Glaring at him, Elrabin clenched his fists and started to launch himself, but just as he moved, the other youth drew a sticker and pointed it straight at him.

The sticker's blade was long and needle-thin, fashioned of blue steel, and quite deadly. The sight of it stopped Elrabin in his tracks. For a moment he couldn't take his eyes off it. He forgot to breathe, forgot how angry he was.

Instead, he shifted his gaze to the other end of the alley, the only way out.

"Stand still," the youth said curtly. He was still examining the card and didn't even glance at Elrabin. He didn't have to.

The sticker held Elrabin in place as effectively as a side-arm would have.

Elrabin knew the streets, knew the thugs and punks who prowled them, knew they had territories, knew they liked to steal from the independents, like himself. Elrabin realized he'd better forget his rage and fear and concentrate on using his wits. This Kelth might just decide to kill him, either on a whim or to enforce a lesson.

"Please," Elrabin whispered. "Take it, okay? Let me go. I got nothing else—"

"You got no tongue, you, if you don't be quiet."

Elrabin shut up, his mouth dry, his heart pounding.

Finally, the Kelth quit looking at the card and shoved it in his pocket with a scowl. "Stupid," he said flatly. He was lean and fit, with light tan fur that darkened on the back of his skull and single, upright ear. His stony eyes held all the age he hadn't lived yet.

"This card you stole from the Viis, you. Got a limiter on it. Got an encoder on it. A fence wouldn't pay two city credits for it. Junk."

He snarled in Elrabin's face, making him flinch.

"Okay," Elrabin said, trying to find enough air to keep

his voice steady. "So it's junk. You got it. Now let me go."

"Why? So you can go back and hang around the arena for the crowd turnout? Who you with?"

Elrabin blinked at him and didn't answer.

The youth stepped closer, the sunlight harsh on his white scar, his revealed teeth glinting. "Who you with? Who sent you to our territory?"

Elrabin drew a sharp breath. Maybe it would help if he claimed to belong to a gang. A powerful gang, bloody and violent enough to frighten this menace away. But Elrabin's mind went blank. He couldn't think of any names. His wits all seemed to be hanging on the sharp tip of the sticker.

Finally he shook his head.

Anger flared in the scarred youth's eyes. He moved fast, crowding Elrabin back against the wall and holding him pinned there with the sticker at his throat. "I got no time for you, stupid. You talk fast, or die here, die now."

The tip of the sticker pressed against Elrabin's throat. He couldn't even swallow against it. Panting for breath, he tried to speak and couldn't.

"Well?"

"No one."

"What?"

"No one! No one sent me," Elrabin said, babbling now. He despised himself but he couldn't help it. "No gang. By myself. Just trying to survive."

The scarred Kelth frowned. "Expect me to believe that? Huh!"

"True!" Elrabin said as forcefully as he could. "I've got no scars, no tattoos. I don't belong to—"

"Shut up."

Elrabin snapped his teeth together and said nothing else. He wished he knew more about fighting, wished he could throw off his captor and pound him into the dirt, wished he could just twist free and run for it.

But he hurt too bad, and his stomach was flapping empty

against his spine, and his knees kept going weak and wobbly on him. His heart pounded too fast, making him dizzy. He shivered, feeling the heat run down his arm, followed by a chill that shook his bones.

His captor stepped back from him so suddenly Elrabin nearly fell. "You sick?"

Elrabin slumped to his knees, shivering and trying not to moan. "Yeah."

Alarm filled the scarred youth's eyes. He backed away. "What kind of sick? Dry cough? Street pox? Quivers?"

Elrabin shook his head. He was tired, but he couldn't give way to his misery. He had to speak up or he might find himself executed because of misguided mercy.

"No," he said, dragging his head up to meet the other youth's eyes. "My arm. I had my implant removed. It's infected."

The Kelth whistled through his teeth in sudden respect. Coming closer again, he dropped to his haunches in front of Elrabin. "You cut it yourself?"

"No. Behind Commerce Street."

"Bad place, that. Bad move. Stupid move."

Elrabin cradled his aching arm in his lap. "Yeah."

"Maybe your arm'll fall off, if you don't take care of it."

"I could have gotten some medicine if you hadn't stolen that card from me. I was going to fence it and—"

The Kelth scratched his ear, unmoved. He'd called the card junk, but he didn't give it back. "Where you from? What street?"

"Nowhere," Elrabin said bitterly.

"You got no gang, you?"

"No. I work alone."

"You a babe, that's what you are. You a citizen." He made it sound like a disease.

Elrabin bared his teeth. He wasn't going to take that kind of insult from anyone. "Wrong on both counts."

"Maybe. You wanted? Gotta be, you taking your implant out. What you wanted for?"

Elrabin looked away. He wasn't going to explain. "Does it matter?"

"No. What's your name?"

"Elrabin."

The Kelth nodded, mouthing it to himself as though committing it to memory. "Yeah, a citizen name, all right. You talk fancy, like a grifter. You look like a grifter, except for that coat. Even a Zrhel wouldn't wear a rag like that."

Elrabin said nothing.

"Got family?"

"No."

"Okay. I'm Scar."

The two youths looked at each other. Elrabin wasn't sure this sharing of names was a friendly overture. Maybe Scar just wanted his name so he could turn him in. He was nosy enough to be a snitch.

"You're a bad thief, you know that?" Scar continued. "I spotted you easy. The patrollers, they be too lazy to care around the arena, most days. Barthul's got them paid off, yeah. So you're lucky today."

"Yeah, really lucky," Elrabin said, averting his gaze. The afternoon was wearing on, and he had no hope now of getting anything to eat. He shivered and squinted his eyes, feeling too miserable to care.

Scar tapped his shoulder. "I'll give you advice, stupid. The way you work, you'll lose a hand soon."

Elrabin rolled his eyes. This was advice? "Thanks."

"Shut up," Scar said. "Listen good. The arena is Barthul's turf, see? Stay away from it. This crowd belongs to Barthul. You can't steal here."

"So where do I go?"

Scar shrugged. "Nothing to me, where you go. Just get away from our turf. And stay away."

Elrabin frowned. He wasn't afraid now, but he was feeling hopeless. He'd pretty much cleaned out the area where he'd been staying, and knew he had to keep moving around. Although this wasn't the first time he'd had to avoid gang territory, it was the first time he'd been robbed and nearly had his throat cut.

He shivered, knowing he wasn't doing a very good job of making it on his own, not in this end of the city, far from the districts he knew best.

"All the turf around here's been staked out," he said. "Where do independents go?"

Scar laughed harshly and backed his single ear. "Elrabin, you are so stupid, you got to be likable. Independents? That's a word, that is."

"So where do they go, the ones like me, who don't belong to gangs?"

The friendliness in Scar's eyes faded. He rose to his feet and turned away.

Desperate for help, Elrabin staggered upright also. "Please!" he cried. "It's just a question. Can't you tell me something?"

"I'll tell you," Scar said unpleasantly. "Independents go to the arrest tank, that's where. Independents get their hands cut off, or they go into hard labor. How you lived this long, you being so stupid?"

"Could I be in your gang?"

The request popped out of Elrabin's mouth before he knew he was going to ask it. He waited, feeling this might be his last hope.

Refusal filled Scar's face. Even before he started shaking his head, Elrabin stepped forward.

"I'll learn anything I have to. I'll do anything I'm told. I need a place to go. I'm too sick to keep going on my own. I need help."

"Ain't no help," Scar said flatly. "By the law of the streets, you live or you die."

"But your gang, you hang out together. You belong together. You have a place, a hole—"

"You wired?" Scar asked with fresh suspicion.

"No! You searched me, remember?"

The alarm faded from Scar's eyes. "Yeah, okay."

"Please. I have a lot of skills, not just grifting. Just let me—"

"Not my decision," Scar broke in. "Not my gang."

"This Barthul, then. Where is he? Will you take me to him and ask?"

"No."

"Scar, please! You took my card. I have nothing left. I haven't eaten in—"

"Shut up!" Scar said, and turned away. He strode down the alley without looking back.

Elrabin watched him go, feeling all his hope drain away. He hated begging, but he had no other option. The last thing he wanted was to belong to a gang, but he needed help. There had to be some way to get it, some way to reach this Scar, who seemed half-sympathetic at times under his rough exterior.

After a moment, Elrabin forced himself to stagger after Scar. But he couldn't find the strength to run and catch up, and when Scar turned the corner and disappeared from sight, panic filled Elrabin's throat.

Shouting, he stumbled into a shuffling run, feeling his knees wobble under him, feeling the fever burning hotter in his blood. He made it to the corner before he fell, dropping to his knees and slumping with his shoulder against the wall.

He was shaking all over, and his breathing came harsh and uneven. His strength failed him, and he knew he couldn't go any farther. He lay shivering and helpless, his strength leaking out of him and taking his will with it. He would lie here until someone killed him or until a patroller picked him up. Either way he was finished.

With his last ounce of strength he lifted his head and looked down the street in hopes of seeing Scar coming back for him.

But Scar was gone as though he had never been. Another

thief, faster, bigger, and more ruthless. The predators always won.

Shivering, Elrabin let his head slump to the pavement and lay there. It was over.

CHAPTER TWELVE

Elrabin roused to the feel of rough hands searching him. Groaning, he grabbed for the edge of consciousness and tried to roll over.

Thin, high-pitched voices squeaked in alarm. "Quick! Quick!"

The hands ripped out his pockets and shucked him out of his tattered coat, rolling him across the ground.

His swollen arm whacked against something hard and seemed to explode. Sucking in a breath, Elrabin held on to the agony, using it to drive himself up from the mists.

Blinking, he came fully to and found himself kneeling on the dirty pavement, clutching his arm and gritting his teeth. Realizing he'd been robbed, he swore long and low to himself.

"Damned, dirty Skeks."

He could still smell their stink on him. Disgusted, he pushed himself to his feet. It took three tries before he made it upright; then he stood swaying with his head down, hanging on by sheer grit.

He wasn't giving up, not for anyone.

Drawing in a deep breath, he forced his head up and staggered forward. He wasn't certain where he was going yet, but he knew he had to keep moving. He didn't want to be picked up in a vagrant sweep and sold.

It was dark, but how late he did not know. Most of the streetlights in this district were burned out, which suited him fine. He staggered along slowly, weaving his way and keeping to the shadows. Whenever he heard footsteps, he froze and hid in the darkness, refusing to move until the pedestrian walked on.

Occasionally a skimmer flew by, sometimes a litter, but traffic was light. That told him the hour must be late.

He made it back to the plaza which skirted the arena and found the area deserted. Only the wind remained, playing with trash among the benches, lampposts, and small, ornamental trees. Elrabin paused there to rest, leaning against a pillar. He could smell the burned remains of concession food still lingering on the air.

His hunger rose up inside him like a wildness. Dropping to his knees, Elrabin scratched in the trash until he found a greasy food wrapper. He unfolded it with trembling fingers, licked the wrapper ravenously, then ate it.

A light snapped on, dazzling his eyes.

Blinded, Elrabin lifted his arm to shield his vision and squinted. He glimpsed a shape coming toward him, and tried to flee.

But he was too slow and too weak to run.

He was caught before he even gained his feet.

"What you got?" a familiar voice demanded. "What you eating, you?"

"Scar!"

Elrabin gazed up at the silhouette standing over him and felt a rush of fresh fear. Scar had warned him away once. This time he might kill.

The light clicked off. Scar kicked him in the haunch, nearly knocking him over. "You again," he said in disgust. "The down-luck grifter."

Elrabin tried to answer, but Scar leaned over him and grabbed the remnants of the food wrapper from his hand.

"What you eating?" he demanded a second time. "The wrapper? Huh? You eating that, stupid?"

The scorn in his voice was like a whip. Elrabin hunkered down in raw humiliation and could not answer.

"It's cold tonight. Where's your coat?" Scar asked him, throwing the wrapper away. The wind caught it, sending it pinwheeling across the plaza. "You sell your coat, stupid?"

"Skeks took it," Elrabin answered sullenly. He knew now that Scar wouldn't help him. He was done asking. "Robbed me while I was passed out."

Scar growled without sympathy. "What you expect, lying in the gutter?"

"What's it to you?" Elrabin retorted. "What do you care?"

"Don't care. You're trespassing again."

Fury gave Elrabin the strength to climb to his feet. He faced Scar in the darkness. "So now I can't even walk across a public plaza? Do the stones belong to you? Does the air? Excuse me, but I didn't know. I thought you just owned all the marks that come here in the afternoons—"

Scar flipped him to the ground before Elrabin realized what was happening. Throwing himself on top of Elrabin, Scar pinned his throat with a forearm and growled long and low.

Feeling Scar's hot breath ruffle his fur, knowing Scar's teeth were just centimeters away from his throat, Elrabin froze. He didn't even breathe.

"So you can be quiet," Scar said finally. "And here I thought you didn't have no sense at all. You be too stupid to live, you know that?"

"Yeah, and maybe I don't care," Elrabin shot back.

Scar growled again, and Elrabin figured he was finished now. But instead of taking out his throat, Scar uttered a strange low laugh and rolled off Elrabin. "Get up."

Racked by fresh shivers, Elrabin lay there. "What for? I haven't got anything else you can steal."

Scar kicked him hard, making him yelp. "Shut up and get on your feet. Get up!"

He kicked Elrabin again, and with a groan Elrabin dragged himself upright. Scar gripped him and marched him forward.

"Where we going?" Elrabin asked.

"What do you care?" Scar replied grimly, marching him along. "You wanted me to take you someplace, yeah, you wanted that. So I'm taking you."

Suspicion flared inside Elrabin's chest. "You turning me in? Or giving me a home?"

Scar's laugh was unpleasant. "Yeah, a home. You call it that, stupid. You call it anything you want."

Elrabin planted his feet, halting so abruptly that he nearly threw Scar off balance. "If you turn me in, I'll turn you in," he said desperately. "I'll tell the patrollers that you work for—"

"Shut up!"

Snapping, Scar lunged for him, but Elrabin dodged. He got two steps before Scar caught him and gave him a shaking that made him dizzy.

"Keep walking," Scar said gruffly. "You threaten me or Barthul again, yeah, I'll use my sticker on you."

"I—"

"Quiet! Maybe Barthul can use you as a runner."

Fresh alarm filled Elrabin. This wasn't what he'd had in mind when he'd asked for help. "Dust? No way!" he said sharply. "I won't risk the death penalty for—"

"You'll risk anything you're told to risk. You'll do what you're told."

"But I—"

Scar nipped his ear, sending a sharp flare of pain into Elrabin's skull. "First thing you learn, stupid, is you keep quiet when you're told, and maybe you won't get your tongue cut out. You do what you're told, and you do it quick. No double action on the side. No pulling in the patrollers. You stay in the territory you're told to stay in."

Elrabin tried to shut out the gruff lecture, without success. He was being given the rules, whether he liked them or not. But strict rules, strictly enforced, were a way of life he understood. Cuvein's simple ones had provided him with structure these last ten years. Despite his fear of Scar and gangs in general, Elrabin felt something inside him responding to what Scar was saying.

Less than an hour later, Elrabin found himself being dragged down a short flight of crumbling steps into deserted basement lodgings.

Inside, a rickety set of wooden steps led even lower beneath the ground. At the bottom, Scar eyed a bulky Aaroun standing guard with an illegal sidearm and spoke a single word that was incomprehensible to Elrabin.

The Aaroun sniffed Elrabin suspiciously but let them pass. They walked over a magnetic plate, and the scan registered nothing on Elrabin. Scar's tense shoulders slumped a little.

"So you ain't wired after all," he said, and gave Elrabin a grudging little twist of a grin. "Guess you be what you been saying."

"Of course." Elrabin glared at him. "If I'm running a scam, no one catches—"

"Sure." Scar narrowed his eyes. "Bragging don't mean dirt here. You keep your scams to yourself."

They walked on along a roughly hewn tunnel, their footsteps barely echoing.

"Patrollers train undercover agents all the time and send them in," Scar said. "We always catch them. We're careful, see?"

Elrabin nodded. After a moment, Scar pulled out a food bar from his pocket and handed it over. Elrabin snatched it without even a word of thanks and wolfed it down in three bites, barely chewing as he gulped it. Then he licked the wrapper to get every last crumb.

Scar watched him eat from the corner of his eye but said

nothing. Pausing before a door, he opened it and shoved Elrabin inside.

The tiny room contained nothing save a dim light globe in the ceiling overhead, a stool, and a small cabinet. Elrabin looked around, then glanced over his shoulder at Scar.

"What—"

But Scar retreated without a word, slammed the door shut, and bolted it, effectively locking Elrabin inside.

Alarmed again, Elrabin pounded on the door and shouted, but Scar was gone.

After a moment Elrabin gave up calling to him. He circled the small room and thumped the cabinet, which was locked. How stupid could he be, telling a stranger his real name, letting himself be led right into a trap. Now he was locked in, and all Scar had to do was sell him down the—

The door opened without warning. Scar stood there. With him was a short, rotund Myal with a shaggy black and gold mane that hung over his dark, beady eyes.

"Barthul," Scar said by way of scant introduction.

The Myal advanced bowlegged into the room, sticking out his paunch, and cocked his head as he looked Elrabin over. His eyes were cold and shrewd, utterly without mercy. "What's your real name?" he asked at last. "What's your registration number?"

Elrabin met his gaze with all the defiance he had left. "If I'd wanted that known, I wouldn't have had my implant cut out."

"Try again," Scar said quietly. It was a warning.

Elrabin said nothing.

Barthul croaked out a laugh and curled his prehensile tail tightly against his backside. "He's useless. Too old for training. Too sick. Look at his eyes. He's no fighter."

Elrabin squared his shoulders with his last remnants of pride. "I can run any gambling table you got. I can mark Junta cards. I can work the—"

"Useless." Barthul turned his back on Elrabin and started to walk out.

Scar was leaning against the wall, cleaning his claws with the tip of his sticker. He let Barthul get to the doorway before he said, "How about a dust runner?"

Barthul halted on the threshold and stared at Scar incredulously. "A runner? Him?"

"Why not?"

"He's got worker grade stamped all over him. Look at him. He couldn't fool a patroller one minute."

"Doesn't have to. Clean him up. Put him on the citizen run, yeah, and let him work that route. He looks employed, acts honest, blends right in with the rest of the citizens, only he's out in plain sight. Might work. The patrollers ain't expecting that."

It was the most Scar had ever said at once since Elrabin had met him. Elrabin stared at the youth, astonished that Scar was actually speaking up for him, trying to get him a job. Not that it mattered.

"I'll do anything but sell dust," Elrabin said. "I can get you into any dock warehouse you—"

"Nah," Barthul said, cutting him off with a gesture. "Docks ain't my turf. Stay away from there." He stared hard at Scar. "You think so?"

"Sure," Scar said easily, still cleaning his claws. "Worth a try, once he's straightened out."

Elrabin glared at them both. "Look. I asked for a job, but not—"

Barthul grimaced, making a curt gesture. "Too much trouble. Kill the *nolo*."

"Wait!" Elrabin said, lifting his hands even as Scar's eyes went intense, cold, and scary. Inside, Elrabin was cursing himself for getting into this. "My apologies. I can learn your rules. Selling dust is better than starving. And I need your protection."

Barthul and Scar stared at him a long, tense moment. "Glad you see it our way," Barthul said. Peeling up his broad lip, he dug out a string of food from between his teeth and flicked it away. Then he gestured at Scar, who went back to leaning against the wall.

Elrabin stared at the youth doubtfully. Could he just switch it on and off—the willingness to kill? Did taking life mean so little to him that he actually didn't care one way or another?

Elrabin panted. "I'll follow orders," he said, feeling ashamed of himself. But desperation canceled out good intentions every time.

"See?" Scar said.

"Nah," Barthul replied. "This one's a *nolo,* a fool."

"So?"

Scar grinned in his lopsided, insolent way, and after a moment Barthul tilted back his head and guffawed, holding his round sides. "I got you," he said in approval. "Run a double blind and bluff them."

"Yeah."

Barthul nodded and slapped Scar on the shoulder. "Good, good," he said. "Train him and put him on the run."

He handed Scar a slim pouch of something, and Scar slipped it out of sight fast into his pocket. Satisfaction gleamed in Scar's eyes and he went on smiling to himself as Barthul walked out.

Elrabin watched Scar warily. "So I'm in?" he said.

The smile faded from Scar's eyes. He looked almost angry again. "Yeah, no thanks to you," he said with a growl. "You really that stupid or is it fever you got?"

Choosing not to answer that one, Elrabin glanced around. "Do I stay here?"

"No." Scar walked over to the cabinet and unlocked the top drawer with a quick punch of numbers on the keypad that he concealed from Elrabin with his body.

The drawer popped open, and Scar pulled out a basin and a couple of medical packets in bright pink foil.

Seeing them, Elrabin's eyes widened. Those were medical packets from an actual Viis clinic, the kind of place he couldn't afford back in good times, even if they admitted abiru, which they didn't. He watched Scar's nimble hands break the seals and spill out the stolen contents.

"Real medicine," Elrabin breathed, impressed. This wasn't the synthetic, cheap stuff. This would do him good. He couldn't believe Scar's generosity. "Thank you."

"Don't thank me," Scar said irritably. He slapped a medicine patch onto Elrabin's left shoulder with more force than was necessary for it to stick.

The effect on Elrabin's bloodstream was immediate and soothing. He stopped bracing himself against the pain, feeling it fade, and let out his breath in a long whoosh.

Scar put the basin in Elrabin's lap and draped his septic arm across it. "Hold still. This ain't pretty, but it works."

He swiped the needle-thin blade of his sticker with disinfectant and slashed down the infected streak in Elrabin's arm. Despite the painkiller, Elrabin felt the cut burn through him.

He jerked in a breath, but Scar glared at him and after his initial flinch Elrabin didn't move again.

Blood, bright and filled with angry pus, splattered into the basin. Scar opened the infected incision with another quick, sure slash of his blade, as delicate and precise with it as a surgeon. Then he uncapped a bottle of brown liquid and poured it liberally over the cuts.

Elrabin expected that to hurt like fire, but it didn't. The liquid felt cool and soothing. He relaxed again as the drugs took hold in his system, and without concern watched himself bleed into the bowl.

After a short time, Scar bandaged him, ripped off the painkiller patch, and applied something else instead. He emptied and cleaned the basin, and threw out the used foil packets. Locking the cabinet once more, he hoisted Elrabin to his feet.

"You come," he said, supporting most of Elrabin's weight.

Elrabin was floating. If his feet moved at all, he couldn't

feel them. They went along the tunnel to another room, a larger one fitted with several bunks. Most of them were occupied. Snoring buzzed in the room.

Scar lowered Elrabin to a bunk and tossed a blanket over him. "You sleep," he ordered. "In morning, no fever. You be ready to work, yeah?"

"Yeah," Elrabin mumbled drowsily. He wanted to find the words to thank Scar for his help, but his tongue felt too large and clumsy to talk now.

Scar stood over him a moment longer, a silent, slim shadow in the gloom. "Yeah," he said softly, his tone low and grim. "Stupid little citizen. Think you found a home. You ain't found nothing but trouble."

Elrabin heard Scar's voice from far away, a sound too distant to listen to. "Scar?" he said, seeking reassurance.

Scar leaned over him and put his hand briefly on Elrabin's brow, where Magathin used to lick him when he was little. "Sleep," Scar said gruffly, and walked away.

CHAPTER THIRTEEN

The Kaa shifted on his high-backed chair and sighed. Kneeling at his feet, Ampris dared steal a quick peek at his face, then quickly looked down again. He looked so bleak, like a stranger. With all her heart she wanted to ask about Israi, but she dared say nothing. Without turning her head, she tried to look toward Israi's bed to see how her friend was doing, but the angle was all wrong.

"Ampris." The Kaa's deep voice made her jump. "This is a terrible day."

Gaveid prodded her again with his staff, and Ampris bowed lower until her head nearly touched the floor. "Yes, sire," she whispered. Because she was Aaroun and not Viis, she could not call him Imperial Father as the others at court did. "A very terrible day."

"You are beloved of the Imperial Daughter," the Kaa said. "For her sake, we will allow you to tell us what occurred on the side of the mountain."

Although stern, his voice held no anger, no accusation. Relieved, Ampris looked up. "Will she be all right? Is she badly hurt?"

The Kaa's rill lifted, and Chancellor Gaveid cleared his throat in hasty warning.

Ampris gulped and lowered her eyes at once.

"It is the Imperial Father who asks the questions," Gaveid told her. "Not you."

She nodded, keeping her gaze down. "I'm sorry," she whispered, trying not to whimper.

Silence fell over the room, and the chancellor sighed. "Perhaps another approach is needed, sire."

The Kaa gestured assent and leaned his head back wearily against his chair.

"Ampris," Gaveid said in a gentle voice, "why did you and the Imperial Daughter avoid the main trail?"

It was easier to talk to the chancellor than the Kaa. In relief, Ampris turned to Gaveid. "The shortcut is quicker and more fun."

"It is dangerous."

Ampris shrugged. "We've been up it before."

The Kaa made a faint sound but gestured for the chancellor to continue.

"Was it your idea to take the Imperial Daughter up this trail?"

"No," Ampris answered honestly. "We were trying to hurry to avoid Lady Lenith. We were going on a picnic, you see, and she would have had us spend the afternoon doing needle art or something boring."

"Why did the Imperial Daughter not take her guards as she was supposed to?"

Ampris backed her ears, wondering how to explain the obvious to an adult. "We were *pretending*," she said at last. "It's hard to do that with them along."

"Why did you urge the Imperial Daughter to keep climbing when Lord Fazhmind called out to her to return?"

"But I didn't."

Gaveid's cynical yellow eyes grew quite cold, and he inflated his air sacs. "On the contrary, cub," he said very gently. "Lord Fazhmind witnessed you doing exactly that."

"I didn't."

"Denial does not alter what he has said. The Imperial Daughter walked before you up the trail, as was proper, until Lord Fazhmind called out. Then you pushed ahead of her and pulled her onto the rocks after you."

"Oh, that," Ampris said, comprehending now. "We were wearing these silly old costumes, as part of our pretending, but they were too long and awfully in the way."

"Most unsuitable garments," the chancellor agreed. His eyes watched her like a raptul's.

"So I took mine off, but Israi—the sri-Kaa—kept hers on. I'm a better climber than she is, so I climbed to the ledge first so I could pull her up after me. She knows I am stronger and said it would be easier for me to assist her that way than to boost her from behind."

"I see. And again, you did this by the sri-Kaa's order?"

"Well . . ." Ampris frowned, trying to remember. "Yes, or perhaps I suggested it and she agreed to it. All I know is, we didn't want to go back down. We were going to hide from Lord Fazhmind."

The Kaa flicked out his tongue, and both Ampris and Gaveid glanced at him.

He gestured impatiently. "Continue."

Gaveid bowed. "Now, Ampris, about the—"

"But if Lord Fazhmind says that I made Israi climb up the rocks, that isn't so," Ampris said hotly. "He was too far down the mountain to see everything that happened. He couldn't hear what was said—we wanted to get away from him, so we were hurrying too fast. The sri-Kaa started climbing above the ledge by herself, without waiting for me to help her. I didn't see how she slipped, but suddenly she was falling. If I hadn't—"

She stopped, panting and near tears, reliving the horror of that moment in her mind.

"Yes?" the chancellor prodded. "If you hadn't what?"

"If I hadn't caught her by the leg, she would have gone over the ledge and maybe been killed. When she fainted, I thought she *was* dead." Tears choked Ampris's voice, and she could no longer hold them back. "I got Moscar—"

"A servant, sire," Gaveid said in a quick aside.

"We wrapped her in a blanket, and he started carrying her down the mountain. That's all that happened. It wasn't anyone's fault. She slipped." Ampris sniffed and licked away the tears dampening her muzzle. "If Lord Fazhmind wants to blame anyone, let it be himself for following us—"

"Silence," Gaveid snapped. "You are here to give an account of yourself, not to accuse your betters."

From the bed, Israi moaned.

At once the Kaa shot from his chair and hurried to her side. He bent over her, stroking her rill as he murmured to her.

"Ampris," Israi called.

Ampris ran to her, eluding the chancellor's grab at her shoulder.

Israi lay curled among her nest of pillows, looking the color of dust beneath a bandage across her left temple. Her arms and hands were bruised and scraped. Her green eyes were heavy with drugs, but she smiled when she saw Ampris crowding next to the Kaa's side.

"Ampris," she whispered again, and tried to stretch out her hand.

Ampris would have moved closer to touch her fingers, but the Kaa gripped her shoulder, holding her back.

"You must rest, precious one," he said, his voice thick with emotion. "Go back to sleep."

Israi looked at him, blinking slowly, her green eyes clouded and dull. "I heard you talking. Don't be angry. I didn't wait for her to help me. I didn't take off the robe like she . . . urged me to." Israi's eyes drifted closed. "My fault," she murmured, and fell asleep.

The Kaa bent over her and blew gently across her ear dimple, then straightened and stood staring down at Ampris. This time she met his gaze without fear.

He stared at her for what seemed like forever before

something indefinable shifted in the depths of his brilliant blue eyes. "We see," he said. "Very well."

Turning from the bedside, he walked away. Ampris took a step after him.

"May I stay with her, sire?"

The Kaa paused in mid-stride and glanced back. "It is what she would wish."

He walked on, and his guards hastened to open the doors for him. In the outer sitting room, muffled commotion rose up as the ladies jumped to their feet and asked questions. The physician returned to Israi's bedside, and the doors were closed, shutting out the noise.

Gaveid stood on the crimson runner of carpet and beckoned to Ampris, who joined him.

"As faithful as ever," he murmured. "You have been a good companion for the sri-Kaa, despite all the consternation you have caused."

Ampris grinned.

"But it is not enough to be a simple follower," he admonished her. "Doing whatever she suggests, and agreeing to her schemes. The sri-Kaa is headstrong and impetuous. She runs with a very light rein indeed, and in his devoted love for her, the Kaa has perhaps been too lenient. I believe you have some common sense in that Aaroun head of yours. Do you?"

Perhaps a hundred years spanned between their ages, yet at that moment Ampris felt in complete accord with the chancellor. "I think so, Lord Gaveid," she said.

"Time you both grew up a little. The freedom of taschunenhal is passing."

Ampris backed her ears. She didn't want to hear what he was saying, yet at the same time she knew he was right. It was frightening, but Israi's injuries were frightening too.

"Lord Fazhmind has no influence with the sri-Kaa, and Lady Lenith very little," Gaveid continued. "You, on the other hand, are her most intimate companion. And although you are young, I believe you capable of using good sense when it comes to these escapades. Persuade her toward more caution, toward safer adventures.''

''But she says what we will do—''

''Does she?'' Lord Gaveid flicked out his tongue. ''Does she think of everything?''

Ampris met his wise gaze and could not lie. Reluctantly she shook her head.

''Ah,'' he said. ''Then you understand me.''

He turned to go, and Ampris looked from him to the physician, who was running a scanner over Israi. She ran after Gaveid. ''Please, my lord. Is she going to die?''

''Hmm?'' He paused reluctantly and raised his rill when he realized she was clutching his sleeve.

Ampris released him and stepped back. ''Please. No one will tell me anything.''

''No, of course she isn't going to die. She has a broken rib and some painful cuts and scrapes. According to the physician, her beauty will not be marred by these injuries.'' Gaveid's cynical eyes softened a moment and he patted Ampris on the head. ''You weep for the sri-Kaa, little one?''

Ampris wiped her eyes, too overwhelmed with relief to speak.

''Ah,'' he said, his tone strange. ''In all the imperial court, who cares more deeply than a half-domesticated Aaroun? Truly, the Imperial Daughter chose well in you, cub. I trust she will always remember your value.''

''Of course.'' Ampris didn't understand him. It was as though he spoke with hidden meanings to his words. ''I will always be her friend. Always. And she mine. We *promised*.''

''Ah.'' He patted her head again. ''Stay with her, cub. She calls for you every time she wakes.''

Israi recovered very quickly, while everyone spoiled her and brought her presents as tokens of their good wishes. The Kaa visited her twice daily. Lord Fazhmind and Lady

Lenith were banned from the sickroom, and Israi gloated over this.

"They have been dismissed from my service," she said. "I am sure of it. Don't you think so, Ampris? Oh, I hope so. They are tedious, both of them."

This hope proved to be unfounded. But it was the physician's recommendation that Israi be released from her lessons and responsibilities until summer, to ensure a complete recovery of both body and spirit. Thus, Lady Lenith was given leave to visit her family. Lord Fazhmind remained at court, but without assigned duties.

When Israi was deemed well enough to travel, the Kaa returned to the imperial palace at Vir. By then, the buds were beginning to swell in the palace gardens as harbingers of spring. All talk focused on the coming Festival. Ladies at court grew absentminded and silly, neglecting their duties and giggling at the least provocation. Ambassadors brought new wives to the Kaa, who made his selections and sent the others to his country estates.

Ampris and Israi ran free, roaming the palace at will, keeping whatever hours they chose, eating whatever they liked, doing what they pleased. They had no routine, no lessons, no one to hinder their fun.

Subi, the old Kelth nursemaid, grumbled and tried to impose order, but they only laughed at her.

The physician's methods apparently worked. Israi not only healed without a blemish, but she blossomed as well. She grew several inches that spring, and her coloring acquired a new glow that gave her beauty a hint of coming maturity. She was at the age where most adolescent Viis females become gawky and impossible. But Israi remained graceful, slender, and lovely. Her voice deepened slightly, becoming more melodic than ever. The slope of her jaw, the brightness of her teeth, the brilliance of her eyes, the arch of her throat arrested the gaze of everyone who saw her. New courtiers, upon catching a glimpse of her, often lost the thread of their conversations. Older courtiers gazed at her with knowing looks, murmuring behind their fans.

The sri-Kaa was growing up.

But neither Israi nor Ampris were ready to acknowledge that. They had these last few months of freedom, as though tas-chunenhal and all its magic had been given an extension, and they were determined to make the most of it.

They played harder than ever, giggling and pulling pranks on everyone in the palace except the Kaa and Chancellor Gaveid. Even the lesser chancellors and ministers were not exempt.

Visitors of minor importance discovered unpleasant surprises in their beds. Hot water was mysteriously cut off from all the bathing chambers for an entire day. Wives found bitter salt in their desserts because pranksters had substituted it for sweetener in the kitchens. Lord Fazhmind found soilworms in his drinking cup and exploding powder in his kerchiefs. Bizarre, alien music was piped into his bedchamber in the dead of night, giving him nightmares.

The majordomo of the palace, in charge of the immense and complex preparations for Sahvrazaa, lived in agonized fear that the pranksters would sabotage the banquets and ruin his life.

Complaints ran rife in the palace, yet no one dared demand punishment. The Kaa himself, vaguely aware that Israi was up to considerable mischief, merely remarked that it was splendid she felt so energetic. Therefore, nothing could be done to stop her, and everyone prayed that she would soon tire of these games and leave them in peace.

Then Lady Zureal arrived at court, and the pranks stopped cold.

Ampris and Israi were lying idly in the shade near the garden pool one day when Ampris heard a commotion from inside. She sat up, listening.

"More new candidates for the wives court have arrived," she said eagerly. "Do you want to go and look at them?"

Israi rolled onto her side and draped her arm across her

eye. "No," she said, sounding bored. "I am sleepy."

"May I go?"

Israi lifted her arm just enough to shoot Ampris a look of exasperation. "Why do you care about them? New wives are always silly. They overdress and wear too much perfume. All they can do is giggle and stare at themselves in the mirrors."

"I want to see what they are wearing. I want to see their jewels," Ampris said.

Israi flicked out her tongue and said nothing.

Ampris stared at her a moment. Israi had been in a strange mood all day, grouchy and lazy. All she wanted to do was lie by the pool, and Ampris was bored. Anything, even staring at fine court ladies, was preferable to this.

"Please?" Ampris asked.

"Yes, yes, go," Israi said with irritation. "At least then you will be quiet and I can nap in peace."

Her words were unkind, for Ampris had not been chattering to her. Ampris let it pass, however, and bounded up before Israi could change her mind.

She trotted through the loggia and its welcome shade, then entered through open doors into the long gallery. Her feet made no sound on the polished stone floors, and she hurried to catch up with the courtiers gathering in the main audience hall to observe the official arrival and presentation of this last batch of imperial brides.

Ampris elbowed her way through the crowd, and the onlookers reluctantly made way for her to edge to the front, where she could see without hindrance. In the past month Ampris had suddenly shot up in height, growing gawky and ill at ease with her changing body. She found herself clumsy when she had never been so before. Her hands and feet did not seem to belong to her. She had outgrown her clothes twice, making Subi grumble about the cost and bother of replacements. And she was hungry all the time, constantly craving meat, which was not allowed her. Lady Lenith said she was getting too big. Feeling ugly and in-

creasingly self-conscious, Ampris sometimes worried that
Israi would send her away for having changed so much.

Now, she took care not to venture too near the most
important courtiers or to stand too close to the carpet runner
stretching from the main entrance to the Kaa's throne. She
ignored the whispers from those who disapproved of her
appearing in public when Israi was not present to command
her.

However, the imminent presentation of the brides created
a general air of excitement that soon eclipsed Ampris's
presence. The hall filled with whispering and speculation,
and as always Ampris enjoyed watching and listening. She
didn't understand why Israi wanted to miss the fun.

New spring fashions among Viis females dictated a fuller
sweep in the skirts of court gowns, creating an angular line
in the back that completely concealed their tails and made
their upper bodies look slender and long. Ampris liked the
new style, although she was grateful she didn't have to
dress in such a way.

The hall smelled of fragrant white flowers, the Kaa's
favorite, and soft flyta music played in the background.
Then ceremonial chimes sounded, and a procession of sing-
ers in green cloaks entered, tossing flower petals as they
came. Behind them walked the brides, veiled and gowned
in breathtaking regalia. Each female was escorted by her
sponsoring ambassador, in full court uniform.

One by one, they were led to the foot of the throne. A
page uttered each lady's name, and the ambassador unveiled her before the Kaa. She bowed low and presented a
small gift token, then stood with blushing rill and downcast
eyes while the Kaa scrutinized her. Beside the Kaa stood a
minister with a data screen of bloodlines and family histories, constantly murmuring information to the sovereign.

The Kaa never hurried his selection, allowing anticipation to fill the hall as everyone watched breathlessly. All
the brides were here as the result of long and delicate ne-
gotiations that went on throughout the year. However, those

personally selected by the Kaa today would remain at court with the supreme standing of favorite wife. Each would be specially courted by the Kaa in the next few weeks as Festival approached, and on the special day, the favored few would go to the sacred Chamber of Hatching to lay their eggs. Those not smiled at today would be taken away from court, forever to live pampered, secluded lives, but far from the Kaa and his circle.

The last bride was presented and unveiled. A collective *aah* rose from the watching courtiers.

"The Lady Zureal," announced the ambassador, and she bowed to the Kaa.

Even Ampris caught her breath, for Zureal was lovely. Green-skinned with delicate bone structure and graceful movements, she possessed large, tilted eyes of an exotic shade of amethyst. As the Kaa stared at her, she extended her rill above its jeweled collar, and it blushed a matching hue of delicate purple.

"Lady Zureal is newly adult, sire," the ambassador said. "She begs you to accept this token of her devotion."

The Kaa rose to his feet—a sign of great honor—and smiled at the lady. He took her gift with his own hand, making the spectators gasp and nudge each other. His gaze never left the lady's sweet countenance.

"We are well-pleased," he said, and her rill blushed again.

Taking her hand, he led her away without warning. He did not bother to dismiss the courtiers, to take his farewell from the ambassadors, or to give even a second glance to the other brides, who stood stricken with drooping rills.

Stunned silence filled the hall, then as the Kaa vanished with his new favorite, a loud buzz arose.

"Well," said a courtier near Ampris. *"Well."*

"Indeed," agreed another. "Have you ever seen her equal?"

"She almost rivals the sri-Kaa's beauty."

"Almost! I would venture that she surpasses it."

Ampris waited to hear no more. Bursting with the news, she went rushing back to the garden to tell Israi all that she had seen.

"Oh, hush," Israi said, still bored and cranky. "I told you I care nothing for these creatures. There is a new favorite every year. It means nothing."

"But Lady Zureal is beautiful," Ampris said in excitement. "Such coloring. Everyone is talking about her. And the Kaa could not take his gaze from her. Truly, she is exotic. She blushes purple, not indigo."

"Purple!" Israi sat up and flicked out her tongue in disgust. "I have never heard of something so silly. Who could be enchanted with that?"

"But it matches the color of her eyes. She is different." Israi's rill darkened. "How different?"

"Like nothing ever seen. Everyone—"

"I am not interested in the opinions of the court," Israi said sharply. "Is she *really* beautiful?"

Ampris sighed and nodded. "Breathtaking."

A strange light appeared in Israi's eyes. "More beautiful than I?"

Ampris had not foreseen that question. She hesitated, warned too late by Israi's darkening rill. "Well, she is different," she said clumsily.

"As you said."

"No one could be more beautiful than you, Israi," Ampris said out of loyalty, yet . . . "It is hard to explain. She moves like she's gliding on water. When you're adult, you'll also—"

"Also!" Israi said in a huff, jumping to her feet. She kicked her pillows into the pool, where they bobbed and floated like fat, blood-red water blossoms. "There is no *also!* How dare you compare her to me!"

"That isn't what I meant," Ampris said hastily, trying to avert the coming tantrum. "I was trying to explain that she's—"

"I don't wish to discuss her further," Israi said. "Which

is better, a lady who walks like she's gliding on water—or me, when I have been compared to the lightness of a summer's breeze?''

''You, of course. You're magnificent,'' Ampris said, trying to soothe her. ''After all, you're golden-skinned and she's only—''

''What?'' Israi demanded. ''What is her color? Blue?''

''Green,'' Ampris said, and waited.

Israi's eyes widened, then narrowed. She tilted her head to one side. ''Green?'' she asked smugly.

Ampris nodded. ''Green.''

Israi hooted in triumph. ''The most *common* hue! Then she is nothing compared to me. Nothing!''

''Well, no, but her combination is striking,'' Ampris said.

''Phoo,'' Israi said, dismissing this quibble. ''Striking combinations fade. In a year, she'll be nothing at all out of the ordinary. I'll even wager that she's had her rill altered, for it to turn such a hue.''

Ampris gasped in shock. ''Would she dare?''

''Oh, yes, she would,'' Israi said with all the wisdom of being both older and more sophisticated. ''I've heard how the wives talk. There is so much competition among brides to be selected as favorites that they'll do anything, submit themselves to *any* procedure, in order to enhance their looks. When my father finds out, she'll be exiled faster than she can blink.''

It seemed a shame to Ampris, for Lady Zureal really was pretty, but she wasn't about to say so to Israi. The near-tantrum had been averted, and Ampris wasn't going to risk another.

''Come on!'' Israi grabbed Ampris's hand, and together they ran from the garden.

''Where are we going?'' Ampris asked, taking care not to outrun Israi.

''Somewhere different to think. I need a plan.''

''What sort of plan?''

"I want to play the ultimate prank, and I need inspiration."

Ampris couldn't keep herself from sighing. "Haven't we played enough pranks?"

"But this one will be supreme," Israi said, her green eyes glowing.

"Fazhmind isn't even funny to watch anymore," Ampris said, bored with the idea. "He just yells and his rill turns red."

"We aren't going to bother with Fazhmind," Israi said with scorn.

"Who, then?"

Israi laughed and yanked Ampris to a halt behind a carved stone pillar. She put her finger between her nostrils in warning and glanced around to make sure no one could overhear.

"The Lady Zureal," she whispered.

"What?"

"Don't look so shocked. She's the perfect target."

"But—but she's a bride. Festival is coming!"

"Yes, isn't that perfect? No one will expect us to pick on her."

"But that's unkind."

Israi stared at her. "Ampris! Are you on my side, or hers?"

"Yours, of course."

"Then stop objecting. I want to think up something that will drive her away."

"But if she's the new—"

"Hush! We'll make her hysterical and silly. She'll plead to be sent away. It will be wonderful!"

Ampris didn't like what she was hearing. She looked at her friend in dismay. "You mean, just because Lady Zureal is beautiful, you want to drive her away from court? You don't want her to be a possible rival to you in looks? Is that why?"

Israi's rill snapped up. "How dare you say such a thing

to me. You are not allowed to question me.''

Ampris flinched, but she didn't back down. ''Then who will, if I do not?''

''You *are* on her side,'' Israi said in outrage. ''You like her better than me.''

''Of course not. I couldn't,'' Ampris said. ''It's just that if you pick on her, you make her important. And you're the sri-Kaa, while she's only a wife. Shouldn't you be kind, if you're—''

''Get away from me,'' Israi said, furious. ''You've turned against me. You think I'm wrong. You won't help me. Then go fawn over her, if that's what you want. Go!''

''But, Israi—''

Israi snapped at her blindly, and missed. Hissing, the sri-Kaa pushed away from Ampris and ran off, leaving Ampris to stare after her in dismay.

''You argue with sri-Kaa?'' Subi said from behind Ampris. ''Bad, you are.''

Ampris turned to the old nursemaid, whose fur smelled of cleaning powder and age. ''You overheard us?''

''I hear enough.''

Frustration welled up inside Ampris. ''I don't understand her. She doesn't have to be jealous of Zureal. It's silly.''

''Nothing is silly when you are young Viis female, growing up.''

Shocked, Ampris stared wide-eyed at the old Kelth. ''She isn't growing up. Not yet!''

''The time is coming. She is not of age yet to have eggs, but she feels the urges of Festival this year. They confuse her. She does not understand what she feels yet, but next year or the year after that, she will. It will be better then.''

''I don't feel any urges,'' Ampris said. Yet even as she spoke she wondered, for she was much bigger than she used to be, and more impatient. Sometimes she ached and felt restless. Was this growing up? ''Festival is just a time to dress in fancy clothes and have fun,'' she insisted.

Subi bared her yellowed teeth. "That is because you are not Viis."

"Well, I'm glad. If you have to throw fits and yell at people and hate everyone, I'd rather be Aaroun and never grow up," Ampris said. "I don't see why she has to act this way."

Subi gave Ampris a little push. "You go find her. Play with her. Make her happy again. This anger, it will pass."

"She doesn't want to be my friend anymore. She's angry with me."

"Not with you. At what she feels. Make her happy, Ampris. That is your responsibility."

Backing her ears, Ampris struggled to make Subi understand that things weren't that simple. Israi was acting like a stranger, and Ampris didn't think she could reach her.

"Agree with her. Play her games," Subi said, almost as though she could read Ampris's mind. "Let her run free. Don't stop her in whatever she wants to do."

Ampris blinked. "You're always saying we should have rules."

"This is her last spring to be ta-chune," Subi said. "When she becomes vi-adult, all will be different."

"But—"

"Run after her, now, and play what she wants. It is not your place to be her guide or conscience."

That was just the opposite of what Chancellor Gaveid had said. Ampris didn't bother trying to sort it out. What mattered was that Israi was angry with her. Subi's advice made sense, and soon Ampris was running through the palace to catch up with her and try again to be the faithful, unquestioning companion that Israi wanted her to be.

CHAPTER FOURTEEN

Israi wasn't in sight. She could have gone anywhere within the vast palace complex. She was adept at following old passageways, sneaking along the servant routes, and evading just about anyone who wanted to find her. But she could not hide from Ampris, who tracked her scent from the wives court, through the main public section, and on along the old concourse that led into the original structures, where restoration work was now in progress.

Slaves of all races hammered, cut, carved, and polished in a ceaseless cacophony, punctuated by shouted instructions from supervisors and the architects.

The area smelled of paint, heated metal, and laborer sweat. A fine coating of white dust covered everything. Two specialized construction robots worked independently, hoisting support beams and soldering bolts into place. But Ampris saw a line of dead robots stacked in a discard heap along one wall. She wasn't surprised. Most machinery like that was antiquated and failed to work well. The Viis, especially the Kaa, preferred hand labor. It provided a special quality to whatever was being constructed. Indeed, the restoration process seemed to require extensive amounts of

skilled handcrafting, for Ampris saw such workers everywhere.

At present, most of the work was focused on what had
been the original throne room. As she scurried past, Ampris
caught a glimpse of a vast chamber every bit as large as
the audience hall currently in use. Scaffolding filled the
throne room from floor to ceiling, and workers swarmed up
and down with buckets and tools. Plasterers and carvers
crouched at the very top of the scaffolding with their shoulders hunched against the vaulting beams, busy restoring the
ceiling to its former magnificence. At a distance from the
scaffolding, a Myal balanced on tall stilts with his prehensile tail stuck out behind him for balance was skillfully
applying gold leaf to the delicate leaves carved into a wall
panel. A Viis architect stood in the center of the room,
wearing the white cape of his profession and pointing to a
holographic schematic as he explained something to a second Viis in an artist's sash. The two were arguing vehe-
mently, frequently stabbing their fingers into the holo image
or making sweeping gestures at the ceiling far overhead.

Israi was not in there. Sneezing against the dust, Ampris
hurried on.

It was hard to follow Israi's trail through the construction
zone. Chemical and construction smells overlaid Israi's
scent, and Ampris found it difficult to imagine why the sri-
Kaa would come to such a dirty and noisy section of the
palace.

She turned a corner and saw Israi standing next to a pillar
swathed with drop cloths. The sri-Kaa had her back partially to Ampris and did not see her approach. Israi was
scowling into the distance, and her green eyes held deep
unhappiness.

Remembering what Subi had said, Ampris walked up to
her and nuzzled the back of her rill with simple affection.

"I'm sorry," Ampris said. "I was wrong to argue with
you. Please forgive me."

Israi flashed her an angry glare and turned away. Her slender back was rigid, her rill dark indigo.

"Please," Ampris said, anxious to make amends. "I shall do anything you say. Let's think up a way to really ruin Lady Zureal's happiness."

Israi glared at her again. "Don't say it like that," she said. "Why must you sympathize with her?"

"I don't," Ampris said, holding back a sigh. She'd erred again, but she wasn't sure how. "I'm on your side. I promise. Maybe we could put dye into her cosmetics and turn her face a strange color."

Israi released a gusty sigh and walked on without looking back.

Ampris frowned, patiently following at Israi's heels. Israi said nothing, but that was all right. If she was still angry, she would have ordered Ampris to leave her. It took time for Israi's temper to cool. Soon she would be full of smiles and mischief again, and all would be well.

The farther they walked, the cleaner and quieter the passageway became. The construction noise faded behind them, and there was only the smell of clean, polished stone and new plaster. Relieved, Ampris blew through her nostrils to clear them.

Ahead, the passageway ended at a closed set of doors beneath an archway of dressed stone. Above it hung an inscription that Ampris could not read.

Israi paused, tipping back her head to look at it. "Knowledge is for the many," she read aloud. "What a quaint saying."

"What language is it?" Ampris asked.

"Viis, silly."

"But I can't read it."

"Old Viis," Israi said impatiently. "Two thousand years ago. When this palace was first built."

"Oh."

Ampris squinted at the letters, but they were no more decipherable than before.

"The year four hundred ninety-five, in the third dynasty of the Vrahd," said a quiet voice from behind them. "That's when that quotation was chiseled into the stone and a library was established to hold the palace records."

Ampris and Israi turned, and found a Myal standing there with a neatly wrapped package in his hands.

Ampris sniffed and knew the package held his lunch. She could smell a fruit medley tossed in a light vinaigrette mixed with stouraseeds and honey.

He was short, coming no taller than her shoulder, although he was adult. He had stippled black and silver fur, very distinguished, and a full silver mane floated in silky strands about his intelligent face. Something alert and kind in his black eyes made Ampris like him immediately.

He carried his long prehensile tail neatly curled and tucked up against his hindquarters. His short, bowed legs and soft pouchy belly made him look like a scholar.

Israi wore her haughty expression, standing straight and tall with her head held high. Her green eyes glittered in sudden tension.

Ampris took one look at her and stepped quietly between her friend and this stranger. Although he was only a Myal, and probably harmless, Ampris found her heart beating faster.

It was one thing to run freely about the safe confines of the new palace, with guards stationed at the doors to provide unobtrusive protection and courtiers and attendants always nearby. It was another thing to venture here, deep into the old palace, with its unknown corners, construction laborers, locked-away sections that were completely fallen into ruin and disuse, and lack of security. Ampris found herself very conscious of Israi's vulnerability. Without attendants of any kind, the sri-Kaa had only Ampris as protection.

The fur on Ampris's neck bristled, and she stood ready to defend her friend.

"Who are you?" Ampris asked, making the question a challenge.

The Myal smiled in a gentle, friendly way. He made no threatening moves, and seemed either unaware of or uninterested in their alarm. "Bish is my name," he said. "Chief archivist of the libraries and records."

He spoke his answer in the Viis language, not in slave patois. Ampris thought she was the only abiru allowed to speak Viis. She took immediate offense.

"Bow when you speak," she said sharply. "Are you Viis, to speak in the tongue of your masters? Keep your eyes down. Show respect to the sri-Kaa!"

Bish's dark eyes widened. He gasped slightly and gave Israi a deep bow. "Forgive me," he said with the utmost respect in his tone, although he still spoke Viis. "The sri Kaa I did not recognize. No one informed us of an official visit."

Ampris's temper grew hot. From deep in her throat came a rumbling growl.

"Ampris!" Israi said in swift rebuke. "Stop that. He is an archivist and researcher. He has the right to use our language."

Ampris blinked, feeling both undermined and foolish. "Why?"

Israi flicked out her tongue, and Ampris bowed her head, letting the question drop at once.

Already she knew the answer. Bish could speak Viis because it was allowed by the complexities of court protocol. Archivists, whatever they were, clearly had privileges.

"Well, Bish," Israi said, doing her best to achieve the lofty tones of ennui affected by so many courtiers, "we have come unannounced in an unofficial capacity. What in the Archives will you show us?"

Bish bowed low again. "The sri-Kaa honors me with the presence of herself and her golden pet. Of course. I should have immediately recognized the golden pair of such renown. For such an error, may I be forgiven? As for the

Archives, the entire collection stands at the Imperial
Daughter's disposal. All can be seen, if the Imperial Daughter has time."

Israi gave him a dignified gesture, and Ampris struggled
to hold back a giggle. She knew how much Israi loved to
play the grand lady, and this silly Myal believed every bit
of it. Ampris knew Israi would let Bish chatter on with his
boring lectures until the tour was actually started, then she
would back out and leave him standing there looking foolish, puzzled as to how he had offended.

Stepping around them, Bish approached the doors and
spoke a clear command in coded words.

A light flashed upon him from overhead, scanning him.
Then the doors unlocked and swung slowly open.

Bish hurried inside and bowed to Israi again. "Please
enter."

Ampris met Israi's eyes and saw the mischief gleaming
there. Again, she stifled a giggle. "Isn't he boring?" she
whispered. "Are you actually going in?"

Israi blinked at her in their secret look. "Yes," she whispered back. "I want ideas for our next project."

They laughed together.

"Please," Bish said. "Come inside."

Another worry touched Ampris, and she tugged at Israi's
sleeve. "Is it safe? Without your guards?"

"Don't be so protective. Of course it's safe." With her
head held high, Israi swept inside.

Ampris followed, and the doors swung shut automatically behind her.

"The Archives were the first part of the restoration project to be completed," Bish said proudly. He gestured at
the room around them. "This main exhibit chamber and
two other areas are redone. Our offices have been updated,
and my staff is busy cataloging an incredible warren of old
materials. It will take us years to sort through everything.
A fabulous opportunity for study lies here."

At first Ampris wondered when they planned to fill this

empty room, then as Bish and Israi walked on, with Bish chatting and pointing out various items to the sri-Kaa, she realized the room was *supposed* to be empty. Only what hung on the walls held any importance.

She glanced around and caught her breath. Panel after panel of constellation maps depicted various populated worlds within the far-flung Viis empire. Despite the political and civics lessons Ampris had yawned her way through, for the first time she received a very clear, graphic grasp of just how immense the Viis holdings were.

Beyond the constellation panels hung holograms of planets rotating in midair, delineated perfectly to scale, with continents and oceans sliding beneath the clouds of atmosphere.

Israi stopped between two spinning planets and laughed. "Rogis Four and Mynchepop . . . Father *loves* Mynchepop. He speaks of it often. He has promised me that when I reach adulthood I may travel there."

"From all accounts it is a world of breathtaking beauty," Bish said agreeably.

He glanced at Ampris and pointed at another planet, a small, dusty brown world that spun slowly as though tired. A slender band of water encircled its equator. The rest was solid landmass.

"Homeworld of the Aarouns," he said quietly to Ampris, his black eyes bright and watchful. "The origin point of your race, young cub."

Startled, Ampris frowned at him, then stared at the planet in curiosity. It was an ugly world, especially when compared to others with interesting continents mottled green between large blue oceans.

She wondered what it had been like to live on such a small, brown world, and could not imagine it. Still, Aarouns had come from it. Her ancestors had once walked its ground and breathed its air. The idea of it intrigued her. For the first time, she could visualize the homeworld as an actual place.

"What is it called?" she asked.

"Bish!" Israi said imperiously before he could reply. "I wish to examine the jewelry collection. My father has told me much about the old State jewels, but I have never seen them."

Bish bowed to her at once. "Yes, of course. They are locked in the special vaults on a floor below this one. Let us go down."

But as he spoke, he glanced at Ampris again and touched a button on the projector base beneath the planet hologram. Aaroun homeworld vanished and in its stead appeared a vista of open sky tinged a pearly-gray hue with wide grasslands spread beneath it. Hot, dry wind gusted into Ampris's face, and she smelled a mingled wealth of new scents: the bitter, herbal scent of the tall grass, the hot arid ground, and an animal scent—perhaps that of a small fearful rodent. Instincts inside her quickened automatically. Her mouth watered with an unfamiliar anticipation. Her nose twitched, attuning itself as she located the rodent nibbling at the roots of the grass stems. She focused on it, feeling her muscles ripple across her back. It was prey.

"Ampris!" Israi said sharply. "Have you gone deaf? Come at once."

Startled, and with a feeling of disorientation, Ampris came back to the here and now.

Bish pushed a button, and the grasslands vanished, leaving only the spinning planet in their place.

Ampris frowned in disappointment, finding herself yearning to see more.

"Come," Bish said gently to her. "There are other things to show you."

Again she followed Israi and Bish, this time down a narrow spiraling staircase into a darker, more cramped region of small exhibit rooms, offices, and cleaning chambers that held long tables stacked with rotting fabrics and rusted artifacts. They walked past a library holding scroll cases, bound volumes, fragile tape spools, disks preserved in clear cases, and endless racks of sivo data crystals.

Ampris's head swiveled constantly as she stared, fascinated by the wealth of things here. She expected Israi to stop at any moment and turn back. That was, after all, the game. But Bish was still chattering about the jewels, describing them and their vivid histories, along with accounts of the imperial personages who had worn them. Israi was rapt, as though she had forgotten the prank she wanted to pull.

Just before they reached the vault, Bish paused and opened a door that revealed a dim, shadowy room. "Perhaps you would care to look inside here," he said to Ampris in his gentle way.

His eyes, however, bored into her with an intensity she did not understand.

"What is there?" Israi asked sharply, her rill half-raised. "Why do you send my Ampris there?"

Bish turned back to the sri-Kaa and bowed. "I thought she might find it interesting. It has information on her people. Why should an Aaroun care about the jewels which will one day be the exclusive property of the sri-Kaa?"

Israi lowered her rill and flicked Ampris a casual glance of permission. "Go in there, and see your history," she said, and turned away.

There was a derisive, almost contemptuous note in her voice as she spoke. Ampris did not mind it. She knew that none of the slave races had illustrious histories, nothing to compare with the advanced Viis civilization and its glory.

Still, perhaps there might be something as interesting as the hologram of the grasslands had been. Obediently Ampris stepped into the room.

At first it looked dusty and poorly lit. She saw a jumbled stack of things on the long table. Sighing, she walked over to look at the pictures on the wall. Some were authentic paintings. Others were computer-generated reconstructions. She saw portraits of Aarouns of all ages and colors, their long-lashed eyes staring gravely at her from the past. There was something unusual about them, something she could not quite define.

Unless . . . She suddenly realized how bold their eyes were, how free. They stood straight, without the hunch of submission. They looked fearless and content.

A lump filled her throat, choking her before she swallowed it away. She looked at other pictures, seeing settlements, towns, and individual houses. The architectural styles seemed simple—squares and rectangles, mud brick and stucco construction, natural shelters both functional and efficient that were appropriate to the landscape. She found herself studying one house that was larger and far more elaborate than the rest. Low to the ground, it surrounded a courtyard and loggia. A simple pool of water adorned the courtyard. Aaroun youngsters crouched there among clay pots of flowers. She could see the carved pebbles in the cubs' hands, and the game board they played with.

Again a lump filled her throat. All her life she'd believed her people to be nothing. She'd never understood that once they had been separate and independent of the Viis empire, with their own lifestyles and their own customs.

She moved on to another display, and learned about birth celebrations, adulthood rituals, wedding ceremonies, and funerals. Then she came to a display case that lit automatically when she approached. Within, a necklace hung suspended. At first she saw nothing special about it, for compared to Israi's jewelry this piece looked simple and plain. A leather thong, brittle with age, was strung through a small disk with radiating points, like a sun. The center of the disk held a smooth, clear stone—almost as clear as glass, except she could see minute flecks and inclusions within it. Squinting for a closer look, Ampris thought for a split second that she saw a spark of radiance come to life in the transparent stone's center. Her heartbeat quickened in response, and she felt suddenly breathless, although she knew not why. Then the fleeting radiance vanished, and it was just an old amulet hanging on an age-worn thong of leather, nothing special at all.

"That is an Eye of Clarity."

Ampris turned and saw Bish standing in the doorway, alone.

"The sri-Kaa occupies herself in trying on necklaces in the vault," he said before Ampris could ask. He walked into the room on his short bowed legs, his black eyes intent on her. "Have you ever seen an Eye of Clarity before?"

Feeling overwhelmed and confused by all she'd seen in this room, Ampris shook her head. "It looks like an old amulet. Why—"

"Ah, but it is so much more. In centuries past, our greatest, most visionary leaders all wore Eyes of Clarity."

"Myal leaders?"

He shook back his mane. His dark eyes glowed, luminous and intense. "Not just Myals, but Aarouns as well. And others. The Eyes of Clarity belong to no single culture or race."

"I've never seen one before or even heard of them," she said, wondering why he spoke so passionately about the old artifact. "The Viis courtiers in the palace don't wear them. Nor do the chancellors, and they are very important."

Bish snorted. "No Viis can wear this."

"You mean no Viis *would* wear it," she said, turning her gaze on the simple necklace again. "It's not pretty enough."

"Pretty?" he echoed, affronted. "Alas, young cub, have the Viis corrupted you so that you judge value by superficial standards? Rub the age-tarnish from its surface, and it will shine as much as any Viis trinket. Exchange the leather cord for a delicate chain of gold, and would it not look fine?"

"I guess so," Ampris said, not sure why he was so offended.

He stared at her long and hard. "How the Viis have clouded your young mind."

She stared right back. "I have been trained to appreciate art and aesthetics. I meant you no insult. All I said was it wouldn't appeal to a Viis."

"It is not meant to," he said with some asperity. "No Viis can wear one, even if its appearance did not offend Viis aesthetics."

"Why not?"

"That is a mystery. I cannot provide you with an answer. But it is so. And what the Viis themselves cannot use, they never value."

His criticism made Ampris uneasy. She glanced at the door and tried to change the subject. "What was the Eye of Clarity used for?"

"Ah," Bish said, and his voice held a tinge of awe. "It holds great power and wisdom. When a wearer proves him or herself worthy, an Eye of Clarity will share its secrets."

Ampris frowned at the old amulet, not certain she believed anything he was saying. "How do you become worthy?"

Bish spread out his expressive hands in a slight shrug. "Alas, such knowledge is lost."

"I thought so." Bored, Ampris headed for the door.

He blocked her path, however. "Please, young cub. Do not be so skeptical, so impatient. I can teach you much about your kind, if you will allow me."

"I take my lessons with the sri-Kaa," Ampris said haughtily, then felt a rush of shame at having spoken so rudely.

He regarded her a long moment in silence, with his hands folded over his rounded belly. Ampris was the first to drop her gaze.

"I ask pardon," she said quietly. "I have spoken to you with disrespect."

"You have much spirit, much fire in your soul, young cub. Even if it sometimes leads you to speak rashly, at least it has not been crushed." Bish smiled at her in forgiveness. Taking her by the shoulders, he turned her around to once more face the display case containing the Eye of Clarity.

"The oldest writings indicate that the key to understanding its power lies inside each wearer," he said as though they'd never gotten off the subject. "A journey of sorts."

Ampris swallowed a sigh. Bish was just like Israi's tutor, dull and persistent, lecturing on forever. But having apologized once for showing bad manners, she forced herself to be polite this time. "What kind of power?" she asked. "Do you mean it can make things blow up? Can it start fires?"

"To be great or powerful is not always to be destructive," Bish replied patiently. "According to the legends, the Eyes of Clarity were once pathways to the very center of that which powers the universe. Can you tame that?"

She blinked at him and did not answer.

"Well," he said and smiled in his gentle way. "So little is now taught, handed down in song from Aaroun mother to daughter. Did your mother never sing to you, golden one?"

Ampris's eyes widened. No one had ever called her that before. Or had they? A whisper of memory brushed through her mind, elusive, resisting capture. She backed her ears, shaking old thoughts away. She wasn't going to think about the Scary Time if she could help it.

"I have no mother," she said, and even to her ears her voice sounded harsh and flat. "The sri-Kaa raised me. I am forever indebted to her for her kindness and benevolence."

"Yes," he said, his voice softer and more gentle than ever. "Then it is good you have come here to learn your heritage." He gestured at the exhibits filling the room. "You are heir to all this, and much more."

Ampris backed her ears in puzzlement. "This belongs to the Kaa."

"To *you*, Ampris. Your heritage belongs to you and to all other Aarouns," he said. "The artifacts the Kaa may own, but your history, your ancestry, and your lost culture he does not own. Such intangibles can be the richest possessions of all. They are yours.''

She said nothing. Such words were intoxicating, yet they sounded like treason.

He walked over to one of the history panels and pointed at a name. ''Read here about Zimbarl, leader of the Heva clan in the northern hemisphere. He was responsible for pulling the scattered Aaroun tribes together into a unified nation. He created a country, established laws, civilized people into working together instead of against each other. Under his leadership and vision, your people took giant strides forward. For centuries Zimbarl was a hero. Have you ever heard of him?''

Ampris shook her head. She drank in what Bish was telling her, and was suddenly eager to hear more. ''Zimbarl was a hero,'' she echoed. ''Like Havlmehd the Great.''

Bish laughed, curling back his broad lips and shaking his mane. ''Yes,'' he said. ''You know only the typical Viis heroes, and none of your own?''

Shame filled Ampris. Although his voice held no censure, she felt as though she'd been judged and found wanting. ''Why shouldn't I know about the Viis heroes? They are great legends. I hear about them all the time. They have accomplished much that is worthy.''

''Of course. But look here.'' He pointed at another panel. ''Read about Nithlived, an Aaroun priestess. In the final Aaroun uprising, she rallied her people. They would have thrown off the Viis yoke forever had the Viis not cracked open their sun's center. The Viis starforces directed the sun's terrible energy against the Aaroun homeworld.''

Appalled, Ampris stared at him. She could not believe such a terrible story was true. ''The Viis would not do such a thing.''

Bish's eyes were grave. ''But they did. Your people make proud fighters, young cub. They resisted and would not surrender themselves, as other races did. They did not fall prey to the trickery and lies that brought the downfall of my own kind. No, the Aarouns wanted to remain free and independent. They fought, but they could not win. Their world of grassland and hunting was laid waste. Every living thing not evacuated from the planet was destroyed. Now it is bare, blasted rock, spinning in erratic orbit around its dead sun. This the Viis did to your homeworld, golden one.''

Ampris tried to imagine it and couldn't. She tried to sort out what she felt and couldn't. She had never been to the homeworld of her ancestors. She had never walked it, had never breathed its scents . . . until a few minutes ago, when she had experienced the hologram in the exhibit room. Still, to think about the obliteration of an entire living world chilled her. There could not exist such cruelty, yet into her mind came the dreadful memory of the trophy room in the Kaa's mountain lodge, where Aaroun heads hung mounted as grisly reminders of another uprising, and another failure.

Shaken, Ampris glanced around and once again saw the portraits of Aarouns long dead. Their eyes seemed to look right into her, seemed to be pleading for her to do something, as the ghosts of her nightmares pleaded.

The room was suddenly too hot, too close. She backed up a step, the fur on her neck bristling.

Bish seemed unaware of her distress. He gestured at another exhibit. ''But there are other things to learn besides events of politics and war. See this? Did you know that an Aaroun female named Lutishan invented the flyta? That is a very great accomplishment indeed.''

''Impossible!'' Ampris said in instant objection, distracted from her distress, as perhaps he had intended. ''The flyta is a Viis musical instrument.''

''Oh, yes, it features in most of today's music. It is very popular at court,'' Bish agreed mildly. ''But the Viis did not invent it. They found it when they discovered your homeworld. Like many things from many worlds, the flyta was absorbed into the culture of the empire.''

She still wasn't sure she could believe an Aaroun had

actually created the flyta. And yet, a sense of pride surged through her. She stared at Bish, almost smiling. "Really?"

He smiled back. "Really."

So it was true. She hugged the knowledge inside her, thrilled by it. That meant her people were intelligent, accomplished, and cultured too. Like the Viis, only . . .

"Why isn't this known?" she asked. "Why is it kept secret?"

"It is not secret," he replied. "Few Viis know the origins of what they borrow and assimilate into their everyday lives. Even fewer care. The empire conquers many worlds, taking the best they have to offer and discarding the rest." He straightened his tail momentarily, then coiled it around his left leg. "This is the way of tyranny."

Her eyes widened, and again she backed away from him. She did not like him, she decided. Each time she began to find his information interesting, he pushed some treasonous or disconcerting statement at her. She could get into trouble listening to him. "I should go now," she said. "I must not stay absent from the sri-Kaa's side."

"Will you return?"

"I don't know. The sri-Kaa doesn't—"

"By yourself, will you return?" he asked.

She stared at him, slightly alarmed by his question. Why did he study her so intently? He seemed to expect something from her, something she did not understand.

"Have you any periods of freedom? Time of your own, apart from the sri-Kaa's activities?" he persisted. "Are you not interested in learning more about your people? The Aarouns have been a conquered race for less than two hundred years. Before that, they were independent and progressive, inventing their own technology, advancing at their own pace. Are you not curious about them, Ampris?"

"Yes," she said warily, and it was the truth. None of this had ever been told to her before. She'd always thought Aarouns had been slaves forever. Now her mind felt expanded by this radical new information. She needed to get away and think it over.

"Then come back," he urged her. "By yourself. I can teach you much."

"You are Myal," she said. "Not Aaroun. Why do you care about my race instead of your own?"

Impatience flickered in his eyes before he smiled again. "The history of my race is not lost. Nor should the history of other races be lost. You are special, Ampris. The first Aaroun, the first of *any* of the abiru, to be raised in the imperial household. You, alone of all Aarouns, are permitted to speak Viis because you *belong* to that household."

"You can speak Viis," Ampris protested.

"Because of my position, because of my work," he said. "Not because of who I am."

"But—"

"You are a special friend to the next ruler of the empire," he said, his gaze boring into her. "This gives you great opportunity. Your influence, used wisely, could be of great help to your people, my people, *all* the abiru races. Think of it, Ampris. To you, so much is available."

His eyes were blazing with a fervor that alarmed her.

She hurried toward the door. "I must go," she said.

"Ampris," he called after her.

She wanted to rush out, but something in his tone made her pause. She glanced back reluctantly.

"Come again," he said, gesturing at the room. "There is so much more to show you, so much more than you can imagine."

She backed her ears.

"Please," he said. "Will you return?"

"Perhaps," she said, unwilling to promise.

"Ah." He smiled as though satisfied, and the intensity in his gaze faded. Folding his hands together over his little paunch, he gave her a slight bow. "For now, that is sufficient. Knowledge cannot be forced upon another. What you have learned today, you will think about. When you are ready to learn more, you will come back."

She stared at him, uncertain of what to say, then turned and fled.

Israi was emerging from the vault, looking pleased and content. A pendant of a pebble-sized Gaza stone hung on a gold chain about her neck.

"Ampris, good," Israi said. "I was just about to call you. See what I am wearing?" she asked.

Ampris obediently admired the fiery green facets of the jewel. "But are you allowed to take it?" she asked.

Israi's eyes flashed. "Of course. Am I not sri-Kaa?"

"But does not everything here belong to the Kaa your father?" Ampris asked. "I do not wish you to be punished."

Israi sighed and stamped her foot. "I *hate* this," she said, and yanked off the necklace. "How long must I wait until I can do as I please?"

She tossed the necklace on the floor and walked past Bish, who stared at the discarded jewelry with astonished eyes. He hurried to scoop it up and handed it to another Myal, who had appeared with a folded paper in his hands.

Taking the paper, Bish caught up with Israi and bowed. "For the Imperial Daughter, as requested."

She nodded at Ampris, who took the paper for her.

"Thank you," Ampris said for her.

Bish's black eyes shifted to Ampris. Again he seemed to want to say something to her, but he merely bowed. "To serve has been an honor. The Impérial Daughter and her companion are always welcome."

Israi left the Archives in haughty silence, her expression petulant. Ampris walked beside her, saying nothing. She wasn't sure if Israi was annoyed with her specifically or just put out because she couldn't keep the necklace.

Right then, Ampris hardly cared. She was too busy thinking about the things Bish had told her. All her life, she had believed that Aarouns were barely useful barbarians able to do manual labor and not much else, less-than-bright creatures tolerated for their strength and stamina alone.

For the first time she realized she didn't have to feel ashamed of being Aaroun. Her people had once had their own culture, their own art, their own intelligence, and their own future, before the Viis had conquered them and robbed them of everything, even their memories.

Ampris glanced at Israi, bursting to tell her friend of what she had discovered. "Israi," she said at last, her voice swelling with excitement, "I have so much to tell you about what I saw."

Israi took the paper from her hands. "Hmm?" she said absently, unfolding it as they hurried through the construction zone without pausing. "The Aaroun exhibit? Poor Ampris, I'm sorry about that. I shouldn't have let him put you in that room by yourself. Were you bored? Are you upset because you didn't see the jewels?"

"No, I—"

"They were boring too," Israi said, cutting off Ampris's answer. "Old, uncleaned, and out-of-date." She crumpled the paper in her hands and tossed it on the floor. "That was an inventory list of them, prepared especially for me." She laughed with scorn. "How silly."

Ampris refrained from mentioning the necklace Israi had wanted. "Why did you look at them so long?"

Israi flicked her tongue and changed the subject. "Could you believe that Myal? What a strange one! He actually thought we were interested in his ancient information. How useless to preserve such things. And you, sweet Ampris, you didn't even complain about being stuck in there with bits of old grass and mud."

Ampris blinked. "There wasn't—"

"After all, there is nothing to learn from the ancient pasts of the abiru races," Israi continued. "Nothing! The notion of the Archives is quaint, but I'm sure only my father and the Myals care anything about it. I certainly don't."

"Some of it was interesting," Ampris said in a small voice.

"Was it?" Israi paused to stroke her rill and rearrange its folds above her collar. "Perhaps as a curiosity. Wasn't the Aaroun homeworld ugly? I could barely stand to look at it. Now Mynchepop is reputed to be lovely. Fortunately we weren't forced to destroy entire landmasses in order to gain their cooperation." She laughed. "They are—"

"What do you mean?" Ampris asked, feeling the hair stand up along her spine. Bish's words about the fate of her homeworld came back to her, and she felt suddenly desperate to silence her friend. "It isn't so. Landmasses—continents—can't be—they wouldn't be—"

Pride filled Israi's face. "Yes, of course it can be done. My father explained it to me only a few days past. Really, the procedure is a very simple matter, especially with our advanced technology."

"Israi, I would rather not—"

"Don't be squeamish," Israi said, not heeding Ampris's protest. "Why should it matter to you? That planet was destroyed centuries ago, and it was never your home. My father says that our fleet comes up to a world, surveys it to see if it has anything useful to offer us, then we request their surrender. If they refuse, we can attack them from space. You know, slag continents with such intense heat all the vegetation is burned off and nothing can grow or live there. We also decimate entire populations, although that isn't cost-effective if the people can be used in some manner. We can poison the oceans, or even rip away their atmosphere. Usually they surrender when we threaten them. Only the stupid ones resist."

"I understand," Ampris said quickly, anxious to stop the explanation. She thought of the Aaroun portraits she had seen—intelligent, happy faces of purpose and vision—and felt sick to her stomach. How could the Viis be so arrogant, so dismissive of others? How could Israi be proud of it?

Israi squeezed her arm and gave a little skip. "I am glad

we came down here. Ampris, I have a brilliant idea of what we can do to Lady Zureal. Listen . . .''

She pulled Ampris close and whispered plans in her ear. Ampris listened and smiled, but her heart was not in it. All she could think about were the proud faces in the pictures, faces that had been burned to dust and ashes.

CHAPTER FIFTEEN

That night, while Israi slept soundly in her nest of cushions, Ampris crept from her cot and left the bedchamber. On silent feet she moved past the dozing attendants and slipped into the narrow study alcove where Israi usually worked on her lessons. Pulling the door shut silently, Ampris felt her way through the shadows, taking care not to stumble over the chairs, and opened the tall window by the desk.

Moonlight streamed in, bathing the alcove in its pearly luminescence. In the distance Ampris could see the fat, pale orb shimmering its reflection on the river's surface, but she was not interested in the view.

Instead, she turned on the data screen and called up Information. At night she often used Israi's study tools to privately supplement her own education. As long as no one caught her, she could study what she liked, as thoroughly as she wished, without being interrupted and directed by Israi's whims.

Her favorite subject was Architecture, with Mathematics and Natronics running a close second and third. But tonight she called up History and sought the entry for Aaroun.

The screen shimmered a moment, then displayed in vivid graphics a male of her species. Impatiently skipping this subentry, Ampris cross-indexed her request to Aaroun homeworld. As she entered the request, it occurred to her that she did not know the planet's name. She felt ashamed of her ignorance.

An astronomy map shimmered onto the screen with an arrow pointing to where the planet should have been. /AR-ROUN HOMEWORLD,\ read the caption across the bottom of the screen. /LOCATION IN SARGAS SOLAR SYSTEM, GALACTIC CENTER SEVEN POINT NINE NINE BY SEVEN. THIRD WORLD IN SYSTEM. INCAPABLE OF SUPPORTING LIFE.\

Anger slithered through her heart, but she ignored the emotion and asked for a cross-reference to Sargas III.

No response registered from the equipment for a long time. Then finally, a new caption crawled across the screen. /INFORMATION DELETED BY ORDER OF HIGH COUNCIL.\

Frustrated, Ampris glared at it, but she knew an information deletion could not be countermanded. Trying to dig further might even alert Security, although she doubted they would dare to shut down any activity requests that came from the sri-Kaa's data screen.

Instead, she requested information on Zimbarl. Again there was a long pause. Again the answer came: /INFORMATION DELETED BY ORDER OF HIGH COUNCIL.\

She requested information on Nithlived, and received the same reply. Snarling to herself, she asked about the Heva clan.

This time, she received a split screen of captions and new graphics of a fawn-colored Aaroun female with brown spots and a light brown mask across her eyes. The female was mature, well into her middle years by the heavy bulk and musculature of her neck and shoulders. Her eyes were keen and far-seeing.

/HEVA CLAN,\ read the caption on the right side of the screen. /TRIBAL DESIGNATION FOR THE SPECIES ARROUN, CARNIVORES ORIGINATING IN SARGAS SYSTEM, TECHNOL-OGY GRADE THREE. SOCIOLOGICAL PATTERN INDICATES

THIRTY CLANS WITHIN FIVE PRIMARY TRIBES. HEVA CLAN IS \

Ampris frowned when the screen failed to automatically scroll. She touched it with her fingertip, but it did not respond. She touched it again. The screen went blank, except for one blinking message:

/INFORMATION DELETED BY ORDER OF HIGH COUNCIL.\

Growling to herself, Ampris tried every cross-reference in the index she could think of, and came up with nothing else. Then she heard a faint sound outside the door.

Swift as thought, she shut off the screen and closed the window. Blanketed by the resulting darkness, she crouched on the floor with her back against a cabinet.

The door swung open.

Ampris drew in a swift breath and held it, feeling her heart thump harder. The shadows were thick. She could not see who stood at the doorway. No light shone for either of them. Neither breathing nor moving, Ampris let her nostrils widen to take scent.

She smelled skin oil, a special blend of cynribal, koi-kai, and ohl favored by Lady Lenith. But the chief lady in waiting usually retired to her own apartments at night, leaving lesser attendants to guard the sri-Kaa's sleep. That meant someone else had been dipping into Lady Lenith's perfume pots.

Who would dare?

No one, save Israi herself.

Relieved, Ampris caught the sri-Kaa's true skin scent beneath the cloying perfume and started to speak.

But an instinctive sense of caution held her silent. She realized that as long as the lights stayed off, she could not be seen in the thick pool of shadows where she was hiding. And although Israi probably would not punish her for using the data screen without permission, Ampris did not want to explain what she had been looking up or why. And so she stayed silent on her haunches, while the memory of Israi's carelessly cruel words in the Archives throbbed through her mind.

It was all true, Ampris thought. Everything Bish had told her was true. The Viis had captured, plundered, enslaved, and conquered the Aarouns. They had destroyed everything they did not take, leaving nothing for the Aarouns to go home to. They had even taken the planet's name.

Israi did not care.

No Viis cared.

For the first time in her life, Ampris felt a gulf widening between her and her friend. For no matter how true and wonderful a friend Israi was, she would always be Viis, a descendant of atrocity and conquest. And no matter how long Ampris lived in the palace, favored, and pampered, and loved, she would always be Aaroun, descendant of slaves.

"Your heritage is here," Bish had told her in the Archives. "It belongs to you, Ampris."

She crouched in the shadows, waiting for Israi to speak her name and demand she come forth. But although Israi's scent altered slightly with heat, indicating she sensed that Ampris was in there hiding from her, Israi said nothing. After a long, long moment, she softly closed the door and went away.

Ampris let out her breath, but felt no relief. Something was happening between them. She did not know what it was. She did not want to know what it meant. Perhaps Israi had always known she sneaked in here to use the data screen at night. Perhaps not. Ampris realized, however, that she would never dare slip in here again. Israi's very silence was a warning.

But I will know the answers to my questions, Ampris thought. *I must learn more about my people.*

The next day, when Israi joined the Kaa for a private lesson, Ampris stole away to the Archives. She found Bish bent over a table of dirt-encrusted artifacts, carefully cleaning an object with a tiny brush.

"Teach me," she said without even a greeting, making him start and whirl around. "I want to learn more about my people. When did we come to be slaves? Two hundred years ago? What did we do before then? Did we have our own space travel, our own technology? What happened to—"

"Gently, young cub," Bish said, holding up his hands. "Gently. So many questions. So much impatience. Let us deal with one subject at a time."

"I don't have much time," Ampris said impatiently. "I must go back soon or I will be missed. Almost every entry in the data screen has been deleted. I can find out *nothing* about—"

Bish's lips parted in a broad smile. He drew a small object from his pocket and handed it to her.

It was a sivo data crystal. Ampris hefted it on her palm, then curled her fingers around it. She felt as though she had been handed a treasure trove. "How much information does it contain?" she asked.

"The crystal is full," he replied, shaking back his mane. "You have many days' worth of learning in your hand, golden one. Learn it well—"

"I'll listen to it tonight—"

"Slowly," he said in warning, his tail whipping out behind him in alarm. "Listen to it slowly, in small bits. Do not rush your lessons."

"But I—"

"Honor your people's history," he said, his voice suddenly stern. "Treat this with care. Do not tell anyone I have given this to you. Do you understand?"

His tone and the fierce look in his eyes alarmed her. She blinked at him, clutching the crystal in her hand. "Is it forbidden for me to have this?" she asked in a small voice.

"It is."

Her mouth went dry, and she found herself panting. She wished she had never come back, had never let her curiosity carry her past common sense. She tried to return it to him. "I will commit no treason."

"But you already have," Bish said, very softly. He looked at her with compassion, seeing the fear that dawned in her eyes. "When you sought deleted information on the data screen. When you came here just now, asking questions. Even when you listened to me uttering forbidden names yesterday."

She gasped and turned her back to him. "I didn't know they were forbidden. I didn't—"

"Ampris," he said. "Fear is not for one such as you. Look at me."

She froze, her heart hammering hard. She would be arrested, dragged from Israi's side, and thrown into the Pit of Questioning. She would be slaughtered, her head and hands cut off, and—

"Ampris," Bish said more forcefully, "turn around."

She complied with great reluctance, tempted to dash the sivo crystal on the floor and break it into pieces. Already Israi knew. She had to know. She had come to the alcove door, but she had not spoken. Yet if she had not spoken, what did that mean? Was it a warning, as Ampris had first thought? Or did it mean she gave her permission for Ampris to learn?

Relief swept Ampris with such intensity it was almost painful. She met Bish's eyes and saw open concern in his gentle gaze.

"Ah," he said with a blink. "You have found your courage again."

Ampris nodded. "I think so."

"That is well. Take care with this. Show it to no one, not even the sri-Kaa."

Ampris nodded again. "When must I return it? Tomorrow?"

"No. Do not come again so soon. I told you to study the contents slowly. Take your time, young cub. Impatience is no virtue."

She frowned at the crystal within her fist. "Are you saying this is all the information you have?"

"Study that, then come for more." Bish sighed. "You must learn not to make assumptions, golden one. You must learn wisdom if you are to save your people."

Her ears snapped forward, and she stared at him. "What?"

"A great opportunity is yours," he said. "You are rare and unusual. You are surely our hope."

"What do you—"

"You have been raised with the sri-Kaa herself," he said as though she hadn't interrupted. "One day when she ascends to the throne, perhaps you will be there with her."

"Of course," Ampris said blankly. "I shall always be with Israi."

"Never, in all the long mingled histories of the abiru folk, has something like this happened," Bish said, his dark eyes glowing. "You will one day be in a position to give much help to your people, and to all the abiru folk. Perhaps you are Zimbarl or Nithlived come again."

She shivered at his words. "I don't understand."

"Perhaps in you the abiru races will find a new symbol of hope. Perhaps in years to come you will rally them for rebellion."

Fresh alarm flared inside her. Ampris backed up a step. "I am not a traitor," she said angrily, and shook her fist at him. "If this contains only lies to twist my thinking, I will surely throw it in the river. No matter what you tell me, I will never turn against Israi or the Kaa—"

"This has not been asked of you," Bish replied, just as sharply. "We do not seek war, Ampris. We want freedom. Freedom as a gift one day from the sri-Kaa. You can persuade her, Ampris. You must."

"But—"

"Not now, little one. Not now," he said, spreading out his hands in a calming gesture. "Forgive me for speaking about that which must wait for the future. You are very young. There is time for all that must be learned first. Freedom is not gained in an instant. Nor is it ever granted easily."

He seemed to be talking to himself more than to her. Ampris stared at him, swallowing an involuntary growl of unease in her throat. His words both exhilarated and frightened her. She wished she had never come here, never followed Israi here yesterday, never returned on her own today. But her feet seemed to have taken to a path that she could not step away from. She wanted to jump back, to keep things as they had always been. But already everything seemed to be changing.

"I should not have come," Ampris said, backing away now. "I think you have misinterpreted my interest in old history." She laid the sivo crystal on the corner of the artifact table and turned away. "I must go."

"Afraid to see if destiny's hand lies on your shoulder, young cub?"

His question came at her in mocking challenge. She stiffened her spine and spun around with her teeth bared.

"I am not afraid," she said, squaring her shoulders instinctively to make herself look bigger.

His dark eyes flashed, and he pointed at the crystal with the tip of his tail. "Then take it and make use of it. Or live in ignorance, like the Aaroun slaves outside the palace. It is your choice."

Anger filled her, and with it came defiance mixed with a rush of arrogance. She was nothing like the slaves. She was friend of the sri-Kaa. He had no right to compare her to those lesser creatures.

Huffing to herself, she hesitated a moment, longing to leave and never come back. But he had piqued her curiosity too much yesterday. She wanted to know more. She craved it as she craved cool water on a summer's day. And she had come here to get it, after all.

In the end, she gave up struggling with herself. Darting forward, she grabbed the crystal off the table and tucked it into her pocket.

Bish smiled and bowed to her. "Excellent. Go forth and study, my young cub. I look forward to the moment you return with more questions."

Ampris shot him one last look and rushed out, heading back to the part of the palace where she belonged. When she reached Israi's quarters, she prowled around until the cleaning maids left the bedchamber, then pulled out her small chest of belongings from beneath her cot and concealed the sivo crystal among her pebble collection. As she closed the pouch containing them and tucked it back beneath her other meager treasures, Ampris growled thoughtfully to herself. She would study the contents of the crystal, to assuage her curiosity, but she did not think she would go back to Bish again.

The old Myal was half-crazed, no doubt from too many years of breathing dust and studying the ancient texts of dead people.

And yet . . . destiny? To lead the abiru folk to freedom? What if Bish's words were true?

Considering this, Ampris smoothed her palms across the lid of the chest and shoved it back into place. For a moment she dreamed of the fierce priestess Nithlived, rallying the people, leading them in a great march . . .

To where?

Sargas III was a bare, blasted rock spinning in space. They could not go back to it.

The visions faded from her head, and Ampris rubbed her muzzle with a sigh over her own foolishness. Perhaps madness was contagious. If she wasn't careful, she might catch some of it from Bish.

"Ampris!" one of the ladies in waiting called to her from the sitting room. "What are you doing in there? The sri-Kaa awaits your presence immediately. Come at once."

And she forgot her dreams in running to do as she was bid.

*   *   *

Hours later, Bish left his worktable and descended deeper into the oldest, most shadowed passageways of the Archives. Stretching for klick after klick, the underground sections of the Great Library of the Kaas now held row after row of crumbling documents, priceless treasures of knowledge fading to dust before it could be transferred to new, more stable media of data storage. He could work a lifetime here and never save more than a fraction of it.

But tonight Bish's thoughts revolved around another matter. When he reached a small conference chamber where only antiquated torches burned to provide illumination because to use modern sources of light would have alerted Security to the chamber's existence—and use—he found a quiet gathering of six other Myals waiting for him.

Their muted conversations faded at his arrival. Anticipation filled the air. Bright-eyed and smiling, they watched him take his seat. Bish stared at the floor, unable to meet such eager gazes.

"Well?" Prynan, the youngest, asked. He was forever impatient and usually the first to speak on any matter. "Did she come back? Did she listen?"

"She came." Bish swallowed a sigh.

Around him, they broke into exclamations of triumph and excitement.

Old Lomat raised his hands in the air. "At last. At last it can begin," he said. "I have lived to see its beginning. Now I can face the end of my life's journey without regret."

"Wait!" Bish said sharply, unable to let them celebrate unchecked. His sense of guilt weighed heavily on his shoulders. "My brothers, it is premature to rejoice yet. I fear I have spoiled everything."

Silence fell upon the shadowy room like a thudding weight. The torchlight flickered unevenly across their faces, shining reflections in their eyes.

"What happened?" Lomat asked, the quaver of old age

heard plainly in his voice. "Bish, you must tell us."

Bish lowered his gaze from theirs, remorse bitter in his throat. "I spoke too much too soon. In my excitement, I said she was surely destined to free us. I am sorry, my brothers. My unbridled tongue has frightened the cub. I fear we have lost her."

The others exchanged glances while Bish berated himself internally once again. He wanted to cut off his mane in shame. They had trusted him to speak to the golden one, believing in his judgment, but he had blundered like an untried novice. Prating of destiny and freedom, leading her straight into the jaws of treason.

He groaned aloud. "This required delicacy and tact. I wished to entice her along the path of knowledge, but instead I dumped everything at her feet. I said too much. I frightened her away."

"But she came to you alone, did she not?" Prynan asked, breaking another silence. "She came. That shows the cub has courage."

"Yes," Lomat agreed. "She listened, did she not?"

"She listened," Bish said bleakly. "To too much."

"The truth may frighten, but it never does lasting harm," Lomat said.

"Did the cub take the crystal?" Avnal asked from the back.

Hope touched Bish's heart, the only hope he had left after his mistakes. He straightened his shoulders. "She did. But not without much coaxing on my part. Will she ever—"

"It is in her possession. She will use it," Lomat said with certainty. "Let us not fear. The seeds have been planted. If our cause is favored, those seeds will grow." He came and linked his long tail with Bish's, coiling them tightly together. "You did the task allotted you, Brother Bish. The rest is up to her now, if she is the one."

CHAPTER SIXTEEN

Twelve sunsets thereafter, the bells of Sahvrazaa Festival began to toll across the city. A glorious blaze of coral, green, and dusky lavender filled the sky, and the setting sun turned the surface of the Cuna Da'r River to molten copper. Melodious and loud, the bells pealed joyously from the spires. The Viis populace came pouring from shops and houses to cheer, to fling silk scarves in the air so that the wind caught them and sent them sailing forth. They greeted the viis males from other communities arriving on foot in large ceremonial processions.

In the palace, all was merriment and excitement. Fragrant festoons of flowers draped across every doorway and window in the wives court, and there was much hastening to and fro, much calling to attendants, much slamming of doors and giddy laughter and even arguments of excitement.

Gowned in green silk and wearing a rill collar studded with delicate river pearls, Israi tiptoed across her bedchamber in her new sandals and listened at the door, then nodded at Ampris.

Her golden fur cleaned and fluffed to perfection, Ampris wore a scratchy garland of fragrant yellow lileas around her neck. At Israi's signal, Ampris rolled back the rug on the floor and opened the secret hiding place. She withdrew a slender crystal vial with a stopper carved in the knot that symbolized love.

Ampris could not help but sniff at the stopper, inhaling the musky fragrance of the perfume inside. The scent of it was intoxicating, overwhelming. It made Ampris's tongue curl against the roof of her mouth and her eyes roll back in her head.

"Ampris!" Israi whispered angrily. "Stop that! I have told you several times. I shall not tell you again."

Abashed, Ampris lowered the vial and came hurrying to Israi with it. She handed it over, panting with anticipation. Israi carefully placed it inside the tiny wrist bag that matched her gown and that was supposed to hold her fan, her gold toothpick, and any dainty gifts that might be given to her this evening at the banquet.

Tonight was the first time Israi would be sitting at the table with her father, a public announcement to the court that she was now to be considered vi-adult, old enough for inclusion at select functions. It was a heady time, the moment every young Viis female dreamed of, when she officially stepped onto the threshold of adulthood and waited poised to cross it.

Israi was glowing with excitement, her rill flushed, her breathing rapid, and her vivid green eyes brighter than the stars just starting to appear in the evening sky.

"Don't let it spill," Ampris said as she watched her friend's unsteady fingers fit the perfume vial into the wrist bag.

"Gods, no," Israi breathed. She secured it and drew the cords to close the top of the bag.

Her eyes flashed at Ampris, and they held not just anticipation but triumph as well. "The moment is at hand," she said breathlessly. "Within hours, my enemy will know how I can strike."

Ampris nodded, her own heart thumping fast with excitement. "She will never live down the embarrassment."

Together they gripped hands and laughed.

"Now," Israi said quickly. "Remember to stay alert and watch for my signal. If my father will allow me to approach his precious *favorite,* I shall give her the gift with my own hand. But if not, then you must slip it from my wrist bag during the dancing and smuggle it into her bedchamber. Can you do it?"

Ampris drew a deep breath, ready to take on any task Israi set for her. "Yes."

"Good." Israi ran to activate the wall mirror and swiftly checked her appearance one last time. Her eyes were glittering with more malice than mischief. "Have you heard the latest gossip? It seems the Master of the Hatching has been instructed to allow Zureal to lay her eggs in a separate place from the others. That way my father will know which are hers." Israi slapped her palm against the mirror, making its energy field bulge and crackle. Fury blazed across her rill, turning it dark blue. "Imagine it! If he should choose a new sri-Kaa from her brood, I could be ripped from my place in an instant."

Dismayed, Ampris ran to her and stroked her rill, trying to make it lower. "No, no," she said, trying to soothe Israi's distress. "It cannot happen. It will not happen. You are his favorite. He has named you so. He will not change."

"But *she* fills his eyes now," Israi said, making a rasping sound in the back of her throat. The variegated skin of green and blue around her eyes turned pale. "It is she he sends for. I have not spoken to him since she came."

"That will soon change," Ampris assured her. "We have seen to that."

Israi nodded, trying to control her breathing. She gripped her wrist bag fiercely. "This has to work," she said. "It has to!"

"It will. Compose yourself. You mustn't let anyone see how much you care."

"No, you are right." Israi dabbed at her face and lowered her rill in a visible effort to achieve calm. "My dearest Ampris, what would I do without you?"

Ampris grinned at her. "Just keep thinking about how this potion is going to work. That will support your composure."

Israi burst into laughter and finished repairs to her complexion. "Yes, indeed."

They were still giggling when the doors opened and Lady Lenith swept inside. Gowned in resplendent magenta and dripping with numerous jeweled necklaces and bracelets, Lady Lenith bowed deeply to Israi.

"By the Imperial Daughter's leave," she said. "A gift-bearing messenger has come from Lady Zureal."

Israi's eyes dilated, and Ampris barely suppressed a gasp. She watched Israi, seeing a blush spread up her rill. *Keep your temper,* Ampris thought, never taking her gaze off her friend. *Do not spoil this chance.*

"How—how delightful," Israi said, layering honeyed tones over the constraint in her voice. "Permit the messenger to enter."

Lady Lenith turned aside and clapped her hands. At once a servant entered, cringing low in respect, eyes carefully averted. The servant carried a package in festive wrapping.

Israi glanced at Ampris and gestured imperiously. Ampris went and took the package.

"Compliments of Lady Zureal," the servant said.

Israi smiled. She nodded again to Ampris, who opened the package. Inside was a holographic cube filled with pretty but juvenile images. Ampris held it up.

Israi's smile suddenly looked as though it had been set in plaster. "How pretty," she said in a flat voice. "Please convey my thanks to Lady Zureal."

The servant bowed and hurried out. For a moment there was only taut silence in the room. Then Lady Lenith walked over to Ampris and took the cube from her hand.

She held it up, turning it this way and that. "It was well-meant," she said.

Israi whirled around and took it from her, smashing it to the floor in fury. "Well-meant!" she shouted. "I am vi-adult, and she knows it! I'm not a hatchling, to be given something like this."

"It was the gesture of the gift which must be held charming," Lady Lenith corrected her. "A most agreeable revival of an old custom, this exchange of gifts between moth—"

"Mother?" Israi said with a dangerous flash of her tiny, razor-sharp teeth. "Zureal is *not* my mother. She may have displaced Lady Myneith as First Wife, but she will never be—"

"Still," Lady Lenith interrupted in her cool manner, "no insult was intended, and the Imperial Daughter should not lose her temper. Instead, why not consider the intent behind the gesture and respond to that?"

"Intent?" Israi stood there with her eyes narrowed, breathing hard as she visibly battled her temper. "Oh, yes, Lady Lenith. I think I understand the *intent* very well."

"It is perhaps unwise to read too much into this," Lady Lenith said mildly. "Zureal is not a complex person. I am sure her motives are kind generosity, nothing more."

"Yes," Israi said flatly. "No doubt." Her gaze went to Ampris. "Then I should give her a gift in return, should I not?"

Lady Lenith gestured approval. "Why, Israi, that is splendid of you. Very grown up."

Still looking at Ampris, Israi flicked her tongue in and out rapidly. "I meant to give her something at the banquet, but this is better. Don't you think?"

Ampris's eyes widened as she understood.

Lady Lenith, oblivious to the hidden meaning beneath Israi's words, replied, "Why, yes. It is charming to exchange gifts of affection in private before the festivities officially commence. So very appropriate. I am proud of you."

Israi drew the vial from her wrist bag and held it up carefully. "Ampris," she said.

Hardly daring to breathe lest she burst into gleeful laughter, Ampris walked forward and took the vial from Israi's slender fingers. The light shone through its clear sides, burnishing the pale amber liquid inside. What they had gone through to get it—petitioning for permission to leave the palace and setting out with guards and escorts to an obscure little shop just off the Avenue of Triumph. The potion had been prepared for a very generous sum. Israi had spent her entire allowance for the quarter on this, and she was counting on it to work.

Now, Israi's gaze bored into Ampris. "You will take this straight to the chambers of Lady Zureal," she commanded. "Give it to the lady herself and no other. Make her understand that it comes from me."

They had argued about this before, with Ampris insisting that the perfume should be an anonymous gift. But Israi considered the rivalry she felt with Lady Zureal to be war, and she would not heed caution. She wanted Zureal to know they were enemies, and after tonight that would certainly be very clear.

"Ampris," Israi said sharply. "Put it directly into her hands."

Ampris took a deep breath. "Yes, Israi," she said.

"And hurry. You must catch her before she leaves for the banquet."

Ampris nodded and went out the door with the precious weapon, while behind her she overheard Lady Lenith praising Israi again for her courtesy and generosity.

Stifling a snort of laughter, Ampris hurried out into the corridor and headed straight to the chambers of Lady Zureal.

There, the attendants stopped her, flicking out their aristocratic Viis tongues with disdain.

"What do *you* want here?" one asked.

"I am sent by the sri-Kaa," Ampris said with dignity. She had dealt with disdainful courtiers and ladies in waiting all her life. "I bring the Imperial Daughter's compliments to Lady Zureal in the form of an advent gift.''

"How nice," the female said, holding out her hand. "I shall give it to her."

Ampris clutched the perfume vial firmly. "My instructions are to give it to the lady personally."

They all laughed.

"Nonsense," the female in charge said, spreading her rill. "You are an unworthy slave. Give it to me, and I shall see that Lady Zureal receives it."

Ampris growled at her. "You insult the sri-Kaa! You would keep her gift for yourself."

Anger filled the female's eyes. "You little—"

"What is it, Mavia?" a melodic voice asked from the other room in the suite. "Who are you talking to?"

The doors opened, and Lady Zureal stood revealed in the soft lamplight. She wore a loose dressing robe that did not conceal the swelling in her body from the eggs she carried. Her pale green skin was radiant, and her amethyst eyes gazed upon Ampris with kindness.

"Oh," she said, and smiled. "Are you not the pet of the sri-Kaa?"

The lady's charm was irresistible. She had a trick of fastening her tilted eyes on someone and making them feel they were the only creature in the universe at that moment. Ampris found herself smiling back, then realized what she was doing and hastily walked forward with a bow.

"Yes, my lady," she said politely. "I bring greetings of Festival from the sri-Kaa. She sends you a gift tonight in hopes that you will lay many eggs."

Pleasure sent an amethyst blush up the lady's rill. "How charming! That dear chune. I am as enchanted with her as is her esteemed father." She held out her hand with a graceful droop to her wrist. "Please bring it to me."

Ampris obeyed, concealing her glee at how well the plan was working so far. And yet, as she handed over the perfume and received yet another smile from Zureal, Ampris felt a quiver of regret pass through her.

Zureal really was nice, she thought. Not conceited or temperamental at all, like so many of the wives. Although she had become an instant favorite, clearly besotting the Kaa and creating much gossip thereby, she did not seem vain about it. She had not given herself airs or tried to place herself higher than her position allowed. Ampris wished that Israi did not hate Zureal so much. She almost found herself warning Zureal not to wear the perfume, and had to bite her tongue.

Meanwhile, Zureal was sniffing the stopper. Heady fragrance filled the room, and she quickly replaced it. With little exclamations, the others gathered around her.

"What is it? I have never smelled anything quite like it."

Ampris met Zureal's gaze with growing discomfort. "The sri-Kaa had it specially formulated for you," she replied. "I must go."

"Thank her," Lady Zureal said with sincerity. "This is a lovely gift indeed."

Ampris bowed, suddenly desperate to get out of there. But Lady Zureal reached out to stop her and stroked Ampris's head between her ears.

"You are lovely too," she said kindly. "What are you called?"

"Ampris."

"You look very pretty tonight, with your collar of flowers. Will you be permitted to see any of the banquet?"

Ampris drew herself up with pride. "I am attending," she said. "The sri-Kaa will recline tonight at the table as a vi-adult, and I am permitted to stand behind her."

Zureal's lovely eyes dilated in dismay. "Oh, dear," she said, letting her rill fall. "I had not realized. That is—I am pleased at such an honor for the sri-Kaa. But I thought her younger."

"No," Ampris said flatly, enjoying Zureal's discomfiture. "She is not."

"Then I have erred with her Festival gift," Zureal said.

"Mavia, we must find something else. Was the sri-Kaa insulted by the cube? I have seen her so little, and everyone talks so indulgently about her pranks and immature behavior. I'm afraid I thought her quite a chune."

Embarrassment flooded Ampris. She dropped her gaze, understanding how a stranger might misconstrue Israi's recent wild behavior. Yes, Israi had been running about the palace as free and wild as she pleased. But that was over. As soon as Festival ended, lessons and the old routine would recommence. But Ampris did not know how to explain all of that to Zureal, who was directing Mavia to look for a pretty scarf or bracelet.

"Here," she said, pressing a crimson and blue scarf into Ampris's hands. "Give her this, and ask her to come to me when Festival is over. We must talk, she and I, must come to know each other and understand each other better. I want to be friends with her. And she is now at the age when she may wish to be friends with someone a little older. Tell her these things, Ampris, and give her my apology for the mistake."

Horrified, Ampris stared at the scarf in her hands. It was beautiful, costly, exactly the sort of thing Israi would love. And yet, that hateful bottle of perfume was being carried away to a place of honor on Zureal's dressing table. Ampris stared at it, wishing she could find a way to run after Mavia and knock it from her hand.

She was ashamed of herself and more ashamed of Israi, who had judged this female with prejudice and meanness of spirit. Israi was acting from petty motives, exactly like a selfish hatchling. And Zureal did not deserve her spite.

"I—I—"

"Yes, Ampris," Zureal said with a dismissive gesture. "I know I have given you a long message, but do try to convey as much of it as you can to your mistress. Run along now. I have much to do to get ready."

Ampris bowed and backed away from her, wanting to tell her the truth, yet not knowing how.

"Oh, and Ampris?"

Ampris glanced up. "Yes, my lady?"

Zureal beamed at her. "Tell the sri-Kaa that I shall wear her lovely perfume tonight. In fact, I'm going to put it on now."

Heat flashed through Ampris. She opened her mouth to protest, but Mavia and the other attendants shoved her outside into the corridor. The door shut firmly, and the chance was lost.

Ampris stood there, clutching the fine scarf, knowing it would never be worn. Israi was going to get into such awful trouble.

Worried, she debated what to do. It was too late now to stop Zureal from putting on the potion. That meant Israi's only hope was to confess everything immediately to the Kaa, explain why it had all come about, and ask for his pardon, as well as the forbearance of the Lady Zureal.

Growling to herself, Ampris hurried away. Israi was going to get into terrible, terrible trouble.

"Apologize?" Israi's voice rose sharply, causing several courtiers to glance in her direction. Spreading her rill and turning her back on them, she bent low and whispered furiously in Ampris's ear, "Never! Never! Never! You have lost your wits."

"But, Israi—"

The sri-Kaa turned away from Ampris and walked deeper into the crowded audience hall. The entire court was slowly assembling there, waiting for the signal to enter the banquet chamber. Courtiers bowed to Israi as she walked past them, and Ampris hurried in her wake.

Finally Israi paused near a column, poising herself with her head held high. Her eyes were glittering, and her rill extended far above its collar. Despite her youth she looked magnificent, and formidable.

"She didn't understand," Ampris said, catching up. "She sent me back with a beautiful gift, and—"

"I don't want to hear this," Israi said, her voice emphatic and flat. "You were seduced by her charm, as is everyone. But I refuse."

"Israi—"

Israi turned on Ampris with a flash of her eyes. "Silence!" she commanded. "Keep your place."

The harsh rebuke stung Ampris deeply. She clamped her jaws shut and said nothing more. Her eyes reproached Israi for being so unjust. After all, she was only trying to help.

Then Israi gazed at the assembly and did not look at Ampris again.

Trumpets sounded in a fanfare that stopped the general babble of conversation. Courtiers turned to face the tall open doors where guards in green cloaks were filing through to stand in a double row. A command rang out, and the guards drew ceremonial swords, holding them in an arch.

The Kaa appeared, tall and resplendent in a rill collar of solid gold and a coat of myriad colors that swirled and changed with his every movement. His bronze skin gleamed with supple health, and if the lamplight caught it just right it looked iridescent. Never had he looked more virile or magnificent.

A sigh of reverence passed through the crowd, and everyone bowed low.

The Kaa walked beneath the arch of swords, followed by Lady Zureal, Lady Myneith, Lady Abiya, and the other favorite wives. The trumpets sounded again, and the crowd surged forward to follow them into the banquet chamber, their chatter swelling up and drowning out the music that began to play.

Heralds and stewards scurried in all directions to guide banqueters to their correct places. Circular arrangements of reclining couches filled the room, with the most important circles being closest to the Kaa's.

On a spacious dais at one end of the banquet chamber, the couches for the imperial party were arranged around a low, round table of costly wood. The Kaa's couch was draped in crimson velvet bound at the corners with fat bullion tassels. Israi was positioned on the Kaa's right; Lady Zureal took her place on his left. Lightly rubbing her jaw with a delicate motion, Lady Zureal allowed her attendants to arrange the folds of her gown, then sent a smile in Israi's direction.

Israi nodded to her and sent a perfunctory smile back.

The other wives took their places with much giggling and rustling of their elaborate gowns. They were all swollen with eggs, slow-moving, and treated with extra solicitude by attendants, servers, and the Kaa himself.

Ampris stood at the foot of Israi's couch, both proud at the privilege of being present at such an important occasion and deeply apprehensive of what was about to occur.

She let her gaze stray to Lady Zureal, wondering if the potion was working yet.

"Ampris," Israi said.

At once Ampris hurried to take a small dish from the sri-Kaa's hand.

"These spiced antas are particularly good," Israi said, her eyes dancing. "See that Lady Zureal tries them."

Ampris presented them to Lady Zureal with a bow. She couldn't take her eyes off the lady's jaw, where her delicate skin was beginning to mottle yellow and pale green.

"Antas?" the Kaa said with interest, taking a morsel off the dish Ampris held. He popped it into his mouth and gazed at Zureal with deep tenderness in his eyes. "Delicious. Try it, our dearest."

Lady Zureal seemed distracted and uncomfortable, but she inclined her head to the Kaa and took an anta. More yellow splotches were breaking out across her forehead and below her ear dimples. Her wrists looked puffy and splotchy as well.

The Kaa stared at her. "Are you feeling unwell?"

Lady Zureal murmured something inaudible and rubbed at her wrist and then her face. The rubbing seemed to make the breakouts worse. "I don't know," she said, rubbing harder. "I feel very strange."

Watching in horrified fascination, Ampris stepped back. She glanced at Israi, who flicked out her tongue in satisfaction.

The Kaa continued to stare at his favorite, who was now making soft little cries of distress and constantly rubbing her face and throat. "What is wrong?" he asked her.

"I don't know!" she cried.

He gestured, and attendants hurried forward. "Assist Lady Zureal. She is ill."

The courtiers had begun to notice. Several were staring, and someone pointed. "Look at her face!"

Lady Zureal gasped and put her palms against her jaws.

Israi buried her face against her cushions for a moment, then looked up. "How ugly!" she said in a loud voice. "What a dreadful rash. It quite destroys her beauty."

Lady Zureal began to rock from side to side, making a rasping sound in the back of her throat.

Her attendants hurried to surround her, assisting her to her feet and leading her away.

Also standing, the Kaa summoned a steward. "Send for the physician, immediately."

"At once, sire." The steward vanished at a run.

The whole banquet chamber filled with buzzing speculation. Courtiers stopped eating and rose to their feet because the Kaa was standing. They stared as Lady Zureal was ushered out.

"Cover me," she kept saying, her voice raw with shame. "Cover me."

Murmuring soothing platitudes, her ladies veiled her face with scarves and vanished with her.

The Kaa stood there, puffing his air sacs in and out, until Chancellor Gaveid approached him.

"It would be best, sire, to resume the banquet as though nothing is wrong."

The Kaa made an impatient gesture. "She is ill. Disease

has struck her on the eve of Festival. Her eggs could be in jeopardy.''

"A small rash, sire," Gaveid said soothingly. "Let us not overreact and cause unseemly gossip."

The Kaa nodded reluctantly and glanced at Ampris, who froze in place. Her heart suddenly pounded, and she was certain he was going to accuse her then and there.

But his gaze shifted away, and he returned to his couch. The other wives plied him with questions and speculations, their chatter serving to distract him.

Israi kept on eating, keeping her gaze away from her father, but Ampris could see the grin that kept straying across her face. Beneath her gown, her tail switched from side to side.

Ampris wanted to nip her. She was going to give everything away if she didn't master her composure. The rash had been everything the potion maker had promised. Those large yellow blotches were perfect. Lady Zureal had been publicly humiliated, but Ampris felt no satisfaction. Instead, she felt shame and worry, and she wished Israi would not gloat so much.

After several minutes word was brought to the Kaa that the lady was not seriously ill. The cause of the rash remained a mystery, but it accompanied no fever. Perhaps too much excitement had distressed the lady.

"The lady is resting now. Her physicians have given her a sedative. All is well."

Israi glanced at Ampris and smiled in satisfaction, then turned to the Kaa and touched his sleeve.

"There, Father," she said brightly. "All is well. You know how high-strung and delicate some of the southerners can be."

He was still puffing his air sacs. "It would seem so."

"Put it from your mind this evening. She is comfortable now. Tomorrow all will be well," Israi said. "I want to ask you about the processional and what surprises have been planned."

Her chatter went on, occupying the Kaa's attention and distracting him from fretting over Lady Zureal. Several times during the long evening Ampris caught Chancellor Gaveid looking at Israi in approval.

Ampris had to admit that her friend was in perfect form tonight. Gone was the wild behavior and rudeness that Israi so often exhibited. Tonight she appeared poised, accomplished, articulate. Her comments were witty and displayed her educated mind well. She acted mature for her years, and only Ampris knew the truth.

Israi was happiest when playing a role, as she did tonight. When she had charmed and impressed everyone, including her preoccupied father, she finally took her leave at the proper time, heeding Lady Lenith's discreet signal without any protests.

"It is the hour of my retirement," she announced with a pretty little sigh, tilting her head to show the Kaa her regret before she rose from her couch with lithe grace. "Enjoy the remainder of the revels, Father."

She leaned over and blew in his ear canal, and he patted her hand in return.

"Well done, Daughter," he said with pride. "You have comported yourself well. We are most pleased with how much you have grown up."

Israi glowed at his praise, and a blush colored her rill. She bowed low, then with shining eyes turned to the wives and wished them well on the morrow.

Then she hurried out, with Ampris faithfully at her heels. Many of the courtiers bowed to her in open admiration, and Israi's eyes glittered with satisfaction.

Israi's ladies in waiting had to trot to keep up with her. As soon as the tall doors to the banquet chamber closed, Israi tipped back her head and unleashed a peal of laughter.

"We did it, Ampris. It was perfect!" she crowed.

Mortified, Ampris longed to shush her.

Naturally Lady Lenith's suspicions were immediately aroused. "I suspected the Imperial Daughter was too well-behaved tonight," she said, eyeing them both. "What prank have you pulled now?"

Israi threw up her hands and spun around and around until her gown belled around her legs. Without answering Lady Lenith, she laughed again and then ran to her chambers, leaving her attendants far behind.

Slamming shut the door, Israi whirled around and gripped Ampris by both hands. "We did it!" she said. "Public humiliation and embarrassment for that silly, vain puff of nothing! Ha!"

Giving Ampris a swift hug, she pushed away and began to dance across her sitting room.

Lady Lenith entered with the attendants and saw Ampris pulling off her scratchy flower garland while Israi danced in glee.

"Undress me!" Israi commanded even as she eluded the attendants' approach. "I am ready for bed. It has been a perfect day, and a splendid evening."

The attendants looked at each other, and even Subi—standing in the doorway of the bathing chamber—shook her head.

"Too much wine," someone said.

They surrounded Israi and eventually managed to undress, bathe, and bed her. When the lamps were turned down low, and Ampris lay curled on her cot at the foot of Israi's round bed, she could still hear Israi humming and chuckling to herself. Ampris closed her eyes, trying to shut out the sound. She wished she could join in Israi's happiness, but her feeling of guilt and shame wouldn't go away. It was one thing to pick on Fazhmind, who was pompous, horrid, and deserving of what he got. But Lady Zureal hadn't deserved this, and Ampris felt cruel. They had gone too far tonight, and she wished she knew how they could undo it.

CHAPTER SEVENTEEN

The doors crashed open with a loud bang, awakening Ampris.

She sat bolt upright, alarmed and blinking, trying to claw her way awake.

In the dim gray light of dawn that illuminated Israi's bedchamber, a tall figure in long robes stood silhouetted in the doorway.

An instinctive growl rumbled in Ampris's throat even as she recognized the Kaa. Horrified at herself, she clamped her hands over her muzzle and scrambled out of bed as he came striding forward.

He didn't even appear to notice Ampris's presence. His whole attention was focused on Israi, who sat up and yawned.

"Father?" she said drowsily.

The Kaa's eyes blazed at her, and his rill stood at full extension without the support of a collar. It glowed a dull crimson, and Ampris's heart sank.

He had found out.

"Israi, get up," he said. Every word was terse and cold.

His tone got through to Israi. Yawning and rubbing her

head, she obeyed him and stood there in her sleeping robe, disheveled and half-awake.

"What did you give her?" he demanded.

Israi blinked at him and finally focused. She opened her mouth, and for a moment Ampris thought she was going to be evasive or at least pretend not to know what he was talking about.

But he was too angry. Towering above his daughter, he stood there with his air sacs inflated, his rill at full extension, and his tail switching from side to side beneath his robe. Pouches of exhaustion bagged beneath his eyes, which never left Israi's face.

Meeting that furious gaze, Israi slowly drew herself upright and squared her shoulders.

"I gave her perfume," she replied.

He snarled an oath that made Israi's rill go pale. "What was *in* the perfume? Encetylide," he said, answering his own question before Israi could. "An odorless compound that reacts chemically with the skin, causing swelling, discoloration, and severe itching."

Israi dared smile. "Yes, like itching powder, except it blotches the skin."

"How much did you pay the perfumer for this illegal transaction?"

"Twenty imperials," she said.

Ampris couldn't believe how unconcerned, how confident she was. Israi stood there, impervious to the Kaa's anger.

"Rather a stiff price to pay for a prank," he said.

She shrugged. "Perhaps. It took all my allowance to persuade him."

"You didn't pay him enough," the Kaa said in a voice so low it was almost a growl.

"Why do you say that?"

"Because we ordered his neck broken this morning when he confessed. And twenty imperials is a very small inheritance for his wife and family to console themselves with."

Ampris's jaw dropped open, and she felt cold inside with shock.

Israi stared at her father, her rill flat on her shoulders. Finally she said, "You *killed* him? For a silly prank? I don't believe it."

"Believe it!" he roared, his voice rising suddenly in volume. "You caused Zureal distress—"

"Her own vanity caused the distress," Israi said dismissively. "All the court does is talk about how beautiful she is, and she believes every word. Take away her beauty for a few hours, and she is reduced to a crying, pathetic heap. She is nothing but a vain and silly creature."

The Kaa's hand shot out and gripped Israi by the shoulder. He shook her, hard.

"Father!" Israi said in alarm, gasping in pain. "You're hurting me."

"Are we?" he said through his teeth. "And what of Zureal's hurt, our daughter?"

"She'll get over it as soon as the blotches go away—"

"Will she? Will she get over the loss of her eggs in the night?"

Israi stared at him, looking stunned. "What?"

He released her, giving her a little shove against the bed as he turned away. Back and forth he paced, his tongue flicking rapidly, his rill redder than ever, his eyes raw with rage and grief. "Yes, Israi, yes!" he said. "She miscarried."

Israi stood in silence, several expressions chasing themselves across her face. "Oh, Father," she said quietly at last.

"Do you know how dangerous it is to miscarry this late in term? The physicians worked for hours, trying to save them . . . and her."

Israi's eyes dilated, but it was Ampris who asked in a shaky voice, "Is she dead?"

He didn't look up, didn't appear to notice who it was he answered. "No," he said, still pacing. "But she is gravely ill. The eggs could not be saved. They ruptured inside her and—''

Breaking off abruptly, he turned and strode to the window.

Ampris's heart grieved for him and the lost hatchlings. She was well-aware of how precious offspring were to the Viis, who had fewer and fewer every year. The dropping birthrate concerned everyone, and now this tragedy had struck on the opening day of Festival, a time when everyone should have been rejoicing as eggs were laid both here in the palace and out in the public hatchery in the city.

More than that, Ampris felt sorry for lovely Zureal, who was young, kindhearted, and caught up in the joy of her first days at court. Zureal hadn't deserved this tragedy.

''But it's all so silly,'' Israi said into the silence. Her voice was cool and unconcerned. ''Such a terrible, tragic response to a simple prank—''

''It was not a simple prank!'' the Kaa said, turning on her so violently she shrank back. ''Above all else, Daughter, do not lie about that.''

''But—''

''You have been jealous of Zureal since the day of her arrival. You have refused to greet her, to speak to her, or to be kind to her. Simple courtesies are part of your responsibilities. You know that!''

''I was courteous,'' Israi said, blinking rapidly as a blush deepened in her rill. ''I exchanged gifts—''

''You set her up for intense public humiliation at her first official function.''

''If she is going to be at court, she must learn—''

''Silence!'' the Kaa roared.

Eyes dilated, Israi stood there, breathing hard with shock. ''You are angry with me,'' she said in astonishment.

Even Ampris stared at him, amazed. She had never seen the Kaa lose his imperial composure. She had never heard him raise his voice, and certainly he had never spoken to Israi like this before.

"It is not your place, Israi, to dictate what our wives will and will not learn," he said, raging. "You are sri-Kaa, but that does not set you so high you are above every consequence. You will be punished, Daughter. It is *you* who will learn."

"Father, no!" Israi protested in dismay. She held out her hands. "I meant no harm to the eggs. For this, I will apologize—"

"For that, but nothing else," he said flatly, glaring at her.

Israi blinked at him. "I don't understand."

"We think you do."

"The blotches are not permanent," Israi said finally. "She will recover her looks in a day or two."

Disappointment filled his eyes. "Is this our beautiful daughter?" he asked. "Is her heart so cold, so petty, that she feels neither pity nor remorse?"

Israi flicked out her tongue. "Very well, Father, if you wish I will speak to Zureal personally—"

"We think not."

"Then what is it you wish from me?"

The Kaa allowed his rill to lower. "All your life you have been spoiled and indulged. We loved you, Israi, so very much. Too much, it seems. We have given you everything, and you repay us with behavior unworthy of even a barbarian."

Her rill flushed, and anger touched her eyes. "Father, that is very harsh."

"Harsh?" he repeated in a mild voice that sent a shiver through Ampris. "We have never shown you harshness. Perhaps it is time we did. The Imperial Daughter has been shielded from grief and loss such as that which she has inflicted. Now that will change."

Israi looked uneasy. "It is unfair to punish me for her overreaction."

The Kaa lifted his hand to silence her. "Never again will we hear you assign blame to Lady Zureal. The blame is yours, and you will learn what it means to feel sorry. You will suffer as Zureal has suffered."

Israi backed away from him. "Father!" she said in protest. "Surely you aren't going to make me wear that perfume."

"Guards!" he shouted, and they appeared at once from the sitting room. The Kaa swung around and pointed straight at Ampris.

"That Aaroun is the only thing you appear to care about besides yourself," he said while Ampris gasped in dawning horror. "You will lose her as we have lost our unborn eggs. Grieve for *her* as we grieve for them."

Fearfully Ampris backed away, but the guards pounced on her before she could elude them. Growling, she snapped and struggled, but they held her firmly.

Israi stared. "You wouldn't take Ampris away from me," she said in disbelief. "I don't believe it."

The Kaa's face might have been carved from stone. Grief raged unchecked in his eyes. He pointed at the door and said to his guards, "Dispose of her at once."

Ampris howled in fear, and Israi surged forward, screaming.

The guards, however, held the sri-Kaa back as Ampris was carried out, kicking and struggling. She could hear Israi pleading, could hear her cries, but more guards came to shut and bolt the doors to Israi's bedchamber, locking the sri-Kaa in.

The reality of their separation sank in. Yet Ampris refused to accept it. No one could take her away from Israi. No one.

Ampris loosed a guttural roar from deep inside her throat and lunged at the guard on her left. Her teeth snapped closed on his rill and she shook her head with all her might, ripping the flesh with a spurt of blood that tasted sour and alien on her tongue.

The guard screamed, and his companion hammered a blow across Ampris's shoulders that drove her to her knees.

With her ears flattened to her skull, she hardly felt the blow and heeded nothing save the fury pounding through her. Pivoting on her knees, she swiped with her claws, going for the guard's tail. Body armor protected it, however, and they dragged her upright, one holding her while the other hit her repeatedly.

Stunned, her wits spinning, Ampris lunged again with her teeth bared, but missed this time. They dragged her out bodily into the corridor, where courtiers had begun to appear, gawking in curiosity.

Lady Lenith emerged from her own small quarters, swathed in robes and looking bleary-eyed.

Ampris surged toward her, only to be pulled back by the guards. "Lady Lenith!" she called out. "Have mercy on me!"

Lady Lenith came hurrying forward. "Ampris? What is this?" she demanded. "What's amiss?"

A sergeant at arms stepped between her and Ampris. "We're acting on the Kaa's direct order, my lady," he said. "Do not interfere."

Another guard rushed up with a restraint bar and muzzle. The latter he rammed down over Ampris's head. Whirling, she butted him with her skull before he could switch on the restraint field, and ripped at his body armor with her claws.

"Get back, my lady!" the sergeant said, sweeping Lady Lenith aside. "Guards, restrain this savage at once!"

Battered to the floor, Ampris snarled and struggled with all her might, but she was no match for the training of palace guards. Within minutes the restraint bar was clamped across her wrists and a control on her muzzle was switched on. A force field shimmered around her, engulfing her. Her muscles spasmed and then locked up. Immobile, she lay there helplessly, unable to even speak.

The guard she'd wounded swabbed at the blood dripping from his rill and swore, low and furiously.

Behind them, Israi was still pounding on her locked doors and shouting. Hearing her muffled cries, Ampris struggled to rise, but the restraints held her fast. Fear returned to her as the guards dragged her upright. Her gaze went to Lady Lenith, beseeching her silently for aid. But Lady Lenith said nothing in Ampris's defense.

Fazhmind came up, robed in vivid purple and fanning himself. A little purple cap of silk perched atop his head. It looked so ridiculous Ampris wanted to laugh, but she couldn't. Tears welled up in her eyes, blurring her vision. She wished now she'd never played any tricks on him. She wished she'd never bitten him when she was little. Maybe then he would have had pity on her now.

"The mercy of the gods befall us!" he said, extending his rill. "This creature has finally turned on her illustrious mistress like the savage beast she is. Hear the wounded cries of the sri-Kaa."

Around him the courtiers murmured in outrage and shock, while fresh fury filled Ampris. Glaring at Fazhmind, she strained against the force field which imprisoned her, longing to sink her teeth into his sour old hide. How dare he say such lies. She would never harm Israi—never.

"The sri-Kaa is well," the sergeant hastened to announce before the crowd could panic. "Step aside, and let us carry out our orders."

The courtiers parted, and Ampris was dragged bodily away. No one spoke in her defense. No one protested this cruel separation ordered by the Kaa.

Ampris wanted to cry out, to call to them again for mercy. These were people she'd known all her life. People who had trained her and helped raise her. Even if she didn't like them, they were family. And now they refused to save her.

Bitter tears stung Ampris's eyes. She couldn't believe it. And yet, the guards were carrying her away like garbage to be thrown out.

"From the first day I predicted this trouble," Fazhmind said loudly. "Did I not say she would grow up into an unruly beast? Yes, I said it. I warned the Kaa repeatedly, and now I am proven right. Good riddance!''

Ampris shut her eyes, hating him, hating the Kaa, hating everyone who stood in the palace corridors and watched her go by. But even those who stared and whispered could not distract her from the awful words that kept echoing in her head: *Dispose of her at once.*

Cold words, uttered without mercy by the Kaa, whom she had reverenced and admired with all her heart. She had been a loyal, faithful subject. She had been petted by him, had received his smiles, had benefited all her life from his kindness. And now, he had turned on her, without justice, without regard for anything except his own loss.

She wanted to cry, to howl, to empty herself in her terror. Yet the restraint field kept her from doing any of those things. There was only her pounding heart and the shortness of breath in her lungs as she was carried into the service area behind the palace.

A transport waited there, already loaded with slaves deemed too old, too stupid, or too untrainable. A Gorlican slave merchant stood next to it, studying a manifest. The torso shell beneath his tunic was mottled orange and brown, and beneath his mask, his beaked mouth opened and closed while he counted to himself.

''One more for the load,'' the guards called to him.

The slaver glanced up, took a second look at Ampris, and came forward with a sudden gleam of interest in his yellow eyes. ''This one sure?'' he asked.

The guards removed her earring of ownership and the restraints, then tossed her onto the transport. She fell bodily against a whimpering Myal and was thrust off with a sharp elbow.

''She goes,'' the guards said, and walked away without looking back.

The slaver slammed the hatch shut and peered in at Ampris. ''Very pretty,'' he said in approval. ''Very good quality. You must have been a bad Aaroun, to get yourself thrown out, eh?''

Racked with misery, Ampris averted her gaze from him and wished with all her heart for Israi to come running to get her. The sri-Kaa would not let this happen to her. She knew Israi would find a way to appease her father and make him relent.

She watched the rear entrance, certain that it would open and the guards would return for her. Or that Subi would come. Or—

With a whine of its engines, the transport lifted above the ground and swung around, laboring beneath the load it carried. It flew away, and Ampris's hopes were left behind in the deserted service alley.

The first time Elrabin made a dust run he was so scared he thought his fur might fall out. The next time he found the danger a thrill. After that, it fell into an easy routine.

Elrabin was offered a taste his first day. Like they thought him so stupid he didn't know what it was. He never explained that he hated the sight and smell of it, or that he knew every grade on the streets and half the suppliers in the ghetto network. He was too relieved at not having to sell it himself. Delivery wasn't so bad, although the risks— and the penalties if caught with it—were plenty.

Scar's training was simple. "I give you these credit vouchers, see?" he said, handing over four thin disks, each one smaller in diameter than Elrabin's palm and in four different colors that signified numerical amounts.

Elrabin stared at them, trying not to gasp out loud. They represented more money than his da had won in a lifetime's gambling and grifting. Elrabin had never dreamed there could be so much money, at least not resting in his hand.

"They're marked," Scar said sharply, watching him. "You take off with them, you'll be dead in two hours. You follow?"

Panting, Elrabin nodded. He did not ask how he would be watched. He believed what Scar said.

"Good. You go to the Street of Two Faces, down on the south side. You know where that is?"

"I can find it."

"You go straight there, to the tattoo shop called Feilee's. Say it back to me."

"Feilee's," Elrabin repeated impatiently. "On the Street of Two Faces. I've got it."

"You go in, ask for Feilee in the back, and don't flash those disks! You'll get your throat slit quicker than you can blink, see?"

Elrabin's ears twitched nervously. He nodded.

"Go in back and talk to Feilee. No one else. Show him the disks. Tell him you're from Barthul. If he don't believe you, tell him the password I gave you this morning. You remember it?"

Elrabin repeated the strange words, feeling his fur prickle as he said them. He knew running dust could get him killed if a patroller spotted him. He still wished he'd never agreed to this. Like he had a choice. Like he would ever have a choice again. He belonged to Barthul now, and he might as well be a slave.

"You give Feilee the disks," Scar said, "and take whatever he gives you. Bring it back here tonight."

Elrabin blinked in surprise. "Tonight? Why not as soon as I get it?"

Scar bared his yellowed teeth. "Stupid! You think patrollers don't watch Feilee's? They know it's a drop-off point. You got to lose the tail you'll be picking up as soon as you walk out."

Fear filled Elrabin's entrails, making them burn. For a moment he thought he would be sick. He thought of the patrollers he had escaped in the Street of Regard, not because he was clever or slick, but because they had let him go. He remembered Cuvein's face, defeated and afraid. He remembered his own humiliation and helplessness when he'd faced the wrist cutters. How well would he face a death penalty?

Scar nipped his ear. "You listening, fool? Hey!"

Elrabin blinked away his memories and rubbed his smarting ear. "Yeah, I'm listening," he said. "I'm supposed to lose the patrollers. Any instructions on that?"

"You figure it out. That's your job," Scar said, swiveling his one ear. "Just don't bring them here."

"I won't," Elrabin said, but he was tempted to do exactly that.

Scar stared at him a moment, evaluating him, looking doubtful. "You goof this, you're dead. You follow me?"

"I follow."

"Then go."

His mouth dry and his ears burning with determination, Elrabin left Barthul's stronghold and set out through the city streets. It took him half the day to find Feilee's grubby little shop. Once he had the dust bags weighing down his pockets, he stepped out feeling as though he wore a sign that said ARREST ME!

He found his tail immediately. It was a surveillance scanner that floated along after him in plain sight. Elrabin nearly panicked and ran for it, but he knew that would be stupid. He kept cool, strolling along in crowds of other pedestrians. After two blocks, the scanner reached the end of its signal tether and dropped him to float back to its post.

Elrabin managed to breathe slightly easier, but in a few minutes he discovered another tail, one far less obvious than the first.

He lost it with a couple of tricks. After that, he figured he was clear, but he took every precaution he could think up. He came back to Barthul's at dark, exhausted and stressed from dodging all day. He wasn't followed, and he faced Scar triumphantly, his chest bursting with pride at his accomplishment.

Scar took the bags from him and tossed them in the trash.

Elrabin stared in dismay. "What're you doing?"

Scar laughed at him. "Just a test run, fool. Nothing but dirt you been carrying all day."

Elrabin took a step back, trying to understand. Dirt? He had been carrying dirt all day? He had been worrying himself gray trying to do a good job, and for nothing?

Furious, he glared at Scar and started to speak, but Scar grabbed him by the front of his new coat and yanked him close.

Scar's eyes narrowed to dangerous slits, and he bared his teeth. "You got something to complain about, stupid?"

The threat, unspoken, hung clearly between them. Elrabin swallowed his anger, although it pained him all the way down. Panting hard, he struggled with himself, then said in a meek voice, "No, I got no complaint."

Scar shoved him away, nearly making him stagger. "That's good. Get out of my way. You'll make a real run tomorrow."

"Maybe," Elrabin shot off as Scar started to walk away. "And maybe you'll set me up to be a fool again."

Scar turned on him fast and slammed him against the wall so hard all the breath was knocked from Elrabin.

Wheezing for air, he found Scar's teeth on his throat. Terrified, Elrabin froze a moment, then stretched out his fingers in hopes of grabbing Scar's sticker. He never reached it, however.

Scar released him with a growl, his eyes holding cold, flat death. "Never question me," he said in a voice that made Elrabin shiver. "If I send you out every day to bring home rocks, you'll do it. If I tell you to drink from the sewers, you'll do it. I saved your puny life, and you *owe* me. You are *mine*. You follow?"

Choking with anger and fear, Elrabin heard Scar's words through the roaring in his ears. He made a strangled sound, not trusting himself to say the correct thing.

Scar punched him in the stomach with his fist, doubling him over.

Coughing and gasping, Elrabin sagged to his knees. His stomach hurt, and he couldn't do anything but fight against throwing up. His whole body was trembling, and it took him a while before he was able to pull himself together.

Finally he looked up, but Scar was gone. Some of the others were watching him, grinning and nudging each other.

Humiliation made Elrabin swing his gaze away. He staggered upright and thought about leaving. He could take their precious dust and sell it on the black market, then turn in Barthul's location to the patrollers. Sure, the gang would come after him, but he figured he could hide. He wasn't as stupid as Scar thought.

But at the same time he remembered how close he'd come to starving on his own. Maybe he wasn't as clever as *he* thought. The smell of hot food filled the air, and he dropped his idea of running away. It wouldn't prove anything to Scar, and it would only leave him without a place to go. He wasn't ready for that. Not yet. He figured tomorrow had to get better.

It did.

Soon Elrabin had a regular collection of delivery routes. He did whatever Scar told him, and soon Scar stopped threatening him and picking on him. Scar even occasionally dropped him a word of praise or a little nod of approval.

Such rewards made Elrabin swell with pride. He found himself increasingly eager to please Scar. The other thieves and runners in the gang stayed aloof, insulting him whenever he tried to join their tri-dice games in the evenings. Lonely, missing his da and the old life, Elrabin kept to himself and tried to believe things would get better. At least he had food and shelter. He had a job, although he wasn't paid. Scar told him he had to pass his apprenticeship first before he could take a cut. Elrabin even gathered his courage and asked Scar one day to teach him how to handle a sticker.

Scar laughed at him, but obliged with a lesson.

Elrabin was too eager and too clumsy. He ended up cut. Yelping, he jumped back, giving up the fight.

Scar cleaned his sticker and put it away with a little snarl of disgust. "Hopeless," he said, and walked off.

Dejected, Elrabin wrapped up his bleeding hand. He wasn't really cut out to be a fighter, he admitted to himself. No matter how much he wanted to be like Scar, he knew that surface imitations were all he could achieve. He would never have the other youth's killer instincts or steely ruthlessness. He didn't have what it took, and he didn't know how to acquire it.

But the next day Scar sought him out. Expecting to get his orders, Elrabin faced Scar and tried to look ready and competent. At least he could run dust. Maybe, if he ever gained acceptance, he'd ask Barthul to let him open a gambling shop.

"Which route today?" he asked.

Scar shook his head. "Something different. Come with me."

With no more explanation than that, Scar led him across the ghetto. Then they slipped through the gates and headed toward Keskia and the better districts of the city. Elrabin was bursting with a mixture of curiosity and pride. For the first time he and Scar were working together. Elrabin knew Scar could never be his friend, but at least he had companionship. He was tired of solitude and loneliness.

Happy, he bounced along beside Scar. "I figured you were mad at me after yesterday," he said.

Scar kept up a fast, ground-eating stride. He grunted.

"Will you give me another lesson sometime?" Elrabin asked.

Scar backed his one ear.

Elrabin strode along beside him for a few moments, then tried a different tack. "Where we going?"

Scar growled. He refused to look at Elrabin. "Big job today."

"Yeah, I guess so. You don't go along on runs much, do you, Scar?"

Scar dodged a female Viis pedestrian who had stopped

to rummage in her market basket. He didn't reply to Elrabin's question.

"So how big a job we got?" Elrabin asked. "What are we going to do? Where are we going?"

Scar stopped so abruptly Elrabin had to skip sideways to avoid crashing into him. Scar glared at him. "Shut up," he said. "Just shut up."

He walked on, and Elrabin rushed to catch up with him. Elrabin was used to Scar's unpredictable moods by now, so he didn't let today's bad temper upset him. He was just glad to be along, and proud that Scar had chosen him as his helper. Maybe after today, the others wouldn't be so hard to get along with. Maybe this was a big part of passing his apprenticeship and soon he'd be accepted by everyone in Barthul's gang.

Leaving the broad avenue, they turned into a series of alleys that grew increasingly narrow and dilapidated. Skek eyes glowed in the shadows behind sewer grates, watching them walk by. Seeing the old loading zones, rusted bars across doors that looked as though they hadn't been opened in years, decayed pavement, crumbling bricks, and trash blown aimlessly by the wind, Elrabin kept his senses alert and drew closer to Scar's heels. He saw the gang symbols painted on a corner and shivered. They were intruding into someone else's territory. Not for the first time he wished he carried a weapon like Scar.

The other Kelth turned a corner and stopped with his back pressed to the wall. Elrabin copied him, and they stood there, silent and listening, for several seconds. Scar gestured for Elrabin to follow, and they moved on in silence until Scar came to a door no higher than his knees.

Crouching before it, he knocked once, twice, three times in a distinctive pattern. Then he glanced up at Elrabin. "Keep watch."

Elrabin drew a deep breath and swung around to face the way they'd come. His ears shifted constantly, alert and nervous. He was scared, and he wanted to whine deep in his throat.

The small door opened from inside, and Elrabin jumped. He turned around, trying to hide his nervous reaction.

A slender Viis with mottled blue and green skin and no more than a vestigial rill crept out and straightened to face them. He was one of the Rejects, the subclass of Viis deemed too ugly or malformed to live in normal Viis society. The Rejects existed on the fringes, scavenging, scrounging, competing with the abiru for scarce food and unsteady work.

Elrabin didn't like the Rejects, finding most of them borderline psychotic and sour. They hated everyone, including themselves, for they had to cope with the abhorrence they received from all privileged Viis. A few were decent, but even they thought themselves superior to the abiru. Elrabin had watched little bands of Rejects begging near the gladiator arena. They were pathetic, cringing up to people with their tattered hoods drawn closely about their faces. Most normal Viis wouldn't even toss them a transit token.

Scar murmured something too soft and quick to catch. The Reject looked at him and Elrabin, then replied. Scar nodded, and handed over credit vouchers.

The Reject palmed them swiftly and crawled back through the low door.

Scar waited a second, then reached inside the cavity. Drawing out a bag, he tossed it to Elrabin, who barely caught it in time. He tossed a second bag to Elrabin, then drew out two more and tucked them into his own pockets.

The door slammed shut, and Scar climbed to his feet. He glanced at Elrabin. "You ready?"

Elrabin felt breathless. He stuffed the bags into his pockets. "What do I do?"

"Double blind," Scar replied, glancing around. "We're running a bluff, see?"

Elrabin didn't understand, but he knew Scar hated to be

asked too many questions. "What do I do?" he asked again.

Scar met his eyes a moment, then slid his gaze away. "We leave this alley and split up. You take your usual precautions. Circle around, then drop the dust at Feilee's, see?"

Elrabin panted in excitement. "Sure," he said eagerly. "This time I'm delivering—"

"Yeah, you got it." Scar touched his shoulder with a rare sign of affection. "Now, try to look casual. Try to look the *same* when you go in. Don't tip off the surveillance, you. Don't be stupid."

Elrabin scratched his ear. "I understand. I'll do it exactly right. I'll wait until they are changing the signal loads in the scanners, and then I'll go in. Surveillance always gets fuzzy about then. I'll—"

"Yeah, you'll be fine." Scar checked his pockets. "I'll go to that corner there and wait. You go out of the alley first, ahead of me. See?"

Elrabin bared his teeth, feeling the chance of a lifetime in his pocket. If he wanted to betray Barthul's gang, this was the day to do it. Or he could wait. Maybe he didn't want to put himself back on his own dodge just yet. He waved at Scar. "See you tonight."

"Yeah, fool. Tonight. Go."

Elrabin trotted away, then steadied himself down to a normal stride. He glanced back once at Scar, flashed him another grin, then moved out into the alley, keeping alert, feeling competent and sure of himself. For a few seconds he could hear the quiet echo of Scar's footsteps behind him. Then the sound faded. Elrabin glanced back and did not see Scar.

Admiration swelled through him. Scar was definitely good, almost as good at vanishing as Cuvein had been.

"Stop right there!"

The voice, stern with authority, came blaring at Elrabin from nowhere. Startled, he whirled around and found himself staring up at a sniffer floating over his head. Elrabin couldn't believe it. Where had that thing come from? How had it found him so fast?

Knowing he didn't want to find out, he dodged to one side and started to run.

"Stop! Do not resist arrest!"

The mechanized voice called after him, but Elrabin ignored it. He streaked down the alley, determined to break free before patrollers could catch up with their toy. Under his breath he was cursing. He glanced back once, wondering if Scar had been netted in a similar trap.

The sniffer blared a siren, its shrill sound making him yelp and run faster. It was following him, all right, keeping pace easily. He swore at it, knowing he had to lose this thing and fast. It couldn't lock onto his implant, but it could sight-follow him.

Worse, the large streets of this district were fairly respectable. He couldn't go running through groups of pedestrians without bringing too much of the wrong kind of attention to himself.

Skidding to a halt, Elrabin crouched and scooped up some broken chunks of pavement. He hurled one at the sniffer, missed, and hurled another one. This time his missile hit the sniffer squarely, knocking it off-kilter. The siren faltered, then resumed. Elrabin hit it again, knocking it into a building. The machinery belched smoke and crumpled to the ground.

Running to it, Elrabin stamped on its delicate casing, cracking it and crushing the parts inside.

Then he hurried on, telling himself to be scared later. He had to think now. He had to *move*.

But just as he reached the mouth of the alley, three patrollers in black uniforms stepped across his path. Elrabin whirled to double back, but something hit him between the shoulder blades with enough force to knock him off his feet.

Crying out, he skidded across the pavement and found

himself lying facedown beneath a crushing weight. He couldn't move. His muscles were stiffening, becoming paralyzed. Elrabin groaned to himself. He'd been stunned. He was helpless now, with no hope of moving at all, much less getting away. They had him, and he was carrying two full bags of dust. That meant death, with no appeal and no reprieve.

He was too frightened to even yelp when the patrollers reached him and dragged him upright. They patted him down roughly for weapons, found none, and pulled the bags from his pockets. Elrabin stopped breathing. The patrollers had the right to shoot him here and now. Possession of this much illegal substance marked him as a supplier.

Sometimes, though, the patrollers wanted to toy with their victims first. They might torture him. They might drag him off to prison or—

The patrollers slit open one of the bags, and black soil poured out. The patrollers stared at it, and Elrabin stared at it. He started breathing again, started hoping.

"Gods, what is this?" one of the patrollers asked in disgust.

"It's dirt, ordinary dirt," another one said.

The first crouched and pinched some in his gloved fingers. He opened his visor and flicked out his tongue to it. "Dirt," he confirmed.

Relief swept through Elrabin. "Nothing illegal about carrying dirt, is there?" he asked, his voice groggy and garbled by the stun effect.

One of them struck him. "Silence!"

They searched him again, and this time one of them picked a tiny transmitter off the back of his shoulder. "Look at this. He was marked for us."

The others swore, and Elrabin's relief came crashing down. He stared at it, refusing to believe his own suspicions.

"A double blind," one of the patrollers said in disgust.

"We were bluffed as neat and slick as though we just hatched out of the egg. Damn."

Elrabin backed his ears. He remembered how grouchy Scar had been today, how Scar had refused to meet his eyes for very long. Scar had planned this from the first, had set him up to be caught. That unexpected pat on the shoulder had concealed his planting of the transmitter. Scar had betrayed him, had intended to betray him from the hour he'd persuaded Barthul to let Elrabin join the gang. Elrabin realized he had stupidly allowed Scar to make him into an expendable tool—one used and then discarded.

Bitterness soured his mouth. He should have betrayed Scar first, only—

"Where did you get this?" the patrollers asked him. "Who gave you these bags? Who put this transmitter on you?"

Elrabin clamped his jaws shut and refused to answer. If he mentioned Barthul's name here, the patrollers would take it as proof of his guilt, nothing more.

They shook him hard enough to rattle his teeth.

"Don't be stupid," the patrollers told him. "You're caught, either way. You might as well talk. Protecting your partner won't help you now."

"I have nothing to say," Elrabin muttered. "Carrying dirt is not illegal."

"Working as an accomplice to a dust runner is."

Elrabin's gaze flashed up in mock outrage. "You can't prove that."

"We don't have to prove anything. You resisted arrest. We received word a drop was going down in this alley, and out you came like a Skek. You also destroyed patroller property, and that is a Class F felony."

"Nothing," Elrabin said in defiance, trying to bluff. "I've done nothing."

The patrollers looked at each other. "We can kill him anyway, then say it was a mistake," one of them suggested.

"Too much paperwork involved," another said.

The third one stared at Elrabin without mercy. His Viis eyes were cold. "Put him in the slave market. Sell him to labor and recoup our expenses that way. It'll pay for a new sniffer and we won't have to file a loss-of-equipment form."

Desperate, realizing his da's fate was happening to him, Elrabin tried to struggle, but the stun effect still held him pinned. He could do nothing but wriggle slightly. "You can't sell me!" he said. "I got rights as a grade-two citizen. I'm free."

"Yes, free to starve. Free to steal and cause trouble. Even hard-labor slaves eat better than you, little grade-two citizen." The patroller flicked his fingers at the others. "Sell him."

CHAPTER EIGHTEEN

With its engine rumbling loudly, the transport lurched and veered through sluggish traffic. Other newer, sleeker transports passed it on all sides. Their cargo was secured beneath opaque bubbles, sometimes with force fields shimmering over them for extra security. The Gorlican slaver's old transport, however, had cheap crates stacked behind the driver's seat, while in the back cargo area, wire mesh served as sides and top.

Wedged between several bodies and the side of the cargo hold, Ampris gripped the rusting mesh and stared bleakly at the passing streets. Any chance to leave the palace was rare. Ampris had always been curious about the city, wondering how many people lived in it, and what they did all day. From hints and passing comments, she realized that common folk must lead lives far different from those at the palace. But today, she took little interest in the sights around her.

The transport flew down one block of the famous Zehava—the richest shopping district of the galaxy, renowned for its floating walkways and multileveled shops containing priceless wares of every description—before a traffic monitor blew a siren and warned it off.

Accordingly the transport veered sharply away and lumbered through less affluent, more industrialized streets. Traffic congestion grew steadily thicker. Horns blared at slim racing skimmers that flitted illegally in and out, narrowly missing the slower litters and transports, and creating havoc as they went.

Ampris turned her head to watch a pair of them dart by, racing for a few meters only to separate to avoid an oncoming transit module. Horns blared again, then the skimmers were gone, leaving only a curling wake of jetted exhaust behind them.

Israi would have admired them. Of late she had mentioned that she would like to have a skimmer of her own, something small and sleek. She had said that perhaps she would even teach Ampris to fly it.

Now such plans were like smoke, vanishing before they could be grasped. It was impossible to believe this was happening. Ampris kept telling herself this was reality and no dream, but it was too awful to comprehend.

An elbow dug into Ampris's ribs, prodding her from her thoughts.

"Look!" said a jeering voice in the slave patois. "It be the pampered pet herself. Ain't so pampered now, be you?"

Ampris turned around to meet the scornful eyes of an Aaroun male. Striped in shades of beige and brown, he held his right hand cradled protectively against his midriff. A clumsy splint and bandage covered the appendage.

When he caught her staring at it, he lifted his hand and waved it under her nose. She caught a sickly-sweet smell of rotting flesh.

"Won't heal, will it?" he said. "Had me a good spot in the gardening corps. Did, till a scythe near cut it off. Now I'm useless. Cripples can't work. Some high-and-mighty Viis lord or lady might see me and be offended."

He stuck his furred face close to Ampris's and glared at her. His breath stank of meat. "What'd you do, you, to make offense? Threw you out with the rest of us garbage, didn't they?''

Fresh sorrow welled up inside Ampris. ''It's a mistake,'' she said. ''They have to relent.''

He drew back and bared his teeth, while some of the others laughed bitterly. ''Have to relent,'' he said, mocking her. ''Relent? What kind of uppity Viis word is that, you?''

Ampris said, ''It means to—''

He nipped her ear, and someone laughed.

Shocked, Ampris stared at them.

The Aaroun leaned closer. ''Don't teach me nothing, you! Got no place over me, now. Be garbage like the rest of us. You learn to keep quiet.''

Looking at their hostile faces, Ampris trembled and resisted the urge to rub her aching ear. She refused to give him the satisfaction of knowing he'd hurt her. As for the others, now staring at her, why did they all look so angry and bitter? Why did they resent her? She wasn't to blame for their troubles.

When she said nothing, did nothing in response, the Aaroun bared his teeth again, looking more scornful than ever.

''Fancy *pet*,'' he said, making the word sound dirty and vile. ''But you be pet no more, you.''

''Yeah!'' put in a Kelth female, so old one of her eyes had filmed over and her muzzle had turned gray. ''No more pet you be, eh? No more fancy food. No more fancy treats or fancy clothes or fancy life, no!'' She laughed gleefully, her one good eye glittering with malice.

Ampris stared at her, then at all of them. ''Why are you all so angry at me?'' she asked. ''I've done nothing to any of you—''

They roared and surged toward her, making the transport dip to one side. Pummeled and bitten, Ampris crouched low with her hands folded over her head as protection.

''Done nothing, that be right,'' the Aaroun male said.

''Lazy pet!'' the old Kelth added.

''Never worked a day,'' said someone else.

"Never known a kick in the ribs," said a fourth voice.

"Or how it hurts, goin' without that supper."

They went on hurling accusations at her, and their rough, angry words hurt. The slaves closed in on her, dragging her upright and pounding on her again.

Growling in her throat, Ampris tried to fight back, but there were too many of them.

Then the transport lurched to a violent halt that threw several of them off their feet. The Aaroun male landed on top of Ampris, his heavy weight nearly squashing her.

She grunted and flailed, but he took his time getting up and made sure he stepped on her fingers and kicked her in the process. Curling up in pain, Ampris lay on her side while the others were herded off by Gorlicans. Their cruelty left her dazed. All she wanted to do was hide from everyone and be left alone.

But Gorlicans wearing stained leather jerkins over their torso shells and masks came stepping inside the cargo hold, their eyes glowing yellow as they shouted at her in ill temper. Using their long staffs, they prodded Ampris upright and sent her staggering down a loading ramp and into a narrow chute at the rear of an assorted group of slaves. There were four times the number that had been on her transport.

Ampris tried to hang back from anyone she recognized, but the Gorlicans kept prodding her hard with their staffs, snapping and grumbling at her as they forced her into the group.

Everyone was shoving and pushing, packed too close in the chute, shuffling forward yet unable to move fast enough to avoid the staffs and shock-whips of their handlers.

Bruised and jostled, Ampris concentrated on keeping her balance. She was afraid if she fell down she would be trampled to death.

Behind her another load of slaves came rushing down the loading ramp and into the chute, packing her in even more tightly. Her fear increased, but there was nowhere to go except forward.

Gorlicans stood lined up on either side of the chute, poking the slaves through the slats. Other Gorlicans paced overhead on a metal catwalk, their bootsteps making the mesh ring out.

The noise was deafening—all shouts and confusing commands. The stench nearly choked her. She had never smelled such filth in her life. Dust hung in the air like a fog, choking them, and the handlers kept shouting and pushing, confusing Ampris and making her panic.

A shock-whip lashed across the shoulders of a slave jostling next to her. Ampris heard the sizzle of impact and smelled his singed fur and flesh. The slave yelped and dodged sideways into Ampris, nearly knocking her down.

She grabbed at the slats of the chute for balance, but a Gorlican on the other side of it snarled at her and rapped his staff across her fingers.

Pain flared through her hand, and she snatched it back, whimpering. Cradling it against her stomach, she fought back her tears. It felt broken, the pain pulsing fire in the delicate bones of her hand. Thinking of the Aaroun gardener who'd been so bitter over his infected hand, Ampris gritted her teeth and flexed her fingers. So her hand was not broken, but, gods, how it hurt.

A staff thudded against her shoulder blades. "Move on!" came the command, and Ampris shuffled forward.

Ahead, the Gorlicans were opening small gates in the sides of the chute. With whips and shouts, they sorted through the jostling slaves, dividing them by size, breed, and age.

A staff struck Ampris in the back again, driving her forward with three others, but almost immediately a gate snapped across the chute in front of her, blocking her path. The yells increased in volume, and the slaves with Ampris milled around her in growing confusion.

"Her! Her!"

A Gorlican stood over her on the catwalk above her head. He poked his staff down to tap her on the shoulder. Ampris glanced up and froze in her tracks.

"Tell me what you want me to do!" she yelled in exasperation.

He didn't answer. The handlers on the ground thrust their staffs through the sides of the chute, separating the other slaves from her.

The gate blocking the chute snapped out of the way, and Ampris was prodded forward.

She ran, panting for breath and hearing the shouts of triumph. The gate slammed quickly behind her, cutting her off from everyone else.

For a few seconds she was alone in this section of the chute, alone except for the Gorlican who ran along the catwalk overhead, keeping pace with her easily. He was chanting something and tapping his staff on the mesh above her. The noise and rhythm jangled her nerves. She wanted to scream at him to stop.

Instead she halted abruptly, letting him run a few paces ahead of her. Gasping for breath, she whirled around and tried to run back the way she'd come, but the Gorlican overtook her in moments. His shock-whip lashed out ahead of her, sizzling and snapping centimeters from her nose.

Terrified, Ampris turned back and ran in the direction he wanted. He kept pace with her, yelling as though to urge her on faster.

More Gorlicans were waiting a short distance ahead, perched on the top rail in a huddle, making tallies on handheld data screens. At her approach, they scattered and ran to open another gate.

Going through it, Ampris turned and ran down a smaller chute, then through yet another gate, and another, until she was driven out into a large circular pen of smooth welded mesh topped with the same material.

Behind her the gate slammed shut and was bolted. The

Gorlicans yelled in satisfaction and ran back toward the chutes.

Breathing hard—more from fear than from exertion—Ampris realized they were through with her for the moment. She looked around, trying to steady herself, and saw that the pen held a central mound of fresh straw and a few scattered pails of water. Around the perimeter stood five benches cut from heavy blocks of stone and carved with graffiti. A few of the pen's occupants sat on them. The rest stood huddled in small groups at the opposite side from Ampris.

No one looked at her.

Finding this odd, she frowned and started to walk toward them. Then she stopped herself and veered away toward a deserted section of the pen. She remembered what had happened to her in the transport. It was better if she kept to herself.

Her legs were trembling. Crouching with her back to the fence, Ampris hugged herself and fought back her tears. She sensed this was not a place to show vulnerability. And yet, again and again through her mind flashed images of Israi's pretty apartment in the palace, the soothing, distant splashing of the fountains, the clean, polished stone floors, the well-trained slaves that were unobtrusive and silent, the fragrant scents of flowers and perfumes. How long had it been—an hour, two hours since she'd been ripped from her safe world? She'd lost all track of time.

Here, a foul stench hung over the chutes and pens that stretched on one side as far as she could see. On the other side, gray stone walls rose in a grim, solid barrier. Cries of misery rose from the other pens. In the distance, the Gorlicans yelled and banged their staffs ceaselessly.

Surveillance scanners swiveled constantly from every angle, keeping watch. A Gorlican handler walked diagonally across the top of her pen, alarming Ampris until she realized he was just a guard.

More slaves came through the chutes. Most of them

surged past the pen containing Ampris. She didn't want to watch, and yet she couldn't help herself.

The sorting and unloading went on all day. Now and then, the gate to Ampris's pen opened and a slave or two were pushed inside, but most of the new arrivals went into other pens farther down the row.

As the day progressed, the noise grew louder. Clouds of dust left a haze in the air. The slaves either stood quietly, their heads low in subjection, or paced restlessly, shouted, and banged on the fences.

No one came with food until sunset. By then Ampris was so ravenous she abandoned her sense of caution and rushed forward with the others to a long metal trough. Gorlicans dumped pails of food into the trough and jeered while the slaves jostled and fought over the best pieces.

Ampris, being younger and smaller than most, had trouble elbowing her way through the crowd, but she finally reached the trough and peered into it eagerly.

It held scraps of half-rotted food, produce past its prime, hunks of stale bread, and meat globes.

Repulsed, Ampris drew back. A Zrhel pushed her aside with a greasy wing and began to pick over the food rapidly, nibbling a sample, then tossing it back into the trough. He picked up something else and tasted it, swore, tossed it back in, and reached for another piece.

Ampris stared in disgust, losing the rest of her appetite. "Must you do that?" she asked.

The Zrhel ignored her, nibbling and scratching itself. It dropped a few feathers in the trough and did not pick them out.

"Get away!" Ampris shouted at him. "You're ruining the food. Have you no manners?"

The Zrhel turned his head to stare straight into her eyes. Beneath a bald, domed head his face was pinched and intelligent, with keen, defiant eyes above a hooked nose. Still meeting her gaze, he belched loudly, then turned his attention back to picking through the food.

Ampris backed away, leaving the Zrhel alone at the trough. She crossed the pen, and some of the others laughed at her.

One female Kelth was gnawing on a rock-hard crust of bread. She grinned at Ampris. "Get your food before the Zrhel reaches the trough. You'll learn."

Ampris returned to her solitary spot, her stomach growling in frantic insistence. Trying to ignore her misery, she sank down and stared at the stars beginning to twinkle in the spring sky overhead.

It was a long, lonely night.

The next day, more slaves arrived and were crowded into the pens. Ampris watched the proceedings, telling herself this nightmare had to end soon. Surely the Kaa would relent and allow her to go home.

But every time the gate to her pen opened, it was to push in more arrivals. No one came for her.

Ampris's spirits drooped, but she told herself to trust in Israi. Surely the sri-Kaa would find a way to get her back.

By afternoon, however, she wasn't quite as sure. Exhausted and hot from sitting in the relentless sun, Ampris watched yet another batch of newcomers come stumbling into her pen.

It was getting very crowded now. She kept to herself, grateful to be left alone.

Then a group of three Aarouns with spotted fur and heavy shoulders gathered around her. Their eyes held only hostility, and their short round ears were flat to their skulls.

The one in the center gestured at her. "Clear out, female," he said.

Ampris bared her teeth. "Why should I—"

They grabbed her and shoved her away bodily, causing her to stumble into a nearly grown Kelth, who growled in warning.

Ampris moved back swiftly and turned on the Aaroun

males who had taken her place. Angry, she started toward them, but the Kelth gripped her arm.

"Don't," he said in quiet warning. "You can't take them."

The idea of fighting them fueled her anger. "They have no right to—"

He pulled her away. "Come over here."

She tried to twist free of his grasp, but he tightened his hold.

She struggled harder. "Let go of me."

"Don't cause trouble. Stay quiet," he told her.

"Let go of me!"

He glared at her. "You cause trouble, you cause a fight, the handlers'll take you out and flay you. Want that, Goldie?"

Shocked, Ampris didn't know whether to believe him or not. "How do you know?"

He rolled his eyes at her, a dirty youth with brindled, matted fur, alert, upright ears, and streetwise eyes. He seemed to know everything, and she knew nothing.

On the opposite side of the pen, a short distance from the benches, he elbowed a way for them next to the fence and crouched there.

"Here is better," he said. He tugged at her wrist. "Sit. Make yourself slack."

His coat was made of cheap, shiny cloth. It looked new, yet it was already fraying at cuffs and collar. One sleeve was torn. A curious odor hung on him, something spicy and attractive, but somehow repellent. She had never smelled anything like it before. Her instincts told her to avoid him.

Yet, his light brown eyes held a hint of kindness, the first she'd encountered in this place.

She sat on the ground beside him, a little wary of her newfound friend.

He was looking her over too, his gaze keen and appraising. "You look pretty pampered, Goldie. Ever been in the slave market before?"

"No."

"Knew it." He rubbed his muzzle in a quick nervous gesture. "Me neither."

The confession made him somehow more likable. Ampris edged closer. "This is a horrible place."

He glanced around. "Yeah, maybe. I'm called Elrabin. How about yourself?"

"Ampris."

"Suits you, Goldie. Kind of fancy and . . . pretty," he added almost shyly.

Ampris smiled.

He smiled back. "When do they grill the grub?"

She stared at him without comprehension. "I beg your pardon?"

"Food," he snapped in exasperation. "You understand that?"

"Oh. We're fed at sunset." Ampris wrinkled her nose. "It's terrible."

He grunted and didn't seem to believe her.

"I'm telling the truth," she said. "It's like garbage thrown away from the kitchens. Rotted, molded, stale—"

"Sounds like a feast," he said, and made smacking sounds.

She couldn't tell if he was joking or serious. "I couldn't eat it last night. Now all I can think about is food. I've never been this hungry before."

The sympathy died in Elrabin's eyes. "Hungry? You been without food how long? A day? That's nothing, Goldie."

"It's horrible!" she said. "You know nothing about how it feels to be—"

"Shut up," he said fiercely. "Don't look down your nose at me! You're fat and sleek. You—"

"I am *not* fat!" she said with indignation. "I am in perfect condition."

He scowled, unimpressed, and flung open his coat. "Feel my ribs."

She hesitated, staring at him.

With a little growl of impatience, Elrabin seized her hand and thrust it against his side. She felt knobby ribs under his pelt of rough hair, with practically no flesh in between.

"Yeah," he said, "and I been eating regular since I became a runner. Before that, I picked up garbage off the streets, fighting Skeks for it."

"Skeks!" she said in horror.

He tilted his head to one side. "Where do you come from? You don't know nothing. You don't look like you've worked."

"Worked?" She shook her head. "Of course not."

"In this life, you either work, Goldie, or you steal."

She straightened in indignation. "I am no thief. I would never take—"

"Stuff the howl," he said in sharp scorn.

"What?"

"Be quiet." Elrabin glanced around swiftly to see if anyone was paying attention to them. "You better learn faster, Goldie, or you're finished. You follow?"

She frowned. "I'm not going to be here long. They'll send for me."

"Who? The fancy Viis family that owned you?"

Ampris lifted her chin with pride. "I am Ampris, closest friend and companion of the sri-Kaa."

She expected him to be impressed, but his expression didn't change.

He didn't say anything either.

His refusal to believe her was an insult. "I lived in the palace," she insisted. "All my life I have been at the sri-Kaa's side."

"So?"

She drew an impatient breath. "I have permission to speak Viis. I can read and write. I have—"

"So what'd you do?"

She stopped her boasting and blinked at him. "Do? Why, whatever the Imperial Daughter wanted to do. We—"

"No, stupid. You must have done something wrong. Something to get you sent here."

Ampris felt fresh sorrow turn over inside her. She backed her ears.

"Just another of life's injustices," he said. His words were sympathetic, but his tone came out raw with anger. "You do your best and you still get slagged. You think you know someone, but you never do. It's all a lie, Goldie. Everything is a lie."

The bitterness in his voice was belied by the apprehension she saw lurking in his eyes. She understood then that his words were mostly bravado. Underneath his roughness, he was just as scared as she.

"Why are you here?" she asked.

The faraway look in his eyes faded, to be replaced by anger. "I'm here on an arrest charge."

Ampris had never talked to anyone who'd been arrested before. She stared at him. "Are you a thief?"

Elrabin bared his teeth. "Nah. I'm above that, unless forced to it. I've played the cons and the scams with the best. Then I got in a spot, had to fall in with a gang, see? Had to work for them. So I became a dust runner."

Ampris found him very strange, and not at all understandable. "Why would you run with dust?"

He threw back his head with shrill yips of laughter. "Gods, you're no more streetwise than a newborn lit. How've you survived this long, not knowing anything?"

Then his eyes narrowed, and he gave her no chance to answer. "You honest?" he asked. "You talking straight about living in the palace, and all that?"

She nodded. "Everything is so different here."

"Yeah, I guess it is." He looked at the crowded pen, at the milling, uneasy occupants, at the filth, at the fence.

Overhead, a group of Gorlicans walked across the top of the pen, pausing to point and gesture in earnest discussion.

Elrabin watched them a moment, then lowered his gaze to meet Ampris's. "Those are buyers," he said grimly. "They're looking us over before the auction."

"What auction?" Ampris said. "I don't understand anything here. Please explain it to me."

He shifted his gaze away from hers and started drawing aimlessly in the dust. "Never been sold before," he muttered, and his voice sounded scared now. "Never worn an ownership number."

She thought of her pretty ownership earring with Israi's cartouche. Her ear felt naked and light without it. "It doesn't have to be bad."

He made no answer.

His fear increased Ampris's own. She reached out and gently took his hand in hers.

"What's going to become of us?" she asked.

Elrabin wouldn't look at her, but he didn't draw his hand away. "We'll go in the sale," he said, his voice tight and low. "We'll be sold in the common market. They have different auctions for house slaves and highly skilled workers like that Zrhel over there."

Ampris's fingers tightened on his. "I remember being taken from my mother when I was very young, just a few days old. Now it's like that is happening all over again. Israi is my family. I thought she would have come for me by now."

Panting, he sent her a glance of pity. "So you're really the one," he whispered. "The one I've heard talked about. I even saw you once on the vid broadcast, riding in a parade or something. You're the Imperial Daughter's pet."

"I am her *friend*," Ampris said with pride.

"So why did she get angry at you and throw you out?"

"She didn't. It was the Kaa."

"So what did you do to the Kaa?"

"Nothing," Ampris said with a sigh. "I was taken away to punish Israi for one of her pranks."

Elrabin pricked his ears at her. "So they punished you for something she did?"

Ampris dropped her gaze. "I—I guess so."

"That stinks."

Agreement made Ampris's ears droop. "Yes," she said, very softly.

"Still think she's your friend?"

She didn't like his criticizing Israi. "It wasn't her fault. The Kaa decreed the punishment."

"So why didn't he punish Israi?"

The hair rose on the back of Ampris's neck. "Don't call her that. You do not have permission to—"

"Oh, slag that," he said rudely. "She's the one who should be punished, not you. She did the prank, so what good does it do to be rough on you?"

Ampris found herself agreeing, and that scared her. "If anyone hears you speaking against the Kaa, you will lose your tongue. Maybe your head." She thought of the trophy room at the mountain lodge, and shuddered.

"So I lose my tongue," he said with scorn, although his ears swiveled nervously. "Is that worse than having my hand cut off if I'm caught stealing? Or being sold into hard labor tomorrow at auction? I'll spend the rest of my life hauling stones until my back snaps and I'm thrown into the sewers to rot. And for what? The Kaa owns machines that could rebuild his precious old buildings in a few months. But, no, he wants everything done by hand the way it used to be. So he enslaves entire races to do the work. He tears families apart, the way he tore apart yours. He walks on our backs and crushes the life from us. He lets transit systems decay and buildings fall down and jump gates fail, all because he cares more about the past than he does the present."

"Stop it!" Ampris cried, horrified by what came spewing from Elrabin. "You don't know what you're saying. I know that past kaas have been cruel, but this one is good and kind. He cares about his subjects."

Elrabin yipped with derision. "He cares nothing! Before she died, my mother worked herself to a shadow for sub-grade wages and low food allotments that wouldn't feed the lits. My da—"

"That is a problem of society," Ampris said, quoting a courtier she had once overheard. "Chancellor Gaveid says that—"

"Him? All the commentators on the vids say he's against abiru reforms. He's our enemy."

Ampris drew back. "You don't know him. You've never met him."

Elrabin stared at her as though he could not believe what he saw. "You sit here, in the dirt, in an auction pen *where they sent you,* and you defend them. Worse, you talk like a Viis—all pride and emptiness, blind to the way things really are. What kind of Aaroun are you?"

Ampris felt as though all the wind had been crushed from her. Speechless, she stared back at him. Her mind wound back to the data crystal Bish had given her about the once-proud history of her people. She thought about the fate of her ancestors, how they had been torn from their homes and made into slaves to serve Viis society. She thought about her own trust and security, shattered in a moment by the Kaa's terrible wrath. Not even Israi had been able to save her from this place.

"You're right," she said softly, bowing her head so that Elrabin could not see her shame. Retracting her claws, she curled her hands into fists. "I just want to go home."

Despite the sympathy in Elrabin's eyes, his expression remained bleak. "That will never happen, Goldie. You might as well face it. Aarouns are meant for labor. No matter how pretty you are, your easy life is over."

She turned away from him, her heart pounding. "I won't believe that. They have to relent. They have to!"

"Why should they?"

Battling her tangled emotions, she couldn't answer.

He touched her shoulder. "I'm sorry to carry you the

bad news, Goldie, but you have to face it. Sooner or later we all come to the wall.''

She shook her head. ''I have lived all my life with them. They treated me like . . . like a part of—''

''You're not Viis,'' he said firmly. ''You know that. No matter if the Imperial Daughter played with you or how many privileges you enjoyed, it's over. Gods, I can't even imagine the life you've led. Everything you wanted. Food every day. Jewels to wear. Some slave waiting on you hand and foot. But it's not real, Goldie.''

He gestured across the pen to where the Zrhel was scratching his feathers and belching as a way of passing the time. ''*This* is real. This stink hole is where you belong, and I belong, and all of us belong. Anything else is a dream, a cloud in the mind.''

Tears welled up in her eyes, hot and stinging. ''I want the dream,'' she whispered. ''I've lived in it too long. I want to go back.''

''You don't belong there. You never did. And now they've put you out and closed the gates. Accept it—''

''No!'' she said. She glared at him, furious now. ''I will *never* accept it. Israi will send for me. I know she will. She promised to always take care of me, and she will keep that promise.''

''Believe in nothing, Goldie. The Viis keep only the promises they want to keep. They are liars, tyrants, and users. Everything they do is a lie. Everything you've always known is a lie.''

''You're wrong,'' Ampris said. ''They're not *all* like that.''

''Sure,'' he said, swiveling his ears and moving away from her. ''So tell me again why you're here.''

And Ampris was left with nothing else to say.

CHAPTER NINETEEN

At sunset, Ampris stayed crouched beside the fence while the others crowded and fought at the food trough. Ampris refused to fight over the bad-quality food. She certainly had no intention of eating it, no matter how strongly her stomach gnawed against her backbone. She was beginning to feel dizzy sometimes, but she didn't care. In the morning, she told herself, the palace guards would come for her. They would take her home, and Subi would feed her civa cakes and spicemeats, as much as she wanted, and then she would have a bath. This place would be a forgotten nightmare, fading swiftly from her mind.

If only she could drive it away now. She turned her back to the pen, staring through the fence at the walls beyond. The squabbling, the screeching, the stench of too many unwashed bodies too close together . . . she hated all of it.

A claw-tipped hand gripped her shoulder, startling her to such a degree that she cried out. She whirled around, her heart pounding, then saw it was only Elrabin.

She relaxed, letting out her breath in a rumble. "You scared me."

"You're like a cub," he said gruffly, placing a chunk of

greasy meat in her hand. "Never turn your back on folk. Always keep watch."

"I have no enemies here," she said, and then thought of the palace slaves who had beaten her during the ride in the transport. She was glad none of them were in this pen.

Elrabin dropped to his haunches beside her and pulled a second chunk of meat from his pocket. He sniffed it, then started gnawing on it. "Enemies can come from nowhere," he said, and shot her a sideways look. "So you're speaking to me again?"

"Not willingly." She tried to hand him her piece of meat. "No, thank you."

"Don't be stupid. Eat it before someone takes it from you." He bit off another piece, chewed, and swallowed. "Sniff it for maggots, then eat around them. Don't look at it."

Ampris stared at the meat in disgust and dropped it on the ground. "It has maggots in it? I can't eat such a thing."

Swearing, Elrabin snatched the meat off the ground and thrust it deep in his pocket. "That was stupid," he said angrily. "Stupid, stupid, stupid. Never refuse food. *Never*. If you want to live, then you got to learn."

"I will eat tomorrow when I go home," Ampris said.

Elrabin scowled at her, then went back to eating. He ate his piece and hers, hunched up and wary as though he expected someone to take it from him.

Ampris listened to her stomach growl and decided perhaps he was right about her being stupid. He had been kind to bring her food, and she'd insulted him with her refusal.

Sighing, she finally said, "I'm sorry."

He licked his mouth and belched. "No good being sorry now. I ate your share."

"Never mind that. It was very kind of you to try and help me. Really it was. I'm sorry I didn't thank you properly for your care and concern."

Still he wouldn't look at her. "It's gone. Too late to get more, no matter how sorry you are."

"I know. I'm not asking for the meat." She looked at him with exasperation. "I'm apologizing, not begging."

"Yeah." He turned to face her. "Never met anyone like you. Abiru but not abiru. You got education. You talk fancy. You're special, Goldie."

She felt suddenly shy and embarrassed, yet warm inside. "Thank you."

"I got no one now," he said as the twilight shadows closed around them. "My family's gone. As for my friends, they're nothing. Never were my friends. Never were." He scowled. "Don't want no more friends."

"You've been a friend to me today," Ampris said shyly. "Thank you for that."

"Quit thanking me," he said gruffly. "And I ain't your friend."

She didn't want to argue with him, so she changed the subject. "What will happen tomorrow?"

"You got to be ready for the auction," he said. "You got to find a way to take the shame of it, Goldie. Otherwise, you won't make it. You follow me?"

Dread rose inside her, and she tried to ignore it. "I think so. Only maybe—"

"Stop it!" He reached out and gripped her hand hard. "Stop thinking maybe. There's only now—what is right now. You follow? You got to be strong inside yourself. You can't let them break you. You can't let them beat you. Not inside, where it counts." He pressed his fist against his heart. "It's the only way to survive."

"I'm afraid," she said with a shiver, thinking about his words.

Around them, the other captives were talking among themselves or pacing. It was a restless night; tension could be felt in the air. Someone wailed in a distant pen, and was silenced.

Ampris realized that Elrabin was right. She'd been fooling no one but herself with her optimism.

"I'm afraid too," Elrabin admitted softly. "I always said

I was too smart to get caught. Only, I was wrong. I let myself trust again, when all the time I knew better. Now I get to pay for that. Sold out. The law of the streets. Sell out someone before they sell you.'' He glanced at her. ''Maybe it's the law of the palace too.''

''No! Israi stood up for me.''

''But she didn't rescue you.''

Ampris backed her ears and said nothing else. She couldn't keep denying it forever.

''When you're sold to someone,'' she said in a soft voice, ''what happens?''

''Depends. What kind of labor you go to. What you're trained for.'' Elrabin drew on the ground for a few seconds, although it was too dark to see the pattern. ''The auction ain't a good place, Goldie. Good places are private merchants, private sales. The auction ain't good.''

She wanted to ask more, but Elrabin abruptly turned his back on her and curled himself on the ground. ''Get some sleep,'' he said.

In the morning, the Gorlicans, yelling and snapping open gates, had them up at dawn. Whips cracked and sizzled on all sides. They were prodded back into the chute, urged along at a swift trot and crowded too close together.

Ampris stumbled and would have fallen had Elrabin not steadied her.

She was dizzy with thirst and hunger, feeling light-headed and frightened. Colors and shapes looked alien today. Noises were too loud or too soft. Her knees felt unable to support her, yet she forced herself to keep up.

Elrabin kept shaking his head and muttering gloomy things about being the first lot on the block. Ampris tried to hang on to her failing courage.

She didn't know what to expect, but the humiliations she'd encountered up till now—being treated like a non-sentient animal, being forced to live dirty, being forced to eat garbage—were nothing compared to what lay ahead of her.

When she came staggering up a ramp onto a tall stone platform surrounded by a gallery of seats filled with spectators, her hide felt too tight for her body and her skin began to burn beneath her fur.

Surveillance cameras mounted on the walls swiveled this way and that. The top of the market was open to the sky, and the newly risen sun shone dazzling light over Ampris.

Gorlican buyers and agents whistled when they saw her. They stamped their round feet and began talking rapidly into their comms.

Shoved into a single-file line behind Elrabin, Ampris walked across the platform with the other slaves in her lot. They were forced to stop and face the spectators, then were prodded into a narrow holding pen on the other side.

The handlers used staffs to separate one reddish-gold Myal from the others and sent him shuffling back onto the platform alone. The auctioneer opened the bidding while buyers crowded around the holding pen with avaricious eyes.

Every few minutes, the auctioneer cried, "Sold!" The handlers would select another slave from the pen, and the process would start again.

Appalled, Ampris watched each slave go through humiliating physical examinations. Some submitted tamely, standing with faces averted in shame. Others fought and were whipped. The speed and efficiency of the handlers and auctioneer kept everything moving fast, too fast.

Elrabin stood beside Ampris, close enough that she could feel him trembling. She saw that his eyes were wet and shiny.

He panted, and his ears moved constantly.

When Ampris touched his arm gently in reassurance, he jumped.

Embarrassment clouded his eyes, and he dropped his gaze from hers.

"Why are they so cruel?" Ampris asked in a soft voice.

"Why do they take so much joy in hurting, in shaming us?"

Elrabin shrugged. "My father was sold into hard labor," he said in a low voice. "I swore to myself that I would never share his fate. I thought I was too smart, too clever to get caught. Now . . ." He let his voice trail off.

The handlers opened the holding pen and a long hook reached through the milling slaves to catch Elrabin's collar.

"No!" Ampris cried out, and reached for him.

Another handler struck her in the stomach with a staff, knocking her off her feet.

Winded, she rolled onto her knees and wheezed for breath. She felt nauseated, and she couldn't straighten from the pain in her stomach.

By the time she staggered to her feet, Elrabin was being forced from the pen. He fought every step of the way, panic and fury mingling in his howls. The handlers put a restraint noose around his throat and another around his arms, binding them. Still, it took three Gorlicans to push him onto the block.

"Hey, hey!" the auctioneer said loudly, his voice echoing over the speaker system. He waved his flag for the spectators' attention. "A fine young Kelth, full-grown or close to it. A lifetime of work in his muscles, eh? Bids are open!"

The bidding went swiftly, too much so for Ampris to comprehend.

"Sold!" the auctioneer said a few seconds later. A price flashed on the information board above his head. "To Utar Dan Gladiator School."

The handlers shoved Elrabin off the block, pushing him from Ampris's sight. She realized suddenly that she would never see him again. She hadn't even thanked him again for his kindness. She hadn't even said good-bye.

Grief swelled inside her. Frantically she threw herself against the mesh side of the pen. "Elrabin!" she shouted at the top of her lungs. "Elrabin!"

But he was gone from sight, already whisked away by the efficient system.

Ampris clung to the fence, still calling his name.

The auctioneer glared at her and gestured for the handlers to bring her out.

Ampris tried to run from them, but a shock-whip flicked across her shoulders. The sizzle of pain locked her in mid-step, and she stumbled to her knees with her mouth open in a silent cry of agony.

They grabbed her by her arms and dragged her upright, slinging her around and pushing her from the pen. At the steps leading up to the block, one of the handlers pushed his masked face close to hers.

She smelled his hot, fetid breath as his glowing yellow eyes bored deep into hers. Repulsed and frightened, she tried to draw back, but he leaned closer.

"You good property," he said in a hoarse, guttural voice. "You bring good price. Walk straight. No cry. No show pain. No cause trouble."

She quivered in his hold, wanting to spit in his face, wanting to claw and bite.

His eyes glowed brighter. "Good look. Spirit raise value."

"You—"

But they shoved her up the steps onto the block and fitted her feet into two depressions that locked onto her with vise-like strength, holding her fast. The handlers vanished, and the spectators shouted with interest and questions.

The auctioneer's voice boomed over the speakers: "A fine specimen of the Aaroun breed. Young enough to be trained. Strong and straight. We can certify no bones have been broken. Complete health and a high level of intelligence. Regard the quality of this grade-twelve pelt, how thick and lustrous it is. Unusual coloring, with no spots or stripes. This young female can be used to infuse your breeding stock with new vigor."

Ampris shut out what he was saying. It was too awful,

too embarrassing. Drenched with shame, she stood there before the tiers of spectators with her ears flat to her skull and her claws digging into her palms. She wanted to die.

She had never been put on display like this before, had never been stared at this way. They did not treat her as a person, but instead as a piece of property to be bought or sold. In their eyes, she was only goods, priced merchandise. For the first time in her life, she knew what it meant to be a slave.

Humiliation burned inside her. She wanted to throw back her head and roar at them. She wanted to break free of her bonds and attack the auctioneer, to bite him until he was silenced. She wanted to charge at the agents who were putting in swift calls to potential buyers over their comms. If she were grown, bigger and stronger, she thought, she could get loose somehow and make them all sorry.

Then, just when she thought things couldn't get worse, the auctioneer activated a control at his podium and sent her turning slowly around and around like wares on display in a shop.

Both shamed and furious, she fought back tears and instead held herself proudly in defense. She reminded herself that she was the friend of the sri-Kaa. She had eaten from the Imperial Daughter's plate, had walked everywhere the Imperial Daughter walked, had spent her life in the palace as one of the favored. She had sometimes been permitted to lean against the Kaa's knee when he read to his young daughter. In these things, Ampris took her pride and her identity. Even if she had lost everything else, even if she had been turned against by all those whom she loved, she could at least cling to the court protocols that she had been so rigorously taught.

Thus, she stood straight and tall, holding her head high. She stared at no one, and let nothing cross her face despite the pounding of her heart and the dryness on her tongue.

Murmurs of appreciation ran through the crowd. The auctioneer beamed.

Gorlican handlers came forward to hold up Ampris's arms, calling out measurements of reach, then of height and weight. One blew on her fur to certify its quality. Although Ampris resisted, they forced open her mouth to examine her teeth.

"None missing," the auctioneer reported to the crowd. "None rotted."

Then she was spun around again, rotating until she had to close her eyes to keep from getting dizzy.

"A prize of the very highest quality," the auctioneer boomed over the speaker system. "Such an opportunity comes to the market rarely. As you know, the best slaves are usually sold through private agents. But she—"

"What is her provenance?" shouted someone.

"I certify her as a legal acquisition," the auctioneer said smoothly. "Now, let's open the bidding at—"

"Stop in the name of the sri-Kaa!" called out a stern voice in ringing tones.

Ampris opened her eyes as the spectators craned to look. The auctioneer's voice faltered.

Ampris saw a squadron of Viis guards wearing palace green come striding into the market. Their captain swept one glance around the place, then trotted up the steps and went straight to the auctioneer.

The loudspeakers were snapped off. The information board went blank. Amid the buzz of speculation, Ampris went on rotating around and around. Her hopes rose like bubbles. She had known all along that Israi would find a way to save her.

"We're in the middle of a sale," the auctioneer complained. "Bidding is at—"

"I am not interested in your activities," the captain said in a sharp voice. He produced a gold disk of authority, and the auctioneer froze in place at the very sight of it.

"Yes, of—of course," the auctioneer said. "Whatever—"

"This Aaroun is the property of the sri-Kaa, wrongfully

taken from the palace. She is to be released at once.''

The auctioneer's mouth fell open. ''But, Captain, I must protest this high-handed—''

''Do you dispute the sri-Kaa's authority?''

The auctioneer quailed. ''No! Not at all. Not in the least. Please do not misunderstand me. But—but are you certain *this* Aaroun is the one you seek? Her value is extremely high, and a mistake of identity could cost me thousands of—''

''I am not interested in your costs. This Aaroun is the property of the sri-Kaa. It is a Class A felony to sell her without authority. Do you wish to be arrested for theft and—''

''No!'' The auctioneer made placating gestures. ''Not at all. I will make no protests. Such a fine young creature, but alas, some mistake must have been made. I do not understand how she came to be here. There is no ownership earring, no means of—Please, take her. Take her!''

He said the last sentence almost as an oath, snarling as he spoke, and pushed the controls that stopped Ampris from rotating. Her foot restraints released her, and she stumbled across the platform to the captain, eager to be taken away.

''The sri-Kaa has sent for me?'' she asked.

The captain's glance was cursory. ''Come at once.''

Intense relief swept Ampris. Israi had not failed her after all. She was saved.

Turning to join the other guards, Ampris saw the world suddenly tilt and spin around her. Everything went blank, and when she blinked back to consciousness it was to find herself aboard a skimmer with its siren blaring. They surged through the open traffic lane that other vehicles cleared for them.

Ampris blinked and sat up, holding her head, which felt very strange and light. She had the feeling that if it weren't attached, it might float off and be lost. Worse, a restrictive tug of cable hampered her movements. She discovered that she was wearing a broad collar around her throat, and a wide cuff around each wrist and ankle. Restraint cables, inactivated, snaked between each point, effectively binding her.

Jerking the cable between her wrists, she sat bolt upright, fighting a fresh bout of vertigo. "What happened?" she mumbled. "Why am I restrained?"

The captain sat next to her, his cloak fluttering in the wind. His attention seemed focused on the driver of the skimmer, as though he would have preferred to pilot it himself. At her question, he turned his brilliant Viis eyes upon her. "Aside from a routine beating, what special injuries have they inflicted on you?"

"I don't know," Ampris said in confusion. Her head ached, and she felt terrible. "I'm hungry. I—"

The captain flicked his fingers, and an underling opened a compartment from which he produced a bottle of puriska fruit juice and a packet of wafers.

Ampris consumed the food avidly, ignoring the fact that such snacks were usually denied her. Although everything tasted too sweet, she was too hungry and thirsty to care. She licked every crumb and finished the juice to the final drop.

Only then did she happen to glance up and see the palace spires in the distance . . . behind them. Her head swiveled around in alarm. "Where are we going? Why am I bound like this? I wish to be taken to the sri-Kaa at once."

"Silence," the captain snapped. "You do not give the orders here."

Ampris glared at him. "And you will treat the companion of the sri-Kaa with respect."

His rill reddened, but his gaze did not shift from hers. "It is beneath me to argue with a half-grown Aaroun. Keep silent as you have been commanded, or I will muzzle you."

She was already bound like a criminal. The muzzle would be the final humiliation. She had no desire to wear one. Still, she did not understand where they were taking

her. Unless . . . "Am I being stolen?" she asked, backing
her ears.

The captain uttered a Viis laugh, so contemptuous it cut
like glass, and flicked out his tongue at her. The other
guards laughed too.

Ampris swallowed a growl and glared at the passing
buildings. "Where are we going?" she demanded, sitting
erect in her seat. "Why do you not return me to the sri-
Kaa?"

The captain's look of amusement faded. Again he flicked
his fingers, and a muzzle was taken from a storage compartment. Seeing it, Ampris stiffened and howled in protest,
but the muzzle was crammed on her head and switched on.
She opened her mouth, panting hard, but she could not utter
a sound. Her throat felt as though it was being squeezed,
although she could still breathe. Miserable and frightened,
she no longer knew what to think as the skimmer flew
farther and farther from the palace.

Still blaring its siren, the skimmer crossed traffic lanes
and dipped beneath a congested snarl at an intersection.
Looking down, Ampris saw a district of faded glory.
Houses of great age, with outdated architectural details,
stood crammed together along narrow streets. Clusters of
shops filled little squares. Ampris saw a tiny public garden
surrounded by a security force field. Viis chunen played
there under the casual watch of their nursemaids.

The skimmer veered again, just as a loud boom rattled
the buildings and made Ampris jump. A gleaming shuttle
launched into the sky, and to her horror Ampris realized
they were approaching one of the terminals. Incoming shuttles circled far overhead, and the boom of takeoffs came
almost constantly.

Ampris panted harder, unable to scream her protests. She
couldn't believe this was happening. How could these
guards steal her so openly? Why should they dare? Did they
not fear the wrath of Israi when this crime was discovered?
She jerked at her bindings until the captain glared at her

and threatened to activate the entire restraint field. Glaring back, Ampris tried to stand up, ready to hurl herself bodily off the skimmer as it entered the approach-traffic channel that led into Vir Station Four, the cargo terminal that served both domestic and offworld flights.

Swearing, the captain grabbed her by her collar and hauled her back into her seat so hard it jolted her bones. "Be still," he said, his rill a deep red. He yanked her close enough for her to see the finest pebble-grain of his facial skin, and his eyes bored into hers. "You will cause no trouble," he said in a low, furious voice for her ears alone. "You are here because the sri-Kaa has commanded you to be here. Why she cares about your fate, no one knows, but she wishes you to have a good home with a worthy family."

Listening to him, still unable to speak, Ampris felt her eyes fill with tears. She did not believe him. She could not. Israi would not give her away. What was he saying?

"She has braved the wrath of the Kaa on your miserable behalf," the captain said. "She has persuaded him to relent, and she even abased herself to present a formal public apology to the Lady Zureal for what happened."

Ampris closed her eyes a moment, awash with feelings of relief and bewilderment. If Israi had done all that, why then was Ampris here?

"Now, will you behave?" the captain said sternly. "I do not wish to beat you, but I will if you do not remember your training and act in a subdued manner."

Opening her eyes, Ampris felt a shuddering jolt pass through the skimmer as it was locked into a tractor field and pulled through the approach channel into the terminal itself. Spans of trium alloy vaulted high overhead, supporting panels of tinted glass through which the sky looked green. The terminal echoed with noise as robots labeled cargo pods and tossed them onto moving belts.

Ampris forced herself to meet the captain's merciless eyes. She still did not understand.

He switched off the restraint field on her muzzle, and she sagged, coughing in relief.

"You will be treated better if you arrive looking and acting like a slave of refinement and proper training," he said to her. The skimmer halted with a bump, and the other guards jumped off onto a dock platform. The captain rose to his feet and stared down at her. "Or you can remain savage, clamped in a restraint field, and find yourself sold as soon as you arrive."

Ampris held out her bound wrists. "Take them off, please," she said, forcing her voice to be meek.

He flicked out his tongue. "You must wear the cables during the shuttle flight. Regulations," he said. "My advice is to act as though they are unnecessary. It is to your advantage."

She realized he was trying, in his own way, to be kind. Her heart lurched inside her, and she found herself still unable to believe this was happening. "She is sending me away from her?" Ampris asked plaintively. "I do not understand."

The captain raised his rill with visible impatience and looked past her at the other guards. They had secured an empty cargo pod and were waiting.

The captain handed Ampris a holocube. "This will explain," he said. "Now get in the pod and behave. It's a short flight to Malraaket. You will prosper there if you use good sense."

Clutching the holocube, which bore Israi's seal, Ampris started to speak, but the captain gave a signal and the guards hauled Ampris off the skimmer and pushed her into the pod.

She howled, trying to climb out, but a ruthless hand shoved her down and the two halves of the pod were snapped shut around her, closing her in.

Furious and frightened, she pounded on the sides, but it did no good. In seconds, she felt a thump from outside as her pod was labeled, then she was bounced onto a belt and borne away into the controlled chaos of the cargo hold.

She could not escape the pod, and Ampris stopped pounding on it as she was jolted along. Instead, she switched on the holocube, desperate for answers.

A second later, Israi's lovely face shimmered in the air before her. Israi's radiant eyes were dimmed with sadness. "My dearest companion," she said, and the sound of her voice made Ampris weep in longing. "I have pleaded long and hard for your return, but your own treachery has made my efforts futile. I thought I knew you, my golden Ampris, but I was mistaken. The guards found a sivo crystal of forbidden information in your belongings chest, and my duty is clear."

"No!" Ampris cried aloud as though the image of Israi could hear her. "I didn't listen to all of it. I never took the time."

"Chancellor Gaveid says you cannot be trusted close to my imperial person," Israi continued. "But because I loved you once, I—"

"You love me still," Ampris said. "You must!"

"—I cannot allow you to be destroyed as the Imperial Father commanded. Therefore, I have arranged for you to be placed in the home of a family of Lady Lenith's distant acquaintance. Perhaps there you can begin again. Enclosed with this message is a token of my regard. It has no real worth, but comes from the Aaroun culture, which you apparently value more than my company. Shame be on you, Ampris, for breaking our happiness. Good-bye."

"No!" Ampris cried, but the image vanished.

She played it again while her pod was being loaded onto a shuttle. And again during the flight. And again upon arrival while her pod was unloaded. By then she had memorized every word of Israi's parting message. Israi's tone held a finality that crushed Ampris's heart.

But it was so unfair. Ampris had done nothing wrong, nothing treacherous. The crystal's information held only history about the Aarouns. What harm lay in that? How could Israi say she was no longer faithful, no longer to be trusted?

Worst of all, how could Israi blame her for what had happened, when the prank against Lady Zureal had been Israi's idea in the first place? Ampris had tried to stop her friend and failed. Why, as Elrabin had pointed out, should she be punished? Why should she carry sole blame?

Twisting the bottom of the holocube, she opened its compartment and withdrew a necklace on a cheap metal chain. She held it up, and recognized the disk-shaped amulet with its distinctive center of clear stone.

"An Eye of Clarity," she said aloud in astonishment.

Worthless, according to Israi. Precious beyond all measure, according to Bish.

Holding it in her hand, Ampris bowed her head in bitterness and thought of what she'd lost—the way of life she'd always known, the friend she'd loved from her earliest memories. For all of that, the Eye of Clarity seemed a very poor exchange.

And Ampris wept.

CHAPTER TWENTY

The port of Malraaket was capital of the southern continent, smaller than Vir and lacking both the imperial city's size and galactic importance. Located on a wedge of land between a wide, sluggish river and the broad sweep of sea beyond, Malraaket rose in a glittering jumble of spires and domes painted every bright color imaginable. Balconies jutted out beneath the windows, many of them lush with blooming, vining plants that spilled vivid hues of pink and magenta down the sides of buildings. Seabirds wheeled around the eves of houses. Fat poufers strutted on the rooftops, cooing to themselves. Bells rang, traffic blared, incoming sea vessels whooped approach sirens to warn off outgoing barges. The activity never seemed to slacken.

Uninterested in politics or the governance of a vast empire, and therefore free of a heavy bureaucratic burden, Malraaket supported a flourishing trade center for merchants of all kinds. Importers and exporters of exotic goods thronged the vast complex that was its cargo terminal. Dozens of dialects and languages filled the air with a racket that punctuated the general noise of the city itself—all of it making Ampris's head spin. Parked on a pickup dock beside an impressive stack of crates that smelled of spices, her restraint cables fastened to a bolt clip stout enough to hold tonnage, Ampris sat in the broiling sun, panting in the heat, and unsure of what was to befall her next. She'd been waiting two hours, with nothing to do but count incoming shuttle flights, and it looked like the family Israi had sold her to had no desire to come fetch her.

From her vantage point, she could glimpse the sea through a gap between distant buildings. But although she was awed by its vast size—it stretched to the horizon and beyond—its scent impressed her more. She had never before smelled such a briny fragrance, or one so mingled with the odor of fish and other sea creatures. Oh, she was used to the strong scent of the Cuna Da'r River, with its muddy, reed-strewn banks. But the sea . . . inhaling deeply, Ampris closed her eyes and felt her senses surge toward the glittering water. It was raw, primitive, elemental. It drew her in some mysterious way, awakened strange urges inside her, made her blood throb heavily in her veins. She wanted to roam. She wanted to explore. She wanted to hunt.

But the cables held her in place. She was tied too short to allow her to stand and stretch her legs. And there wasn't a finger's breadth of shade.

Periodically a Viis dock guard swathed in a white robe of strange coarse-woven fabric would walk past her and make a notation on his manifest. This time, Ampris gazed up at him. "If no one comes to pick me up, what will happen—"

With a wordless exclamation, the guard unclipped a short bar from his belt and struck her with it. Knocked flat on her back, her chest and shoulder burning with pain, Ampris struggled for breath.

The guard stamped his booted foot on her wrist, pinning her there. His rill, bright red, stood out in a broad flare around his face. "Abiru trash," he said in a voice hoarse with anger. "Defile my language again with your unworthy tongue, and I'll cut it out."

She lay there, shocked and fighting back tears, and with

a mutter the guard strode on. Slowly Ampris righted herself
and brushed off her fur. She swallowed her whimper of
pain, refusing to surrender to it, and told herself she must
remember not to speak Viis again. Only it was more familiar to her than the abiru patois that the slaves spoke. She
had spoken Viis all her life, privileged by the wish of the
sri-Kaa, and it was ingrained in her.

Yet she knew she must break the habit, or suffer more
beatings and attacks. She had to remember that Israi no
longer protected her. She was simply a slave now, and she
belonged to someone else.

Fresh grief welled up into her throat, and she had to
struggle to control it. Her pride would not allow her to sit
out here on display, weeping openly and feeling sorry for
herself. If this was her fate, then she must cope with it and
find what good she could in the situation. She was certain
Israi had found kind, decent people to take her in. There
had to be a reason why they had not yet come to get her.

The sun had begun to sink beyond the outermost flank
of the city, a great fiery orb that still radiated heat, before
someone came striding onto the dock and stamped to a halt
before her.

Ampris gazed up, squinting into the stern visage of an
aging Viis male, surely a lun-adult in his sixth life cycle,
garbed in pale coarse cloth and carrying a claims tag that
he matched to the one dangling from Ampris's collar. Two
bulky Aaroun males in loose sleeveless jerkins stood behind
him.

"Stand up," the Viis said to Ampris in strangely accented patois.

"I cannot," she replied.

Red darkened his rill and he whipped her across the chest
with a slim baton that stung. "Obey me at once, you both-
ersome creature! I will have none of your foreign insolence."

Swallowing a growl, Ampris backed her ears and rose to

a semicrouched stance which was as far as her cables would allow.

"Straighten up," he snapped at her. "Are you crippled, you wretched beast? Stand straight before me, that I may see you properly."

Ampris shifted her feet, trying not to lose her temper. "I cannot," she said. "The cable is too short."

From behind the Viis, one of the Aarouns looked at her and silently shook his head. But his warning came too late. The Viis whipped her repeatedly with short, stinging blows until she was shuddering from both pain and the effort to hold herself back from biting him.

"Insolent and disobedient," he said at last, stopping his attack while she stood crouched before him with her head held low and her breathing harsh and ragged. "Small wonder you were thrown out of the palace."

Ampris's head snapped up and she opened her mouth, only to stop herself from speaking at the last instant.

The Viis glared at her, his air sacs inflating. "Improperly trained as well," he said at last, looking disappointed when she said nothing. He slashed the air with his baton, then put it away and curled his green-skinned, bony hands into fists. "Can you serve table?"

"Yes," Ampris mumbled, aching from his blows. Her pride revived within her, and she lifted her head to meet his gaze. "I served the sri-Kaa at—"

"Silence! None of your boasting will be tolerated here. You serve the Hahveen family now. Your loyalty will be to them. Your thoughts will be to please them. None but their wishes matter to you. Do you understand, you simpleton?"

"Yes," Ampris said, pushing down her seething resentment. He was every bit as petty and horrid as Lord Fazhmind, and there was nothing she could do to escape him.

"Better," he said grudgingly, and drew himself erect. "Remember your place. Keep silent unless you are addressed directly. Answer only what you are asked. Do precisely what you are told."

She said nothing in response, and he flicked out his tongue in displeasure and swung away from her. Gesturing at the two Aarouns, he said, "Bring her," and strode away.

In the gathering twilight, she could see neither Aaroun clearly, except that they were full-grown adults. One of them held her arm while the other one unsnapped her tether. Ampris straightened fully with a soft groan of relief.

"That is Kevarsh, steward of the household," the largest Aaroun told her in a voice as soft as the evening breeze. He spoke the patois in a peculiar singsong rhythm that was far different from the way it was spoken in Vir. "He will punish you with great pleasure if you do not learn your duties quickly."

"How will I—"

"Hush," the Aaroun warned her, his voice so soft now she could barely hear it. "I am called Faln, but we are not permitted to chatter while on duty."

Ampris backed her ears, unaccustomed to taking orders from anyone but Israi and Lady Lenith. She didn't like it, but she realized Faln meant well.

He pointed at his silent companion, who opened his mouth. In the shadows Ampris could not see anything clearly except a faint gleam of light reflecting off his teeth.

"Gur has no tongue," Faln told her. "Always talking, this one, until they silenced him for good. Now come."

The Hahveen family lived in a narrow, three-storied house jammed between similar dwellings on the Street of Thoughts. Arriving in darkness, Ampris received only a confused impression of lights blazing from tall, rectangular windows before she was shoved through a side entrance on the ground floor, whisked down a narrow hallway smelling of cleanser and stored food, and placed inside a tiny cell containing a sagging cot, a peg with a servant's tabard hanging on it, and a small three-legged table supporting a bowl of cold mush. Gur removed her restraints, and while

Ampris was flexing her arms in relief, her escorts slammed and locked the door to her quarters, leaving her in solitude.

She was glad to be alone. Hungry, she ate the mush, even though it was tasteless and congealed into a cold lump. Once more she played the holocube with Israi's parting message, aching to be home with her beloved friend. If only she could reach Israi, could somehow explain about the crystal, she was certain she would be forgiven and allowed to return.

The cot provided no comfort, despite the fact that she kept telling herself it was better than sleeping on the ground in the auction pens. She slept fitfully and awoke stiff-necked and sore from her beatings. Muffled noises in the distance told her the household was up.

Minutes later, her door opened without warning and a female Kelth stood there, clad in a yellow servant's tabard, teeth bared impatiently, ears pricked forward. "Aren't you ready?" she asked without preamble. She pointed at the tabard hanging on the peg. "Put that on, and look sharp. Kevarsh allows no tardiness."

Ampris grabbed the article of clothing and pulled it on over her head. "My name is Ampris," she said. "What is—"

"No time for chatter," the Kelth broke in, glancing over her shoulder. She beckoned impatiently. "Quickly."

Emerging from her tiny cell, Ampris was grabbed by her elbow and hastened into a spacious, low-ceilinged room that held the kitchen, stored casks of wine with import marks stamped on their sides, long worktables, and an accounts office.

It was from the latter that Kevarsh emerged scant seconds after the Kelth shoved Ampris into line with the other servants. Rowed in front of the ovens, they stood in silence for the Viis steward's scowling inspection. Counting from the corner of her eye, Ampris saw six servants all together, including herself. There was a short Myal female, bowleg-ged and swathed in a cook's apron. She stood at the head of the line, probably as servant of highest rank. Her red mane floated silkily about her face, and she endured Kevarsh's inspection with her tail coiled tight against her leg. Kevarsh eyed her closely but said nothing to her. Next stood two Kelths, one the female who had fetched Ampris this morning, the other a half-grown lit male, thin and silver-furred. He reminded Ampris of Elrabin. Kevarsh reprimanded the female Kelth sharply for some ill-completed task, calling her Hama, and berating her until she stood with head bowed and ears flat. The youth's tabard sat crooked on his shoulders. He took a scolding for that.

Standing at the end of the line next to Gur, Ampris surreptitiously straightened her own tabard. She caught the mute Aaroun watching her from the corner of his eye. He gave her a tiny, gentle smile that made her smile back.

By now Kevarsh stood before Faln. He and Gur were clearly used for outside, heavy work. "The master has need of you to unload the new spools of cloth that arrived in yesterday's shipment," Kevarsh said. He glanced at the timekeeper on the wall and extended his rill. "See that you work quickly and finish the task by midday. It will please the master if the cloth is ready for the dye vats by the time he returns. Also, the mistress still wants the nursery painted, and that must be finished by the time she returns today from the hatchery. You are fools, both of you, but surely you can accomplish these simple assignments."

Faln bowed his head respectfully, and Kevarsh moved to stand before Ampris, his scathing old glare raking her up and down before he produced an ownership earring and fastened it through her ear.

Ampris held herself stiffly, not flinching despite his roughness. She thought of how proudly she had worn Israi's pretty gold cartouche. This ring was made of plain iron, with her new master's name inscribed on a tarnished tag. She knew, without being told, that this ring had been worn by other slaves before her. The thought of it made her nauseous, but she held herself under control.

"This is the new addition to our household," Kevarsh announced. "Ampris, she is called. She is vain and a boastful liar. You are not to believe what she says."

Backing her ears at his unjust charge, Ampris opened her mouth to protest, then remembered she was not permitted to speak unless directly addressed. Prickling with resentment, she held her tongue, but Kevarsh's sharp eyes did not miss her inner struggle.

"Lazy and insolent as well," he continued. "Hama, you will be in charge of her training."

Hama's head snapped up, and she bared her teeth. "If I may remind the steward—I am to be nursemaid to the new hatchling. My duties are—"

"There will be time for you to train her," Kevarsh broke in, his rill flaming red at the interruption. "Jenai will be more than adequate to handle the new hatchling in addition to the other chunen."

"But the mistress said that I should—"

"Silence!" Kevarsh shouted. He pulled out his baton and whipped her with it.

Watching, Ampris flinched in sympathy, but none of the others watched. When the whipping was over, silence hung thick in the kitchen. Hama stood with her gaze lowered and her ears flat. Only a ridge of hair standing erect on her neck betrayed her emotions.

"You will train Ampris in addition to your other duties," Kevarsh said. "The family wishes her to serve at table, but start her on cleaning detail. She looks too clumsy to be entrusted with goblets and fine plates." Swinging his baton through the air hard enough to make it whistle, he stepped back and glared at all of them. "Get to work."

The servants dispersed, each heading to his or her assigned tasks. Hama gripped Ampris by the front of her tabard and pulled her over to a stone vat. She showed Ampris how to take a pail from the neat stack next to the vat; how to hold it beneath the spigot, which spewed water automatically; and how to use the pail to fill the floor-sweep, an antiquated, dented machine blackened with tarnish and soap scum. Switching it on, she clamped Ampris's hands around the grips, and the heavy vibration shook Ampris all the way to her shoulders.

"Sweep it back and forth," Hama instructed her. "Use steady strokes. Make sure you don't miss any spots. Do the entire ground floor, except for the food storerooms. And don't go into the hallway that leads to the courtyard. You are not permitted outside yet. When you are finished, we'll see what's next for you."

Ampris stared at her in amazement, not at all certain she wanted to be turned loose with this heavy old machine that gurgled and churned internally as it heated the cleaning water. "But when will we have our breakfast? I—"

Hama's eyes narrowed, and she bared her teeth. "Breakfast?" she repeated as though she didn't know what the word meant. "You will be fed at midday, with the others. Truly did Kevarsh speak, in saying you are spoiled and lazy. Only the *family* eats breakfast. Now get to work, and make sure you don't let the line feed too much water onto the floor at once."

By midday, however, Ampris had not come close to being finished with her assignment. The kitchen floor was but half-done. Puddles dotted the pavers where she'd spilled too much water. She'd left haphazard streaks in the corners, and was still trying to get the machine to suck up a tangled pile of wet lint that it had unexpectedly belched out. Her hands were swelling from the heavy vibration of the machine, and her shoulders and back ached from the work. She was starving and sore, and when Kevarsh saw what she'd done, he flew into a rage and screamed at her in a tirade that left her shaken and trembling.

"Fool! Incompetent idiot! No food for you today until this is done properly."

Red-rilled and swearing, he stamped away. Ampris stood there, feeling humiliated, while the other servants refused to look at her. Silence fell over the kitchen, broken only by

Hama's sigh as she wiped her hands on her tabard and came forward.

"Already you are causing us trouble," she muttered. She took the floor-sweep from Ampris and demonstrated again how to use it. "Fill it with clean water and start over. Maybe while you watch us eat, you will be inspired to do your work properly."

Ampris swallowed back her disappointment. She was so hungry she wanted to beg Hama to relent and slip her food against Kevarsh's orders, but caution warned her to stay quiet. Still, there was no ignoring the delicious scents coming from the large ovens. And she was so tired she could not think.

"I'm sorry," she said, knowing from her training at court that excuses could not be offered. "I will learn to do this, Hama."

The Kelth barely glanced at her, but Ampris thought for a moment she detected a faint softening in Hama's gaze. "You had better," Hama said in warning. "There are worse jobs than cleaning floors. And I must go upstairs this afternoon to receive the new hatchling."

Ampris smiled, thinking of the little one's arrival. "Did the mistress lay many eggs during Festival?"

Hama's eyes widened, and she nipped Ampris on the ear. "Hush, you fool! Never say anything about the mistress!"

Rubbing her smarting ear, Ampris stared at Hama in puzzlement. "But I—"

"She cannot lay eggs at all," Hama said in a fierce whisper, her ears swiveling nervously as she glanced around to be sure Kevarsh was not in sight. "You will be flogged if anyone hears you refer to her tragedy."

"Then the little one is adopted?" Ampris persisted.

Hama stared at her in astonishment. "All hatchlings are shared, without knowledge of who actually laid their egg. Where have you lived, that you do not know the custom?"

"In the palace of the Kaa, things are done differently."

Hama's ears flattened to her skull. "Keep such comments to yourself," she said angrily. "We care nothing for how things are done in the palace of the Kaa."

"Hama!" called the cook. "Come and eat your portion."

Hama glared at Ampris. "Get back to work. Do not let me see you staring at us while we eat. And I warn you, if I am punished because you cannot perform a simple cleaning task, I will beat you worse than Kevarsh will beat me."

It took Ampris until nightfall, but she finally finished the floors. By the time she swished water through the floor-sweep to clean it and put it in its place, she was trembling so from weariness that she could hardly stand upright. Her shoulders felt as though they'd been wired to a block of wood. She could barely lift her arms, and her hands were swollen and aching.

Without asking permission, she drank deeply from the spigot, earning herself an outraged swat from the cook's ladle. When Hama handed her a plate of cold leftovers, she nearly dropped it.

"Eat quickly," Hama said impatiently. "It is almost time for lights out."

The Myal cook opened the oven doors to allow them to finish cooling, gave an order to the lit who was hanging up the freshly scrubbed pots, and came over to stand beside Ampris.

Coiling her tail against her leg, the cook glared at Ampris. "Eat faster," she said. "I want that plate clean and shelved. My old feet are ready for their rest."

Ampris choked down the rest of her food. She was still chewing the last morsel when the cook grabbed her plate and handed it to the lit to clean.

"Now get to your room," the cook said to Ampris. "We're too tired to wait for you all night."

Ampris trudged out, too exhausted to argue, and Hama and the cook followed. The lights faded on the room— scrubbed, shining, and everything in perfect order. At the door to Ampris's tiny cell, Hama paused beside her and put her hand on Ampris's aching shoulder.

Appreciative of that small gesture of comfort, Ampris dragged out a smile for the Kelth. But Hama's grip changed to a shove that pushed Ampris inside. Stumbling in surprise, Ampris turned back, only to see Hama grip the door and slam it closed. The lock turned, and Ampris was left alone and friendless in her quarters.

After that, her days passed in a weary blur. Buried in the constant learning of new tasks, Ampris scrubbed and fetched and carried and polished. She knew nothing about work, and Hama and the others grew increasingly annoyed with her for being so ignorant and untrained. Ampris learned to master her temper, to hold her tongue, and to do as she was told. She learned to ask no questions, to keep her gaze down submissively, to make no protests.

Yet she made constant mistakes, which brought her beatings and skipped meals. When she was fed, she never got enough. As a young, growing Aaroun, she required double the quotient an adult female would eat, and Kevarsh complained unceasingly about the expense of feeding her.

"The mistress wanted an Aaroun raised in the imperial palace," Kevarsh would say shrilly, puffing out his air sacs. "The mistress must have an Aaroun from Vir. Never mind that it is a useless sack of flesh and fur, hopelessly stupid, endlessly hungry, and impossibly untrainable."

Hama, bustling up and down the stairs between her double tasks as new nursemaid and Ampris's keeper, grew thin and short-tempered during the passing days. She demanded all kinds of tempting delicacies from the cook to feed the hatchling, who was said to have a delicate stomach and fretful appetite.

"I will not let this one die, like the last new one put in Jenai's care," Hama declared. She was ambitious to succeed Jenai, who had been chief nursemaid since the arrival of the oldest daughter in the household.

"Make tiny civa cakes," Ampris suggested. "Flavor

them with nectar and honey instead of the usual spices. Make them only the size of your fingertip. That should tempt him to eat.''

Both Hama and the cook stared at Ampris in astonishment. Ampris bent her attention back to her scrubbing. As punishment for having broken a tray, she was doing scullion duty today. The lit, whose name was Ralvik, had been taken outside with the Aarouns to unload a new shipment of cloth for the master's warehouse. Ampris expected Hama to scold her for speaking without permission, but, neither of them seemed to have much imagination and she was tired of listening to them dither over a problem that seemed so easily solved.

"Can you bake some, as Ampris suggests?" Hama asked.

The cook curled her broad lips down thoughtfully, hesitated, then slid her gaze over to Ampris. "They would be too moist without the usual spices."

Ampris went on scrubbing, although inside she was pleased that for the first time she was being included in a conversation. "Bake them longer, keeping the heat low so they do not cook too fast and become tough. The extra moisture will make them tender, which is what the hatchling should like."

"This I will attempt," the cook said. Turning away on her short, bowed legs, she began rummaging for bowls and ingredients, humming to herself with her tail coiled happily.

Hama rubbed her muzzle and stared at Ampris a moment in silence. Finally she came over and stood beside the vat filled with steaming, soapy water and stacks of pots. Wielding her whirring scrubber with newly acquired skill, Ampris went on working, taking care not to splash Hama.

"How do you know to try this?" Hama asked, her tone grudging.

Ampris glanced at her, wondering if a truthful answer would bring more punishment for boasting.

"A trick of the palace?" Hama said.

Ampris nodded. "I saw it done in the imperial nursery. They also use kivini fruit, very ripe and mashed, to tempt the finicky ones."

"Kivini is very expensive."

Ampris had no idea of what things cost, so she said nothing.

"I will suggest it to the mistress," Hama said. "We cannot bring home such an expensive item from market without her permission. Kevarsh would never authorize it if I ask him." She bared her teeth and glanced warily at the closed door of the steward's office. Ampris knew that he napped inside it every afternoon instead of overseeing the work as he was supposed to. "He is such a fool."

Ampris grinned, and Hama gave her a brief smile in return.

"Thank you, Ampris," she said.

"When will I be allowed to work upstairs?" Ampris asked, hoping that Hama was softening toward her at last.

But Hama's expression closed at once like a slammed door. "You are not ready to be seen by the family. Your training is not good enough."

"But I—"

"Get back to work," Hama snapped, and hurried away.

Sighing, Ampris rinsed another pot and set it aside. She was determined to get upstairs, because she wanted to find the opportunity to call Israi on the linkup. It was the only way she could think of to reach her friend and beg for mercy. She knew that if she could only talk directly to Israi she would be able to persuade her beloved companion to relent and let her come home.

But first she had to reach the equipment, and to do that she had to be allowed inside the family's quarters. If the mistress wasn't so besotted with her new hatchling, she mused, probably she would have sent for Ampris by now, just to see what she looked like.

Work harder, Ampris told herself. *Keep finding ways to be useful to Hama. She has to relent eventually.*

The specially made civa cakes pleased the hatchling, who began to eat more and thrive. Hama bustled back and forth, grinning to herself. Ampris waited for a sign of gratitude, but Hama gave her nothing.

As Ampris settled into the routine of the household, she soon saw how inefficiently Kevarsh ran things. The amount of waste in food, materials, and labor appalled Ampris. He forgot details, could not schedule duties efficiently, made poor decisions or procrastinated until a crisis was created. Then he screamed and whipped and punished, blaming the servants for his own mistakes. Because of this, the servants usually listened to his orders, then waited until he was out of sight before trying to do their tasks differently. Even so, Ampris often saw ways to streamline their tasks.

"If Ralvik set out the ingredients ahead of time, grouping them next to the correct pot, here, here, and here, in a line in the order that you would need them, could the preparation for the family's dinner not be shortened?" Ampris asked the cook one evening during general cleanup.

The cook glared at her. "Who asked for your interference? Are you trained as a cook? Do you know how to tempt Viis appetites?"

"No," Ampris said quietly. "Forgive me for my interference."

But the next day while she was carrying out rolled rugs into the courtyard to beat the dust from them, she saw the cook instructing Ralvik to group pots and foods ahead of time as Ampris had suggested. Smiling to herself, Ampris went outside with her heavy load.

Now that she was allowed outdoors occasionally, she felt as though her dreary life had improved greatly. The courtyard was a utilitarian square lacking any ornamentation, a space to buffer the back of the house from the cloth warehouse behind it, where the master's business was conducted. Although the warehouse was sealed, with all its equipment carefully vented, now and then a noxious odor escaped from the dyeing vats to poison the air and cause

some member of the family upstairs in the house to slam
the windows shut.

Today as Ampris finished carrying her rugs outside, she
saw Faln and Gur at work in the courtyard, unloading long,
massive spools of cloth from a cargo flat floating on its
antigrav unit and fitting the spool bolts onto robot carters
that lumbered back and forth between the courtyard and the
warehouse.

Spying her, Gur waved and ambled over to grin widely
in greeting.

"Hello, Gur," Ampris said shyly. Although the big Aaroun was much older than she, he was always kind. She
considered him her only friend in this place.

He gave her a friendly rub between the ears and tapped
her amulet with his fingertip. She held it up on its chain,
making the sunlight flash through the clear stone in the
center, and Gur watched it in simple delight. He never lost
his fascination with the Eye of Clarity. She had asked him
once if he knew what it was, but he'd shaken his head.

"Gur!" Faln called impatiently. "Do you want a flog-
ging? Come back to work."

Gur waggled his broad rump in cheerful insult and fin-
gered the amulet a moment longer. Then he gave Ampris
his gentle smile and by way of thanks shook out the largest
of her rugs with an effortless snap that made dust fly in all
directions.

"Gur!" Faln shouted again, but Gur ignored him.

Faln switched off the robot and came hurrying over.
Grabbing Gur's muscular arm, he pointed at their load of
cloth. Gur ignored him and went on shaking the rug.

Faln turned to Ampris in visible disgust. "A mountain I
might as well ask to move. You come and help in his
place."

Ampris stopped grinning and blinked in dismay. "But I
can't lift one of those spools."

"Try then. It's the only way to get him back where he
belongs, the oaf."

Hoisting her end of the spool with a grunt, Ampris found that it weighed as much as she feared. Her shoulder joints popped with the strain, but she was able to handle her end without dropping it. They got it fitted onto the robot, which Faln switched on and sent lurching into the warehouse.

While they waited for the other robot to return, he gave Ampris a nod of approval. "See? You can do more than you think, golden one. You are growing fast. This kind of work will make you grow more."

Basking in his praise, she reached more readily for the next spool of cloth, although its weight made her muscles shake.

"Good," Faln said while she panted and blinked the dizzy spots from her vision. "One more—"

"What is this madness?" Kevarsh shrieked across the courtyard. He came striding toward them, his rill a crimson frame around his face, his hands uplifted to the air. "The gods take my reason before the lot of you drive me to madness! Gur shaking rugs like a housemaid, and the table server unloading cloth? Stop it! Stop it at once!"

Ampris came around the robot and stood beside Faln, silent and with lowered eyes. Kevarsh grabbed her by the arm and yanked her away from Faln.

"I knew you would be trouble," he muttered as he pushed her back across the courtyard. "Were it up to me, that golden hide of yours would be hanging on the wall as decoration right now."

Ampris glared at him, but kept silent. This old Viis was a fool, and every day he proved it more.

"Get inside," he said. "Report to Hama at once."

"Hama is upstairs in the nursery," Ampris said. "It is her time with the—"

"Silence!" he said, striking her with his baton. "Did I request your opinion? Will you never learn obedience? Go! Go!"

Ampris hurried past Gur, who still stood in the midst of the rugs. Behind her she heard Kevarsh scolding him, then

the angry whistle of the baton striking him again and again.
Her heart burned with anger against this petty tyrant, and
she wished Gur would pick him up and break him in half
as he deserved. But she knew Gur would stand there, docile
under the abuse, offering no resistance. Without looking
back, for she could not bear to see the beating, Ampris ran
inside.

Much to her surprise, however, Hama was downstairs
looking for her. Ampris had finally received her summons
to the upper floors of the house.

"Here," Hama said, rushing about to thrust a clean, em-
broidered tabard at Ampris, who came to a halt, thrilled to
the tips of her ears by the chance of finally being taken to
the family.

At last everyone would see that she wasn't stupid and
untrained. No indeed. Ampris understood how to be a companion, how to fetch pretty cushions for a lady's back, how
to applaud the efforts of musicians, how to follow discreetly
during strolls in the gardens. Not that the Hahveen family
had a garden really large enough to stroll through. But at
the moment, nothing mattered except the chance to return
to a form of life that was familiar.

"Hurry! You must not keep Sana Mashaal waiting,"
Hama ordered, and with a thumping heart Ampris changed
tabards and smoothed her golden fur.

She couldn't stop herself from grinning, and she barely
listened to the stream of instructions coming from Hama.
No one had to teach her etiquette or protocol. She had mastered those intricacies in the imperial palace, and now all
her recently lost confidence was returning to her.

Holding her head high, she rejoined Kevarsh, who had
finished beating Gur and come inside. He glared at her,
inspected her tabard just to delay matters, then finally led
her upstairs.

If the first floor of the house held workrooms and servants' quarters, the rest of the house was reserved exclu-
sively for the family. The second floor held public rooms

where guests were received and family members spent their leisure hours. The third floor held the private baths and bedchambers.

Kevarsh walked proudly before her, his rill extended high and his fat tail swaying slightly from side to side beneath the long hem of his coat. As she followed, glimpsing rooms through open doorways, some of Ampris's initial excitement began to fade at the obvious and surprising lack of taste, refinement, and wealth.

The displayed art was mediocre at best. Carpets underfoot were faded, worn, and far from the best quality. The furnishings, of great age and thus clearly inherited, stood about in gloomy rooms. The hangings were out-of-date, in colors that made Ampris wince. Flower bouquets made a pretty detail, except that they should have been changed daily and clearly had not been.

Ampris looked at her surroundings in disappointment that quelled her excitement. It seemed that Kevarsh was as incompetent at running the household abovestairs as he was below. Had he been a steward at the palace, he would have been dismissed long ago.

Their gazes met and locked. Hers must have revealed her thoughts too much, for a red stain crept up his rill. Hatred puckered his face, and he flicked out his tongue.

"Come at once," he whispered in a scornful tone. "Do not dawdle when the mistress is expecting you."

Ampris walked forward, following him into a receiving room where three adult Viis females and one vi-adult female all reclined on couches around a tray of sweets and tall drinks of fermented melon juice. This room was brightened by a tall window overlooking the street, opened to let in a warm breeze that stirred sheer gauze hangings in a pleasing way. The furnishings here were more delicate and modern than what Ampris had seen before, yet her discerning eye detected cheap construction disguised with faux gilt.

Kevarsh made his obeisance to the gathering while one

female—blue-skinned with a rill in variegated hues of green, blue, and lavender—broke off her conversation and deigned to look at him.

"Ah, my steward," Mashaal said. She spoke Viis in the accent of the southern continent, reminding Ampris of Lady Zureal. "You have brought our new acquisition? Good. Come forward."

Still bowing, he sidled forward, beckoning for Ampris to follow. She approached, head erect and shoulders straight in the court fashion. Meeting Mashaal's startled yellow eyes directly, Ampris smiled and made her obeisance with perfection as Lady Lenith had taught her.

"Ah." A sigh circled the Viis females, and Mashaal preened and flicked out her tongue with pride.

"As Aarouns go, she is a beauty," Mashaal pointed out. She gestured to Kevarsh, who in turn whispered to Ampris.

"Turn around for the mistress," he said. "Display yourself."

Ampris blinked, and a hot tide of humiliation surged through her skin beneath her fur. In silence, she pivoted as directed, then stood there with her gaze lowered while Mashaal boasted.

"She was the pet of the sri-Kaa, you know. Quite spoiled, I am sure, but my husband spares no expense to please me, and when she was put into private sale, I had to have her."

"But she looks nearly grown," one of the guests ventured, fanning herself. "Is it wise to have an adult female Aaroun on the premises? You know how they can be."

Mashaal shrugged and smoothed a fold of her garish pink gown of synthetic silk. Her jewels were real, but of very poor quality, glittering cheaply in the sunlight. "I am assured that she is large for her actual age. When she matures, we will test her temperament then. Should she cause trouble, she can always be sold."

The vi-adult female, as slender as Israi but with skin a dark shade of green streaked with yellow, left her couch and approached Ampris to examine her more closely with spoiled, petulant eyes.

Her gaze shifted to Kevarsh. "Will she bite?"

He bowed. "No, indeed, Misa Lameel. She is most gentle."

Lameel smiled and extended her slim fingers to give Ampris a tentative stroke. Ampris did not move, and Lameel's caresses grew bolder. She wore a gown of plain cloth that was fashionable but poorly cut. Her rill collar was imitation gold and far too ornate for one her age. She wore skin oil perfumed with cheap synthetics, a copy of one of the fashionable fragrances. The smell tickled Ampris's nostrils, and she struggled not to sneeze.

"Her fur is pretty," Lameel said. "She shall be my pet."

Ampris's heart sank a fraction. Companion to this ill-dressed, gawky female, who couldn't approach Israi's perfection no matter how much she tried? The Hahveens were nothing but middle-class Viis lacking rank or taste. They pretended to have the wealth and sophistication of the true aristocrats by copying their betters with cheap imitations and giving themselves airs far beyond their actual standing. They were tawdry and pathetic. Ampris despised them on sight.

"My pet," Lameel said more insistently. She tugged Ampris's ear hard enough to hurt.

Ampris glared at her, swallowing the involuntary growl that filled her throat.

Lameel met her gaze with one like steel. "You are my pet now. You will adore me. You will crouch at my feet when I receive callers. You will follow at my heels, faithful and true."

Conscious of everyone's staring at her, Ampris bowed to this arrogant vi-adult in silent compliance, but her heart was boiling. Lameel would never take Israi's place. Love could not be commanded.

Lameel flicked out her tongue and clapped her hands. "Kevarsh, what tricks can she do?"

Before the bowing steward could answer, Mashaal intervened. "My dear, your esteemed father did not purchase this expensive slave to be your pet. He bought her to serve our table when we entertain his business associates."

Lameel's rill extended, turning dark blue as it stiffened. "I want her, and she belongs to me!" she screamed.

The guests sat up wide-eyed, and Mashaal flicked her fingers at Kevarsh. "Take the Aaroun out," she said.

The steward obeyed, shooing Ampris outside and closing the door on Lameel's tantrum.

Ampris smiled slightly in memory. "She resembles the sri-Kaa in temper, if nothing else."

Kevarsh hissed at her. "Silence! You will make no comparisons. You will do no boasting. There will be no dinner for you tonight. You may starve while you serve the family their meal. And if you drop one goblet or break one plate, I will have you flogged. Now go downstairs and resume your work."

CHAPTER TWENTY-ONE

In the darkness of the sleeping house, Ampris crept shadowlike through the third-floor rooms. Holding her breath, the fur on her neck standing erect in fear, she listened a moment to the whistling snores coming from Lameel's bedchamber, then crept past it and the large nursery where the pair of chunen—five and three years out of the egg, respectively—slept curled together with an affection they never showed each other during their waking hours. Jenai, the chief nursemaid, was a Kelth who slept with one eye and both ears open, ever vigilant for a whimper or cry from the fretful hatchling.

Successfully passing the nursery, Ampris reached the end of the corridor and pressed herself against the wall outside the master's office. Silently she counted seconds while the sensor beam on the door blinked its red light in warning.

It had taken her a month to figure out the security system in the house, which was activated only at night. A month of careful observation and spying without appearing to pay attention to anything save her duties.

Using the linkup in the vid room on the second floor had been her initial goal. But that linkup made only local calls within the city limits. In order to reach Vir, Ampris needed the linkup located in the master's private office, a room kept locked and secured, a room annexed directly to his bedchamber.

The security sensor was programmed to monitor motion only, lacking the sophisticated monitors for heat detection and carbon dioxide emissions that would have sounded an alarm immediately. Furthermore, the motion detector was limited to its shortest distance setting, due to the office's proximity to the nursery and the occasional tendency of the chunen to prowl in their sleep. The detector worked in twenty-second cycles. Therefore, all Ampris had to do was watch the blinking red light, count carefully, and match her movements to its timing.

She and Israi had learned these skills from the many pranks they had pulled over the years, bypassing guards, monitors, and individual body alarms to play tricks on hapless courtiers who thought themselves safe in their own beds.

But this was no prank, and Ampris could not begin to imagine the severity of her punishment if she were to get caught.

Her breathing grew shaky, and for a moment she lost count.

Then she pulled her wits together and forced herself to concentrate. This was no time to lose her nerve, not when she was so close.

The blinking light glowed steady, and Ampris slid forward, crouching beneath the device on the door and waiting for the blinking cycle to stop again. When it did, she shot upright, clamped her hand swiftly over the sensor, and flipped off the switch on the edge of the casing.

Only then did she let herself sag in relief, drawing in breath after breath, her heart still thudding too fast. A flicker of satisfaction came to life inside her. *Easy.*

But she knew she mustn't gloat yet.

Carefully she turned the latch, and smiled to herself when it opened. So she was right in thinking the sensor automatically locked and unlocked the door. This was a very cheap security system indeed.

But that was to her advantage, and she could not waste time criticizing the miserly ways of her master.

Easing her way inside, she shut the door behind her and stood still to get her bearings.

A glimmer of moonlight shone through the window, and gradually her vision adjusted to the shapes and shadows around her. She had feared the passageway between the office and the master's bedchamber would be open, but she discovered it closed.

She smiled to herself, letting hope off its leash. The gods were giving her luck with this. Surely success was meant to be hers.

With stealthy movements, she located the linkup and activated it. Light from its screen flickered over her face and hands. She put in the call to the imperial palace, keeping the voice link switched off, tapping in her message manually as slowly and as quietly as possible.

She directed it to Israi sri-Kaa only, encoding it as a personal message and using the special suffix digits reserved for the imperial family alone. That would allow the message to bypass the usual barricades in the main palace communications center and route it straight to Israi's own linkup.

Ampris had spent many hours mentally composing her message. She kept her explanation simple, stripped to the essentials, and finished with an apology. *I am sorry for any trouble I have caused. Please let me come back to you, for it is at your side that I belong. Ampris.*

Then holding onto her amulet for luck, she pushed the control that would send the message across the world to Israi. And she prayed with all her heart that Israi would read her message and relent.

For three days she waited for a reply—cleaning, fetching, and serving; living on hope. Every sense was attuned to the slightest sound outside, sending her running to the window in certainty that an imperial skimmer had arrived to fetch her.

For six more days she waited, her hope growing thin, while she told herself Israi must be gone from the palace, perhaps on a tour with the Kaa. But the vidcasts mentioned nothing about the Kaa's being on a journey. The court remained in Vir. The news carried standard clips on council meetings, envoys from other worlds, the economic status of the empire, an imperial banquet held in honor of some ambassador Ampris had never heard of.

For a month Ampris waited in daily expectation of a reply from Israi. But none came. She wept on her cot at night, where the darkness would not let her deny the brutal fact that Israi no longer wanted her.

Still, there might yet be an explanation for Israi's silence. Perhaps she had not received the message. It was possible that Lady Lenith combed through even Israi's personal messages. The sri-Kaa was screened from everything remotely upsetting or unpleasant. Ampris believed that Lady Lenith would put her in that category now.

She told herself she must give Israi one more chance. Which meant she must take an even bigger risk and somehow use the linkup during the daytime, when she could activate voice and vid lines and reach out to Israi with a stronger appeal.

Impatiently she bided her time until the opportunity came. On a hot afternoon when the master was working in the warehouse, the mistress and Lameel were out calling on friends, and Jenai and Hama were occupied with getting the three youngest Hahveens to the physician for their annual inoculations, Hama ordered Ampris to go upstairs and restore order to the nursery. She was to clean and straighten, putting everything in place before the mistress returned. Kevarsh was sleeping in his office, following his usual afternoon custom, and Hama saw no reason to disturb him with official permission to assign Ampris to this task.

Concealing her smile of delight, Ampris assured Hama

that she needed no supervision and hurried upstairs into the deserted house as fast as she could run.

She opened the door of the nursery, put down her pail of cleaning equipment, and hurried to the master's office without delay. She had already calculated the time difference between Malraaket and Vir. By now Israi would be finished with her siesta. The timing was perfect.

Hastily, Ampris switched on the linkup and pushed in the imperial code. She knew that by using it her calls were not recorded and would not show up on the master's bills. The machine seemed to take forever to get through. She figured it must be a heavy calling hour, but finally the imperial seal appeared on the screen. Seconds later, Ampris found herself staring into the bored gaze of a Viis operator.

Gasping in surprise, Ampris spoke in Viis. "This is a direct call, on a private channel, to the sri-Kaa."

The operator didn't even blink. "A call from what party?"

Ampris backed her ears. "From me. I—I mean, from Ampris, former companion to the sri-Kaa. I must speak to her at once."

"A direct call is not permitted."

"But you must let me through," Ampris protested. "I am calling on a private channel."

The operator's gaze dropped while she checked something. "Negative. This line is not private."

"But I used the imperial codes—"

The operator's eyes narrowed on Ampris. She leaned closer to the screen. "You, abiru trash, are in violation of communications laws, for which prosecution is swift. I have traced your call from—"

Ampris reared back and broke the link. Switching off the machine, she backed away from it and panted in growing panic. Only members of the imperial family or their designees could utilize the calling codes. Ampris realized her confession had been recorded. Moreover, her call had been traced here, to the master's linkup. If she could have gotten through to Israi, this whole matter could have been cleared up easily. But now . . . what was she going to do?

Ampris battled her rising fear as she tried to think. She knew she could not afford to panic. It was vital to keep her wits. The first thing she had to do—

"What are you doing in here?" shrieked Kevarsh.

Startled, Ampris whirled around and saw him standing in the doorway. His rill stood up stiffly around his face, turning as dark a crimson as she had ever seen it. His eyes blazed at her in a mixture of shock and fury.

"In the master's office," he said, his tail lashing beneath the hem of his coat. "Spying into his business affairs. Stealing—"

"No!" Ampris cried, anxious to stop his accusations. Kevarsh was always willing to jump to conclusions, yet she knew it was forbidden for her to be in here. There was no explanation that could justify her presence. "I wasn't stealing! I—I was told to clean—"

"Liar!" he shouted, rushing at her with his upraised baton. He swung it at her, and Ampris dodged out of reflex. Kevarsh shrieked in outrage. "You dare run from the beating you deserve? You *dare*? I will have you flogged in the courtyard for this. I will have the hide flayed from your back, you savage!"

He swung again, and Ampris blundered her way around the desk to evade him a second time. But his third swing whacked across her upper arm, wringing a howl of pain from her. He viciously struck her again and again, hitting her across muzzle and throat, aiming for her eyes, anywhere vulnerable.

And all the time he kept shouting accusations, railing at her, calling her the vilest names.

Something in Ampris snapped. Perhaps it was the weeks of hard work and inadequate food, the grueling discipline, her grief and pent-up resentments—but everything inside her came boiling up into a fury that erupted in a powerful, full-throated roar.

The noise drowned out Kevarsh's shouting, and he paused in mid-swing as Ampris turned on him with bared fangs. She roared again, her rage like a fire in her veins. Her fear dropped away, and she lunged at him with claws and snapping teeth.

Kevarsh's rill dropped limply onto his shoulders, and with an inarticulate squeak he bounded aside to put the desk between him and her. "Get back!" he shouted at her, slashing defensively with the baton. "It is forbidden to turn on your master."

She grabbed the baton and tore it from his hands. Breaking it in half, she flung the pieces away. "You are not my master," she growled. "You do not own me. You do not command me. I pray you will live long enough to catch the Dancing Death, you old fool."

"And you are doomed to the labor camps!" he shouted back. "You'll pay for this. You'll crawl on your belly and cry out for death before they're through with you. You'll wish your heathen mother had killed you at birth rather than suffer the torture and degradation that every stinking abiru deserves."

Shoving the desk aside with a strength she didn't know she possessed, she came at him, knowing nothing but the desire to snap his scrawny neck in her jaws. She wanted to hear him squeal for mercy before she shook the life from him.

Backing up hastily, Kevarsh grabbed the nearest object off the desk and flung it at her. It struck Ampris in the shoulder, heavy enough to slow her. Kevarsh scrambled sideways and reached the linkup before Ampris could stop him. An alarm sounded, startling her.

"The patrollers will deal with you," Kevarsh told her, his rill as red as his eyes were wild. He flicked out his tongue at her, laughing in triumph. "You fool, they will cut off your hands for stealing, and you will—"

Ampris tackled him with the full weight of her body, driving him down in a flailing tangle of limbs and tail. He hit the polished floor hard, his head thumping like a ripe melon, then lay still and crumpled beneath her.

The sudden silence beneath the whooping alarm drove back her anger. She blinked, gulping in air, and for a moment could not think of what to do. If she'd killed him, then her life was finished.

Fresh fear gripped her, shaking her from her daze. This was no time to sit here and shake. The patrollers would be arriving at any minute, and they would give her no chance to explain.

She'd committed how many crimes already? Using her master's equipment without permission, calling the palace, striking a Viis, maybe killing a Viis. She knew the laws were harsh and absolute. Any abiru attack against a Viis, any instance of a slave's turning against master, brought death. There was no appeal from such a penalty. The patrollers would probably shoot her on sight.

Getting to her feet, she stared down at Kevarsh. He did not move. She could not tell if he even breathed. But although she walked and breathed, she was already dead herself.

Condemned by her own actions.

Ampris turned and fled, racing through the corridor to the stairs. Ralvik and the cook stood gawking at the foot of the steps. Ampris came thundering down and pushed past them without pausing.

"Ampris!" the Myal cook called after her. "What have you done?"

From the courtyard outside came the sound of shouts and commotion. Glancing back, Ampris saw the master striding inside, his coattails swinging behind him, followed by Faln and Gur. Those two were her friends, but even Gur would seize and hold her if the master ordered it.

The alarm went on shrieking, piercing her skull, drowning out the master's questions as he hurried closer. From the street outside the opposite end of the house, Ampris heard the approaching wail of a patroller siren.

She looked right and left, then bolted straight ahead into the kitchen. As she ran she grabbed up a large pot and swung it by its handle with all her might. She smashed open the window above the water vat, sending shards of glass raining down over her head and shoulders, and climbed out. Dropping into the dusty tufts of grass outside, she crouched a moment, then ran, veering around the end of the building, through the courtyard, and out into the service alley beyond.

Behind her, the shouts and sirens seemed to grow louder, then faded as Ampris rounded a corner and ran even faster. She darted out into a larger street, one thronged with foot traffic and peddlers pushing wares on antigrav carts, and was swallowed up in the noise and confusion, leaving pursuit behind her.

She ran until she was panting and dizzy in the heat. She ran until suspicious stares from pedestrians brought her back to her senses. Only then did she slow down, tucking her hands beneath her tabard the way other servants did as they went on errands. With her ownership ring in her ear and her tabard on, she looked respectable and harmless. But inside she was a throbbing tangle of fear and worry. What was she going to do now? How could she live? Where could she go? Returning to Israi was impossible, even if she could somehow steal aboard a shuttle and return to Vir, which she could not. It was only a matter of time before her likeness was flashed on every vidcast in Malraaket. She was distinctive for an Aaroun, easily recognizable. The patrollers would find her unless she found a place to hide, and soon. But where?

Knowing nothing about the city, Ampris wandered without direction, taking care only to avoid any patrollers she saw. Gradually the streets grew smaller and the buildings more dilapidated. She saw no abiru wearing tabards and discarded her own by rolling it into a ball and wadding it through a gap in a sewer grate. Far below, she heard a Skek gibbering in glee as it scuttled off into the smelly darkness with its prize.

Ampris dusted off her hands with satisfaction. She felt as though a weight had been lifted from her shoulders. Without hesitation she took off the ownership ring and flung it into the sewer as well. For a moment she felt light and free. She stretched her arms high above her head toward the sky, where the sun was beginning to set, and ignored the warning rumble of hunger in her stomach. There had to be a way to live without belonging to someone's household. Other abiru folk did it; at least she had heard they did.

The first thing she had to do was disguise herself somehow, then seek employment. She was not going to despair. She was not going to listen to her fears, or pay attention to the memory of Kevarsh's crumpled figure lying on the floor.

Condemned to death. Condemned to death. The refrain ran constantly through her thoughts, and she pushed it away. She could not worry about that now. She had to—

The only warning she had was a faint whistling sound through the air overhead; then a net settled its heavy folds over her. Startled, she had no idea at first what was happening, until panic gripped her and she whirled around to fight her way out. But the net was impossible to escape. The more she struggled against it, the more its folds wrapped around her. Something snaked around her legs, binding her before she could elude it, and she was yanked hard off her feet.

She fell onto her side with a jolt that knocked the wind from her lungs. While she was struggling to breathe and hang on to consciousness, she was rolled up in the net and trussed securely.

It happened so fast, so expertly that Ampris could not believe she had been caught. Yet there she lay, helpless and doomed. Her escape had been all too short and futile. Her hopes might as well have been flung into the sewer along with the rest of her identity. A howl of fear filled her throat, and Ampris closed it off with the last remnants of her pride. She squeezed shut her eyes to fight back tears, refusing to let the patrollers see her terror.

"Well, well," said a Viis voice, a smug, self-satisfied voice. "Let's see what we've caught this time, Holonth."

A booted foot toed her and rolled her over. Ampris opened her eyes, but it was no black-armored patroller who stood over her. Instead, she found herself staring up at a Viis male garbed in loose trousers and a coat the color of dust. A hood lay in folds about his throat, partially obscuring his rill. He carried a stun-stick in his belt, surely, she figured, a weapon illegal for civilians to own. Ampris gazed at him in astonishment, but she felt no relief. Instinctively she knew this male was no rescuer. He smelled of greed and self-interest beneath the sour fragrance of Viis skin. His gaze examined her without mercy.

His companion joined him and crouched down on one knee to stare at Ampris more closely. Holonth's large head was covered with a smelly mat of brown hair that hung beneath his jaw in a heavy beard. Flies buzzed around him, and even as he grinned at her his broad, ugly tongue snaked from his mouth up into one of his nostrils.

Ampris nearly choked on the stench of him. "A Toth," she whispered in repugnance.

"Young one," Holonth said, his voice thick and stupid. "Strong and healthy."

"Exactly," the Viis said in satisfaction. He flicked out his tongue, then glanced around at the deserted street. "Bad time to linger. Let's get her loaded."

Ampris growled and snapped, but Holonth hoisted her up and flung her across his powerful shoulder. Helpless and afraid, Ampris squirmed all she could and lifted her head to glare at the Viis.

"Where are you taking me?" she demanded in patois. "You have no right to—"

"An educated Aaroun," the Viis said with amusement.

He laughed softly to himself even as his gaze swept alertly from side to side as though he expected trouble. "One who has run away from her rich household. A pity you threw away your ownership ring before we caught up with you. We could have ransomed you back to your owner."

Ampris again lifted her head to glare at him. The bobbing motion of the street beneath her was making her dizzy. "Is that how you make your living, catching runaway slaves?"

"Such a mouth," he said to Holonth, who grunted. "Such a rebellious nature. I'm surprised your tongue hasn't been cut out by now. Still, I suppose you could tell me the name of your master."

"No," Ampris snapped.

"Have you been a wicked slave?" he asked her, still using that mocking tone. "Have you run away to avoid being punished?"

"You're Viis," she retorted with scorn of her own. "You know all things. Why should I answer?"

He hit her for that, making her head ring. By the time she recovered her wits, she was being stuffed bodily into a cage in the cargo end of a skimmer. The cage smelled of blood. Her fear came rushing back.

Ampris howled. "Let me out! I do not belong to you! Let me out!"

"Shut up!" the Viis told her angrily as he climbed into the driver's seat and revved the skimmer's engines. "If you cause trouble, I'll let Holonth beat you."

Believing the threat, Ampris fell silent. Still bound inside the net, she sagged wearily against the side of the cage. What had she done to herself, she wondered in rising despair. All she had wanted to do was talk to Israi one last time. Was that so wrong? And now, she found herself descending from one disaster to another. She had thought her life was at the bottom when she'd scrubbed floors for the Hahveens. Now she knew how wrong she'd been. Things could have been much worse. They already were.

Holonth climbed into the skimmer, his weight making it

tip dangerously. The Viis gunned it forward, flying fast through the twilight-shadowed streets while he speculated aloud.

"We can sell her to the slave market, but she won't bring a good price," he said. "The market is too soft this time of year."

"Pelt is good," Holonth told him.

"You think we should take her to the meat merchants and have her skinned?" The Viis laughed, puffing out his air sacs. "Oh, yes, she would make a pretty rug for the floor."

Listening to them, Ampris curled herself as small as she could and tried not to whimper. They wanted her to be afraid; she could tell by the mocking tone lingering in the Viis's voice. He was playing with her, the way a predator toys with its victim before the kill.

Memories, old and long-buried, came to life along the edges of her mind. She thought suddenly of the Scary Time, and another Viis who had smelled of cruelty and greed, who came in terror, with Toths at his side. It was her earliest memory of life, a terrible one she wished she could forget.

Now it seemed life had cycled back to the beginning. She gripped her amulet in her fist and tried not to shiver. The amulet grew warm within the curl of her palm, as though her emotions had brought it to life. For a moment it burned against her skin.

Astonished, Ampris uncurled her fingers and stared at it.

The clear center of the Eye of Clarity was glowing with a fiery white radiance.

But as soon as she looked at it, the radiance faded, and the amulet grew cool and lifeless again. It was just an old artifact that no one understood anymore.

Wondering, Ampris stared at it and momentarily forgot her plight. What force, exactly, did the amulet contain? She wished Bish had told her more than his few vague hints. She wished she knew how to control it, how to use it to

gain her release. But it was not under her command. It lay
on her palm, mysterious and unfathomable, useless to her.

Sighing, she let it swing free around her neck once more.

The skimmer was slowing, and Ampris lifted her head
in alarm. Many of the buildings in this section of the city
stood dark and deserted. The place lay under an unnatural
quiet, unlike the ceaseless noise so common in the rest of
Malraaket. The air held the stench of garbage, decay, and
rotting vegetation.

The skimmer backed up to a pair of sagging, rusted
doors, and hovered on park. Holonth got off and stood
guard with his weapon drawn, chewing his cud and flicking
his large ears. The Viis pounded on the doors.

After a long while, a peephole squeaked open cautiously.
Soft words were exchanged, then the peephole banged shut.
The Viis stepped back, glancing around uneasily. Holonth
stopped chewing. The quiet grew thick and tense.

Then the large doors creaked open with the grating protest of rusty hinges. A dank, shadowy expanse loomed beyond them. The Viis trader conferred again with an
individual swathed in a heavy cloak and hood. Both of them
glanced furtively at Ampris.

"I'll have to see her first," a voice in a foreign accent
said firmly.

The trader murmured again, and they haggled a long
while before the trader gave in.

"All right," he said, the tension gone from his voice.
"Holonth, bring her out."

The Toth unlocked the cage and dragged Ampris out by
her feet. She squirmed and snarled, wishing she could break
free of her bonds just enough to bite him. He picked her
up and carried her inside as though she weighed nothing.

A few quick slashes of his knife, and the ropes holding
her fell away. Holonth gripped the net and unrolled her with
an expert yank, spilling her onto the floor. She came up
snarling and wild, only to be pinned by a spotlight that
shone right in her eyes, blinding her.

The cloaked figure circled her, his boots clicking softly on the hard floor. Ampris circled with him, a growl constant in her throat, her fur standing on end. She smelled death on him, and she was afraid.

"What's her age?" the cloaked figure asked.

"Fourteen, sixteen?"

"Perhaps," the cloaked one said doubtfully. "We could get a better estimate from her teeth."

The Viis who had captured her laughed. "I'm not holding her down for that. She's showing enough teeth already."

Ampris lunged, and quick as thought the Viis tapped her with his stun-stick.

The jolt zapped through her, bringing a hot flash of pain and numbness that dropped her to the floor. She lay there, panting and whimpering to herself, too stunned at first to quite realize what had happened.

"Plenty of spirit in her," the Viis said. "A female Aaroun in the first stages of puberty. It's the perfect time to train her for the arena."

"Perhaps, but is she trainable?" the cloaked figure asked.

"That's your job," the Viis said impatiently. "She's smart. She's educated, by the way she speaks. Her accent marks her from the north. Vir, perhaps. She's well-bred and solid muscle."

"Thin for her size."

"She can be fattened up. What do you say? Ninety imperials?"

Ampris gasped at the price, and both of them looked at her.

"She understands Viis," the cloaked one said.

"Of course. She's a house servant."

"Sixty imperials."

"Sixty!" the Viis said in outrage.

"She's stolen property."

"I'm no thief. I caught her on the streets."

"You could make more if you took her back to her rightful owner."

"No earring," the Viis said smugly.

"Which you removed," the cloaked one said in soft accusation.

"I—"

"Sixty-five. It's a decent price for a creature off the streets, with no known bloodlines, no provenance at all."

"Eighty," the Viis argued. "She's well-boned and strong. Lots of spirit and intelligent besides."

"Those cause the most trouble. If she's a runaway, she'll always be trying to escape."

"She can't get away from you," the Viis said. "Besides, the troublemakers are the best fighters. I've won enough bets on your gladiators to learn that. Seventy-five imperials will make her the property of the Bizsi Mo'ad."

The cloaked one hesitated. Lying there at their feet, Ampris felt a new sense of shock. The Bizsi Mo'ad was the most famous gladiator school in the empire, renowned for turning out fierce, capable fighters for the arena games.

Shame flooded her at the thought of being sold to such a barbarous organization. She was no fighter. She was . . .

Ampris stopped her thoughts. She was an abiru slave without an owner, without a home. She had been cast out by the person she loved most in the world, by the person who had promised to always take care of her. Now she was an outlaw, being hunted through the streets of Malraaket by the patrollers, who would serve her to a very harsh form of justice indeed.

Very well. She had no say in this bargain tonight except in her heart. And her heart grew hard inside her chest while the cloaked one considered and the Viis trader held his rill high in anticipation. She could learn to be dangerous. She could learn to be a fighter. She could learn to hate and to kill. What good was sitting in a garden, trying to act civilized? All her life, she'd striven to conform to the Viis way of life, and where had it gotten her?

Ampris backed her ears. For the first time today she allowed herself to savor that savage thrill she'd felt while attacking the steward. He'd deserved her attack, and it had felt good. Yes, she could be a fighter, a good one. She knew it in the very flex of her strong young muscles.

All her life, the courtiers in the imperial palace had called her a savage beast, ignoring her gentle spirit, her trusting nature, and her loyal heart. Right now her heart felt as hard as stone. Ampris growled to herself. She would become all they accused her of being—savage and wild. She would survive, but never again would she trust.

That was, if the representative of the Bizsi Mo'ad bought her tonight.

She turned her head and looked up at him, a figure kept mysterious by his cloak and hood. Seventy-five imperials equaled nearly two thousand credits. Could she really be worth that much? Yet, from time to time she and Israi had stolen glimpses of the gladiator games on the vidscreen— it was forbidden for them to watch such bloody sport—and Ampris knew vast sums were wagered on their outcomes.

"Seventy-five," the Viis whispered enticingly. "She's a bargain at that price. Worth every bit of it."

"Seventy," the cloaked one said.

"Done!" The Viis flicked out his tongue and clapped his hands together. "She's yours."

Ampris saw the quick flash of a payment card; then the Viis and his enforcer Holonth were striding outside, swallowed in an instant by the darkness. Ampris heard the skimmer fly away, and she was left at the feet of her new owner.

She made no move, uncertain now of whether to be obedient or to run again.

The cloaked one's hand snaked out, and a noose settled around her throat, yanked tight when she tried to jump to her feet. Gasping for breath, Ampris gripped the thin cord with her fingers and writhed helplessly.

"Be still," she was told, the accented voice harsh and

merciless. "You try again to escape, and I'll choke the life from you."

To emphasize his words, he tightened the noose. Dizzy and gasping for air, her vision blurring, Ampris stopped struggling. At once the noose slackened fractionally, allowing her to suck in a much-needed breath.

Glaring up at her new owner, she said, "Are you so rich you can throw away seventy imperials? Is killing how you discipline your slaves?"

She expected to be throttled again or beaten for her insolence, but instead the cloaked one laughed heartily. The noose slackened a fraction more, but not enough for her to escape it.

"Ah, yes, a troublemaker who can think and reason. Get on your feet, little Aaroun. When we finish your training, you will be worth five times the price I paid tonight."

Rising to her feet, Ampris found herself shackled with restraint bars clamped across her wrists and ankles. Awkwardly she shuffled forward into a cargo pod and crouched as commanded while it was shut around her.

Only then, as she was jounced and transported in a direction she could not see, did Ampris bow her head and let her burning eyes weep. Her defiance was but manufactured to keep her strong, and now it deserted her, leaving her with nothing but fear and uncertainty regarding her future.

She clenched her fists after a moment, however, refusing to let herself weaken further. Backing her ears flat to her skull, she growled to find her courage again.

"I will survive," she vowed softly. "I *will,* no matter what befalls me. And someday, if any justice lies in my path, it will be Israi who weeps for what she threw away. It will be Israi who feels regret for broken promises. No more will I weep for *her.*"